A HARMLESS
A SERIOUS

I'M STANDING in my corset cover and petticoats, pulling a green dress splashed with white poppies from my armoire, when Tess rushes into my room without knocking.

"Cate! Cate, come quick!" she cries.

"What is it?" I ask, drawing the dress down over my head.

"It's Cyclops," she gasps.

Cyclops is the one-eyed teddy bear she's cherished since she was little. "Is he missing?"

"No, he—" She swallows. "Come and see."

I make quick work of the green velvet sash at my waist and hurry after her.

She stands in her doorway until I join her. "Look, Cate, someone—"

Her voice cuts off. I stare at her side of the room: the polka-dotted curtains Mrs. O'Hare sewed for her, the daguerreotype of Mother and Father on her windowsill, the blue quilt on her bed. Cyclops rests on her pillow.

"Someone what?" I prompt.

Tess strides into the room, staring up at the top of her window. "He was *hanging*!"

"Hanging?" I echo, confused.

"Cyclops was hanging from the curtain rod. By a rope. By his neck." She shudders, rushing over to the teddy bear and picking him up gingerly as though he were a spider.

I frown. "Perhaps it was an illusion? Someone playing a trick on you?"

Tess tosses Cyclops onto the bed. "There was a note pinned to his hand that said *You'll be next.* Does that sound like a schoolgirl prank to you?"

OTHER BOOKS YOU MAY ENJOY

THE CAHILL WITCH CHRONICLES

SISTERS' FATE

JESSICA SPOTSWOOD

speak

An Imprint of Penguin Group (USA)

SPEAK
Published by the Penguin Group
Penguin Group (USA) LLC
375 Hudson Street
New York, New York 10014

USA • Canada • UK • Ireland • Australia
New Zealand • India • South Africa • China

penguin.com
A Penguin Random House Company

First published in the United States of America by G. P. Putnam's Sons,
an imprint of Penguin Group (USA) LLC, 2014
Published by Speak, an imprint of Penguin Group (USA) LLC, 2015

THE LIBRARY OF CONGRESS HAS CATALOGED THE G. P. PUTNAM'S SONS EDITION AS FOLLOWS:
Spotswood, Jessica.
Sisters' fate / Jessica Spotswood.
pages cm.—(The Cahill Witch chronicles ; 3)
ISBN 978-0-399-25747-6 (hc)
Summary: "In the final book in the Cahill Witch Chronicles, the Sisters and the Brotherhood
near all-out war as an epidemic breaks out in New London, and the prophecy that one sister
will murder another comes ever closer to fruition."—Provided by publisher.
[1. Witches—Fiction. 2. Sisters—Fiction. 3. Epidemics—Fiction. 4. Prophecies—Fiction.
5. Family life—New England—Fiction. 6. New England—History—20th century—Fiction.]
I. Title.
PZ7.S7643Sis 2014
[Fic]—dc23
2013040026

Speak ISBN 978-0-14-751442-4

Printed in the United States of America

1 3 5 7 9 10 8 6 4 2

To my sisters, Amber & Shannon,
without whom I couldn't have written
all the love & bickering between the Cahill girls.

And to my friends Jenn, Jill, Liz, & Laura,
who—like Cate's—have become the sisters of my heart.

SISTERS'
FATE

PROLOGUE
FIVE MINUTES AGO

Brenna is dancing up the marble *steps to the front door, and I'm following her when there's a sound—flesh smacking against wet pavement—and I turn. Finn's on his hands and knees; he's tripped over the curb. He picks himself up, pokes his glasses into place, and walks back toward his carriage, but his gait lacks its usual gangly grace. He pauses, examining the carriage, looking as though he's puzzled by it.*

"Are you all right?" I call down.

He looks up at me, then ducks his head. His ears are red with embarrassment. "I'm sorry, miss—is this my carriage?"

His voice is awkward, formal. As though he's speaking to a stranger.

His words echo in my head: I'm sorry, miss.

I thought I was numb before. This is worse. I don't

understand. I glance around the empty street. It's only Brenna and me and Maura here—

Maura.

My sister stands on the sidewalk, eyes narrowed at Finn. My Finn.

She wouldn't do this.

Not my own sister.

CHAPTER
1

I LEAVE MAURA IN THE SWIRLING SNOW and ice. I cannot look at her scheming face one moment longer, or I will not be responsible for my actions.

Inside the convent, I lean against the heavy wooden door. My black cloak is dripping, but my eyes are dry. It all feels—impossible. Harwood is empty and Zara is dead and Finn won't remember any of it, nor anything about us. Our future has been the touchstone guiding me through this war; the promise that at the end of it we'd be together has driven me forward, even when the odds against us felt insurmountable.

How can I go on without that? Without him?

Tess runs down the hall, flinging herself at me. She must have been listening for the door. "You're back! How did things go at Harwood? I've been so worried, I—" But I'm stiff in her arms, and she draws back, eyes fastened on my face. "What is it?"

"Maura knows you're the oracle." I wrap my arms around myself as if it will prevent me from flying into a thousand pieces. I can't help noticing the streak of scarlet on my right palm.

Zara's blood.

Tess bites her lip. "How could Maura know that?"

My shoulders hunch. "I told her."

"But—" My sister looks stunned. "You promised."

It's not like me to break a promise to my sisters. To anyone, really. I don't give my word lightly.

That's Maura's fault, too. She's made a liar of me.

Tess's blond brows draw together over eyes that have gone as stormy as thunderclouds. "Why would you tell her, after we agreed to wait?"

That truth comes out easily enough. "I wanted to hurt her. I couldn't think of anything else." Maura wanted to be the oracle—the prophesied witch who would save New England—so badly. Badly enough to betray me.

What else did she erase, besides me? For the last few months, Finn's life and mine have been intertwined. He won't understand why his mother closed the bookshop. He'll hate himself for joining the Brotherhood, especially now, with the Brothers subjecting innocent girls to their dungeons, to torture and starvation.

I clench my hands into fists, carving half-moons into my palms. It's either that or scream, and if I start, I don't know when I might stop.

"You wanted to hurt her," Tess repeats, as if it's incomprehensible. She stares at me as though I went away to free the Harwood girls and came back a stranger. "And you used me to do it. You shouldn't—"

"Zara's dead," I interrupt, angry. I am so angry suddenly. "You saw that coming. You could have had the grace to tell me!"

Tears spring into Tess's eyes. "I'm sorry. She asked me not to and I—I was afraid it would distract you. There was nothing you could do to stop it." Her shoulders bow, and she looks much older than twelve. Her sigh pricks at my heart. "Is that why you told Maura? To get back at me?"

"No." Everything is awful but it's not Tess's fault.

"The little one!" Brenna Elliott pops out of the parlor like a spooky jack-in-the-box. "You're safe. I didn't tell. They wanted me to, but I wouldn't, not even when they hit me."

Tess freezes as the mad oracle reaches out and pets her, stroking her blond curls. "Thank you?"

"They broke my fingers." Brenna waggles them in Tess's face. "But the nice crow healed me."

Sister Sophia, she means. Sophia taught me to heal, too. It's the only magic I've ever excelled at. I found satisfaction in nursing—and in proving the Brothers wrong, that not all magic is selfish and wicked.

Tonight I used my gift to stop Zara's heart.

She asked me to help her die with dignity, and I did. But her staring brown eyes and the coppery scent of her breath already haunt me.

"You'll be safe now, too. No one will hurt you here." Tess pats Brenna's arm.

"Rory will be here soon. With her sister." Brenna's eyes flit around like mad blue butterflies. "You and Cate-as-in-fate and the other one. The three sisters."

"Is that Cate?" Alice Auclair strolls around the corner, smiling like the cat that ate the canary. "The Head Council is destroyed. Eleven of the twelve, anyway, including Covington!"

"I've heard." If she's waiting for my congratulations, they won't be forthcoming. Her smile makes my skin crawl. She and Maura and Inez used their mind-magic on the Head Council, ravaging their memories so entirely that they'll be reduced to mewling babies. The Brothers have already been teetering on the edge of violence. Less than a hundred years ago, witches were hunted almost to extinction—and a good many innocent girls were killed in the process. The Brothers have been wanting an excuse to return to their old ways, and now Inez has given them one.

The women of New England will suffer for Inez's foolishness. Anyone a bit too educated, too eccentric, or too outspoken may be murdered outright instead of sent to Harwood. And what can I do to stop it? Nothing. There are tens of thousands of Brothers and only a few hundred witches to fight them. Our only hope is winning the public's favor, and now Inez has mucked that up, too. The Brothers have trained the people to be terrified of mind-magic. After a horrific attack like this, we'll be the monsters in the dark again, the stories told at bedtime to frighten children into good behavior.

Brenna grasps at my sleeve with her bony fingers, startling me out of my reverie. "It's her," she hisses. Her terrified eyes are trained on Alice. "The crow who pecked out all my memories!"

Alice stumbles back, looking from Brenna to me and then back to Brenna. Her porcelain skin flushes patchy and red.

Tess wraps her arm around Brenna, though she only comes up to Brenna's chin. "She won't do it again. It was an accident," she soothes. Brenna whimpers like a child.

Alice turns, ready to retreat. I expect she never thought she'd have to face Brenna again. Her *accident*.

I step forward, blocking her way. "Look at her. Look at what you did."

Alice looks. Takes in Brenna's stained white blouse, her brown sack of a skirt, her tangled chestnut hair. Her emaciated face, one eye still darkened by a bruise where the Brothers hit her for refusing to cooperate. Her skinny scarecrow arms. The livid scars at her wrists from when she tried to kill herself six months ago.

"I'm sorry," Alice whispers. "I didn't mean to."

She tried to make Brenna forget that the Sisters were all witches, but the compulsion went wrong.

Mind-magic is unpredictable that way.

"That's not enough." I take her by the shoulders. "You can't undo it. You can never undo it!"

"Let go of me!" Alice struggles, but I've got a good grip. I give her a little shake.

It's not a small thing to meddle in someone's memory.

Our first kiss, with the Brothers just outside the door and Finn's hands on my waist and feathers in the dark.

Our second, in the gazebo on the hill, with the wind whipping at my hair and the smell of sawdust and wet earth all around us.

Our third, on the day I told him I was a witch and he asked me to marry him anyway.

"Cate!" Tess pulls at my arm.

I relinquish Alice, stepping away. My breath is coming fast, my throat choked with tears that I will not—*will not*—let out. I stare at the wooden floor. At the round green rug wet with snow from my boots.

"Have you gone mad? What's wrong with you?" Alice demands, skittering back down the hall to the sitting room. She pushes through the group of younger girls peering out the door at the commotion.

"What did Maura do?" There's dread in Tess's voice.

I raise my head. "She erased Finn's memory. He doesn't remember me."

Tess raises a hand to her lips. "Why would she do that?"

"She's jealous of what we have. What we *had*," I correct myself. "She wanted me as lonely and bitter as she is. It worked. I'm so angry, I could *kill* her."

Tess stares at me with eyes round as saucers. Those aren't just words. Not since we uncovered the prophecy that one of us will murder another before the turn of the century. I've always found it impossible. We're sisters; we love and protect each other. Nothing is stronger than that.

Nothing *was*.

Brenna peeks out of the sitting room doorway. "That's not how it goes."

"Hush!" Tess snaps, whirling on her.

Tess never snaps.

What has she seen?

"No one is going to kill anyone." Tess grabs my arm again, fingers pinching, trying to tow me toward the steps. There's a touch of desperation in her voice, and I wonder if it's me she's trying to convince, or Brenna, or perhaps herself. "We'll fix this. Let's go upstairs, Cate."

"It can't be fixed." Finn's memories are gone forever; no magic can put them back. Maura betrayed my trust and there's no way to get that back, either. I spot Tess's friend Lucy Wheeler pacing at the other end of the hallway. "And I'm not going to run away from her. Besides, I've got to tell Lucy and the others how things went at Harwood."

I wave Lucy forward, and she comes running, her chipmunk cheeks flushed, eyes full of worry. Before I can open my mouth to tell her that her big sister is fine, that we got her out of the asylum, the front door opens again and girls spill in, all dressed in the black cloaks of the Sisterhood.

"We're home!" My roommate, Rilla, announces the obvious. "The other carriage will be along shortly. They're going in the back."

She's beaming, delighted by our victory. We freed hundreds of girls who were falsely imprisoned in Harwood Asylum. Some of them fled on their own; some are being transported to safe houses in the country; six girls with important talents or ties to the Sisterhood are coming here. They're safe—or safer than they were at Harwood with the Brothers out for blood, at any rate. Zara was the only casualty; our mission was an unqualified success—and yet I can't find any joy in it.

"Grace!" Lucy shrieks.

"Lucy?" Grace Wheeler is a taller, skinnier version of Lucy, with snarled caramel hair and brown eyes too big for her gaunt face.

Lucy hurls herself at her sister, tears streaming down her face. "I thought I'd never see you again!"

"I thought I'd never get out of that place. I thought I'd be there until I died." Grace looks around with trepidation. "You're a—a witch, they said?"

Lucy nods. "All of us. But we're not like the Brothers preach, Grace, we're not bad—"

"I don't care if you dance with the devil every night," says another stranger—an older girl with vivid orange hair and a smattering of freckles. "You're angels as far as I'm concerned, for saving us from that hellhole."

"Caroline," Maud chides. The redhead must be her cousin, then.

Caroline rolls her blue eyes expressively. "I believe in calling a spade a spade. That place was full of rats, and the meat they gave us was crawling often as not, and the Brothers who visited weren't above giving us pretty ones a pinch or two. If we fought back, they gave us extra laudanum."

My eyes flit to the third newcomer, a pretty Indo girl around my age leaning against the hall table, fiddling with the lyre-shaped letter holder. According to the nurses, Parvati was the Brothers' favorite target.

"You're safe now," I assure her. "No one will—"

My words die in my throat as Maura steps out from behind the others. "Welcome to the Sisterhood, girls. I'm Maura Cahill. You're safe here—so long as we can expect your loyalty."

My body goes taut as a bowstring just before the arrow sails home. "Oh, you're a fine one to talk about loyalty!"

"This isn't the time, Cate." Her sapphire skirts rustle as she positions herself in the middle of the hall, a bluebird surrounded by crows. "We'd all be executed if the Brothers discovered what we are. The secrets of the Sisterhood are not shared lightly. Particularly not with outsiders."

"Grace is my *sister*," Lucy protests.

"But she's not a witch." Maura waves a dismissive hand at Grace. "The Sisterhood comes first, Lucy."

Lucy shakes her head, braids dancing. "Not before my own flesh and blood it doesn't."

I give a strangled laugh. "Oh, not according to Maura."

Rilla wrinkles her freckled nose. "I don't see how Maura gets any say in this. She didn't lift a finger to help these girls."

"It was all Cate. Elena and Cate and that marvelous beau of hers." Violet van Buren gives me an arch look, and my stomach twists. "Now I see why you wouldn't give Finn up. My Lord, the way he *looks* at you!"

"Vi—" Tess begins, her fingers fluttering like trapped moths.

"I'd give my eyeteeth to have someone look at me like that." Vi clasps her hands to her bosom, sighing. "It's so romantic. You'll marry him, won't you? When all this is over?"

That's what I wanted. More than anything.

I've kept Finn a secret for weeks. I was afraid that the more people who knew he was spying for the Sisterhood, the more danger he'd be in. But all the girls at Harwood tonight saw him. Now they'll ask me about him and—

I don't know if I can bear that.

"I don't think so," I choke out.

"Why not?" Vi's plummy eyes are puzzled.

"Ask Maura." I jerk my head at her. "Tell them what you did."

Maura won't meet my eyes. "Don't make this about us. There are more important things to discuss." She turns her back on me, and her condescension makes me want to yank her red curls out by the roots. I wish we could settle this as easily as one of our old childhood brawls.

"I'll tell them, then." I step into the center of the hall, the center of attention—a place I've never relished. The words spill out of me, jumbled and passionate. "Finn joined the Brotherhood for me. He hated every minute of it, everything they stand for. He knew I was a witch, and he loved me anyway—no, not *anyway*. He was proud of me. He risked his life to spy for the Sisterhood and to help free you all. If they'd caught him, he would have been executed." I feel as though I'm giving a eulogy, and perhaps I am. "But Sister Inez wanted Maura to prove just how ruthless she could be. She didn't approve of a Brother knowing our secrets. And Maura—she's always been jealous that I had Finn, so she went into his mind and erased me. That's the kind of girl she is—the kind of *sister*. She would betray any one of us in a heartbeat."

Maura stares at me, wordless, cheeks flaming. The other

girls draw away from her as if the brush of her skirts contains some contagion.

"Go, Maura. Go to your room," Tess says finally, her voice low. "Cate shouldn't have to look at you right now. Frankly, I don't want to see you, either."

Maura whirls on her. "Who are you to tell me what to do?"

The oracle. The prophesied one. I want Tess to toss it in Maura's face, but I know she won't. She's not power-mad like Maura or vengeful like me.

Tess purses her lips. "I'm the sister who's still speaking to you."

Maura's face falls. "You haven't even heard my side of things!"

Tess hovers between Maura and me, her gray eyes like knives. "I don't know what you could possibly say that would make me understand why you'd do this."

"Fine. Take her side, like always. I don't need either of you! You'll see." Maura pushes through the crowd of gaping girls and runs upstairs, boots clattering on the wooden steps.

And I'm left feeling—how?

Unsatisfied with my petty vengeance.

Rilla is the first to recover her wits. She takes my hand, hazel eyes full of sympathy. "Come upstairs, Cate. You must be—"

I yank away. "No." She means well—she always does—but her kindness makes me want to fling myself onto the floor and cry.

I look around at the girls gathered in the hall. I can't fall to pieces, because they need me. I'm not the only person

Maura hurt tonight. Even now, the Head Council's subordinates will be finding them, childlike and confused, unable to recall their own names. Tomorrow, New London will be in an uproar against witches, and it will only get worse once the town learns of the mutiny at Harwood.

The Brotherhood *will* strike back. We've got to prepare ourselves for that.

The Harwood girls have been starved and drugged and brutalized. They need a place to heal, and the convent isn't that kind of haven anymore. Not with Sister Cora dead and Inez in charge. She'll do anything to oust the Brothers and put herself in power; she doesn't care who might be destroyed in the process.

But I do.

I've cast off one sister tonight, but now I've got dozens.

I mean to make New England safe for all of them.

My magic rises, sparking through my fingertips. The candles on the hall table burst into flame, followed by the old-fashioned brass candelabras along the hall.

I am tired of hiding what I am. There's got to be a better way. Not Inez's way. Not Brother Covington's, either.

If it's war the Brothers and Maura want, it's war they'll get. I'll fight both of them.

"Welcome to the Sisterhood." I tilt my chin up, meeting each girl's eyes in turn. "As you've probably figured, I'm Cate Cahill, and this is my sister Tess. Let's get you all something to eat, and then we'll show you to your rooms. This is your home now. I'm going to do everything I can to make sure you're protected."

. . .

We get the six Harwood girls settled before the fire in the sitting room, eating yesterday's bread with slabs of butter and strawberry jam, drinking cups of hot cocoa. Once I assure myself that Rilla and Vi will take care of them, I make my way up to the third floor, to Sister Cora's suite.

Sister Gretchen opens the door at my knock. Her hazel eyes are bloodshot and rimmed in red. "Cate. You've heard?"

I nod, brushing a hand through my tangled blond hair. "I'll miss her, but I'm glad she's at peace now."

Gretchen swallows a sob. "I knew it was coming, but I don't quite know what to do without her." She and Cora have been the best of friends since their days studying in the convent school.

"I know." I press her hand. "I'd like to say good-bye, if you don't mind."

"Of course." Gretchen ushers me in, and we cross through Cora's shadowy sitting room to her bedroom. Her body is laid out on the four-poster bed, dressed in a plain black gown. Her white hair cascades over her shoulders; her thin hands are as bare as winter trees without her dozen rings. "I'll give you a moment alone."

"Thank you."

I step closer to the body. Most days, I don't know what I believe insofar as religion, but I suspect Cora's soul is elsewhere now. Instinctively, I glance toward the ceiling, as though expecting to find her spirit floating there.

I've never found much comfort in the notion of my mother watching over me. At her funeral, that was the Brothers'

15

favorite platitude. They stopped short of suggesting I should ask her spirit for guidance. That would be sacrilegious; a girl should turn to her father or her husband or the Brothers themselves for wisdom. But they insisted she would still be looking after me from heaven, thinking that would bring me solace. Mother's instruction to keep my sisters safe weighed heavily enough on me, though; I didn't relish the notion of her spirit peering over my shoulder, judging whether I was doing a good enough job of it.

Sister Cora set me an even bigger task—to protect the entire Sisterhood. Tess may be the prophesied witch, but she's too young to lead, and neither of us trusts Inez to do it for her.

"I won't let Inez ruin everything you worked for," I vow. My voice is soft, swallowed up by the rug and the heavy green curtains pulled shut against the snowy night.

I rather like the idea of Cora looking down on me, I discover. She demanded a great deal, but she made her own mistakes, like with Zara. She'd forgive mine.

The notion gives me courage.

"Thank you," I add. "For believing in me."

I leave her with candles burning on the dressing table to chase away the darkness. In the sitting room, Gretchen is slumped in Cora's green flowered armchair.

"You'll sit up with her?" I ask, and Gretchen nods. "Do you want me to take a turn?"

She shakes her head, gray sausage curls bouncing. "You need your rest. How did things go at Harwood? I should've asked straight off."

"It went well, for the most part." I purse my lips. "Zara's dead. Shot by a guard."

"Oh, Cate." Gretchen's lip wobbles, but she masters it. "I'm sorry to hear it. Zara was a good woman. She would have been a great help to you." Gretchen squares her shoulders, her hazel eyes meeting mine. "If there's anything you need, I'm on your side in this. What Inez did tonight to the Head Council—it wasn't right. It's certainly not what Cora would have wanted."

"There is one thing." I take a deep breath. "I'd like to get word to Brother Brennan. Arrange a meeting as soon as possible." Brennan was Cora's spy on the Head Council. His mind would have been erased tonight along with the others', but Finn slipped herbs into his tea to make him sick and ensure he'd miss the meeting.

I hope that Brennan will be voted the new leader of the Brotherhood. By all accounts, he's a progressive sort. If I can make him understand that not all of us supported Inez, perhaps he'll guide the Brothers along a less vengeful path. It's asking him to forgive a great deal, I know. The men on the Head Council were Brennan's colleagues. Perhaps some were his friends. And unless we can figure out some way to render her powerless, Inez will be in charge of the Sisterhood until Tess comes of age in four years.

"There's a stationery shop, O'Neill's, down in the market district. We left messages for Brennan with the proprietor," Gretchen explains. "You already know the code he and Cora used. I can transcribe a letter for you, if you like, though I daresay Tess could, too." Tess is brilliant at cryptography, just as she is at nearly everything else.

Gretchen unclasps the ruby necklace around her throat. The gold chain pools in her hands, reminding me that Zara's necklace—the locket with Mother's picture inside—still rests in my cloak pocket. As I watch, the ruby transforms into a brass key. "The key will get you into the shop through the back door. We could use magic, of course, but the others have keys and they'll be more likely to trust you if you've got Cora's. In the storage room, there's a staircase to the cellar. That's where they hold the Resistance meetings."

She hands me the key. It's small and cold and slight in my palm, but this intelligence feels momentous. I sink into the chair next to hers. "Resistance meetings?" I echo.

Does she mean to say there are people working in secret against the Brothers, besides witches? Zara alluded to such a thing, and we gambled that they still exist, sending the Harwood refugees to several of their safe houses. I had no notion Cora was involved with them.

Gretchen brushes a hand over her plump cheek. "Brennan isn't the only man in New England who disagrees with the Brothers' methods. The Resistance leaders meet once a week. The next meeting is scheduled for Friday night. I'll go with you, if you like. It won't be an easy thing to win their trust; it took Cora years. They knew she was a witch, but they don't know we all are. And even those who don't mind a witch don't believe a woman their equal. I won't lie to you, Cate. Trying to win over Alistair Merriweather will be no picnic."

I frown. "Who is he?"

Gretchen raises her eyebrows at me. "Good Lord, girl, don't you read? He publishes the *Gazette*."

Truth be told, I've never read the *Gazette*. The *Sentinel* is the official New London newspaper, the Brothers' mouthpiece. It's forbidden to be caught with a copy of any other paper, though I've often seen half-hidden copies of the *Gazette* when we've delivered rations to the poor.

"You should find a copy and educate yourself a bit before you meet him," Gretchen suggests. "If you can get him on your side, it will be a great boon to us. One-fifth of New London reads his paper, as he'll be only too happy to tell you."

I lift my head, a spark of hope racing through me. "That's quite a lot of people unhappy with the Brothers."

"And those are only the ones bold enough to buy the paper. How many borrow it from a neighbor, or can't read to start with?" A wry smile kicks up the corners of Gretchen's mouth. "The poor are frustrated by the new restrictions. Look at the hundreds who protested last month in Richmond Square."

"Half of them were thrown on a prison ship for their trouble," I point out, remembering Mei's sisters. "Don't you think that put a damper on any ideas of rebelling?"

Gretchen shakes her head. "I suspect it only fanned the flames. They protested peacefully enough. That shouldn't be an offense that warrants getting sent away for years, should it? How do you think those unfortunate souls are managing now? Barely, that's how, with the help of family if they've got it, or our charity. The people are angry, especially the working poor. They're looking for leaders."

"Like Tess," I suggest. She's the oracle meant to win the people's hearts back to the witches.

"And you," Gretchen says. "You and Merriweather working together could be a formidable team."

I glance over my shoulder at the half-open door to Cora's bedroom, confidence wavering. If it took Cora years to win over the Resistance leaders, how will I manage it? I'm not half as clever as she was.

"Cora had faith in you, Cate," Gretchen says. "Don't let her down."

I use my magic to transform the brass key back into a ruby, then hang it around my neck. I welcome the weight of it. Like a talisman.

"I won't."

CHAPTER
2

"ATTENTION, GIRLS." INEZ'S VOICE CUTS
through my exhaustion at breakfast the following
morning. "I have a few announcements to make."

I have been studiously avoiding her and the look
of triumph she must surely wear. Her plan is falling
into place. She's destroyed the Head Council. Sister
Cora is dead. Maura proved her loyalty beyond
any shadow of a doubt, and Inez likely thinks it's
broken me.

Let her think it. Her triumph won't last. She will
rule the Sisterhood and New England over my dead
body.

I'm sandwiched between Rilla and Mei at one of
the five long tables that fill the dining room, pushing eggs and ham around my plate. I take a bite of
buttered toast. Tess is sitting at the table behind us

with the younger girls, but I suspect she's keeping a watchful eye on me to make sure I eat.

Inez stands. She's dressed in unrelenting black bombazine, with no ornament save the ivory brooch at her collar. She doesn't look like one of Brenna's crows—more like a predatory hawk with her beak of a nose. I could slice cold butter on her cheekbones.

At the sight of her, my exhaustion fades. Maura erased Finn's memory, but it was at *her* request. Maura's always so blasted desperate for someone to choose *her*, love *her* most, and Inez played on that. I don't absolve Maura of responsibility—but Inez asked it of her.

"To those of you who joined us from Harwood last night, welcome," Inez says, without so much as a smile. "I am sorry for the harm you suffered at the Brothers' hands. I assure you, you will have your chance at vengeance."

I glance down the table, where Parvati's hands are trembling as she holds her fork poised over her eggs. Maud's cousin Caroline is a bit green around the gills. The other new girls—Grace Wheeler, Livvy Price, and Sister Edith's niece Angela—all look shaky and sick. At Harwood, their tea was drugged with laudanum. Now they're reacting to the lack of it. Mei and I dosed them with herbs, but that only keeps the worst of the nausea at bay. These girls don't need vengeance; they need someone to look after them, and the time and space to heal.

"I'm sure you've all heard by now that Sister Cora passed away last night." Inez pauses, and the girls around me cast their faces down. "I make no pretense that Cora and I were friends. We did not agree on how to lead the Sisterhood forward, and I thought her overly cautious." Out of the corner of my eye, I see Gretchen bristling. Inez holds up a hand, the silver ring of the Sisterhood glinting in the early-morning light. "Nonetheless, Cora devoted her life to the Sisterhood, and that is worthy of our respect. Her funeral will take place tomorrow morning at Richmond Cathedral. I expect all of you to attend.

"In accordance with the plan of succession, as the eldest witch capable of mind-magic, I am your new headmistress." Inez's dark eyes meet mine. "The Sisterhood has been divided for years, but I hope you will soon see that I have your best interests at heart. We all have the same aims now, don't we? And the same enemies?"

My fork falls out of my hand and lands on the china plate with a dull clink, and I choke on my indignation. I know who *my* enemies are.

Inez gives a dry chuckle like the crack of an old twig. "Cora put great stock in the prophecy that one of the Cahill sisters would lead us into the next century. She believed that Cate was likeliest to be the oracle. However, it has come to my attention—"

I bite my lip. Is Inez going to cast her support for Maura? There's no more evidence of Maura being an oracle than of me being one.

"It has come to my attention," Inez repeats, relishing the way we all hang on her words, "that it's not Cate who has been blessed by Persephone with visions of the future. It's little Tess. Isn't that right, Tess?"

Everyone swivels in her seat to look at Tess. Except me. I stare at Maura, who gazes down at her lap, her fingers fiddling with the lace tablecloth. I never dreamed she'd tell Inez.

Even now, I give her too much credit.

Tess lifts her pointy chin. "Yes, ma'am."

"How marvelous," Inez practically purrs. "There's never been an oracle who was also a witch, much less a witch capable of mind-magic. I assume you *are* capable of that?"

"Yes, ma'am." Tess flushes from all the attention. I half expect her to squirm and sink in her chair, but she does not; she sits tall and straight, and I feel a swell of pride.

"I see. Well, it wasn't very nice of you to keep it all to yourself." Inez shakes her head, *tsk*ing as though she's scolding a child for stealing a penny candy. "But I understand why you might hesitate to steal the limelight from your sister—"

"It wasn't that," Tess interrupts. "It was a matter of my own safety."

Which has now been thoroughly compromised. Tess is the oracle prophesied to gain the people's favor and bring about a new golden age of magic—or, if she falls into the Brothers' hands, a second Terror. The Brothers have been murdering girls on just the *suspicion* of having visions. And now it's gone from three of us knowing about Tess's prophecies— Tess, Mei, and me—to the entire convent: fifty-odd students, a dozen teachers, and a dozen more governesses. What is Inez playing at?

Inez clasps her hands earnestly to her bosom. "Your secret is safe with us. We are your sisters. We would protect you with our lives!"

Would they really? Is it reasonable to expect them to? What is Tess to the people in this room? She's well liked, certainly, but it's no small thing to sacrifice one's life.

"In any case, I'm delighted to have such a powerful *student*," Inez says, and comprehension floods through me at the way she stresses the word. "Tess is gifted, yes, but she is still a child. A twelve-year-old cannot lead the Sisterhood, particularly not during these troubled times. She'll require guidance, and I am happy to provide it—to rule in her stead, as a sort of regent, until she comes of age and we see if there is any truth to the prophecy."

Tess rakes a hand through her blond curls. I can read her frustration in the way she grinds her jaw, in the tightness of her shoulders. She won't challenge Inez publicly, she's too clever for that, but oh, she loathes being patronized.

"Thank you," she mutters. "I appreciate your support."

"You're quite welcome." Inez prowls down the aisle. "I have one more announcement. Between the Harwood break-out and the strike on the Head Council, the Brotherhood will be up in arms. It is important that, should we be apprehended, we are able to free ourselves, be it through animation or illusion work. Miss Auclair, if you were in a crowd and the Brothers called you out as a witch, what would you do?"

Alice smiles. In the blink of an eye, she becomes a girl with black curls and brown skin and a red plaid dress. "Or, better yet," she murmurs, and a moment later, she's transformed into a stocky Chinese boy with a shock of black hair and a denim shirt.

"Brava, Miss Auclair!" Inez claps. Alice has always been

her prize pupil. Rilla is even better at illusions, but she's not half so obsequious. "We do not know how the Brothers will retaliate, girls, but I feel sure that they will. It will be increasingly difficult to avoid their notice. I am changing your schedules to double up on illusions and animation classes. Art, music, botany, and other electives will be postponed until further notice."

Rilla flings a hand into the air. "Will you continue as illusions teacher as well as headmistress?"

"I shall teach the advanced classes in the mornings. Miss Auclair will teach the introductory ones in the afternoons." Inez lays a bony hand on Alice's shoulder, and Alice—transforming back into her pretty blond self—preens.

I glance at the table behind me. Rebekah Reed looks as though she's swallowed a lemon, and Lucy is cringing. Alice is a bully, and the younger girls already get the worst of it.

"Why Alice?" Mei demands. "Why not Rilla?"

"Rilla would make a wonderful teacher! She's the best in our class!" Pearl adds.

"That's a matter of opinion, isn't it?" Inez snaps. "I am under no obligation to explain staffing decisions to students. However, Miss Auclair will turn seventeen in March and has already announced her intention to become a full member of the Sisterhood. Miss Stephenson's birthday is not until September, and she has made no such guarantee. What good is it to me to train a teacher, only to have her run off and get married?"

Rilla flushes behind her freckles. She's a romantic, yes, but she doesn't have a beau. None of the girls at the convent have. There are not many opportunities to meet boys when one masquerades as a nun in training.

"Now, if there are no further interruptions"—Inez glares at Mei and Pearl—"we are already behind schedule for the day. Miss Kapoor, Miss Price, I would like to see you in my office after morning classes, if you're feeling up to it."

The room explodes into whispers as she turns away, her heels tap-tap-tapping into the hall.

Rilla reaches for the jam. "What does she want with Parvati and Livvy?"

I hand her the sticky jar. "They can do mind-magic." Most of the girls we rescued from Harwood aren't witches, so they're being shepherded to one of three safe houses in the countryside. Grace, Caroline, and Angela are here only by virtue of their connections with students or staff. Parvati and Livvy are here because I found their files in the National Archives and realized how powerful they are. Mind-magic is terribly rare; only my sisters, Alice, Elena, Inez, and I are capable of it.

I'd like to go to Tess and see to it that she's all right, but she's surrounded. Her friends are all pelting her with questions. I catch her eye and she gives me a tiny nod. She can manage this. I head toward Parvati and Livvy.

"Could the two of you come with me for a moment?" Perhaps I can thwart Inez in another way.

Parvati shies away from the hand I put on her shoulder. "Are we in trouble?"

"No, not at all." I give her a reassuring smile. "I just want to talk to you."

Last night we took up a collection of dresses for the new girls. Livvy, a short, buxom brunette, is wearing a pink and red plaid dress of Alice's. I was rather surprised that Alice volunteered it—she's not known for her charity—but Livvy looks well in it. I lent Parvati a navy-blue frock, but it hangs on her skeletal frame like a shroud. Mei's a good hand with a needle; perhaps she can take it in for her.

I guide them upstairs to the room I share with Rilla and gesture for them to sit on my bed. Parvati perches on the edge of the mattress while Livvy kicks off her borrowed red slippers and curls up.

"Why does the headmistress want to see us?" Parvati's hand trembles as she tucks a strand of black hair behind her ear.

"Because of your mind-magic." I drag the bench from the dressing table across the room and sit in front of them. "She'll want to test you."

"Test us how?" Livvy frowns.

My shoulders go tight. "She'll ask you to compel other girls. She asked me to make them walk from the sitting room to her office."

"Did you do it?" There are blue shadows beneath Parvati's eyes.

I shake my head. "I wasn't comfortable going into my friends' minds without their permission."

"But you could have done it, if you'd wanted to? You did mind-magic at Harwood on the nurses, didn't you?" Parvati presses, and I nod. "Will you teach me how? I've never been able to see my compulsion through. The laudanum, I think—it wouldn't let me focus on anything for long."

"I will—though I hope you won't have need of it. I don't think compulsion is to be used lightly. But after—well, after what you've been through . . ." I trail off, flushing. "If it would help you to feel safer—"

"It would help me to know that if I ever see Brother Cabot again, I could compel him to put a bullet through his brain," Parvati says grimly. "I appreciate your delicacy, but Livvy knows. Everyone knows what happened to me and no one came forward to stop it."

"Parvati, I—" Livvy begins, leaning forward.

"I don't blame you for it." Parvati turns to me. "I tried to fight back. Strangled him with his own cravat once, but he slapped me and got away while I was seeing stars. Another time I compelled him to blind himself, but he came out of it right before he stuck the matron's letter opener in his eye. He beat me for it—but it was almost worth it."

"Oh, Parvati." Livvy tries to embrace her, but Parvati shrinks away.

"I don't want your pity," she snaps. "I want vengeance, like Sister Inez promised."

"Sister Inez," I say quietly, "is not to be trusted. I understand that you must—"

"No," Parvati interrupts. Her back is ramrod straight, her legs crossed delicately at the ankles, but anger fairly vibrates through her. "You cannot possibly understand. Not unless you've been there yourself."

I trace the blue pinstripes on my skirt, trying to redirect the conversation. "Inez is leading the Sisterhood into a war we can't win. We're powerful, yes, but we're outnumbered. The prophecy says Tess can win the people to our side—but until then, we need to work with the more moderate Brothers to keep the peace. If Inez continues to do terrible, reckless things, compromise will never be possible."

"Good," Parvati spits, her brown eyes narrowed. "I don't want compromise. How can you expect us to work with Brothers after what they've done to us?"

"They're not all bad," I say, thinking of Finn. Always of Finn. He told me there are moderates within the Brotherhood, men like him who joined to protect their wives or sisters or sweethearts. "And if we don't want inhumane treatment, we can't dole it out. Even if Brother Covington and the others were wrongheaded, they didn't deserve—"

"Wrongheaded?" Parvati leaps to her feet. "That's what you'd call them? You don't think they deserved what was done to them? Do you think *I* deserved what was done to me?"

"No! No, of course not." I jump up, flustered. "I misspoke. They were—are—cruel. But we'll never gain the people's trust Inez's way. Lord knows what else she's plotting. She's such a schemer; I wouldn't trust her to—"

"She's a schemer?" Parvati plants her hands on her thin hips. "You called us up here to undermine her. I suppose you're angry with her on account of what she and Maura did to your beau?" I can't deny that—but it's not only that. Parvati's lip curls in disgust. "I can't believe you were letting a *Brother* court you!"

"He wasn't—you don't understand," I insist. "Finn isn't—"

"You're the one who doesn't understand." Parvati strides across the room and throws open the door. "You've been sheltered all your life. You put yourself in my shoes, and then you tell me what the Brotherhood deserves."

Blast.

Livvy stares at her red slippers. "I should—excuse me, Cate," she mumbles, fleeing after Parvati.

Oh, hell.

I should have asked Elena to be here. She would have known how to finagle such a delicate conversation. Now Parvati thinks I'm a fool who sympathizes with the Brothers, and Inez will have at least one more witch with mind-magic on her side.

I pause beside the window, pushing aside Rilla's yellow curtains and staring at the dreary gray morning. What's happening out there? Are the Brothers already meeting to elect a new leader? A great deal depends on whom they choose and whether he'll lead with vengeance or mercy. Finn predicted they might well vote to resurrect the burnings. I wrap my arms around myself, wishing he were here to comfort me.

I miss him already.

This fall, when I was in New London and he was still in Chatham, I hoped perhaps he was thinking about me, too.

Now he won't even know to miss me.

I push those thoughts away. If I stop moving—stop doing—I'm going to fall apart. I can't give Inez and Maura the satisfaction of that.

I have little faith in the Brotherhood these days, but I've

got to believe most men wouldn't vote to set me on fire if they knew what I could do. It's one thing to lock a girl up in Harwood for the rest of her life; it's quite another to burn her at the stake.

Isn't it?

Are Parvati and Inez right? Will the Brothers go that far?

The prospect of going downstairs, sitting behind a desk, and taking notes seems impossible. How can I concentrate when I don't know what the Brothers are doing or how the people have reacted to Harwood and the attack on the Head Council? I'm sure the *Sentinel* is painting both events with the same brush—dangerous witches on the loose. But what of the *Gazette*? Can Alistair Merriweather see the gulf of difference between what Inez did and freeing innocent girls?

There's a knock on the half-open door.

"Come in," I call, and Tess peers into the room, face scrunched into a frown.

She kicks the door shut behind her and flops onto my bed. "Everyone's staring at me," she announces, her jaw set. "I'd like to throttle Sister Inez. Maura, too."

"I ought to be first in line." I sigh, twisting my hair up into a chignon. "Maura had no right to tell anyone without your permission. But neither did I."

"No, you didn't." Tess scowls. "Still, I forgive you. It was under awfully extenuating circumstances. I know you didn't mean to hurt me."

"I would never," I promise, skewering pins through my hair.

"Maura had time to think about it, though. And Inez made

me look like such a *child*." Tess's eyes narrow. "This is why I wasn't ready to tell. Bekah and Lucy are acting differently around me already. Careful. Like I could break at any moment."

"You won't break," I assure her. "They just found out. Give them some time to get used to the idea."

Tess groans. She's more patient than I am, but that's not saying much. "Don't you see? I won't be just Tess anymore! Everyone will see me as the Oracle now. The Prophesied One."

"It won't be that way forever." I hope not, anyway. I step into my sturdy boots. "I'm going out. Would you like to come with me? Escape the staring for a bit?"

"We have class," Tess reminds me, picking up the history book at the foot of my bed.

"I'm not going. I need to find out whether the Brothers have elected a new leader. And I've got an important errand to run. Sisterhood business." I pick up an ivory envelope lined with green birds—part of a set Tess gave me last Christmas, though who I had to write to then, I don't know—and wave it at her.

She snatches it from me and withdraws the matching ivory paper. A green and blue hummingbird is embossed at the top, and the note itself is written in code—a Caesar cipher of three shifts to the left. "Did you do this yourself?"

I nod. There wasn't much else to do at quarter to five this morning, while Rilla was snoring and I was trying not to think of Finn, so I took a candle down to the library and wrote the note. It took three tries to get it right and then I copied it onto my best stationery. A man like Brother

Brennan might appreciate such niceties. Having never met him, I don't know.

"Does it sound all right?" I ask.

Tess skims the short letter: *Sister Cora has died. I do not trust her successor, who led the attack on the Head Council. It is my hope that you and I can work together for peace. I have Cora's key and look forward to meeting you at tomorrow night's gathering.*

It's unsigned. Even using a code, I'm not fool enough to leave my name for anyone to see.

"It's good." Tess's gray eyes meet mine. "You're going out to deliver it now? Did you already talk to Sister Gretchen?"

I nod. "I'm to leave it with the proprietor of a stationery shop. And Christmas is coming up. Too bad I haven't any idea what you might like."

Tess's smile is its own reward. She could spend days in a stationery store, same as a bookshop.

"I'll miss class for this," she decides, jumping up.

"Good. You can help me figure out how to buy an illegal newspaper, too."

CHAPTER
3

TESS AND I SLIP OUT THE FRONT DOOR unnoticed and make our way through the quiet residential streets. Above us, the sky is shrouded in gray; the roses are withering on our neighbors' gate. After a few blocks, the lawns shrink, the trees become sparse, and the houses grow closer together. Narrow two- and three-story brick buildings are the norm in the market district, with shops on the ground floors and living quarters above. Men of all classes hurry along the cobbled sidewalks. Vendors hawk meat pies and fresh hot bread, offer to shine gentlemen's shoes—and sell newspapers.

I make a beeline for the nearest shouting paperboy. "Witches attack the Head Council! Brother Covington in Richmond Hospital! Jailbreak at Harwood Asylum!" he chants. "Read the horrible news for yourself! Two pennies!"

I fumble in my pocket for coins. "This is the *Sentinel*?" I can't see the masthead because he's waving the paper so furiously in the air. He looks respectable enough, but Mei swore her brother gets the *Gazette* from regular paperboys, bold as you please.

The boy gives me a cheeky grin, black hair falling into his eyes. "Course it is, Sister. What else would I be selling?"

I step closer, lowering my voice. What will he do, arrest me for asking? He can't be older than Tess. "Do you know where I could get the—other paper?"

"I don't know anything about any other paper, Sister." He edges backward, dark eyes darting sideways. "I work for Brother Augustus Richmond, publisher of the *New London Sentinel*. That's the only legal paper in town."

"Of course it is." I smile with a conspiratorial air. "But perhaps you would know where I could procure a copy of—?"

"No, I wouldn't! What kind of trouble are you after?" The paperboy stalks away.

"For heaven's sake, Cate." Tess plucks at my sleeve, sighing. "You're going about it all wrong. He thought you were trying to set him up!"

My face flushes. "Well, what should I do, then?"

"Think. Who reads that paper? Not Sisters or upper-class girls." She tucks her arm through mine, and as we walk through the crowded street, her black cloak turns gray. A moment later, the pink lace hem of her skirt turns into tattered blue wool. Her nice fur muff morphs into worn blue mittens.

"Tess!" I hiss, terrified. I scan the block ahead of us. I don't spot any Brothers, but two of their guards are lounging outside a café. They could have seen her. *Anyone* could have seen her. My heart is racing. It's not like her to be this reckless; this is the sort of thing *Maura* would do.

"I'm not a child," she snaps.

"I know you aren't!" I run a black-gloved hand over my chilled face. "You're very powerful. And very important. Too important to risk your safety like this."

"Because of what I am?" she challenges, coming to a halt outside a flower shop.

"Yes," I admit. But that wasn't my first thought. "And because I love you and I would be lost—utterly lost—if anyone tried to take you away from me."

Tess bites her lip, staring at the imported tulips in the window. "Sometimes I think it would be better for everyone if I *were* arrested."

I grab her arm. "What? Why would you say that?"

Tess doesn't respond. She just tilts her head to the opposite street corner. There's another paperboy lounging against a grocer's window, talking animatedly with three working-class men in jackets and suspenders and blue jeans. "I think he's the one you want."

He's got a bag full of papers slung over his shoulder—a bag with SENTINEL printed on it in wide white letters. "Why do you think that?"

"He's doing a particularly brisk business. Look." Another man comes out of the grocer's with a pouch of tobacco. He lights a pipe and leans against the wall with the others. When he hands the paperboy his pennies, the boy hands him a paper—but even from across the street, I can tell it's thicker than the one I was offered earlier. "The *Gazette* must be tucked inside."

I gape at her, and Tess shakes her head. "You've got to watch before you go blundering into things. Come on, I'll get you your paper. Give me three pennies?"

I comply. "See? I'd be lost without you."

"I'll meet you at the stationery shop," Tess promises, racing across the street.

I follow her at a more sedate, Sisterly pace. Kneeling at the curb, I pretend to retie my bootlaces while Tess strolls toward the group of men. She greets them with words too low for me to hear, exchanges her pennies for a paper, and thanks the paperboy with a grin. The boy—a rascal with tousled blond curls who can't be older than fourteen—stares after her, and the men around him chuckle and say Lord knows what to make him blush.

Tess tucks the paper under her arm and strides off toward O'Neill's Stationery. I follow her. By the time I reach the shop, she's transformed into a demure young Sister again.

"Teresa Elizabeth Cahill," I scold, voice low. "Why, I ought to—"

She strokes a pack of cornflower-blue paper with purple daisies embossed on the top. "What are you going to do, drag me out by my ear?"

I huff and turn away, because she's right and, more abominably, she knows it. I scan the room, tempted to buy something for myself instead to teach her a lesson. I hardly need more writing paper—Tess handles writing to Father—but perhaps a nicer writing implement? I gaze down into the case of fine fountain pens.

Finn would *love* these. The room smells like him, dust and paper and ink. It's only missing the bracing bergamot scent of his tea. I turn in a slow circle, admiring little pots of ink in every color—brown, black, blue, green, purple, red—arranged in tidy rows on the shelves. I run a hand over a stack of thick ivory paper and try to ignore the sting in my throat.

Will everything remind me of him, forever?

"All right," I call to Tess, who's still browsing the rack of ladies' writing papers. "Is that the one you like best?"

Tess smiles slyly. "It is. And perhaps a new pot of ink? I fancy the violet."

"Perhaps for your birthday. *If* you behave!" I snatch up the stationery, already tied with a pink bow, and carry it to the counter.

An old man with a shock of white hair and kind brown eyes greets me. "That's very pretty. For the young lady there?"

"Yes. We're students at the Sisterhood," I explain, watching for his reaction.

There is none. He slides the sheaf of paper into a bag. "Can I help you find anything else?"

I lean against the high counter. "Are you Mr. O'Neill, the proprietor?"

"I am indeed. Been in business here since 1856." He smiles at me. "Is this the first time you've visited us?"

"Yes, but I hope it won't be the last." I glance over my

shoulder. There are two well-to-do matrons examining a display of calling cards, but they seem engrossed in their gossip. "I understand that you and Sister Cora were friends. I wanted to let you know that she passed away last night."

O'Neill bows his snowy head. "I'm sorry to hear it. Cora was a grand lady."

"I admired her very much. In fact, I—I was hoping to take up some of the work she did." I pull the necklace from beneath my cloak, displaying the brass key. "I wanted to leave a note for Brother Brennan."

O'Neill leans over the counter a bit, lowering his voice. "Ah. Then you haven't heard of the trouble he's in."

I shake my head, heart sinking. "What trouble?"

"It's all right there in your paper." He taps a finger against it. "The Head Council was attacked last night and Brennan was absent. Ill, he said. But there was a mutiny at Harwood Asylum, too; all the patients escaped. The nurses don't remember a thing—their memories were all erased—but the body of a witch was found with a man's handkerchief bearing the letter *B*."

"The letter *B*?" I freeze. That's Finn's handkerchief—*B* for *Belastra*—he gave it to Zara when she was coughing up blood.

My first, cruel thought is, *Thank goodness they're blaming Brennan instead.*

"Indeed." There's disapproval in the arch of his gray eyebrows. "The rest of the council has been rendered useless. Not outright murdered, but as good as. O'Shea's taken control until they can arrange a proper vote, and he didn't waste any time accusing Brennan of being in cahoots with the witches."

"Has Brennan been arrested, then?" I try to sort my thoughts. I've got to play this right. Gretchen said O'Neill was a supporter, but—

"No, miss. He's disappeared. No one knows where he might be." O'Neill rubs a hand over his white-stubbled jaw, dropping his eyes. The gesture gives the lie to his words.

"I see." I look over my shoulder. The matrons are tittering, heads bent together, and Tess has moved on to examine the fountain pens. I reach my hand into my pocket and withdraw the note. "I would like to leave this for him. In case he should . . . turn up."

"Here?" O'Neill's eyebrows lift again. "I don't see why he would. That attack last night on the Head Council made us— made *him* look a fool for arguing leniency against the witches. If the Brotherhood can prove he had foreknowledge of it, that's treason. And treason's a killing offense. Any sympathy he had for them—"

"It was—unfortunate, what happened to the council," I interrupt. He has every right to judge us for what Inez and Maura did. "I was Cora's student, Mr. O'Neill. Her protégée, if you will, and—"

"Doesn't sound like Cora's way, what happened." O'Neill shakes his head.

"It wasn't. Nor was it mine. But it's imperative that this note reaches Brother Brennan. So he knows who can be trusted—and who can't."

The old man's brown eyes widen, and he pockets the letter

as the matrons approach the counter. "Well, now. If you put it like that, Sister . . . ?"

"Cate." I pick up the bag for Tess.

He nods. "I'll see you tomorrow night, then, Sister Cate."

It begins to rain as we walk back to the convent. I'm quiet, lost in worry, and Tess has sunk into a black mood of her own. Neither of us brought an umbrella, and though we lengthen our strides, our woolen cloaks are soon soaked through.

I had hoped that by saving Brennan from Inez's attack, I would be positioning him to succeed Brother Covington. I thought we were helping him, not setting him up to be accused of treason.

I shiver into the scratchy wet wool of my hood, remembering the day Brother O'Shea arrested poor Mrs. Anderson. A widow with two children to feed, she'd allowed a customer from her bakery to escort her home. She was taken from her children and sentenced to a prison ship, and O'Shea relished it. He's the type to take pleasure in his power over others. A braggart and a bully.

And then there's Tess. I cast a sidelong look at her. Her steps drag, as though she dreads returning to the convent. My anger sputters out. Would she be safer—happier—back at home in Chatham, where she could bake and read and pretend to be a normal girl? She's seemed happy enough here. A little overwhelmed by the rush of the city, the crush and chatter of all those girls—but thrilled at all the opportunities for learning that the convent provides.

42

The fact is, no matter how much I wish it for her, Tess *isn't* a normal girl. She can't go home and pretend any more than I could. We've got responsibilities that we can't shirk, and I'll have to help her shoulder them as best I can.

We hurry up the marble steps of the convent, shucking our wet cloaks onto the pegs just inside the door. They drip onto the green carpet below. "Let's have a chat in my room, in front of the fire," I suggest, teeth chattering.

Tess holds out her wet pink skirts. "Can I change first?"

I nod. We part ways on the third floor. Tess trudges down the hall to the room she shares with Violet van Buren, while I go into the cheery room I share with Rilla. I unhook the buttons down the front of my gown and let it pool at my feet. Stepping out of my black skirt, I hang it over the hissing radiator to dry. I'm standing in my corset cover and petti-coats, pulling a green dress splashed with white poppies from my armoire, when Tess rushes into my room without knocking.

"Cate! Cate, come quick!" she cries.

"What is it?" I ask, drawing the dress down over my head.

Her face is pale, her eyes shining with tears, and she's still dressed in her wet pink frock. "It's Cyclops," she gasps.

Cyclops is the one-eyed teddy bear she's cherished since she was little. "Is he missing?"

"No, he—" She swallows. "Come and see."

I make quick work of the green velvet sash at my waist and hurry after her.

"Tess? Cate? What's wrong?" Lucy Wheeler and Rebekah Reed are heading toward the stairs, their arms full of books.

"Nothing," Tess lies. She stands in her doorway until I join her. "Look, Cate, someone—"

Her voice cuts off. I stare at her side of the room: the polka-dotted curtains Mrs. O'Hare sewed for her, the daguerreotype of Mother and Father on her windowsill, the blue quilt on her bed. Cyclops rests on her pillow.

"Someone what?" I prompt.

Tess strides into the room, staring up at the top of her window. "He was *hanging*!"

"Hanging?" I echo, confused.

"Cyclops was hanging from the curtain rod. By a rope. By his neck." She shudders, rushing over to the teddy bear and picking him up as gingerly as though he were a spider.

I frown. "Perhaps it was an illusion? Someone playing a trick on you?"

Tess tosses Cyclops onto the bed. "There was a note pinned to his hand that said *You'll be next*. Does that sound like a schoolgirl prank to you?"

"No." It sounds like a threat.

"Who would do that?" Tess whimpers, curling into a wet pink ball.

I sit next to her, rubbing her back in circles. "I don't know. But we'll find out. We'll keep you safe, Tess. I promise."

CHAPTER

4

RICHMOND CATHEDRAL IS THE BROTHERS' pride and joy. It is a place intended for worship, yes, but also for the great pomp and circumstance of state ceremony. Brother Richmond and his first followers hailed from Salisbury in England, and they say our cathedral's design is based on the great cathedral there. Outside, the stone edifice is niched with statues of apostles and the early church fathers. Above us, the spire rises three hundred feet—by law, the tallest building in all of New England. Below us, former Head Council members sleep in the marble crypt.

The cathedral is laid out in the shape of a crucifix. Pointed arches support the high, buttressed ceiling, and the stained glass windows lining the walls are filled with beautiful, terrible illustrations of the

Lord's miracles. Beyond the sanctuary, on the north wall, He ascends to heaven. Before Him, dozens of shining mahogany pews are filled with mourners.

Brother O'Shea, puffed up with new importance, leads the service. It's meant to be an honor, the new head of the Brotherhood delivering her eulogy, but O'Shea knew nothing about Sister Cora. His words, tinny and false as a badly tuned instrument, set my teeth on edge.

"Sister Cora was a good woman, and we mourn her passing. But we must remember that she was an anomaly. It is dangerous to encourage our girls to educate themselves, lest they be distracted, their minds sullied by matters that ought not concern them. True study of the Scriptures must be left to men, whose minds are more capable of discerning the true word of the Lord."

His blue eyes are piercing as he gazes out into the crowd. I cast my face down to hide my outrage. "Most girls cannot manage the"—his nose wrinkles, his long face betraying his distaste—"*independence* that Cora was permitted as a member of the Sisterhood. Women require their husbands' guidance to determine right from wrong. I must admit, I have my doubts about whether the Sisterhood still has a place in New England."

The faces around me are carefully blank, though I know Rilla and Mei must feel the same fury and fear that I do. O'Shea has the power to close the convent and put us all out on the street, or force us into loveless marriages, and he wants us to know it.

"Any deviation from the path raises questions of obedience. Education leads to rebellion. The dangers we face from unscrupulous women—from witches, who believe they are not only our equals but our superiors—has never been greater." Next to me, Rilla bites her lip. "Brother Covington and the other council members lying comatose in Richmond Hospital serve as testament to this. So does Sean Brennan, who is now in hiding, justly fearing the consequences of having freed the witches imprisoned in Harwood. Lord knows what vengeance those madwomen will wreak!"

I glance at the mahogany casket that holds Sister Cora's body. I can't let her down. I've got to find a way to reinstate Brennan into the Brotherhood's good graces—to make it clear that he ran for his life, not out of guilt.

We'll never get anywhere with a tyrant like O'Shea in charge.

After the service, we lead the way through the afternoon gloom to the funeral reception at the convent. Delectable breads and scones and small tea sandwiches march down the dining room tables. With Sister Sophia—the best cook in the Sisterhood—still away, Tess and some of the other girls spent the morning in a flour-drenched frenzy of baking. Tess is in the kitchen now, plating scones and washing dishes. She seems happier today, unafraid, but I can't forget that someone in the Sisterhood wants to do her harm.

The sideboard is stacked with the convent's best gold-and-white china, and Sisters Johanna and Edith bring out pots of steaming tea and chocolate. The pocket doors between the dining room and sitting room are thrown wide. Inez and Gretchen have adopted the roles of mourners-in-chief, greeting guests, reminiscing about Cora's good deeds.

Gretchen's eyes are bloodshot and rimmed in red. Inez's are not.

Our Sisterly uniforms—black bombazine dresses that stretch from throat to wrists to ankles, black heeled boots, and black satin gloves—are well suited to mourning. None of us wants to draw attention to ourselves. We keep our voices respectfully low, gazes cast down demurely.

No one will find any banned texts within the convent's gray stone walls today. The Gothic novels on the bookshelf have been transformed into books of Scripture. The fashion magazines from Dubai and Mexico City have been hidden. In the healing classroom, Bones the skeleton and charts of the human musculature have been locked away.

My eyes catch Maura where she stands with Alice next to the pink velvet settee. The severity of the Sisters' uniform suits my sister; it emphasizes her flame-bright curls and pale skin. As she raises her teacup, her sapphire eyes meet mine. There is nothing of apology in them. Nothing of guilt or contrition.

I want to break her. I want the china cup to explode in her hands, the shards to cut her, staining her creamy skin scarlet.

I want to hurt her the way she's hurt Finn and me. The second I think his name, the dull ache in my chest rises to a roar. His sweetness when I'm snappish. His revelation that my favorite childhood novel was written by a woman. *And a Catherine, no less.* His promise that whatever came next, we would work through it together.

He won't keep that promise. I am the only one who remembers it.

My magic rises, inextricably bound to my anger. It burns
through me. I try to shove it back down, but it sizzles through
my muscles, scorching my throat, singeing my fingertips. My
eyes dart away from my sister's, but it's too late.

Across the room, Maura stifles a cry.

I hurry from the room, but not before I see Alice bend to
pick up the pieces of Maura's cup. Maura's cradling her hand
where the jagged china cut through her thin satin glove. "So
clumsy," she apologizes, her clear voice ringing out like a bell,
and her abashed smile seems to allay everyone's concern. No
one seems to notice that the cup broke in her hands, before
it hit the floor. But Maura knows. At least, she suspects. I can
feel the weight of her eyes on my back, right between my
shoulder blades, following me out into the hall.

I am horrified. At my instinct to do my sister harm. At losing my temper like a reckless child.

"Cate!" a voice says as someone catches my elbow and
draws me into the anatomy classroom. It's Elena. She shuts
the door softly behind us.

"Yes?" My voice is sharp. Did she see what I did?

Well, she's not my governess any longer. She's only a
year and a half older than me; she's got no right to chas-
tise me.

Her chocolate eyes dip to the wooden floor. "I heard what
Maura did."

Oh. I set my jaw. "I don't wish to discuss that."

Elena's brown fingers, lined with silver rings, twist in her skirts. "I'm worried about her. Why would she do something so cruel?"

I laugh without any real mirth. "Isn't it obvious? She was jealous because I had Finn, and she lost you. She can't forgive me for it. Likely she thinks we're even now."

"What happened between Maura and me—" Elena pauses, struggling with the words. "That was my mistake. Not yours. I should have been honest about my feelings, no matter what it cost me."

I slump into a desk. What would my life be like if things had gone that way? I cast my mind back to that dreadful scene in Elena's bedroom at our house. Only two months ago, though it feels a lifetime now. I was so certain that Elena was using Maura.

"Letting Maura think you care for her won't win you any favors if I'm ever in a position of power."

Elena looks at me for a long moment.

Finally, she turns to Maura. Puts a hand on her ruffled cream sleeve. "Maura," she says, "I think you've misunderstood my feelings."

Maura's blue eyes fill with tears. "Don't say that," she begs, taking Elena's other hand. "Don't listen to Cate. Please. I—I love you!"

"I'm flattered by your regard," Elena says, pulling away, "but I don't return it."

Maura reaches out a hand, then lets it fall. The same hand that cradled Elena's face so gently. "But you kissed me!"

Elena shakes her head. "You took me by surprise. It was a mistake."

Maura looks past Elena to me. "You were right," she snaps, running from the room. "Are you happy now?"

I wish I could reach back in time and tell myself to choose differently, because I am the farthest thing from happy I can imagine.

"Well, you weren't honest with Maura," I tell Elena. "And I'm the one being punished for it."

"There has to be more to it than that." She hops onto the desk in front of me, her boots on the chair, elbows propped on her black-clad knees.

"Does there?" I ask. "I thought it was just the way sisters are, always fighting, always jealous. I've been jealous of her, too. Of how clever she is. How pretty. How vivacious. People have always been drawn to her, they—well, you'd know that better than anyone, I suppose."

"I would," Elena agrees. "She may be impulsive, but she's not unkind. Not really. This is Inez's influence. We've got to—"

"No." I trace a finger across the scarred wooden desktop. "If you want her saved from Inez's clutches, you'll have to do it yourself. Maura's not innocent in this. She knew what she was doing. She warned me, in her own way, that we couldn't work with the Brothers anymore. She even told Finn to leave, that he wasn't welcome here with Cora gone."

"But he wouldn't leave you." There's something envious in Elena's eyes.

I sigh. "And Tess is the oracle anyway, so it was all for nothing. Maura will never lead the Sisterhood."

"You're glad of that, aren't you?"

I leap up at the sound of Maura's voice. My muscles go

tight; my jaw clenches. I go to the front of the room, facing the chalkboard, with my back turned to her.

"You kept it from me. How long did you know?" Maura asks.

It takes me a moment to realize she means Tess.

She stalks closer, her boots tap-tap-tapping across the floor like Inez's. I can smell her sweet citrusy scent, from the lemon verbena she dabs at her wrists and throat.

I hear Elena jump down from the desk. "Maura, not now."

"What friends the two of you have become, having these cozy little chats," Maura says. "Who would have thought?"

Jealous again. I curl my fingers into fists. She's so *petty*.

"Cate, I seem to have a cut on my hand. Since you're the one who put it there, I think you ought to heal me."

I turn. Take the five steps across the classroom and grab my sister's bare hand. There's a small red cut on her palm; the bleeding has already stopped. The second I touch her skin, I can feel the injury as well as see it. It's a tiny needling thing.

Maura's watching me, her pink lips pursed. She's always said healing was the most useless form of magic. Naturally. Because it's what I'm good at.

I squeeze her hand, unthinking, and blood trickles across her palm. "Ow," she cries, trying to pull away, but my grip is tight. Instead of stitching the cut closed, I reach out with my magic and rip it open. The cut stretches. Gapes. Becomes a two-inch gash, splashing scarlet onto my own skin.

"Cate!" Elena grabs me, her fingers pinching the soft flesh above my elbow, pulling me away.

My sister stares at me, her blue eyes wide and shocked.

I hurt her. I used my magic—my *healing* magic—to hurt her. On purpose.

I turn, heading for the door.

"Stay away from me." My breath is coming fast, my cheeks flushed. "I don't want to talk to you. I don't even want to *look* at you!"

As I step into the hallway, I hear a crash. Across the hall in the sitting room, the babble of voices continues.

To my left is Inez's classroom. I open the door cautiously.

Alice is on her arse next to an overturned stool. She's got her black skirts flipped up over her knee, and she's massaging her ankle. Ordinary boots won't do for her; she's wearing heeled shoes with decorative buckles. They're new, judging from the shiny, unmarked look of the leather.

"What do you want?" She scrambles to her feet, wincing.

Gracious as always. "I heard you fall. I wanted to see if you were all right."

"I'm fine," she snaps, limping to the nearest desk.

"What on earth were you doing?" My eyes travel up the wall and land on the open brass vent near the ceiling. It connects to the formal parlor next door. "You're spying!" I declare, voice low, rather delighted to have caught her at it. "On whom? What's going on in there?"

Her porcelain cheeks flush. "Sister Inez and Sister Johanna are meeting with Brother O'Shea. About his plans for the Sisterhood. Sister Inez—she said—"

"What? What did she say?" I demand, righting the stool.

Behind me, the door creaks open. Elena and Maura peer

in. "What happened here?" Elena asks. She's carrying a thick roll of bandages. Maura's hand has been wrapped.

"I tripped," Alice says crossly, tucking a stray golden tendril back into her pompadour.

"What were you doing?" Maura asks.

Alice's blue eyes dart between Maura and me. "Nothing," she lies. "I came in to fetch a book and wasn't watching where I was going and walked right into that stool. I twisted my ankle something fierce."

I bite my lip. Alice is the biggest gossip at the convent. Why isn't she rushing to tell Maura what she heard?

"Is Cate going to heal you?" Maura smirks.

When Sister Sophia told me that there was a dark side to healing, I never imagined I'd be capable of using my magic to make someone's pain worse.

Never thought there would be something in me, something small and dark and shameful, that would be *glad* of hurting my own sister.

"Excuse me," I choke out. And then, coward that I am, I flee.

Later that night, Elena and I make our way through the market district, keeping to the shadowy, garbage-strewn alleys that run behind the shops. The air smells of rotting vegetables and spoiled meat, and we surprise more than one person digging through the bins in search of a meal. Up ahead, an open door spills light and music and men. Three sailors meander down the alley, weaving and laughing. Elena clutches my elbow, and we slip into a dark doorway until they pass.

Two doors down, a man with a toothless black smile

whistles at us. "Hey, darlin'," he says, grinning, indiscriminate in his interest. Elena gives him such a look that he scuttles away in the opposite direction.

We cross the street onto a quieter block. The back of O'Neill's Stationery is unassuming; there are no windows, only a wooden door and a small sign directing deliveries. A tiny sliver of lantern light creeps beneath the door. I glance over my shoulder, making sure we're quite alone, before pulling the ruby necklace over my head, transforming it into the key Gretchen gave me, and quickly fitting it into the lock. We slip into the storeroom. Boxes of stationery and calling cards join wedding, funeral, and birth announcements in neat stacks on floor-to-ceiling shelves. The room is small, but utterly organized.

There are three doors: one to the alley, one into the shop, and a third that must lead to the basement and the Resistance meeting.

I loop the necklace back around my neck, nerves swarming like bumblebees, and open the third door. Starting down the steps, I trail my gloved hand over the rickety wooden rail. Elena follows. I blink as my eyes grow adjusted to the light.

In the cellar, seven men lounge around a long table covered with newspapers, mugs of ale, and a few candles. Fear spins spiderwebs down my spine. What if this is some kind of trap? What if they lure us into revealing our witchery and then turn us in? What if, what if, what if—my brain chants the fears.

"Sister Cate." Mr. O'Neill stands. "Welcome."

Are we? The other six men stare at us without rising to

their feet, their faces arranged in solemn, suspicious lines. They do not want us here; that much is clear. But is it because we're witches or because we're women?

"Thank you." I shake his hand, quite businesslike. "Mr. O'Neill, this is Sister Elena. Elena, this is Mr. O'Neill, the proprietor here. And please, call me Cate. I'm not a full member of the Sisterhood yet."

Elena smiles up at him. "Thank you for letting us join you."

"Wasn't aware we had much of a choice." The man at the head of the table stalks over, peering down his patrician nose at us. "Cora gave *her* the key? She's a child! Barely out of short skirts!"

I bristle. I haven't worn short skirts since I was thirteen, and I haven't been a true child since then, either. Not since Mother died and I assumed the responsibility of looking after my sisters.

O'Neill hides a grin behind one wrinkled, liver-spotted hand. "Sister Elena, Cate, this is Alistair Merriweather, publisher and editor in chief of the *Gazette*."

This is Alistair Merriweather? I gape at him. From Gretchen's description, I was expecting some old curmudgeon, but he can't be more than twenty-five himself, and he looks more poet than revolutionary. He's tall and angular, with a square jaw and black hair that flops over his pale forehead. He may be in hiding like Brennan, but he's dressed like a dandy, with a purple silk cravat wrapped around his throat and a brocade vest and black jacket over a snowy white shirt.

"Hugh, this is mad. Surely you see that!" Merriweather throws up his hands. His fingers are streaked with black newsprint and blue ink, which reminds me of Finn. "It was one thing to allow Cora access to our meetings. She brought us valuable intelligence. We may have disagreed at times"—here, O'Neill snorts—"but she was clever enough—for a woman. What can this child offer us?"

Clever enough—for a *woman*? And he calls himself a progressive? I grit my teeth. "I can hear, you know. As for what I've got to offer"—I touch the key around my neck, transforming it back into a ruby. "Magic."

"More witches from within the Sisterhood? How . . . interesting." Merriweather glances at me and then, obviously finding me wanting in some way, he turns to Elena. "Where's Gretchen? I thought she'd be the replacement."

"Sister Gretchen is ill." Elena doesn't wait to be invited to sit at the table. She crosses the room, slim hips swaying, black skirts rustling, and takes an empty chair. "She's been keeping vigil for Cora all week."

"I was sorry to hear of Cora's passing." Merriweather bows his head, and the five men around the table follow suit. "But I've got to confess, I don't see the need to have *any* of you here."

"Any of us?" I ask, voice tart. "Witches, or women?"

"Either. Both." He's got delicate winged brows over those penetrating gray eyes. "I'm not a proponent of giving women the vote. We already face an uphill battle in giving men from every race, every class, and every religion a voice in the new government. Insisting on giving women the vote—or on permitting the practice of magic—will make our battle well near impossible."

"Well, that's a rather defeatist view to take." I prop one hand on my hip. "I thought you were a progressive, sir. Don't you believe in equal rights for everyone?"

"For all *men*." Merriweather paces, his footsteps muffled against the dirt floor. "The common men are the best thinkers of our age. The philosophers and writers, those standing up to fight against—"

"Because you're seldom arrested for it!" I interrupt, temper boiling over. "Women step one toe out of line and we're accused of being witches and thrown into Harwood. More often than not, the women there can't do a lick of magic. It's punishment for wanting more than the cages of wife and mother and daughter that the Brothers would put us in."

There's a pause, and then an older man with muttonchop whiskers laughs, rocking back in his chair and taking a long swallow from his mug. "Sounds familiar, don't it, Alistair?"

"Just like Prue." O'Neill grins, taking the empty seat across from Elena. "Have you heard from her yet?"

"Not yet." Merriweather's jaw clenches.

Who is Prue? A girl he fancies? I can't imagine a woman putting up with him. "We need to work together, Mr. Merriweather," I insist, striding forward. "Witches and all those who oppose the Brotherhood. If we've got any hope of effecting change—"

"After what you did to the Head Council?" Merriweather shakes his head. "Aligning ourselves with the witches is impossible now. You've read my editorial on the attack?" He says it with such faith that even though I have—even though I made a point of it—I am tempted to deny it.

"Yes, and I agree with you. The attack was shortsighted and morally wrong." I sigh. He may be conceited, but I need Merriweather's help. His newspaper reaches a great many men that I cannot, and his good opinion may come in handy. "I opposed it."

His eyes narrow. "Wait—you know who was responsible for it?"

I cross my arms over my chest, fighting the urge to run into the cobwebby corner. "I do."

He moves closer, grasping my elbow in his excitement, heedless of propriety. "Tell me. We'll out them in the paper. What better way to show we don't endorse such tactics?"

I'm tall for a woman, but he must be over six feet, and broad shouldered. I have to remind myself that he isn't trying to restrain me—and that I could toss him across the room in a trice with my magic. "No." I glare down at his fingers on my arm.

"You don't think they deserve punishment?" He releases me. "If that's the case, I don't see how we can possibly—"

"They want to rule New England the way the Brothers do, through fear and intimidation. The best punishment is making sure that doesn't happen. I support the notion of a shared government. Isn't that what you want, too?" I ask.

Merriweather purses his mouth. "It's rare that anyone with true power wants to share it. Whom exactly are you speaking for?"

Elena laughs. The sound draws the attention of every man in the room. "We could deliver at least half the witches in New England. They would follow Cate. Not because she's compelled them or frightened them into it, mind you, but because they respect her. She's sacrificed a great deal to help us."

Not willingly. I would never have given up Finn, had I a choice in it. But she's right. Somehow, in addition to being the girl who engineered the Harwood breakout, I've become something of a tragic romantic heroine. For the last two days, the girls at the convent have been falling over themselves offering me sympathy. Worse, they want to know the details of my romance with Finn, details both too painful and too private to share.

"Half the witches in New England? That is impressive. Almost as impressive as the fifth of the city who buys my newspaper." Merriweather preens, adjusting his cravat, then freezes. "You're not the oracle?"

"How do you know about the oracle?" I wonder how he'd take the news that she actually *is* a child.

"We have sources within the Brotherhood," Merriweather explains. "Don't try to misdirect me."

He turns to Elena and she shakes her head, black curls bouncing. "Do you think we would be so foolish as to send the oracle to a meeting like this?"

"Is she here, in New London? Have her powers manifested?"

"Mr. Merriweather." I sigh. "If I did know, would I hold her safety so lightly as to tell *you*?"

He shoves his hands in his coat pockets. "Tell me just one thing. Did the oracle support the attack on Covington?"

"No. I'm not protecting the people who did that," I insist, glancing around the table. In the wavering candlelight, it's difficult to read the men's faces. Do they agree with Merriweather, that we've got no place here and no hope of one in our own country? "But revealing them right now would put us all in danger and give up secrets better kept hidden for the time being." Like the fact that the Sisterhood is made up entirely of witches.

"What kind of secrets?" Merriweather demands.

I jut my chin at him. "If I told you, they wouldn't stay secrets for long, would they?"

"Stop hounding the girl, Alistair. There are other stories to tell." The muttonchop man crashes his chair back down to all four legs. "That O'Shea is a mean son of a bitch. Interview any family that's ever come in contact with him and they'll tell you."

"We've got to work on clearing Brennan's name," O'Neill adds. "That should be your priority now. I don't agree with the attack on the Head Council, but if we could get Brennan in charge, it'd be a boon for everyone."

"Interview the nurses at Harwood. None of 'em remember seeing Brennan. They don't remember anything. That handkerchief is just—what do you call it?—circumstational evidence," a wiry gray-haired man adds. "Someone could have planted it there, O'Shea himself maybe. He ain't above it."

"Brennan's wife swears he was sick as a dog and didn't leave his house that night. His wife and daughters all vouched for him. That's not good enough for O'Shea and his cronies, though." O'Neill thumps an angry fist against the wooden table.

"Have you spoken with him directly? Did you give him my note?" I ask.

"I did, but he won't be here tonight. Too dangerous coming into the city proper right now. If he's caught—well, I wouldn't put it past O'Shea to have him shot for resisting arrest or some such. He's a sneaky bastard." O'Neill nods at Elena and me. "Pardon the figure of speech."

"He's staying outside New London, then? Nearby? Can you arrange a meeting?" I ask.

"Gentlemen." Merriweather doesn't raise his voice, but all eyes flock to him. "We will continue our investigation and clear Brennan's name. That is the *Gazette*'s highest priority. Never fear—we will find out the truth of this handkerchief."

My eyes fly to the dirt floor, cheeks flushing. He can't find out the truth. Then it will be Finn in trouble, and he won't even know why or how to defend himself. He'll be accused of treason and—

Merriweather runs a hand through his tousled black hair. "Before we share any other confidential information, I think we ought to vote on whether to allow Cate and her cohort a say in the proceedings."

"Vote?" I ask. "I thought we inherited Cora's seat."

"The key, perhaps, but not the right to use it." Merriweather gives an elegant, insufferable shrug. "We'll let you know our decision."

He strides back to the table, taking his seat at the head of it, and it's obvious that we've been dismissed.

Elena stands. "How?"

He smirks, reaching for his mug of ale. "Don't worry. We'll find you."

I want to argue, but it will only make me look childish. Instead, I give a curt nod and follow Elena up the stairs into the storeroom.

We're quiet until we slip out into the freezing midnight air.

"It's only his arrogance getting in the way." A scowl scrunches Elena's pert nose. "We'd be dead useful to him. He's got to see that."

"Does he? He doesn't seem to think very highly of women. We are half the population. The half that no politician has appealed to for a whole century," I add. "If the new government gave women the vote—"

"Would their husbands let them exercise it?" Elena interrupts.

Around us, the back alleys are deserted. I snuggle into my cloak, wondering where the men who were searching the bins for scraps went. Wondering if they've got a warm place to sleep. "I can't think all husbands would be so small-minded."

Finn wouldn't be.

"We could compel Merriweather," Elena suggests. "If he fell in line, they all would."

"I don't want to resort to that. Not if they're to be our allies," I argue.

I don't say what's in my heart: I don't want to compel the Resistance leaders, but if Merriweather's investigation leads him to Finn—if it were the only way to keep Finn safe—I would do it in a heartbeat.

CHAPTER
5

THE FOLLOWING SATURDAY NIGHT IS the Brothers' Christmas bazaar—an annual tradition in New London. Vendors set up booths around the duck pond in Richmond Square Gardens, and the public must buy tickets to enter the gates. The proceeds go to the Sisterhood so that we can deliver extra rations and Christmas presents to the poor.

I'm curled up on my bed, listening to the swish of petticoats as girls run down the hall to borrow brooches or earbobs. They have to wear the black uniform of the Sisterhood, but it's still a night out. They call to each other in bright, excited voices and help one another fix their hair, though it'll be hidden by hoods and blown askew by the sharp December wind.

Tess is sitting at my dressing table, arranging her

pale blond curls in a pompadour. "Are you sure you won't come?"

There was some question as to whether any of us should attend this year, since we're ostensibly in mourning. Wouldn't it be disrespectful to Sister Cora, whose body was laid to rest only a week ago? But we're supposed to have a booth, selling hats and mittens and scarves we knitted ourselves, so Inez decided we should go through with it.

"Quite." I'm not in the mood for a bazaar. "Are you sure you won't stay home? We'll have the place almost to ourselves. We can make cocoa and . . ." I cast about for something that Tess would like. "Play chess?"

"You're terrible at chess." Tess wrinkles her nose. "I'm not going to lock myself up here forever, Cate."

"Not *forever*." I hug my knees to my chin. "Just until things settle down a bit."

"That could be years." She stands, retying the black satin sash at her waist. "I'm going."

"Fine. But no magic. Not for any reason," I say, last week's recklessness still fresh in my mind. "There will be hundreds of Brothers there."

The National Council meeting was supposed to end yesterday, but they've called an emergency extension because of the attack on the Head Council. I felt curiously relieved when I heard of it. Finn's been working as a clerk for Brother Denisof, but now that Denisof's lying comatose in Richmond Hospital, what will he do? Go back to Chatham to teach in the Brothers' school? He might be safer there, but the thought of him being so far away makes my chest ache.

65

"I know that." Tess scowls at me. "I just want one night out. I want to shop for little trinkets for Father and Mrs. O'Hare, and walk around with Lucy and Bekah like a normal girl! Like the world isn't falling in on my head all the time! Is that too much to ask?"

"Of course not. I'm sorry." Chagrined, I press my fingertips to my temple, where a headache is beginning to bloom.

There's a wild rapping on the door and Brenna pokes her head in, her chestnut hair falling in a tangled curtain to her waist. "I need to talk to the little one."

"Are you all right?" I ask. Brenna is wearing a dress of Rory's, though she hasn't the curves to fill it out properly. The vibrant red velvet seems strange on her, like a child playing dress-up.

I wonder how Rory and Sachi are faring. They should be settled into their safe house by now—a farmhouse in the woods of Connecticut. Will they come back to the convent once they've seen the other girls established, or will they opt to stay there?

I never thought I'd miss Rory Elliott's company, but I do. She has a way of making me laugh when I need it most.

"I had a vision. You told me to say when I had a vision." Brenna's all-seeing eyes dominate her narrow face—gaunt from two months of being half starved.

"Yes." Tess glances at me and then away. "Should we go to your room and talk about it?"

I cross my arms over the green ruffles of my bodice, stung by her secrecy. "You can talk about it in front of me."

"Something terrible is going to happen," Brenna says, plucking nervously at her red skirt. "He'll announce it tonight."

"What? Who?" I jump to my feet.

Brenna scrunches up her face, squeezing her eyes shut. "There's a man with a horse face on a stage, in front of lots of people. It's dark out. He says something and they all gasp and you—you're there, little one, and you look sad. And you"—she whirls, pointing at me, almost smacking me in the face—"you're angry."

I'm angry all the time these days; that's no surprise. But it seems I will be going to the bazaar after all. "What does the man say?"

"I can't hear him. He's underwater, like a fish. It's like talking to someone in the ocean." Brenna mimes a breaststroke. "We used to go to the seashore sometimes, Mama and Papa and Jake and me. Before."

Before her father turned her in to the Brothers. Before Alice broke her brain.

"The man was underwater, and he has a horse's head?" Tess asks, clearly perplexed.

"Not a real horse's head, silly!" Brenna giggles. "A great long face. And a shiny bald head."

I take a deep breath, trying to stave off my frustration. This is the trouble with a broken oracle: She can tell us O'Shea will announce something terrible tonight, but not what. "Did you see anything like this?" I ask Tess. She shakes her head. "You haven't had any visions since Zara?"

Tess turns her back to me, but I catch her blush in the mirror over the dressing table. "I don't have to tell you everything."

"I know." I promised myself I wouldn't push her, but it's so hard. "I really don't think you should go tonight, Tess. Not if—"

Tess rolls her eyes at me in the mirror. "I'm not discussing this with you any more. I'm going and that's that. So are you, according to Brenna, so you ought to start getting ready," she snaps. "Come, Brenna. Let me take you back to your room."

She strides out of the room, Brenna dancing after her. Brenna is still skittish with everyone else, cringing like a whipped puppy if anyone touches her or stares—and every- one stares at Brenna. She ran into Alice again yesterday in the hall and screamed like a banshee. For the most part, though, she stays in her room. Tess brings her meals and visits her between classes to keep her company. I don't know what they talk about. Visions, perhaps, trying to piece to- gether how things will play out.

I've just changed into my Sisterly black when Rilla pops back into our room. She's all ready for the bazaar, her short brown curls artfully arranged around her freckled face.

"You've decided to come?" she asks. "You look pretty."

I glare at her. "I do not." I look like a tall, skinny blond vulture in the Sisters' uniform. I always do.

"Hush and take the compliment," she insists, braving a hug. She smells like hot cocoa and the maple candies her mother's always sending from their farm in Vermont. "Are you all right? You seem . . . pricklier than usual."

"I'm fine." I'm not fine. What's O'Shea cooking up now? Hundreds of Brothers will be at the bazaar. Any of us could make a misstep and be arrested. Things seem so on edge. And beyond that—

"Are you worried Finn will be there?" Rilla cuts right to the heart of it.

My breath catches in my throat, and I feel such a coward. Am I that obvious, that pitiful, that everyone can see the truth written on my face?

"I don't know," I whisper, burying my head in my hands. "I miss him. So much. I want to see him but—he won't know me. Not really. It's so awful, Rilla."

Rilla plants her hands on her sturdy hips and gives a fierce little scowl. "I could slap that sister of yours."

"Me too." I give her a weak smile, sliding on a pair of earbobs and glamouring them to look like rubies, to match my new necklace. "But it's done now, isn't it? There's nothing I can do."

"Are you sure of that?" Rilla picks up one of her Gothic novels. "You know, in *The Duke and I,* the duke is in a hunting accident; he falls off his horse and knocks his head and loses his memory. It's amnesia, not magic. But he and the duchess fall in love with each other all over again."

"That's impossible," I say shortly.

"Is it?" Rilla guides me to the dressing table, sits me down, and begins to braid my hair. "If Finn fell in love with you once, what's to say he couldn't do it again? You know him. Know what he likes. You could orchestrate things in your favor."

Hope thrums through my chest, but I quash it. "That

69

seems dishonest. Starting off with secrets between us." Like my parents. Mother erased Father's memory, leaving him unaware that she was a witch and he had three witchy daughters. It kept him safe from the Brothers, but I can't imagine their marriage was ever the same.

Rilla skewers the braids into place around the crown of my head. "You could tell him the truth, then. How you fell in love and what Maura did."

"Just like that?" I snap my fingers. "What if he turned her in?" I shake my head. Furious as I am, I cannot be responsible for Maura ending up—where? Without Harwood, where would they send a witch guilty of mind-magic? She would be executed.

I smooth my black skirts. "And it could be dangerous for him. What if she saw us together? What's to keep her or Inez from attacking him again and leaving him like—like Covington and the others? I can't take that chance."

Rilla's shoulders slump. "I suppose you're right. I just hate to see you so unhappy, Cate."

I stare down at my clenched hands. "Me too."

Hundreds of people mill through Richmond Square Gardens, all bundled up in their winter finery: ladies in fur hoods and men with their collars turned up against the cold. Lanterns swing from majestic red maples, sending light skittering over the crowd. Children run up and down the makeshift aisles playing tag while their mamas examine the merchandise. The bazaar is meant to benefit the poor, but I don't see many of them here. Now that the Brothers have outlawed women working, more families are struggling to make ends meet than ever. They've barely got money for food and shoes and coal, never mind Christmas treats.

The air smells of hot apple cider. People carry roasted chestnuts wrapped in cones of newspaper, and at the far end of the bazaar a hurdy-gurdy man performs with his monkey on a makeshift stage. Earlier, a pair of clowns delighted the audience with their pratfalls and juggling. Next up is a Christmas puppet show, according to the program.

I'm stationed at the Sisters' booth with Rilla, Mei, Vi, and two of the younger girls. The six of us volunteered for the middle shift, while the others wander the aisles and watch the performances.

"Yang would love those." Mei eyes the booth next to ours, where a man and his son sell clockwork toys. "He's always been a great one for taking things apart and putting them back together."

"Why don't you get him one for Christmas?" I suggest.

Mei laughs. "With what? I haven't any pocket money."

Of course. I flush, feeling thoughtless. Unlike Mei and some of the other convent girls, I've never had to worry about money. I fumble in my pocket for coins, then press them into Mei's hand. "Here."

She shakes her head. "No, I couldn't."

"Not for yourself. But for a Christmas gift for your brother, you can," I insist. "You ought to get something for your little sisters, too."

Mei glances wistfully, uneasily, at the coins in my hand. "I don't know."

"Christmas will be hard this year, won't it, without Li and Hua? Get some gifts for the others to make it brighter." Her two middle sisters are serving time on a prison ship for taking part in the Richmond Square protest last month, but she's still got two small sisters and a brother at home. "I've got plenty left to buy presents for Tess and my father." And something for Rilla and for Mei herself. "I'm happy to help, truly."

"It's just a loan. I'll pay it back," Mei promises, taking the coins. "Thank you, Cate."

I smile as she leans over the counter, angling for a better view of the merchandise next door. "Get them now! Before the ones you like are sold."

She looks around our booth, at Vi and Rilla selling mittens and the younger girls huddled in the back whispering. "I'll be right back."

"Take your time." I watch her push out of the booth and dodge other shoppers.

My heart leaps into my throat when a pair of black-cloaked Brothers turns into our aisle. The one on the left is about Finn's height, tall and lean. My pulse hammers in my ears, and I swallow, mouth suddenly dry.

As he strolls toward us, I realize his gait is all wrong. Too purposeful. Finn *ambles*, taking in everything around him with his quick eyes and quicker wit. Still, I wait for the man to get closer and confirm that he isn't wearing spectacles before I look away.

Stupid. It's the fifth time I've done this in the two hours I've been here.

There are hundreds of Brothers in attendance. Even if Finn *is* roaming around the bazaar, we could very well miss each other.

It's not as though he has any cause to seek me out.

I straighten the scarves on my side of the booth. Some are more expert than others. Mei, having grown up with a tailor for a father, has a steady hand and a good eye for color. Pearl and Addie often knit in the evenings while they chat, and their stitches are as meticulous as everything else about them. We've already sold five of Pearl's scarves, all a beautiful, soft gray wool. And Lucy's sister Grace has been sewing nonstop since she arrived from Harwood. The repetitive motions seem to comfort her. She sews. Livvy plays the piano night and day. Sister Edith's niece paints. Caroline chatters at anything, even potted ferns. And Parvati—

What *does* Parvati do? She's been having lessons with Inez, I know that much, and taking her meals with Maura and Alice.

I botched that.

A man's callused hand picks up a small blue scarf, startling me out of my thoughts. "I'd like this one, please."

I glance up, right into the face of the muttonchop man from the Resistance meeting. He smiles at me from behind his gingery whiskers. "Hello, Cate."

"Hello." I glance over my shoulder. Vi and Rilla are busy with other customers; the two younger girls are oblivious.

"The answer is yes, miss," he says. "It was unanimous. Alistair's bark is worse than his bite."

"I'm glad to hear it, Mr. . . . ?" I trail off.

"Moore." He watches as I fold the scarf for him. "I've got a lad at home, nine years old. I hope the world will be a better place by the time he's grown."

"So do I." I take the coins he proffers. "Thank you, Mr. Moore. Have a good night."

"We'll see you on Thursday, then, miss."

I nod and smile as I watch him go.

Mei pops back in, clutching a clockwork dragon. Her round face is troubled. "Have you heard anything about an outbreak of fever? Down near the river?"

"No, but I haven't been in that part of the city since—" I wince. Since I helped Tess on her unsuccessful mission to free the Richmond Square prisoners, including Mei's sisters.

"There have been a handful of deaths already. All in the river district." Mei swipes her bangs out of her black eyes. "At Cora's funeral, one of the nurses from Richmond Hospital mentioned they were overworked. I didn't think much of it at the time, but—"

"Should we volunteer to help?" Since Sister Sophia's off getting the Harwood girls settled at another safe house, we haven't been making our usual rounds at the hospital.

Mei nods. "Perhaps we can stop it before it gets out of hand."

"Of course. Do you want to go look for presents for your sisters? We're not very busy here. Then we can watch the puppet show together."

"Sure," Mei agrees, handing me the toy. "Watch this for me?"

The clockwork dragon is dead clever. I pull on the tiny lever that makes its tail whip back and forth and its mouth open in a silent, ferocious roar.

"Sister Cate?" The words are unfamiliar, but the voice isn't.

I drop the dragon onto the pile of scarves as I turn.

Finn's ears are flushing red, the way they do when he's embarrassed. His brow is furrowed, the space between his eyebrows pulled into the upside-down V that my fingers itch to smooth. His coppery hair is messy as ever, as though he's run his hands through it a dozen times since it last saw a comb.

But behind his wire-rimmed spectacles, his eyes are different. Not full of love or want. He doesn't look at me like I'm *his* anymore.

My heart breaks all over again.

"Brother Belastra." I choke out the words. They feel foreign, too formal on my tongue. "How are you?"

He gives me a smile that reveals the tiny gap between his front teeth, but it's only polite. The smile he'd give a stranger, a customer at the bookshop. "Very well, and you?"

"Fine." I'm not fine. I pull my elbows in tight, folding my arms across my chest. "Are you enjoying the bazaar?"

"Yes. I've been hunting down a gift for my sister." He examines the wares. "Are any of these yours?"

I laugh, short and staccato, before I realize he won't know his question is ridiculous. "Er, no. I'm a terrible seamstress. I prefer to spend my time in the gardens with my hands in the dirt—or now that it's winter, in the conservatory."

It's futile, testing him like this. He won't know. Won't

remember the way he snuck out and met me there and kissed me senseless. But—

"I remember," he says, and hope blooms through me, bright and lovely as an April tulip.

"You do?" My voice is too sharp, too desperate.

"Your father told me. We were—I don't quite remember." Finn frowns, the V in his forehead deepening. "He said you weren't the scholarly sort, that you preferred gardening to books. Funny that you've ended up in the Sisterhood."

Funny? An ache cuts through me, bitterer than the December wind. "I could say the same for you."

Finn glances over his shoulder. There are no Brothers in the vicinity. He gives me another bland smile, but now his eyes are curious. "I've always liked books."

What is the point in this? What am I trying to prove? I know I'm being foolish, and yet—

"But you've never been the Brotherly sort." My voice is so low, he has to lean over the booth to hear it.

He stares at the ground, shifting his feet. "I confess, of late, I'm not entirely certain what sort of man I am." His tone is rich with disgust. What must he be feeling, having found himself a member of the Brotherhood, with no notion of why?

"What do you mean?" I ask, then flush. In his mind, we barely know each other; I've been an occasional customer at his mother's bookshop, nothing more. Nothing to invite confidences. But I can't bear the notion that he's confused and alone and—damn Maura for doing this to him.

"Nothing." Finn straightens, running both hands through his hair. "I'm sorry to have bothered you." His voice has gone starched and his shoulders stiff as he remembers the proprieties.

I reach out, fingertips just brushing his wool cloak. "You're no bother. If I can do anything to help—"

"That's very kind of you. Very—neighborly." He barely glances at me as he pulls his hood up and steps away. "Thank you, Miss Cahill."

Neighborly? I watch him blend back into the crowd, my eyes blurring with tears. Then I kneel, ducking out of sight behind the counter, pretending to riffle through the boxes at my feet.

"Are you all right?" Rilla is at my side, wrapping an arm around me.

This time I can't summon up a lie. "No," I croak, burying my tearstained face in her shoulder.

"Of course. It was a stupid question. Do you want to go home?" she asks.

"I told Mei I'd watch the puppet show with her." And Brenna said something awful would happen. I've got to wait and see what it is.

Rilla smiles. "Mei would understand."

"No, I want to stay. I'll be all right." I struggle to my feet. All around us, people burst into applause while I try to swallow the ache in my throat. "It sounds like the hurdy-gurdy man's finished. Let's go to the stage."

I don't trust myself to be here when Maura shows up for her turn working the booth.

We're halfway to the stage when Brother O'Shea begins to speak. I recognize his loud, affected voice immediately.

77

Other people must, too, because they stop shopping and begin to drift toward the stage by the dozens. Mothers call their children; fathers gather their families close. Along the main thoroughfare, vendors hover outside their booths, keeping wary eyes on customers who listen with merchandise in hand. Whatever dreadful thing Brenna foresaw, it's happening.

Where is Tess? I scan the crowd, searching for her small figure, but there are hundreds of people and too many black cloaks. I walk faster, practically dragging Rilla behind me. At the end of the aisle, Brother O'Shea stands on the makeshift stage, his horsey face stretched into a counterfeit smile.

"Ladies and gentlemen, Brothers and Sisters, I'd like to interrupt our entertainment for just a few moments. As you know, last week there was a mutiny at Harwood Asylum for the Criminally Insane. Hundreds of witches escaped. They were helped by one of our own—Sean Brennan, who has fled the city rather than face justice for his treason." He swaggers across the stage like a man twice his size, and I get the sense that his speech is as rehearsed as his smile. He lacks the appeal of Brother Covington, who—despite his abominable politics—was a warm, charismatic speaker. "These women are a threat to all of New England. I have deployed our National Guardsmen to hunt them down, and I'm pleased to report that over the last week, we have recaptured two dozen witches hiding in empty barns and abandoned homes in the countryside."

My heart plummets, though I knew this might happen. Some of the Harwood patients fled as soon as the doors were open. They were free to make their own choice: come with Sisters to one of three safe houses or try to make it on their own. Over half of them chose the latter.

"If you have any knowledge of the whereabouts of more of these wicked girls, it is your duty to report it immediately." O'Shea's pale blue eyes sweep the crowd. "They may appear weak or confused, even pretend that they were beaten or starved, but this is only a witch's glamour. They are liars and deceivers all. You must harden your hearts against them."

He's clever, I'll give him that. I'd hoped that once I earned Merriweather's trust, I could tell him the truth about what happened at Harwood and he would run an article in the *Gazette* about the terrible conditions there. Now the people will be skeptical.

O'Shea ushers a tall woman onstage. "Don't be afraid, Mrs. Baldwin. Your fellow citizens deserve to hear the truth."

Her blue hood is down so that her fellow citizens can see her honest face. She's a broad woman with steel-colored hair pulled back into a bun and a plump face marred by a strawberry birthmark on her right cheek.

This is the nurse who killed my godmother, Zara Roth.

Who shot her, I correct myself. Technically, *I* killed her.

"What can you tell us about the conditions at Harwood Asylum, Mrs. Baldwin?" O'Shea asks.

"The girls there were well looked after, sir. They had two square meals a day and afternoon tea," she says, and how glad I am that Parvati and Livvy and the others aren't here to witness her lies! Mei pushes up next to me, her jaw set, black eyes snapping. "We had an infirmary with trained nurses to look after them when they were sick. They got fresh air every day, by way of a walk in the courtyard. And we tried to care for their souls as well as their bodies. A Brother came in every week and gave a sermon in the chapel. The girls who were well enough were given little tasks, helping in the garden or the kitchen. Idleness breeds devilry, you know. But those who weren't well enough—why, they didn't have a lick of work to do besides getting better."

"Thank you, Mrs. Baldwin." O'Shea gazes out over the crowd and smiles his thin-lipped, reptilian smile. Around me, people are hanging on every word. Hearing a firsthand tale of Harwood—why, that's much better entertainment than the hurdy-gurdy man! "You saw no evidence of mistreatment, then?"

"No, sir," she lies, folding her hands together in a prayerful manner. "Not once in my twelve years."

"Sounds as though they had it better than many of us who work for a living! Two square meals a day, plus tea, and free room and board!" O'Shea laughs, but it's a harsh, jeering sound. "Now, tell us, Mrs. Baldwin, what happened on the night of the mutiny."

The nurse shudders. "I usually work the day shift, see, so I wasn't even supposed to be there, but Mrs. Snyder's husband sent word she couldn't come on account of her baby was sick. So I was working, and I remember going down to the matron's office to fetch something. And then I sort of woke up with all the other nurses, and we were locked in the ward where the uncooperative girls were kept. We didn't know how we came to be there, but we were awful afraid those girls were going to burn the place down with us still in it. We got down on our knees and prayed, sir. And thank the Lord, the morning watchman came and found us there."

"Thank the Lord!" Brother O'Shea echoes, and the crowd around us offers their gratitude as well. "You're telling me, Mrs. Baldwin, that you have no memory of the mutiny? Someone went into your mind and erased that completely?"

"Yes, sir." The nurse's lip wobbles, her double chins quivering. "And I don't mind saying, it gives me the willies."

"I should imagine so. Knowing that a witch had been poking around in your mind—that would give even the bravest of us the willies!" O'Shea pats her sympathetically on the shoulder. "Thank you for your testimony, Mrs. Baldwin."

She nods and curtsies, scurrying offstage, and I breathe a small sigh of relief. That was ludicrous, but not as horrifying as Brenna made it out to be.

"The night watchman and six other nurses suffered the same mental violation. So, you see why these wicked girls cannot be allowed freedom. Among them are witches of the most evil, deceptive nature. They must be hunted down and punished!" O'Shea punches his fist into his open palm. "Fortunately, last week we were given intelligence that led us straight to a viper's nest. Yesterday, our guards located a farmhouse in Connecticut where no less than thirty-five witches were hiding."

Mei grabs my hand.

"They used magic to resist arrest. They were subdued, however, and are on their way back to New London under heavy guard." The crowd, led by a group of Brothers at the front, claps. O'Shea's grin is a ghastly thing. "Ladies and gentlemen, it has been many years since witches were put to death. It is not a sentence we assign lightly. But today, after much prayer, the National Council voted in favor of reinstating it. The wickedness of the sixty women we have recaptured knows no bounds; they must not be permitted to infect our society, to terrorize our nation, to threaten our safety, for one more day. Some of our soldiers are across the street, beginning to erect a gallows. Tomorrow, at noon, the hangings will begin."

CHAPTER
6

A FEW MEN IN THE CROWD YELL OUT epithets against the witches—but there are no cheers. Has it come to this, that I'm relieved my neighbors don't clap at the prospect of hanging sixty innocent girls? O'Shea swaggers offstage and the puppetry begins, but no one seems in the mood for it. A grave silence has settled over the bazaar.

This—well, this is awful. Brenna was right.

Of course she was.

Tess pushes through the dispersing crowd, Lucy and Bekah trailing after her, their mouths set like straight pins. "Sachi and Rory—" Tess begins.

"I know." They would have been the first to fight back, too, so Lord only knows what condition they're in. I don't imagine the guards would be stinting in their use of force.

We have to stop this, but how? How? The

question pounds like a drumbeat in time with my footsteps crunching against the wide graveled walk. I don't even know where I'm walking. The night is growing late, and the hour or the chill in the air or O'Shea's declaration or all three have people leaving the bazaar in droves, rushing home to the comfort of their own hearths.

The gates are packed with people leaving, so we wander up and down the aisles a bit. Rilla makes a good show of cooing over the merchandise, drawing Bekah and Lucy's attention to jeweled hair clips and cuddly stuffed animals. I buy a cider and press it into Tess's hands.

"I don't want it," she insists, shoving it away. A few drops spill onto my cloak.

"You're pale. Drink," I command, and she sighs and obliges. Even the vendors are beginning to pack up their booths. A few laughs ring out from the puppet show, but most of the children have been taken home. No one seems to be having fun anymore.

We wait while Lucy purchases a hot cake studded with currants and dusted with sugar. Mei is clutching Yang's toy dragon in a death grip. "Did you find something for your sisters?" I ask, and she nods, pulling a packet of colorful hair ribbons from her pocket. They're covered in vivid prints—strawberries, red and white polka dots, and yellow songbirds—that will stand out in her sisters' dark braids.

"Those are pretty," I say. "I bet they'll love them."

Mei's face twists beneath her dark fringe. "Cate, what are we—?"

"Not here." I can't help feeling as though the Brothers' eyes and spies are everywhere. Who told them about the farmhouse in Connecticut? Did a neighbor notice something suspicious? Only the fifteen girls who went on the Harwood mission knew about the safe houses, and most of them wouldn't have had access to the maps—certainly not in enough detail to tell the Brothers. Tess. Me. Sister Mélisande, who was to drive that wagon before Rory and Sachi took her place. Who else?

It couldn't have been one of us. The girls at the other safe houses will be all right. They've got to be.

We've made our way back to the Sisters' booth. I spot Maura's bright curls in the back. Elena is selling mittens at the front.

"*There* you are," Elena says, whirling on me the second her customer's gone, the smile slipping from her face. "Inez and some of the others have already left."

"We'll meet you at home?" I ask, and she nods.

When did I start thinking of the convent as my home, as a safe place to retreat?

And with Inez in charge, how long can that possibly last?

Dozens of girls have gathered in the dining room. They sit slumped in their chairs, chins propped on hands. A few of them sip from cups of tea, but most haven't bothered to take off their cloaks or boots. They're just—waiting. Quietly. With an air of funereal desperation. The only sound is the click of Grace's knitting needles.

When the six of us walk in, faces brighten.

"Cate!" Addie pushes up her spectacles with one finger. "What are we going to do?"

I'd have thought Inez would be down here scheming and denouncing the Brothers, but none of the teachers are present. Perhaps she and the others are locked away in her new office; she moved into Cora's suite of rooms right after the funeral.

"We didn't save them for them to be executed!" Vi's big plummy eyes are furious. "We've got to stop it!"

"How can we?" Alice toys with a strand of golden hair that's escaped from her pompadour. "The Brothers will keep them in the prison in the National Council building, with dozens of guards watching over them all night."

I've been going over our options on the silent walk home, and Alice is right. "We'll have to wait and free them tomorrow, then."

"In front of everyone?" Vi shrinks against the high back of her wooden chair. "But there'll be hundreds of people there!"

She's right, too. Hundreds will show up: a large contingent of Brothers and their guards, plus the curious, the terribly devout, and those who wish to be seen and thought terribly devout. Not to mention anyone with a loved one in Harwood who might be hoping to see her—or *not* see her—among the victims.

"Thousands, maybe," I agree, pulling off my cloak. "But a crowd that size—that's all the better to hide in, isn't it?"

Alice smooths her black velvet skirts. "What are you planning?"

Heeled boots tap, tap, tap their way across the wooden floor behind me. The familiar sound of Inez's approach makes me feel ill. "Whatever it is, Miss Cahill, put it out of your head this minute. The war council has voted not to intervene."

How is that possible? They can't mean to stand by and do *nothing.*

But I see the satisfied gleam in Inez's brown eyes and know that's precisely what she means. Before Cora died, the war council was evenly split—Cora and Gretchen and Sophia versus Inez and her lackeys Evelyn and Johanna. Now, with Sophia away, Gretchen would be the sole dissenting vote. I glance at her as she shuffles into the room, noticing the red that spiderwebs through the whites of her tired eyes. She has aged ten years in the last two weeks.

"You can't mean—you'd just stand by and watch them hanged?" Rilla's stocky body is practically vibrating with indignation.

Inez nods. "Sit down, girls."

I take the nearest chair, with Mei and Rilla at my elbows. Inez strides to the head table. The other teachers sit, but she stands behind her chair like a general before his troops. Her brown hair, graying slightly at the temples, is pulled back severely into a bun at the nape of her neck. In her unrelieved black, with her pinched face, hollow cheeks, and heavy brows, she is not a pretty woman—not even what Father would call handsome—but she commands the room nevertheless.

"This is a terrible thing the Brothers have voted to do," she says. "Anyone suspected of witchery will be killed, without trial. Without being permitted a word in her own defense. Soon, anyone who speaks up on a witch's behalf will be murdered as a sympathizer. What we are witnessing now is the beginning of a second Terror."

The room falls silent, save the crackling of logs in the fireplace. I shiver at the sound, remembering Brother Ishida's words on the night before I left Chatham: *'Twere up to me, I'd resurrect the burnings.*

Well, he's about to get his wish. His daughters will be among the first victims. They'll be hanged, not burnt, but why quibble over methods? Surely he'll be glad to see them dead, a devout man like that.

I look up at Inez. My emotions are churning, sending blood pumping through my veins. My stomach tumbles and my face flushes as my brain scrambles to think up ways to stop this. I will not see Rory and Sachi hanged. But Inez looks—calm. Her hands rest on the back of her wooden chair without trembling.

"They're doing this because of *you*," I say. Several of the younger girls gasp at my impudence. "Because of what you did to the Head Council."

"That's a heavy accusation, Miss Cahill." Inez purses her thin lips. "Do you think this is what I wanted? To see sixty innocent girls suffer? No. Those girls would still be safe in their beds if you and your friends had not freed them."

"Safe in our beds?" Parvati leaps to her feet. "No. We were never *safe* there."

"The fact remains—*I* am hardly responsible for this. If you wish to blame someone for the Brothers' sudden violence,

Miss Cahill, I suggest you look in the mirror." Inez sniffs. "I regret what the Brothers are planning to do, but it is not our obligation to stop it. Most of those girls are not witches. They are not our responsibility."

Sister Edith, the skinny art teacher, steps forward. "If they're not witches, that makes it worse. They're being murdered for crimes we've committed!"

"It's unfortunate," Inez admits, her eyes roving over the huddled group of girls. "But as head of the Sisterhood, my charge during these difficult times is to protect our members. Had it been up to me, I would not have taken in those of you not capable of magic."

Grace puts down her knitting and turns to her sister, panicked. "But I've got nowhere else to go!"

"I don't intend to turn you out onto the street now that you're here, Miss Wheeler." Inez waves a hand, her silver ring glinting orange in the firelight. "But there will be thousands of people gathered tomorrow: Brothers and their guards and people greedy for the spectacle of a mass execution. If we try to stop it, we risk drawing attention to ourselves. It would be tremendously difficult, if not outright impossible, to maintain glamours while doing that much magic. If we were caught, we wouldn't only risk individuals being arrested or executed— we'd risk exposing the entire Sisterhood and every girl in it."

Individuals must be sacrificed for the good of the whole. She doesn't say it, but it hangs there in the air along with the scents of tea and wood smoke. She doesn't give a damn about any one of us, only the power we collectively represent.

And Inez isn't wrong about the risks. It will require very

difficult magic; it's terribly dangerous. But not to even *try*? I couldn't live with myself.

"How does this make us any better than the Brothers?" I demand. "If we could stop it and don't?"

"We don't know for certain that we *could* stop it, do we?" Inez muses. "But the subject is not open for debate."

"I think it should be." Tess stands. "Don't I deserve a vote?"

Murmurs rustle through the room like a wildfire.

"She *is* the oracle." Rilla's words are hardly necessary, but they seem to bolster Tess. She stands taller, shoulders back, pushing pale blond curls away from her heart-shaped face.

Inez puts a skinny finger to her lips. "Did you foresee the Brothers' vote? Their recapture of these prisoners? Anything about tomorrow?"

The whole room seems to hold its breath. Tess's face goes a patchy red. "No."

Inez shrugs. "Then I don't see how being the oracle is relevant. We don't give Brenna Elliott a say, do we?"

"That's a false equivalency. I am hardly in Brenna's position." Tess narrows her gray eyes. "The prophecy says that *I'll* be the one to lead the resurgence of magic."

"Or cause a second Terror." Inez's smile withers. "I haven't forgotten that. You're a bit of a double-edged sword, aren't you? Nor have I forgotten that you are twelve and still sleep with a teddy bear. You have a great deal of growing up to do yet, my dear."

Tess flushes hotter at Inez's condescension, her shoulders slumping.

I rise. "Tess is old enough to know right from wrong, which is something you seem to struggle with."

"I forbid you to interfere, Cate." Inez plants her hands on her bony hips. "Richmond Square will be packed to the gills tomorrow. I doubt that you can save them, and in trying, you'll put us all in danger. I won't allow it."

"You won't *allow* it?" I let out a laugh. "What are you going to do, lock me in a closet? Immobilize me?"

There's a long pause. Inez fidgets with the ivory brooch at her throat, her brown eyes holding mine. "I can't stop you, that's true," she says finally. "But if you get caught, I will not risk other lives to save yours. My first concern, now and always, is the preservation of the Sisterhood."

By the time we've developed a patchwork plan, the sun is only a few hours from rising.

I want as few girls involved as possible. It is, as Inez said, a dangerous thing, made more dangerous by the fact that some of our strongest witches refuse to help. In the end, we decide we'll use only six—Elena, Mélisande, Rilla, Mei, Tess, and me.

I turn to Elena after everyone else has left her bedroom. "Do you think it will work?"

Even Elena, normally so elegant and unflappable, is a bit mussed at three in the morning. She's sprawled on her yellow chintz settee, her head resting against the arm, her brown eyes sleepy. "I hope so, or we'll all be dead," she says, stifling a yawn.

I run my hands through my tangled hair. I took out the aching braids hours ago. "Lovely."

"It's magic, not science," she says. "A lot depends on how quickly Sachi and Rory can think on their feet and what condition the girls are in. If they've been beaten, legs broken, anything like that—"

"They'll never make it." I prop myself against her four-poster bed.

"I hope that isn't the case." Now she does yawn, stretching her arms over her head, catlike. I yawn, too, and open my eyes to find her looking at me with feline watchfulness. "Have you talked to Maura yet?"

I turn away. "You saw what happened when we were in the same room together."

"I saw her provoke you into losing your temper. I don't blame you, Cate. She can be very provoking. But you can't avoid her forever."

"Can't I? Let's see." My voice is all edges. "We can't do any more tonight. Get some sleep."

I slip out of her room and down the hall to my own. Turning the corner, I'm surprised to find Alice huddled outside my door, her head propped against the green flowered wallpaper.

"Finally!" She jumps to her feet. "I've been waiting forever."

"What do you want, Alice? I've got to go to bed. If you're here to argue with me about tomorrow—"

"Surprisingly, no. I need to tell you something." She heads toward the stairs, beckoning me to follow. She's wearing an ivory satin nightgown that just brushes the tops of her bare feet, and her golden hair is tucked into pin curls.

"Is this some sort of trap? Are you going to shove me into a closet?" I demand.

She rolls her eyes. "Don't be absurd."

Her imperiousness grates, but I'm curious, so I follow her down to the formal sitting room. The gaslights on either side of the hearth are lit, there's a fire burning in the grate, and a blanket is piled on one end of the uncomfortable olive settee. "Wait, are you sleeping down here?"

She flushes. "Maura and I are in a fight."

Alice shuts the door, then crosses the room and stretches up on tiptoe to pull the cord that shuts the copper grate. When she's finished with her precautions, she paces to the window.

"Why all the secrecy?" I'm still in my itchy black bombazine, and exhausted enough that the blanket on the settee looks inviting.

"This is important," she snaps. The burgundy drapes are pulled shut, but she pushes one aside and peers out to the street. "After the funeral, Sister Inez spoke privately with Brother O'Shea. I was listening through the grate. That's how I fell off that stool. I was trying to hear better."

"I remember." Alice is an inveterate snoop. We all know that.

Alice presses her knuckles to her lips. She seems genuinely distraught. "Cate, what I heard—the reason I fell—I thought I must have misunderstood. I *prayed* I'd misunderstood. I couldn't imagine . . ."

Suspicion swoops through me. "Alice, what did you hear?"

She turns to face me. "Inez told Brother O'Shea where to find those girls."

Of course she did.

"Did you already know?" Alice asks, and I shake my head. "But you aren't surprised." I shake my head again, blond hair falling over my shoulders. "I think she was bargaining to keep the Sisterhood open, to prove her loyalty. But even then, it doesn't—it doesn't excuse it. She had to know what would happen."

Did Inez know they would all be executed? She must have realized it was a strong possibility. But I think she honestly hopes that if the Brothers are dreadful enough, the people will rise up against them, and the witches will seem a promising alternative. What are a few dozen girls' deaths in comparison to that kind of power?

I almost feel sorry for Alice. She's always been Inez's pet. Before my sisters and I arrived, she was the only pupil at the convent who could do mind-magic. It must be galling to see her hero fall.

"Inez means exactly what she said," I explain, leaning against the marble mantel. "She only cares about the Sisterhood. Specifically, she wants to overthrow the Brothers and put herself in charge. She does not care who gets killed in the process. How is this different from what you did to the Head Council? That's eleven men dead—as good as. You didn't see anything wrong in that."

"But these are *girls.*" Alice sinks onto the brown chair by the fire. Her satin skirt pools against the dun-colored carpet. "The Head Council made our lives a hell. These girls—they've been careless, perhaps, or just unlucky. They don't deserve—"

"You never cared what happened to the Harwood girls before."

"I didn't want them dead!" she shrieks, then claps a hand over her mouth. "If they're all killed tomorrow, it will be my fault, won't it? For not telling you sooner?"

It's still all about her.

But even Alice shouldn't have to think she's responsible for this. "I don't know that we could have gotten word to them in time. It's not your fault, Alice. It's the Brothers', for voting to allow the hangings. It's Inez's, for telling O'Shea where the safe house was."

But who told Inez? Did she compel one of my girls, or do we have a traitor in our midst? It wasn't me. It wasn't Tess. And—strange as it is to admit after our rocky start—I trust Elena implicitly.

Unless Elena confided in Maura—and Maura told Inez.

"Why are you being kind? I know you don't like me."

I shrug. "The truth is, we could use your knack for illusions tomorrow. You say you're sorry? Prove it. Help us stop this."

Alice's hands are clasped together in her lap. "All right."

"Good. Rilla and I will fill you in on the plan before services. You can walk over with us, and we'll sit together in church. I don't want you out of her sight until the whole thing is over, understand? And you'll work with her without arguing?"

Alice nods. "Good night, Cate."

I turn in the doorway, curious despite myself. "Did you tell Maura what you heard? Is that why she threw you out?"

Alice rises and blows out the lamps. The only light comes from the orange ashes in the grate. "She didn't believe me. Accused me of making it up because I was jealous of Inez paying her so much attention."

I walk upstairs in the dark, feeling my way. My sister is so far gone, I don't see any hope of reaching her. Even if I wanted to.

CHAPTER
7

HOW DOES ONE DRESS FOR A HANGING?

I'm wearing my Sisterly black bombazine with black boots and slipping the last hairpins into my chignon when Brenna creeps into my room on silent cat feet. She never seems to walk like a normal person; she's always dancing or twirling or skulking. I jump when I catch her reflection in the mirror above the dressing table.

"Hello, Cate," she says.

"Hello, Brenna." I put my silver brush down. "Is everything all right?"

"You're going to save Rory after church. There'll be fire and lots of people screaming." Brenna creeps closer, until she's standing right behind me. Her breath smells sweet and her fingers are stained red from the raspberry jam she must have spread on her toast. "The guns go *pop-pop-pop.*"

Oh, I hope it will be less dire than she makes it sound. Please Lord, let this work.

"All around the gallows stage, explosions chase the people. And after them in double haste, pop! go the weasels!" Brenna sings. I twist to face her, and she smiles. "The Brothers are weasels. Guns go pop. We mustn't let them pop Rory."

"Er—no." I swallow. "I'll go to church and then to Richmond Square, and I'll bring Rory back home. Don't worry."

Unless, of course, she knows there's something I ought to worry about.

My heart thumps in my chest. Not Rory; please not Rory. She's already had such a rough time of it, with her drunk of a mother and lout of a father.

"I'm dressed for church, too." Brenna pivots. She's been in her cousin's closet again. Today she's wearing a gold dress with red peonies splashed all over the skirt and red fringe at the hem. Truth be told, it looks more like curtains. "I want to help."

"Oh, Brenna, no." I can't be worrying about a mad oracle on top of everything else. "Someone might see you. It isn't safe for you to go out."

Brenna brings a strand of chestnut hair to her mouth and chews on it, staring at me with her eerie blue eyes. "I thought you would say that."

How is it that we've got two oracles, and neither of them are one bit of use in this? I bite my tongue before I say something tart. It isn't as if they can call up visions on command, after all. "Is there something else you wanted, then?"

Brenna shuffles barefoot against the wooden floor. "The little one knows more than she's telling."

I freeze. "What do you mean?"

"Shhh." She mimes locking her lips and throwing away the key. "Promised."

"Tess saw something, and she asked you not to tell me?"

Brenna nods. "It hurts her, keeping secrets from you. I don't want her broken. She's so little yet."

"I know." Downstairs, the grandfather clock begins to chime the half hour, and I stand. "I've got to go now. Church and then saving Rory. I'll bring her home." I pray I'm not telling a lie.

"You will." Brenna's hand whips out, lightning quick, catching mine. Her sharp nails bite into my wrist. "Thank you, Cate."

I tug away. "You're welcome, Brenna."

Sitting through services is torturous. O'Shea himself takes the dais. He speaks at length about hell and the agony that awaits the damned souls of witches. Eventually we're all released, blind as baby mice, blinking into the chilly morning sunshine. About half of the crowd flows out of the cathedral and right across the narrow cobbled street into Richmond Square.

I stroll arm in arm with Tess, boots crunching through the frozen grass as though we're on our way to a picnic instead of a hanging, but I'm careful to note the squadrons of black-and-gold-liveried guards. There are nine guards at each front corner of the square, and I'd bet a third squadron is in position at the back gate.

The Brothers are expecting trouble, and they want us to know it. The guards are armed with guns and bayonets. My fingers tighten on Tess's sleeve, and behind us, I hear Rilla suck in a jagged breath. Alice is chattering on about the money the bazaar raised, as if she's ever cared one whit about the poor. She's good at this deception. I scan the crowd until I find Mei, dressed in an old, battered gray cloak, a mandarin-orange hem peering out beneath. She and Mélisande skipped services to explore the back alleys and plot out ways to shepherd the girls back to the convent.

One of the benefits of a busy city like New London is that no one knows if you attend church or not.

We come around the front of the scaffolding. The gallows are built of rough-hewn oak. Two upright beams support a thick crossbeam, and from that crossbeam hang six nooses. The floor—a platform a dozen feet off the ground—is a trapdoor that will give way when the lever is pushed, and beneath it is a dirt trench to hold the bodies.

I pray there won't be any bodies.

Tess's ungloved fingers tremble on my arm. We're ten feet away from a gallows where our friends are about to be hanged.

We keep walking, joining the crowd farther back. I count the Brothers in their black cloaks—twenty, thirty, forty, more. We are terribly outnumbered.

One Brother turns, and his brown eyes collide with mine. Finn.

My steps falter as he strides toward us. "Good day, Brother Belastra."

Is it my imagination, or does he look disturbed by the salutation? "May I speak to you for a moment, Miss Cahill?"

I nod. "Go ahead and find a spot for us to watch, Tess. I'll be right there."

Finn and I step aside, a few paces from the streaming crowd. His hood is up, but his unruly copper hair peeks out beneath. "I'm not sure how to tell you this, so I'll come straight out with it. Two of the girls being executed today are from Chatham. Sachi Ishida and Rory Elliott."

I fake surprise, my hand hovering over my mouth. "I knew Sachi was arrested last month, but Rory too?"

"She and Sachi have always been thick as thieves." His gaze falls to the brown winter grass. "I thought you would want to know. To prepare yourself."

Oh, I'm as prepared as I can be. I give an uneasy glance at the gallows and then the National Council building next to the cathedral, where, any second now, the prisoners will be escorted out under heavy guard. "Thank you. It's all just awful."

Finn's head snaps up. "I voted against it. Reinstating this." His cherry mouth curls in disgust. "I just—I wanted you to know that. I'm not the kind of man who thinks murder is a solution."

I smile. "I know."

"Do you?" He steps close. Closer than is appropriate, given that we're in full view of half of New London. Behind his spectacles, his brown eyes lock onto mine. "How do you know me so well, Cate Cahill?"

Oh, just that—the sound of my name on his tongue. It makes my toes curl in my boots, my face flush. "I—I've got to go," I mutter. What am I doing, playing at being his friend? "I need to join the other Sisters."

"Wait." His callused fingers are rough against the thin skin at my wrist. My pulse hammers at his touch. "You know something, don't you?"

I should pull away. "I know a great many somethings. I don't know what you mean."

"You're an awful liar." His voice is low, private. Words only I can hear. "Something's happened to me, and I don't know what it is, but you—I was with you when I came to. The night these girls escaped from Harwood."

I glance at the cluster of Brothers near the gallows. Brother Ishida has turned; he's watching us. I yank my arm away, and Finn shoves his hands in his pockets. "I don't know anything about that."

"Sean Brennan's in hiding because he's been accused of treason. I may not remember much, but I know he's a good man. He sure as hell wouldn't have voted for this." Finn looks furious. "Someone set him up and they used me to do it. They found a handkerchief in Harwood on the body of a dead witch. A handkerchief embroidered with a *B*. And it's not Brennan's. I know that because I recognize it. Because it's *mine*."

"Shhh! Are you mad?" I demand. "Do you want to be arrested and strung up yourself?"

"You don't seem shocked." He stares me down. "Was I there at Harwood? Were you?"

He's figured things out quicker than I thought, but I play dumb. "Wouldn't you remember if you were there?"

His eyebrows slant down. "No," he says quietly. "Strangely enough, I don't think I would."

He knows. I work to keep the panic off my face. "We cannot talk about this here."

"Then where? When?" he asks. "Should I call on you this afternoon?"

"No! You can't come to the convent." I glance behind me, seeking out Tess and Rilla. Alice is standing a few feet away from the others, arguing with Maura—but Maura's watching me with Finn. "I can't be seen with you, I— It's dangerous. *Please*, Finn."

He doesn't back down, but his face softens at my use of his given name. "I need answers."

"I understand that, but—you can't risk coming to the convent. It isn't safe." I think quickly. "O'Neill's Stationery. It's on Fifth Street. Meet me in the back alley tonight at ten. Now— go away."

Finn nods. "Very well. I'll see you then."

I hurry to join the others. Maura's vanished back into the crowd, which now fills the square. The audience is penned in on three sides by the tall wrought-iron fence. Unless people are panicked enough to scale it and risk the pointy fleurs-de-lis at the top, the only exits are along the front and the small gate at the back. If all goes according to plan, it's going to be a madhouse.

"What did Maura want?" I ask.

"To accuse me of being a turncoat." Alice looks put out,

her color high, her blue eyes snapping. "What did *he* want?"

"To warn me that we know two of the girls being executed, that they're from Chatham. He thought I might find it *upsetting*," I explain.

"That was kind." Rilla watches Finn stroll back into the crowd of Brothers. There are hundreds of them right down front, ready to watch their vote being carried out. I wonder if their attendance here was mandatory. Surely some of them aren't eager for this spectacle; surely some of them voted, like Finn, against this?

"It looked a bit more personal than that," Alice says.

"It wasn't," I snap. "And I hardly think you're in a position to question *my* loyalty."

I'm spared Alice's reply by the sudden furor. Guards are shepherding the sixty prisoners down the steps of the National Council building and across the street into the square. Despite the cold, the girls aren't wearing cloaks. They're dressed in the same coarse brown skirts and thin white blouses that constituted the Harwood uniform.

Blast. I'd hoped they'd managed to scrounge up other dresses before their capture. It would be easier for them to get lost in the crowd that way. I scan their faces as they get closer, squinting to find Sachi and Rory. They march next to each other, their hands bound behind them. Rory, tall and voluptuous, towers over her petite sister.

Around us, the crowd rustles, craning their necks to see. What do they think? Are they surprised at how young most of the prisoners are, how thin and malnourished? Or do they believe the Brothers' lies that such innocent faces hide the most insidious sins?

The guards clear a path. Can we fend them off? Can this possibly work? I stare at the girls. There are no bruises—at least not where I can see—and they seem remarkably composed. I'd have thought some would be struggling or crying or mumbling prayers.

Alice pinches my upper arm. "They're drugged," she whispers, her breath hot on my ear.

Oh no. I hadn't even considered—but of course. The Brothers must have forced laudanum on the girls, the way they did at Harwood. It accounts for how slow and sleepy the prisoners look, their eyes narrowed into slits against the sunshine.

We can't count on their magic. It's all on us.

The guards herd six of the girls onto the platform and direct the rest into a roped-off holding area to the left of the gallows. Sachi and Rory are in the first group. The more fervent members of the crowd are calling out epithets:

"Damned witches!" a burly, bearded man nearby shouts.

"Devils!" another man yells, making the sign of the cross.

"Go back to hell!" an old woman screams. The effort brings on a fit of coughing that leaves her red-faced, clutching her tattered cloak around her. I purse my lips, remembering Mei's warning about the fever down in the river district. We mustn't be the only people who've heard the rumors; people around the old woman edge away, raising their scarves around their mouths.

"Damned river rats. Ought to hang them right alongside

the witches," the bearded man mutters to his friend, glaring at the sick old woman.

Some enterprising souls have brought rotten food, which they hurl at the girls. Sachi twitches as a pulpy tomato splatters on her brown skirt and splashes her face. I wonder if the Brothers handed it out. The poor people in the crowd haven't got food to spare, not even for something as entertaining as this.

Sachi's dark eyes search the crowd and I wonder if she's looking for me. Does she have faith that I'll stop this? I couldn't prevent her arrest, after all. But her gaze lingers on a figure nearer the front. Her father. How does Brother Ishida feel, seeing both his daughters up on the gallows? Has he hardened his heart so thoroughly that he can stand there with impunity, or does his conscience give a weak stirring?

Lord, but I loathe that man.

Tess grabs my hand. I let my rage rise up, magic stirring my muscles, flexing my fingers against her palm.

The executioners step forward to lift their nooses around the girls' necks.

"Now," Alice says under her breath.

The gallows bursts into flames. Fire leaps across the heavy crossbeam and eats its way down the support beams. Gray smoke curls around the stage, scattering sparks.

It's not real—just an illusion. But it's a convincing one. Together, Alice and Rilla are tremendous.

People begin to flee, shrieking and pushing and shoving toward the exits. O'Shea and his cronies are being shepherded away from the gallows by a squadron of guards, knocking common people aside as they go. I scan the crowd of remaining Brothers for Finn, but he's impossible to make out in the sea of black cloaks.

"Hurry, hurry. It'll be a stampede soon and we'll all be trampled!" a middle-aged woman wails, yanking on her husband's arm. They're rushing toward the back gate, which is closest, but it'll take an age for everyone to fit through that way. It's only wide enough to allow two people at once.

"Someone fetch the fire department, quick, before the whole square goes up!" the bearded man near us shouts.

Onstage, Rory is grinning.

A dark-haired guard reaches for his bayonet. "Witchery!" he roars.

Tess squeezes my hand, and my magic flows into her and merges with her own considerable power. She casts silently, immobilizing the guards. The man with the bayonet has lunged forward; the wicked-looking blade stops just short of Rory's back. It came entirely too close to skewering her. A blond soldier is still holding his noose, frozen in the midst of shoving a skinny dark-haired girl's head toward it. She ducks away.

The ropes that bound the prisoners' wrists are floating through the air like snakes, winding around the guards' chests. If our spell fails, they won't be able to fire their rifles until they're freed. That's Elena's work.

Rory and Sachi grab the dark-haired girl and shout something. All six girls onstage run toward the steps.

The flames are moving quickly, spreading down the legs of the platform, licking at the dead brown grass. I can smell the smoke now—taste it, bitter, in the back of my throat. I can hear the crackle and pop of it. It looks as though the gallows could collapse in a moment, crushing those nearby.

The guards on the ground are hollering. Their rifles are out but they can't get off a good shot—not with half a dozen guards like statues in the way. A squadron moves to intercept the girls, but as Tess casts, the first soldier stops abruptly, frozen in his tracks with one boot on the first step. The man behind him bumps into him, and they all fall to the ground like a stack of dominoes and lie there, unmoving, eyes staring up at the flames coming toward them.

I hope they're scared. I hope they're bloody well *terrified*, thinking they'll be burnt to a crisp.

The girls rush down the stairs. Sachi steps delicately over the guards at the bottom; Rory plants a heel right in one's stomach. They've linked hands with the dark-haired girl between them. I spare a glance for the dozens of other Harwood girls huddled beside the stage, staring with dumbstruck expressions at the fire. Their guard is a quarter what it was. Half the soldiers are trying to control the stampeding crowd; a quarter more are chasing after the fleeing witches.

As I watch, the ropes that bound the girls' hands slither to the ground and then swoop toward the remaining guards. Some of the soldiers fight off the ropes, but Tess immobilizes them as they reach for their rifles. Others make a run for it, and we drop them as they go. They're shoved to the ground and trampled by the crowd. As the girls' laudanum-soaked brains finally grasp their chance at freedom, they begin to run.

Richmond Square is bedlam. All around us, panicked people push and shove and trip over one another, shouting in fear and anger. Tess and I are being jostled, but our hands are firmly linked, fingers interlaced. Alice and Rilla press close behind, the four of us an unmoving unit against the madness.

A man plucks at my sleeve. "Come on, Sisters! We've got to get out of here!"

"What the hell are you doing, standing around like sheep? We're all going to be burnt alive!" his less-chivalrous friend insists.

I risk a glance at them before turning my attention back to the gallows. "Don't you see we're praying? Go!" I snap. If they distract Rilla and Alice, the glamour will give way, and we can't have that yet.

Most of the Brothers are rushing for the exits, but a few are trying to stop the Harwood girls. "Tess," I hiss, but Rilla and Alice beat me to it. A wall of flame leaps across the grass, encircling the flock of Brothers in a fiery prison. Tess and I scan the crowd for more guards, but it's impossible to track them in the crush.

I hear gunshots and wince.

Everyone around us has fled, leaving the middle of the square empty. Behind us, Alice and Rilla are kneeling in the grass, grasping each other's hands as they stare toward the gallows, lips moving as if in prayer. It's a persuasive picture of two devout Sisters.

"We need to get closer," Tess says, and we run, still hand in hand, toward the front of the square. Someone is ringing the fire bell atop the National Council building. Two horse-drawn, steam-powered fire engines pull up, firemen jumping down from the carriages. The machines block the street in front of the cathedral, adding to the chaos. In their hurry to get out of the square, people are pushing so close, they're in danger of being burnt by the steam from the engines or trampled by the horses' hooves.

Up ahead, a Harwood girl is struggling with a man twice her size. Her blouse rips across the shoulder as she tries to free herself. I cast silently, flinging him back, and the girl scrambles away.

Tess drops to her knees and crawls beneath the carriage of one of the fire engines. I follow her, figuring the lack of Sisterly dignity can be forgiven in such an emergency. Children are crying as they're separated from their families. Shopkeepers on the surrounding streets are crawling out their upper windows to wet down their roofs, lest they catch fire from the sparks floating so convincingly on the wind. Throngs of people are flowing down Church Street.

I feel a grim satisfaction at causing such chaos.

As we run, I see a body—one of the Harwood prisoners—lying half in the street, half on the cobbled sidewalk. She's been shot in the head; blood pools on the street around her and mats her long blond hair. She has staring blue eyes and looks strangely familiar. I bite my lip, and then—oh, Lord—I recognize her as the woman I healed in the Harwood infirmary, the one who'd lost her baby girl.

She won't be going home to her sons after all.

Tess tugs on my hand, leading me onto a side street that's

less crowded. Women throw open their windows and lean out, modesty forgotten, as they call to neighbors to try and find out what's happening. Men congregate on the street to share news, then march toward the square to see for themselves. Good. The more curiosity-seekers standing around the fence gawking, the more trouble the remaining guards will have controlling the crowd.

How much longer can Rilla and Alice keep this up?

I've got a stitch in my side and I'm exhausted from casting so many spells in quick succession, but I don't slow my pace. We've got to find the prisoners and get them to safety before our magic runs out. How many have Mei and Mélisande and Elena managed to grab?

I spot four guards dodging into the alley that runs behind Fourth Street and pull Tess after them, sensing trouble. As we round the corner, Tess stops so abruptly, I knock into her.

Up ahead, an abandoned milk wagon blocks the road. Sachi, Rory, and the dark-haired girl who was with them are running pell-mell toward it. "Stop!" shouts one of the guards, but the girls keep running.

I cast silently, trying to immobilize the soldiers, but it doesn't work.

"*Intransito*," I mutter aloud, but nothing happens. My magic gives a weak flicker.

Three of the guards fire their rifles. *Pop-pop-pop,* just like Brenna said, Lord help us. Sachi screams. The skinny dark-haired girl stumbles and knocks into the side of the wagon, clutching her arm. Glass bottles crash and the horses skitter sideways in their harnesses.

I'm almost crying with frustration and panic, and in front of me, Tess is swaying dizzily, bracing her hands on her knees. She cannot be having a vision *now*, can she?

"Tess!" I cry, grabbing her shoulders, trying to draw magic from her, but it doesn't work. Her gray eyes stare right through me, and I don't feel any magic in her. We're going to be too late. I hear boots pounding on the far side of the wagon and it must be another guard coming and I'm so useless; we're all going to be killed. The dark-haired girl ducks under the wagon, reaching out a hand to pull Sachi forward. A guard fires again and I scream it this time, with everything in me: *"Intransito!"*

Two of the guards freeze. Rory turns back at the sound of my voice, hesitating just as another soldier lunges forward with his bayonet and—

"Rory!" It's Brenna, ducking between the brick wall of the shop and the back of the wagon. She flings herself between Rory and the guard, arms outstretched.

Brenna impales herself on the bayonet. It slices into her, *through* her, the *sound—*

"Intransito!" Tess shouts, and the last two soldiers are immobilized a second too late.

"Brenna!" Rory screams. Tess and I run toward them, skirting the guard-statues.

Brenna's pinned to the wagon. Red blossoms across her stomach, mimicking the peonies splashed across her skirt. Where did she come from? How did she find us?

Rory clings to my arm. "Cate, do something! Fix it!"

I swallow. "I can't." Brenna's blue eyes are empty, staring

past us at—what? What was she thinking in her last moments? It happened so fast.

Thank you, Cate. Did she know? Did she see this? How else would she have been here, at the exact right moment?

Rory pulls the rifle from the nearest soldier's frozen hands and turns it on the guard who killed Brenna. He cannot move, but his eyes are aware, terrified, pleading.

"No." I step between them.

"He killed Brenna! He would have killed me!" Rory lifts the rifle to her shoulder, shaking the dark hair from her face.

Sachi puts a restraining hand on Rory's arm. "We have to get out of here before more guards come."

"Get out of the way, Cate," Rory commands, brandishing the bayonet. Tears are slipping silently down her face. "I'm going to run him through, just like he did her."

"No. You're not a murderer. You're better than that," I insist, planting my feet.

"That isn't what Brenna would want," Tess says quietly. She casts a quick glamour over the girls, turning their Harwood uniforms to Sisterly black.

"She's right," I agree. "This morning—she kept talking about saving you, Rory."

"She *knew?*" Rory sobs harder, relaxing her grip on the rifle, allowing Sachi to take it from her and toss it aside.

"We have to go." Tess grabs my hand and gestures down at the guards. "I'm going to erase their memories."

She pulls the magic from me, and this time it feels like squeezing water from a stone. My muscles feel sore, my fingers stiff. My magic flickers and fades until I'm wrung out.

Sachi puts one arm around Rory and leads her through the gap between wagon and wall. I give Brenna one last glance. I hate leaving her like this, but what choice do we have? We can hardly parade her body through the streets. I stagger after my friends, dizzy.

"Are you all right?" the dark-haired girl asks. Behind her spectacles, she has enormous gray eyes. She's clutching her shoulder with one hand, blood on her fingers.

"I should be asking you. You were shot," I point out.

She shrugs. "I think it only nicked me. Stings a bit, but the laudanum helps."

"Here." I pull off my cloak and put it around her shoulders. "Don't want anyone seeing that."

"I suppose not." She holds out her other hand for me to shake. "I've heard a great deal about you, Cate. It's nice to finally meet you. I'm Prudencia Merriweather."

CHAPTER
8

IT'S NOT ENOUGH. IT'S NEVER ENOUGH.

We've saved ten girls. Mei was already waiting with three when we got back to the convent. Mélisande crept through the garden gate with four more shortly after we arrived. That's ten, counting Sachi and Rory and Prue Merriweather.

For that, Brenna is dead and Elena is missing.

It's been hours. The sun is going down now, silhouetting the gabled roofs across the street in gold. Sachi, Rory, and Prue are crammed together on the olive settee in the parlor. I healed Prue's shoulder as soon as my magic came back. One of Mélisande's girls had a wicked-looking slice from a bayonet on her forearm, and another had been trampled in the crowd and twisted her ankle. They'll all be fine, but now I stare out the window, leaning my forehead against the cold glass, stomach tumbling. Where is Elena?

Rilla and Alice got home an hour after we did and that was nerve-racking enough. A group of Brothers had invited them into Richmond Cathedral for prayer and they hadn't felt it prudent to refuse. They both looked foxed when they stumbled in the front door, eyes bleary with exhaustion. Alice nearly swooned in the front hall. Rilla reported they'd seen three corpses on the walk home.

I sent them both to bed. Tried to send Tess, because I could tell from her pinched face and the way she rubbed her temples that she had another headache. She refused to go— Inez has her so afraid of looking weak—but she's sleeping curled up in the silk chair by the fire. Her blond eyelashes flutter rapidly as though she's dreaming. Of what, I wonder? What did she see in that vision?

Brenna said Tess asked her to keep a secret from me. A secret Brenna was afraid would break her. Has it got something to do with the old prophecy—the one about Maura and Tess and me?

Footsteps move down the hall and my heart leaps. Perhaps Elena came in through the garden gate instead? I throw open the door, startling Tess awake.

It's Maura. She sashays into the room in a garish emerald gown I thought pretty a few weeks ago. Now it seems too bright. We should all be in black, mourning for Cora and Brenna.

The dress makes Maura's eyes go grass green and for a moment, as she looks at me and Tess, still flushed from sleep, she seems—relieved. Tension melts out of her stiff shoulders and the downward tilt of her mouth relaxes. Could she be glad we're home safely?

It doesn't last.

"Ten girls," she says, tossing her red curls. "You saved ten out of sixty. Was it worth it?"

"Yes." I glance at the girls on the settee. They've all changed out of their ugly Harwood uniforms. Sachi borrowed a girlish peach brocade of Tess's, Rory's in her own red velvet, and Prue borrowed a dove-gray gown of mine.

"I just paid a visit to the corner grocer at Church and Third. Wanted to hear if there were any consequences for your daring rescue." Maura's fists curl at her sides. "Three of the prisoners were shot and killed anyway. Two bystanders were killed, too. One was a cobbler—father of four, they said—and one was the French ambassador's wife."

I bristle. "I'm not responsible for what the guards did. I thought they'd have the sense not to fire into a crowd."

"A little girl was trampled in the crush. Both her legs were broken. I suppose that wasn't your fault, either?"

My temper snaps. "I didn't step on her. What are you getting at, Maura? How would *you* have managed this? I know you're dying to tell me, so go on."

"I would have let them all hang." Her voice is utterly matter-of-fact.

"Good Lord," Rory mutters.

"It's a good thing for us you're not in charge." Sachi's voice is so withering, I'm surprised Maura doesn't brown at the edges.

I knew Maura backed Inez in this, but to hear her say it so coolly! Anger heats my cheeks. "How can you say such a thing? Sachi and Rory are my friends."

"And that's made you stupid," Maura says. "How much magic did you do out on the street today? You, who were always so cautious, harping on Tess and me about never risking our safety! That time Tess fixed my dress in church, you nearly had a fit. You remember, Tess? But now that you want to play the hero, you've gotten reckless. You were casting illusions left and right to disguise girls and create that fire. And what's worse, you were dressed as Sisters the whole time! How many people could have seen you?"

Tess sits up straight, crossing her ankles. "It would have taken too much magic to glamour ourselves, and split our focus. Looking like Sisters was the best way to escape suspicion. No one stopped us or tried to question us. And we were careful."

"Were you? What if someone was looking out a window and saw you? All it takes is one witness. The Brothers could come knocking at our door any minute." Maura plants her hands on her hips, hooking her fingers through the pink sash at her waist. "You risked us all to save ten girls. And most of them aren't even witches! What use are they?"

"Pardon me?" Prue gasps, obviously unaccustomed to having her personal worth so lightly dismissed.

Maura whirls on Prue, all lovely wide-eyed smile. "I'm forgetting my manners. Who's this? Are you a witch?" she asks, and Prue shakes her head. Maura sighs. "Of course not. Then why did you bring her here, Cate? Are you confused about the purpose of the Sisterhood? We aren't an orphanage. We're not in the business of feeding and clothing strange girls off the street just out of the goodness of our hearts."

"Oh, no one would suspect you of that." I glance out the window. Still no Elena.

"I shan't prevail upon your charity very long. I've got family in the city," Prue says stiffly, and I pray she won't mention Alistair. Is she his cousin? A sister? Surely not his wife; I didn't see a ring on his finger. Whatever the connection, I don't want Maura getting her hooks into Prue.

"At least you all made it back in one piece," Maura grumbles.

There's a long silence. Rory sniffles. The others look down at their laps.

Maura raises her chin. "Who?"

I bite my lip. "Brenna's dead."

Maura's eyebrows shoot heavenward. "You took a mad oracle into a battle?"

"We didn't bring her. She got out. It wasn't Cate's fault," Tess insists.

"Of course not. Nothing ever is." Maura's nose wrinkles in disgust. "Do you hear yourself? You're like a puppet."

"As if you cared one whit about Brenna," I snap. "You wanted to assassinate her weeks ago!"

Tess shoots to her feet. "And you're a fine one to talk about being a puppet, Maura. You haven't had a thought in your head that Inez hasn't put there in weeks!"

I risk another glance out the window at the street. It's empty but for the shadows. Where is Elena?

Maura notices. "Is our conversation boring you, Cate? What are you doing? Who are you looking for?"

I hesitate. Even after everything she's done, my first instinct is not to worry Maura unnecessarily. As if she minds worrying me, breaking my heart and stomping it into pieces.

Sachi speaks first. "Elena isn't back yet."

Maura's smile goes ghoulish. "What do you mean?" Her voice rises, turns shrill. "Where is she?"

"If I knew that, I wouldn't be standing at the window, would I?" I ask.

Maura knots her hands together. "Why aren't you out looking for her?"

Oh. No matter what she'd have us believe, she cares. Somewhere under this brittle exterior, this merciless talk, my sister's still got a heart.

"Elena is the canniest girl I know. I bet she has some of the Harwood girls and they've found a place to hide until after dark. I'm sure she'll be home soon."

"You're sure? If you were so sure, you wouldn't be waiting at the window like that!" Maura throws both hands into the air, and I flinch, thinking she's going to toss me across the room. Has it come to this, that I'm always bracing myself for her attack? "She could be lying dead in the street for all you know!"

"Rilla saw three bodies. She would have said if one of them were Elena," Rory points out helpfully.

"And you accuse *me* of being reckless with people," Maura seethes. "If you've gotten her killed, I'll—"

"You'll what?" My voice is low. "What more would you do to me?"

Her eyes narrow into green slits in her pretty face. "I saw you talking with him this afternoon. Right in the square, bold as brass."

Fear slides down my spine. I parrot the same words I told Alice. "It was nothing. He was warning me that Sachi and Rory were on the list of girls to be executed. Thought I might find it upsetting."

"I can't believe you would have let us hang," Rory complains, tugging at the lace cuffs of her dress.

Maura doesn't take the diversion. "I tried to warn you before, Cate. I told you we couldn't work with Brothers. They're our enemies."

"Oh, don't pretend you did this to protect the Sisterhood. Finn was on *our* side."

"On *your* side, perhaps. It's not the same thing anymore." There's a thread of sadness in Maura's voice, but I'm too far gone to care. "What I did—that's on you. You didn't listen. You're still not listening! Every time you even *look* at him, you're putting him in danger." Maura shakes her head as though I'm too stupid to comprehend what she's saying.

Which is that she'll do it again. She'll hurt Finn, again and again, until there's nothing left of the man I love, until there's nothing left but a shell who can't think for himself.

"Don't. You. Dare." Magic crackles through me, the static electricity of it sparking at my fingertips, lighting me up like fireworks.

"Or what?" Maura thrusts her hand into my face. There's a jagged white line across her palm, a scar from where I hurt her. She could have had someone heal it if she'd wanted; it would have been easy enough. Perhaps she likes the re-minder. "Did Cate tell you what she did? She lost control right in the middle of Cora's funeral reception. Smashed a teacup in my hands. Anyone could have noticed; there were a dozen Brothers there. Afterward I went to her and asked her to heal the cut, and instead she made it worse."

Tess looks at me in shock. I hadn't told her. "Did you really do that?"

"I did, and I feel badly about it." Not bad enough to apolo-gize to Maura, though. "It won't happen again."

Rory tosses her dark hair. "I hardly blame you, if she's going around acting like this all the time."

"A leader can't lose control like that. It's a lesson I've learned the hard way." Maura tuts. "You're weak, Cate. Your misplaced sympathy for those who aren't witches, your feel-ings for Finn—they make you weak."

"No." I think of Finn and for once I'm not sad. I'm *grate-ful.* "Loving the right person, having them love you back—it makes you strong. You want to be better for them—be the woman they see when they look at you—beautiful and brave and clever. You want to live up to that vision, even if—" I take a deep breath. "Even if they don't see you that way any-more. Loving Finn has *never* made me weak, and losing him—I won't let that break me, either. I'm stronger than you think I am."

Rory leans forward, exposing a rather scandalous amount of bosom in her low-cut red gown. "What the hell happened in the last two weeks?"

"Rory! Shhh," Sachi hisses, smacking her sister's arm.

Maura smooths her emerald skirts. "I did it for you. For the Sisterhood."

"Liar. You did it because you were jealous." It will hurt her pride, my saying that in front of the others, but I'm past caring. "If you'd ever really been in love, you would never have done this to me."

Maura's eyes flash. "I was in love and you ruined it and now you've possibly gone and gotten her killed!"

"And how does that feel?" I ask, and Maura sputters. I stalk toward her, edging past Tess in the brown silk chair, and Maura backs away. "It's what you're threatening to do to Finn, isn't it? I don't want to hurt you, Maura. But if you ever do magic on him again, I *will*. I swear it. I will use every ounce of power I have to ensure that you won't ever go near him again."

"Cate!" Tess clutches at my arm, but I shake her off, staring Maura down.

"You'd choose a man over your own sister? Over your promise to Mother to look after us? That used to be the most important thing in the world to you," Maura says.

I set my jaw. "You've made it quite clear you don't need me anymore."

Maura blinks back tears. "I don't. I haven't for ages," she says, and then she flees.

"Maura, wait!" Tess calls. She presses one hand to her temple as if her headache's flared and then runs after Maura. I can hear their footsteps pounding up the stairs.

How does Maura always manage to leave me feeling the villain?

Sachi is at my side, putting an arm around me. "Maura erased Finn's memory?"

I nod. "The night of the Harwood breakout. He doesn't remember me as anything more than a customer in the shop. A neighbor."

Sachi shepherds me to the chair, and I sit. She kneels next to me, her silky black hair brushing my elbow. "You've got to tell him the truth."

"I can't. You heard her. If she sees us together, she'll attack him again. Or Inez would, in a trice." Sachi's dark eyes are full of sympathy. I can hardly bear it. "Who knows what another attack would do to him. He's already so muddled. He approached me earlier because he suspects I've got something to do with it, because I'm a terrible liar, and I'm supposed to meet him tonight—I had to agree to it, to get him to leave me alone—and I don't know what to tell him!"

Sachi puts her hand over mine. "Just tell him the truth. He deserves to know."

"What should I say?" I rub my tired eyes with both fists. "That we were in love, mad as that might seem, and my sister erased his memory? You think that will make him fall right back in love with me?"

I bury my face in my hands. When I resurface, all three girls are watching me. "I'm sorry, Prue, for subjecting you to all this. Do you have sisters?"

"A brother." Prue pushes her spectacles up her nose with her forefinger. The gesture reminds me of Finn.

"Alistair Merriweather's your brother?" I ask.

Prue nods, toying with her long black plait, and I can see

the resemblance, especially in the eyes. She's as pretty as her brother is handsome; it's just hidden behind the spectacles and the clothes that don't quite flatter or fit.

I try to shake off my sadness. "If you'd like to see him, I'll take you to meet him."

Prue frowns, and her glasses slip down her nose again. "You know where he is? He's been in hiding for years."

I stand. "I know where he'll be on Thursday night. I've joined the Resistance movement, and there'll be a meeting."

Rory lets out her loud bark of a laugh. I've missed that sound. "What else have you done in the last two weeks, Cate? It seems you've been quite busy."

Chatting with Sachi, Rory, and Prue restores my spirits. At first I fret about being so candid in front of Prue—an utter stranger—but it's obvious that the three of them have struck up a friendship. I fill them in on the goings-on at the convent, the tension between Inez's faction and ours. Without Tess in the room, I tell them that she's the oracle and beg them not to treat her any differently.

"But she's not—like Brenna?" Rory twirls a finger around her ear, unwilling to speak ill of the dead.

"No. Tess is utterly sane. But she worries about going mad, so no jokes, if you please." I give Rory a stern look.

"Brenna borrowed this dress, didn't she?" Rory's brown eyes fill with tears. "It smells like her. She always loved violets."

I nod. "She did. Tess went out and got her some scented water. They became quite close; Tess was the one who took her meals up and read to her. I think she's more upset about Brenna than she's letting on. I ought to go check on her and make sure Maura hasn't taken her head off."

"We'll stay here and keep a lookout for Elena," Sachi promises, poking at the fire.

"Thank you." I give her a grateful smile.

"Cate, you saved our lives! We ought to be thanking *you*," Rory says.

"Think about what I said," Sachi urges as she lights the gas lamps. "You should tell Finn the truth. You deserve to be happy."

I nod, though I don't know what deserving has to do with it. After all, Brenna hardly deserved her fate.

Still, I ponder it as I walk upstairs to Tess's room. Why am I so reluctant to tell Finn? Is it because of the danger he'd be in from Maura and Inez? Or is it because I'm afraid that, now that he doesn't love me anymore, he'll decide I'm not worth the trouble?

Worse—what if he feels *obliged* to try and love me again? Rilla suggested I could make him. But I didn't *make* him love me the first time. I never employed any of the charming, coy little tricks that girls are meant to use to catch a husband. I was just myself.

What if that isn't enough, a second time around?

I knock at Tess and Vi's door, and Tess calls for me to come in. She's lying on her bed, curled on her side. Cyclops peeks out from beneath the comforter, as though she's just shoved him aside, embarrassed to be caught with such a childish comfort. She shouldn't be. I'd love to have a thing that brought me comfort when I was sad or afraid.

"How did it go with Maura?" I ask.

She pats the space next to her. "Not well. She feels like you've chosen Finn over her."

"Would it be so terrible if I did?" I sit, pulling off my boots so I can tuck my feet under me. "It didn't have to be this way. She's the one making me choose."

"You know Maura. She's always trying to test people, prove that they love her best." Tess fiddles with the black lace at her cuffs. "I'm afraid we've both failed on that score."

"No." I lean forward, angry all over again. "It's not our fault she's got this—this chasm inside her that she's always trying to fill."

"We're not to blame, but we're not helping. She's so hurt, Cate. She feels like everyone chooses you—Mother, Elena, Cora, me. Inez is the only one who keeps choosing Maura." Tess takes a deep breath, holds it, and then slowly lets it out. "I know you won't like this, but I think you ought to go to her. Tell her you didn't mean it, that you aren't giving up on her."

I shake my head. "I do mean it. I *have* given up on her."

Tess massages her temple and continues on as though I haven't spoken, haven't already refused. "I know she acts like she doesn't want you looking out for her, but she needs you."

I give an unladylike snort. "I doubt that very much. I appreciate you trying to make peace, I do, but you've got to stop worrying about us. Your head's bothering you, isn't it? You ought to lie down for a while. I'll come tell you when Elena's back. Unless . . ." I look at Tess's pinched face. "You had a vision this afternoon, didn't you? Right as we came into that alley. Did you see something about Elena?"

"No—I mean, yes, I did have a vision, but it's nothing to do with Elena."

Her eyes have tired shadows under them, and her shoulders are slumped, her jaw clenched. Certainly enough has happened today to account for all that, but Tess's moods have been unpredictable lately. Is it just being twelve, and being an oracle on top of it? Or—I think back to Brenna's warning—has Tess seen something that's weighing on her?

"Did you know that Brenna was going to die?" I whisper. "Like with Zara?"

"No!" Tess shakes her head. "I never imagined—it's only that I think *she* knew. She said something this morning when I brought her breakfast. I didn't think anything of it at the time, but now . . . I think she was saying good-bye."

"Me too. She said—" I pull my knees up to my chest. "She said you're keeping a secret from me. Is it about the prophecy? Did you—did you see me hurting Maura?"

"No." Tess grabs my knee. "It's not that."

"What, then? Brenna—she worried it would break you."

"It feels that way sometimes." Tess gives a sad little laugh. It's too grown-up for a twelve-year-old. Too bitter. "I'm not ready to tell you yet. Give me a little more time?"

I want to press, demand that she tell me everything now.

Is it something to do with Finn? With me? But Tess is clever. I have to trust that she'll tell me when she's ready. When it's right.

"All right," I agree slowly. "But you *will* tell me?"

The look in Tess's eyes is terrible. "I don't see how I can avoid it forever."

CHAPTER
9

I'M BALANCING A PLATE ON MY KNEES, spooning up mashed sweet potatoes, when the front door crashes open. Heart hammering, I jump up so quickly that my napkin and dinner roll go flying to the floor. I set the plate on the tea table and rush out of the parlor into the front hall, Mei right behind me. The rest of the convent is having supper, but we've been in here, worriedly keeping watch for—

Elena. She's propped against the heavy front door as though it's the only thing preventing her from collapse. There are six—no, seven—girls with her, all cloaked in black. One of them sinks to the floor with a moan. Another hobbles to the stairs and sits on the bottom step with the help of two friends. The rest seem overwhelmed, their frightened eyes darting around the gloom of the front hall.

"Thank the Lord," I murmur, torn between the urge to shake Elena and embrace her. "Are you all right? What happened? I've been so worried! It's been *hours.*"

Elena gives me a tired smile. "Will you tend to Jennie and Dora? They're hurt, and my magic . . ." She waves a hand. "Sarah Mae's got a bad bump on her head, too, where some oaf knocked her with the butt of his rifle."

"I'll take a look at it." Mei kneels by the girl on the floor. "Do you think you can make it to the healing classroom? It's right down the hall. I can fix you up there, and I'll ask someone to bring us hot cocoa and some leftover supper."

The girls look at Elena, who nods approval. "Go with Mei. I'll be along in a minute."

They scurry after Mei. Now that I see their faces, I recognize two of them—Jennie Sauter, who's from a farm outside Chatham, and Sarah Mae, a girl I met in the uncooperative ward. The one who buried dead birds on her afternoon constitutionals.

These girls make seventeen. Seventeen prisoners saved out of sixty. That's a sizable portion. I feel a great glad swell of relief that they're here and they're safe.

"What happened?" I ask again.

Elena rubs a weary hand over her face. "As soon as I got out of the square, I grabbed two girls and hid them in the storeroom of a shop on Second Street. I stood in the doorway and plucked more as they went by. A guard was chasing

Dora and it's a mercy he didn't shoot her before I compelled him. Between that and the magic in the square, I couldn't cast for hours. Dora's leg's broken, Jennie's been shot, and Sarah Mae says she's all right but I think she's concussed. I thought it best to wait until it was dark and I was rested enough to disguise them. Loads of guards are still out, though. One saw Dora limping and was about to question us. If it hadn't been for Sarah Mae's quick thinking . . ." Elena shivers. "It was a close call. Too close."

"I'm glad you're all right," I say, a little surprised by the force of my relief. "Is Sarah Mae a witch?"

Elena runs a hand through her black curls, which have come undone from their careful pompadour. They fall over her shoulders in perfect, tight black ringlets, and I realize I've never seen her with her hair down before. "No. She threw a rock that shattered a streetlamp and sent the guard running in the opposite direction. I don't think any of these girls are witches."

"Why would you risk your life for them, then?" Maura stomps around the corner, her face puffy, eyelids pink and swollen from crying.

"Maura—" Elena begins.

"No! I don't care what you're about to say, what reason you have. It's not sufficient. You cannot go around putting yourself in danger like this. I won't allow it!" Maura stamps one foot, clad in a pretty pink slipper that matches the sash at her waist.

I expect Elena to argue with her, to insist that Maura hasn't got any say over what she does or does not do. Instead, a tiny smile plays over her lips. "Is this your way of saying you were worried about me?"

"Of course I was worried about you!" Maura plants her hands on her hips. "I used to think you were clever, you know. But you're nothing but a—a fool! Good Lord, what were you *thinking*?" She turns to me, eyes like ice, and I brace myself. "You weren't thinking, obviously. Just following Cate's orders."

Elena laughs. "Maura. Call me all the names you like, but you can't blame this on Cate."

"Of course she can," I mutter. "She always finds a way."

"You should know better than anyone that I don't follow orders well." Elena's chocolate eyes rest on my sister's face. "Everything I did today, I did because my own conscience told me it was the right thing to do."

"Then you're a complete imbecile," Maura says. "The entire point of being a witch is that we can protect ourselves! Letting yourself get so drained that you couldn't even compel—"

"I'm fine," Elena interrupts, voice soft. She lays a hand on Maura's ruffled emerald sleeve. "I'm safe."

Maura's cheeks go pink. "Well, good." Her eyes fall to the wooden floor. "You're one of the best witches we've got. There are only a handful of us capable of mind-magic, and we'll need all—"

Elena jerks away as though she's been burnt. "*That's* why you were worried? If I'd been murdered, your army would have one less witch with mind-magic?" She shakes her head, curls tumbling, and finally spares a glance for me. "I'm going

133

to check on the girls. They were terrified half out of their minds on the walk here."

She turns the corner in four long, angry strides. Maura sputters. "What—what did I do?"

"If you don't know, then *you're* the imbecile." I pause before following Elena. "She deserves better than you, Maura."

"This is like a scene from one of my novels. Sneaking out for a romantic midnight tryst!" Rilla bounces on the leather seat of the carriage.

"It's only ten o'clock, and it's hardly going to be romantic." I fidget with the button on my black satin glove. "I haven't even figured out what to tell him."

"You should tell him the truth." Rilla peers out between the curtains. "I've never seen so many guards on patrol. I've never been out this late, either. It feels rather scandalous."

"It feels stupid to me," I mutter as the carriage turns into the narrow alley behind the Fifth Street shops. It's late enough that most people should be abed, Rilla and I among them. If Maura knew what I was doing, she would call me seven different kinds of a fool, and she might be right.

I tug on the threads of magic running through my body, twining alongside bone and muscle, but I only feel the barest trace of power. Jennie Sauter lost a great deal of blood, and neither Mei nor Addie were able to patch her up. They worried she might lose the arm. In the end, I was able to heal her, but after all the day's exertions, it sapped what magic I had left. Elena flat-out forbade me to come tonight. But if I missed my meeting with Finn, he would come to the convent; I'm certain of it. And I'd rather risk my own safety than his.

The carriage rolls to a stop. I hop out and help Rilla down into the shadowy alley. The coachman, Robert, sits on the carriage box. "Come back for us in an hour?" I ask.

"Thirty minutes. It's a bad night to be out," he insists with a fatherly frown. He doesn't wait for my agreement before clucking to the horse and heading off.

My hand is tugging on the ruby necklace at my throat when I hear heavy steps turning the corner.

"Halt!" a male voice cries out. I cringe.

The guard is a tall, broad-shouldered man with blond hair and a mustache. He closes the distance between us quickly. "Sisters? What are you doing out at this hour?"

"We . . ." I start, then fall silent as my mind goes blank. I should have prepared a lie. Rilla just stands next to me, her mouth opening and closing like a goldfish.

The guard shoulders his rifle, peering closer. He smells strongly of pipe tobacco. "Unless you ain't really Sisters. I wouldn't be the first man fooled by a witch today. State your business, or I'm taking you to the National Council building for questioning."

What reasonable excuse could good religious girls have for being alone in a back alley at ten o'clock at night? In a fit of inspiration, I remember the woman coughing in the square earlier. "We're paying a call on the sick. A family with the fever." I wave a vague hand toward a house with a light still on.

"To pray for them. With them. They've got a boy who's bad off," Rilla adds, twisting her hands together in a convincing display of distress. "Poor little Johnny. They aren't sure he'll make it through the night."

"Fever's spreading? I thought it was just them river rats coming down with it." The guard looks toward the house, alarmed, and then scowls. "Wait a minute. That don't sound quite right. Why wouldn't you go in the front, instead of sneaking around through the alleys? Where's your carriage?"

"Oh, well, we . . ." Blast. I tug on my magic, frantically sorting through possible plans of escape.

More footsteps turn the corner. The dim moonlight glitters on a pair of glasses. Finn. I breathe a silent prayer as his eyes meet mine, and he takes in the guard and the gun.

"What's this?" He strolls closer. Ambling as if he hasn't a care in the world. But his back is straight, chin up, and I know that look. "You aren't detaining these good Sisters, are you? They're here to meet with me."

"Meet you?" The guard keeps his gun pointed at us. "Then why did they just spin some nonsense about nursing a sick boy?"

Finn gives his gap-toothed grin. "It's a matter of security."

"Security, huh?" The guard raises his thick eyebrows. "Look, what is this all about? If you're out to have some fun with one of them, just say so."

Finn's smile goes tight. "These girls are here to give me information about a suspected witch. They're risking a great deal. I ought to report you for insulting them."

Oh, he's magnificent.

I do my best to look outraged at the notion of having a bit of fun with him, when really I want nothing more than to hurl myself into his arms.

The guard relaxes his hold on the rifle. "I apologize, sir."

"It's not me you should be apologizing to." Finn's voice is low, dangerous. Thrilling.

The guard nods. "I meant no disrespect, Sisters."

"That's all right," Rilla says graciously. "It's been a difficult day."

"You may go," Finn commands. "I'll see them safely home."

The guard goes. As soon as he's out of sight, I rush to the back door of O'Neill's Stationery, the ruby already transforming into a key in my hands. "Quickly, before someone else comes," I urge, ushering them into the dark storeroom.

By the time I've got the door closed and locked behind us, Rilla's lit a candle. Her hands are trembling, sending shadows dancing all around us. "That was a close call."

"Careful, or this place will go up like a tinderbox," Finn warns, eyeing the shelves of stationery.

"Finn, this is Rilla Stephenson, my roommate. Rilla, this is Finn Belastra." I loop the necklace back around my neck. My nerves are still jangling—not so much from the encounter with the guard as from Finn's proximity. He is bound to ask questions that I can't—won't—answer. What if it makes him hate me?

"It's a pleasure to meet you, Miss Stephenson," Finn says. He turns to me. "Is there somewhere private we can talk, Cate?"

My heart gives a silly little flutter. "Why don't you stay here, Rilla, and we'll go down to the cellar?"

"Take your time." Rilla slips a hand into her pocket and pulls out one of her romance novels. "I brought a book."

Finn chuckles, delighted. They're of the same tribe, these two, never without a book in hand. I head downstairs, and he follows me with another candle. He sets it down on the table, shucking off his cloak and laying it over the back of a wooden chair.

"Thank you for coming to our rescue. That could have gone badly." I'm not quite sure what to do with my hands. I toy with Mother's pearl ring, trying not to think about the engagement ring Finn gave me months ago. I gave it back to him when I announced my intention to join the Sisterhood. Where is it now?

He braces his hands against the back of the chair. His rumpled white shirt is rolled up to the elbows, displaying forearms wiry with muscle and spotted with freckles.

I have the absurd urge to trace the patterns they form over his tanned skin.

"Are you a witch?" he asks.

I respect him all the more for coming straight out with it.

I should lie to him. For his own good. I should, but I don't. "Yes," I say quietly. "But I'm not the one who erased your memory. I swear it."

He leans forward, squinting. "How do you know my memory's been erased, then?"

My breath catches. Because I was there when it happened. I know who's responsible. I will never forgive her for it, and yet I still want to protect her. Or Finn. Or myself. My reasoning is cloudy, even to me.

"Because I know you," I say finally.

"Do you?" His voice is soft. "I don't remember much about you at all. It's the most curious thing. Like little pieces of me have been carved right out. I do things, think things, *feel* things, and I don't know why. And then there's the missing time. Hours here and there, whole evenings, just . . . gone." He snaps his ink-stained fingers. "I remember working in Denisof's office that afternoon, helping with some correspondence, and then it's all a blank, right up until I found myself on the convent steps with you. Where was I before that? It's a mystery to me. A vexing one."

The frustration of it is plain in his voice. It twists his lips and furrows his forehead, and I want so badly to fix this, to fix *him*.

"You were with me. At Harwood Asylum."

A grin ghosts across his face. "I helped break out the patients?"

I nod, an answering smile playing over my lips. "You were instrumental."

He turns his head and swears like a sailor. "I knew it! That's why I joined the Brotherhood, isn't it? As a spy?"

His relief breaks my heart. I tap my fingers against the rough wood of the chair nearest me. Anything to keep myself from going to him, throwing my arms around him, and begging his forgiveness.

Begging him to remember me.

"Yes. That, and to keep your mother safe."

"Thank you." His voice is fervent as a prayer; his smile is huge and exuberant. "It's been driving me mad. The letters from my mother—she doesn't come out and say it, but she implies there's another reason for me to be in New London. I've never been what you'd call devout, and Mother—well, you know how she is. She raised me to question things, not follow doctrine. I couldn't think what the hell I was doing in the Brotherhood. Pardon my language."

"It's all right. You—you can say anything to me." The words twist on my tongue, and I must sound like a lovestruck fool. The flickering candlelight casts shadows over his face, illuminating the late-night stubble on his jaw. It reminds me of the other times we've met in secret places: the convent garden, the conservatory, the National Archives. Of the sandpaper feel of his chin against my fingers. Against my mouth.

"We've been working together, then? Me within the Brotherhood, and you within the Sisterhood?" he asks. I nod, weak with longing. "Makes sense. But if I was *helping* the witches, why would— Did you hear that?"

There's a thump from upstairs, followed by a muffled shriek.

"Rilla!" I cry, rushing for the stairs.

"Let me go first." Finn pulls a pistol from his boot.

I follow right on his heels. We creep up the steps quietly, and he flings open the door to reveal Alistair Merriweather standing behind Rilla, his arm wrapped around her throat, his hand clapped over her mouth.

"Mr. Merriweather!" I gasp. "Unhand her at once."

"What the devil?" Merriweather gapes at us.

Finn lowers his pistol. "You know this man?"

Rilla doesn't wait for answers. She bites Merriweather, and

when he releases her, she spins around and knees him in the bollocks. He moans and braces himself against a cabinet full of ink. Rilla grabs the broom leaning in the corner and aims the handle at his head like a baseball bat. Her stance is quite incongruous with her dress, which is yellow and dotted with sunflowers.

"Rilla, it's all right. I know him," I say, though I'm rather tempted to let this play out. Merriweather's a good foot taller than Rilla, but my money's on her.

"It's not all right. He nearly strangled me!" Rilla narrows her hazel eyes at him.

"What exactly are you doing here, Miss Cahill?" Merriweather's dressed in a long, double-breasted olive-green peacoat, with a black cravat wrapped around his throat.

"I could ask you the same thing," I retort, chin up.

"I sleep here sometimes. With Hugh's permission." Merriweather frowns. "That key was not an invitation to come and go as you please. This isn't a space for secret assignations. We've worked for years to——"

Rilla smacks him in the head with the broom handle. Merriweather yelps.

From the look of Finn, though, I'd say he got off lightly. "I resent your insinuation, sir," Finn growls.

"I apologize." Merriweather's gray eyes are fastened warily on Rilla. "Surely you can see how it looks. Perhaps introductions are in order?"

"This is my roommate, Rilla Stephenson, and my—friend, Brother Finn Belastra." I hate the way my voice betrays me. "Rilla, Finn, this is——"

Merriweather grabs my arm and yanks me toward him. "He's a member of the Brotherhood? Good Lord, girl, what are you thinking?"

I pull away. "He's loyal to our causes."

"I helped Cate with the Harwood breakout," Finn adds, and I cast an anxious look at Merriweather. What if he puts two and two together and realizes that the handkerchief was Finn's?

"You took part in that?" Merriweather is staring at me, not Finn. "Wait—were you responsible for what happened in the square today?"

I flush, feeling the weight of Finn's gaze on me. "I had help."

"Good," Finn says. "The idea of those girls being hanged—"

"I know." Our eyes lock, and for a moment it feels—nice. Then I turn back to Merriweather. "Your sister—Prue's safe. She's with friends. I'll bring her to the next Resistance meeting, if you like, so you can see for yourself. If you don't mind using the space for personal assignations." I can't resist the little dig.

Merriweather nods, shoving his hands in his pockets. "I owe you a great debt, Miss Cahill. Prudencia means the world to me."

"Merriweather . . ." Rilla bends down and picks up her novel, which she must have dropped in the struggle. "You're the editor of the *Gazette*, aren't you?"

"*You* read the *Gazette*?" Merriweather gives her a look of disbelief.

Rilla shrugs. "Not normally, but Cate's left it lying around our room lately."

"And what do you think of it?" Merriweather preens like a peacock.

Rilla purses her mouth. "That exposé on O'Shea you ran this week was good—it made him out to be the monster he is, but your paper's still awfully skewed toward what this means for *men*."

"Well, men are the ones who buy the paper," Merriweather mutters.

Rilla reaches up and straightens the yellow feather in her short curls. "Perhaps more women would buy it if you wrote about what concerns them. You ought to talk to some of the girls we broke out of Harwood. You couldn't use their real names, of course, but you could reveal the conditions there. And you should interview some of us, too. Interviews with real witches! *That* would get you some readers."

"I don't have any problems finding readers." Merriweather looks a bit stunned, and I daresay he was expecting praise, not criticism, from this freckled slip of a girl. Then he lowers his voice, gesturing to Rilla. "Wait. She's a witch, too? Is the Sisterhood nothing *but* witches?"

"*She* doesn't much care for being spoken about as though she's not in the room," Rilla says loudly, but her eyes are anxious. "You—you won't print that in your paper, will you?"

"No. I'm not interested in getting you all killed." Merriweather lounges against the cabinet, arms crossed in a condescending posture. "You're a brash woman, Miss Stephenson."

"I've got four brothers. Teaches you to throw a punch and speak up if you want to be heard," Rilla explains, pulling on her cloak over her bright dress. "Cate, we ought to be going. The carriage will be waiting."

"Of course." I'd forgotten all about Robert. "Thursday, then, Mr. Merriweather?"

"What's Thursday?" Finn wonders, and Merriweather looks even more affronted.

"The Resistance leaders meet here." I pull my hood back up over my hair. "They talk about—well, I'm not quite sure. Clearing Brennan's name? Ousting the Brotherhood in favor of a proper democracy? Giving women the right to vote?"

"The last one isn't part of our agenda," Merriweather points out, and Rilla snorts.

"Well, if you could use a spy inside the Brotherhood, I'd be interested in joining up," Finn says.

"It isn't really open for—" Merriweather begins. I can tell that he's going to say no.

"You owe me, for Prue," I interrupt. "Let Finn come to the meetings, and think about Rilla's ideas for the *Gazette*. Please."

"All right." Merriweather spreads his hands out. "If you'll wait a minute, I'll give you the information. *Belastra*, was it?" There's a suspicious glint in his eye.

Rilla peeks her head out the door. "The carriage is waiting, Cate."

Ag. I don't relish the notion of leaving Finn alone with Merriweather. What if he questions Finn about Harwood? He was distracted about Prue earlier, but once he thinks about it, he'll realize that the handkerchief was Finn's and that his memory's been erased and then where will we be?

"I'll see you Thursday?" Finn asks. I nod, and he gives me a gap-toothed grin. "Good. I've got more questions for you."

Rilla and I creep back into the carriage, then into the convent through the back gate, and then upstairs into our room, Rilla grumbling the whole time about "that patronizing egghead Merriweather." We're changing into our nightclothes when a shriek rends the silence.

I freeze. I've been awakened by that shriek before, after Mother died, when Tess used to have regular night terrors.

I'm out the door and running down the hall, heedless of the impropriety. I burst into the room Tess and Vi share without knocking. Tess is sitting up in bed, and she's still in one piece, her face flushed with sleep, her blond hair tumbling out of its plait.

But she's sobbing, her entire body shaking with the force of it.

"What happened?" I ask, but she's buried her face in Cyclops's fur and she's crying too hard to answer. I turn to Vi, who's sitting up and blinking in her bed.

"I don't know. I was sound asleep when she screamed and scared me half to death." Vi throws her covers back and stands up. Her black hair falls in two braids over her shoulders. "Tess, honey, what's wrong? Did you have a nightmare?"

Tess points a wavering finger to the other end of her bed. "It was all around me."

"What?" I ask.

"Fire." Tess wipes away tears with the backs of both hands. "I heard something—a door shut somewhere—and I woke up, and my bed was on fire!"

My stomach plummets, remembering the threat she received a week ago. Nothing's happened since then. But now—

"It was just a nightmare," Vi says soothingly, lighting a candle. "It's no wonder, after everything that's happened today."

"No!" Tess's voice is shrill. "Someone's playing a trick on me. It was real. Or—not real, but an illusion. I felt the heat of it. I smelled the smoke."

"Who would do that?" Rilla asks. She and half a dozen other girls crowd in the doorway. She pulled her yellow dress back on but didn't bother buttoning it up the back.

"You're the oracle," Vi adds, smoothing her wrinkled lavender nightgown. "Who would want to see you hurt? You're too important to all of us."

I turn away from Tess to the girls hovering in the doorway: Rebekah and Lucy and Grace, whose room is to the left, and Parvati and Livvy, whose room is to the right. "Were any of you up and about? Did you see anyone leaving Tess's room?"

"You and Rilla look like you were out," Parvati says.

I flush, glancing down at my ivory petticoats and blue corset. I'd just pulled off my dress and corset cover when Tess screamed. "We're hardly responsible for this."

"Don't tell me you're taking this seriously. It was a child's nightmare!" Parvati insists.

Tess crosses her arms over her chest. "I'm not a child."

Parvati shoots a pointed glance at Cyclops. "Your teddy bear would beg to differ."

"I know what I saw," Tess says, flushing. "It was an illusion. Someone cast it on purpose, to frighten me. Someone's trying to—to get into my mind."

"Well, it seems as though it's working. Didn't the other oracle go mad?"

I turn on Parvati in a rage as Tess starts to cry. "This is the second time someone's threatened her, and I won't have you or anyone else making light of it. A threat to her is a threat to the entire Sisterhood."

Parvati shrugs one bony shoulder. "I seriously doubt anyone here is out to get her. It's been quite a day. They said she had a vision earlier. Perhaps she's cracking up under the stress of it."

Tess cries harder, burying her face against her knees. I resist the urge—just barely—to shove Parvati out the door. She's suffered, I remind myself.

"Everyone out," Vi announces, sensing my tilt toward violence. "Tess needs her rest, and so do I." She marches over to her bed, picks up a tattered stuffed white rabbit, and thrusts it out in front of her. "And for what it's worth, there's nothing wrong with teddy bears. I'm fifteen, and this is my Bunny."

Rilla and the others laugh and file out. Vi flushes but stands her ground, fierce, and I feel a swell of pride. When I came to the convent two months ago, she was one of Alice's lackeys, always currying favor, embarrassed by her father the coachman. She hardly ever said a word for herself. She's grown up a great deal since then.

Parvati hesitates in the doorway. "You want this child to run the Sisterhood? To have a vote on the war council? Truly, Cate?"

"Yes," I say, and shut the door in her face.

"I'm not going mad." Tess sniffles, raising her tearstained face. "Someone is trying to scare me or discredit me or both. I'm sorry for waking everyone. I should have realized straight off that it was an illusion, but it looked so real, and it was hanging right above my bed, and—"

"You've got nothing to apologize for." Vi sits on the edge of Tess's bed and strokes her back while I pace the room angrily. "Anyone would have screamed. It sounds terrifying."

"Perhaps it was Parvati," I suggest. "You heard her."

"I don't know." Vi flips a braid over her shoulder. "She's not very handy with illusions yet. I'm not sure she could have managed something that complicated."

"Who, then?" Would Maura lower herself to torment Tess like this? I don't want to think it, but I can't rule out the possibility. "Tess, do you want to come sleep in my room?"

Tess draws herself up. "I'm not a baby, Cate. I'll be fine."

"I'll look after her," Vi promises. She stands and pushes open the curtains, letting the moonlight spill across the room. "Perhaps you ought to have a little lie-in tomorrow, Tess. I could bring up breakfast for you. I'm sure no one would mind if you missed class just this once."

"No. Please don't coddle me," Tess begs. "That's just what they want—whoever's doing this."

I drop onto the bed next to her. "But you've got to take

care of yourself. I know your visions give you headaches, and now this—"

Tess shrinks away from my ministrations. "I'm fine. Go back to bed."

I bite my lip. "All right. Good night, then."

I glance back at Tess as I close the door behind me. She's pulled the blue quilt up to her chin and turned to face the wall, but I can tell by the way her shoulders are shaking that she's crying again, and trying to hide it.

What else is she hiding from me?

CHAPTER
10

THE NEXT DAY, MEI, ADDIE, PEARL, AND I walk down to Richmond Hospital after classes. We carry doctors' bags stuffed with bandages, Bibles, and medicinal herbs. There are guards on every street corner. With Christmas just a few days away, the shops should be bustling, but a hush has fallen over the city. The gallows still stands in Richmond Square; workers are scrubbing bloodstains from the cobblestones on Church Street. A good portion of the populace is frightened enough to stay home— but is it the escaped witches or the Brothers' over-zealous soldiers that scare them?

When we walk through the front door of the hospital, the fevered stench nearly knocks me over. I breathe in through my mouth, fumbling in my bag for a handkerchief. Next to me, Addie gags.

The lobby is a madhouse. The sick line the walls,

faces red and shiny with sweat. Those too weak to stand have lain down on the cold tiled floor. A nurse spins around, trying to direct a dozen different people at once, and more tug at her sleeves. Three little boys run up and down the hall while babies sit slumped and unnaturally quiet in their mothers' arms.

"Good Lord," Mei whispers. "I heard it was getting bad, but this . . ."

"This is dreadful." I scan the crowd. Judging from their clothes—plain, twice-turned dresses for the women and blue jeans and workmen's shirts for the men—it looks like most of the patients hail from the poor neighborhoods near the river. That makes a terrible sort of sense. They can't afford private physicians, and they live one on top of another, with whole families squished into two-room flats. The fever is bound to spread faster there. And it's not as if those already scrambling to feed their families can take a holiday to rest and recover; likely they keep going until they drop—and infect others when they're out.

Does Merriweather know about this? I've made a point of reading the papers lately and there's been nothing about a possible epidemic in the *Sentinel* or the *Gazette*. People have to be made aware. With Christmas coming up, everyone will be crowded into shops and churches. It could reach a crisis level all too quickly. I cringe, remembering the influenza epidemic of 1887. I was only seven, but I remember how the coffins piled up in the churchyard and the Brothers canceled services for a week, urging us to pray at home for an end to the sickness. Mrs. O'Hare's sister died. So did Rose and

Matthew Collier's baby brother—and dozens of other neighbors. That was just in our small town. What must it have been like in New London?

A nurse clad in a gray dress and a long white apron strides briskly down the hall. When she sees us, she pushes her way through the crowd. "Oh, Sisters, thank the Lord you're finally here! We ran out of beds yesterday and now we've got folks dying on our doorstep. Half of them don't come until it's already too late. We give them valerian to calm them, or salicin to try and break the fever, but there isn't much else we can do. We're being run ragged. I had to send three of my nurses home sick."

"I'm sorry we weren't here sooner. We had no idea it was this bad," I explain.

She clucks, heading up the stairs at a pace so quick, I've nearly got to run to keep up. "Inez has seen it with her own eyes, hasn't she? I've been telling her all week we needed help," she complains. "Lord, I didn't even introduce myself. I'm Mrs. Jarrell."

"I'm Cate." I pause on the landing to catch my breath, introducing the others, and then: "Sister Inez has been here?"

"Every day." The nurse runs a hand through her bobbed, chin-length brown hair. "She's awfully devoted. I suppose you want to see her before you start?"

"No, we—" Addie begins, but I elbow her.

"Yes, please." Now that I think of it, Inez has been missing from the convent most afternoons. She teaches the advanced illusions classes, then disappears. But why? She's not the type to nurse the sick. Not unless there's something in it for her.

We follow the nurse through two of the contagious men's wards. They're full, a patient in every one of the thirty beds. Nurses scramble back and forth, dispensing midafternoon tonics and milk punch. The air is filled with the sound of wet, hacking coughs. As we pass through, an aide delivers two bags bulging with freshly laundered sheets.

Mrs. Jarrell leads us down a hallway with a few private rooms. "She reads to him every day for hours. I doubt he understands a word, but it's kind of her. They don't get many visitors. Sad, really."

She stops before a closed door, and I peer through the window into a dim room with a dozen beds. Four windows line the far wall, but the white curtains are all drawn shut; nine of the men are sleeping. The tenth seems fascinated with his own hands, clenching and unclenching his fists like a baby. Inez sits in a wooden chair, a book of Scripture open on her lap, murmuring prayers over the eleventh bed.

The man in it is none other than William Covington, former head of the Brotherhood.

I press my ear to the glass, straining to hear. Her voice rises and falls, but I can't make out the words. I glance back in, noticing the way her eyes rest on Covington's face, not the Bible, even as her mouth continues to move.

The hair on the nape of my neck prickles. Something about this is wrong. Deeply wrong.

I reach for the doorknob, but Mei grabs my arm. "We shouldn't intrude. She looks so prayerful."

Mrs. Jarrell heads back the way we came. "We've got plenty of work for you. The laundry's come back, so we'll need to change the sheets. If you help the junior nurses with that, it will free me up to talk to the matron and see if we can't find somewhere to put these new patients."

Addie and Pearl follow at her heels like spaniels, while Mei and I lag behind. "We need to find out what Inez is doing," I hiss. "Why would she come to visit Covington and the other council members?"

"Perhaps this is her way of atoning for what she did?" Even Mei sounds dubious.

We cross back over the landing and into the women's wing. Mrs. Jarrell pauses in the first contagious ward to speak with the senior nurse.

"Please," I say. "You can't tell me Inez is praying for their health and recovery, not when she's the one who put them here in the first place."

"Well, confronting her wouldn't do any good. If she's got some nefarious plan, she's not going to confess it straight out." Mei watches as a portly Brother shepherds an old woman toward the nurses. She's small and stooped and dressed in a fine mauve cloak with white rabbit fur at the wrists.

"I'm going to find out what it is. Inez has already hurt enough people."

Mei nods absently, her attention elsewhere. The old woman coughs so hard that strands of iron-gray hair tumble down around her face. The Brother taps the head nurse on the shoulder, interrupting her conversation with Mrs. Jarrell, who steps away. He lowers his booming voice, but snippets of it still carry: "My mother . . . wretched fever . . . see to it that she gets . . ." The head nurse nods and hurries off with the old woman in tow.

Mei scowls. "How do you like that? The rich get prompt treatment—and a private room, no doubt!—while the poor have to wait in line to die."

The Brother sees us staring and doffs his hat. "Good afternoon, Sisters!" he says, crossing the room to join us. "Here to do a bit of nursing?"

Mei casts her face down as I nod. "It is our privilege to help the less fortunate," I parrot.

He wrinkles his bulbous nose, fishing in his pocket for a handkerchief. He pulls one out and presses it to his face. I can smell the pungent, piney scent. "I don't know how you can stand the stench," he confesses. "I wouldn't set foot in the place except my mother's come down with the blasted thing."

Mei peers up at him through her spiky dark lashes. "I'm surprised you didn't call for a private physician. You're obviously a man of means."

"That I am." He smiles proudly. "But private physicians haven't got what Ma needs, do they? She's got to see Brother Kenneally straightaway." He winks one dark eye at us. "Can't have people like us coming down with a thing like this just because some river rats don't know their place! I say we should set up a quarantine till it passes. Keep them all down by the river where they belong."

He is not particularly quiet. I glance around the crowded ward, where women of all ages are racked with coughing and flushed with fever. They're sick, but they're not deaf. A skinny woman with hair like cornsilk is glaring at us, and if looks could kill, we'd all be dead.

"What a marvelous idea," Mei says through gritted teeth.

"I thought so." The Brother grins as his mother reappears, shuffling down the hall. He doffs his hat again. "Well, I've got to be going. Take care, Sisters!"

He saunters away, and I stare at Mei in horror. "I don't—what an awful man."

Mei grabs up a bag of fresh laundry. "I'm not even surprised anymore."

Hours later, we stagger home through the twilight streets. Mei sniffs hungrily as we pass a bakery and the delicious smell of bread wafts out. We missed teatime *and* dinner. "Are you still thinking about Inez?" she demands. "How can you think about anything but food or bed right now? I'm half starved."

My stomach is rumbling, and I'm longing for my bed, too, but I have been dwelling on what we saw in Covington's hospital room. Even as Mei and I changed sheets, dispensed suppers, and made patients comfortable for the night, Inez hardly left my mind.

I was able to calm the more excitable patients, abate their fevers, and ease their breathing, but I couldn't heal them entirely. The fever is tricky; it evaded my magic, shifting away no matter how I tried. I hope my efforts will be enough to set them on the road to recovery—but not so miraculous that a canny nurse notices how our visit coincided with a marked improvement. Doing magic at the hospital is riskier than at

Harwood, where the nurses cared precious little for their patients.

It's such a waste. If we were free to practice our magic openly, we could help so many more people. And it wouldn't be dependent on whether they could pay us or not.

"I can't wait for it to be warm." Pearl shivers into her cloak, her buckteeth chattering. "You know what I'd like right now? A tomato and cheese pie."

Mei groans, and Addie presses her snub nose to the window like a street urchin, her breath fogging the cold glass. "Is that a beef pie? It looks delicious. That's what I'd like."

"Let's get some, then." I fumble in my bag for coins. "My treat. Four beef pies?"

"Bless you," Mei says fervently.

I smile as they rush into the warm bakery. All the stores in the market district are open late this week for holiday shopping. The display windows are decorated with pine boughs, and the spicy scent mingles with succulent meat and oniony gravy and fresh bread.

Father's told us how, when he was a little boy, he and Grandfather cut down pine trees, brought them inside, and decorated them with handmade ornaments and strings of popped corn. They put a feathery angel on top and stacked presents beneath. The year he was ten, though, Christmas trees were forbidden. Too pagan, the Brothers said, like the caroling that neighbors used to do, traveling from house to house with hot cider and song. Christmas Day is for venerating the Lord's birth—for church services in the morning, followed by fasting and quiet contemplation—but at least the Brothers haven't stopped people from feasting and ex-changing gifts on Christmas Eve.

It will be a strange holiday this year, away from home, barely speaking to Maura.

It's late when we get home. We scrub our skin until it's red, and Mei volunteers to boil our dresses. When I pop into the sitting room to look for Tess, Vi tells me she's already retired for the night and doesn't want to be disturbed, even by me. I'm tempted to check on her anyway, but she does need her rest. So do I, for that matter. And yet . . .

My other sister is huddled with Parvati, Genie, and a few others around the pink settee. It seems Alice has fallen per-manently into disfavor. Maura switched rooms again—with Livvy this time—in order to share with Parvati. But Alice seems happy enough now that she and Vi have made up. They sit squashed together in a blue armchair, paging through a fashion magazine from Mexico City. Livvy is playing a lovely sonata on the piano. Sachi is sitting on an ottoman by the fire, while Rory lies on her stomach on the red hooked rug and Prue reads a novel nearby. Pearl is knitting another soft gray scarf—for convalescents in the hospital, sweet girl—while Mei decimates Addie in a game of chess.

Contentment washes over me. Despite Finn—despite Inez's scheming—despite the Brothers' cruelties and the un-certainty of our future—I am not unhappy here. I never dreamed I would have friends like these. Three months ago, I didn't think I could trust anyone in the world save my sisters.

How wrong I was, on both accounts.

I want to fold my tired limbs into a chair and watch Mei maneuver her queen across the board, or throw myself on the floor next to Rory and laugh my worries away. Instead, I cross the room to Maura.

"May I speak with you a moment?"

"You can speak freely in front of my friends," she says, smoothing her sapphire skirts.

"I really can't." I try to keep my voice pleasant. "It'll only take a moment."

"Oh, fine." Maura makes a show of reluctance, though I can read the curiosity on her face. She stands, interlacing her hands behind her back and stretching her shoulders. "Excuse me, girls. I've been summoned."

The girls titter like the brightly colored parrots in the pet shop down on Fourth Street, and I resist the urge to roll my eyes. I lead Maura across the hall into the healing classroom, careful to leave the door open a few inches. Less chance of either of us misbehaving that way.

Maura perches on top of Sister Sophia's desk. "What is it, Cate? I don't appreciate you dragging me away from my friends."

I lean against the wooden cabinet that holds Bones, the skeleton we use for anatomy classes. "Something very strange happened to Tess last night."

"I heard," Maura says. "Not from her, of course. From Parvati. Lord forbid either of you tells me anything."

"What did you hear, exactly?"

Maura adjusts one of the gold combs in her hair. "That

Tess had a nightmare and got hysterical. That you didn't help matters by accusing everyone of being out to get her."

"It wasn't a nightmare." I shiver. "Someone cast the illusion of her bed being on fire. It's the second time someone has tried to frighten her like this. Last time it was in broad daylight. We'd just gotten back from shopping, and she walked into her room to find Cyclops hanging from the curtain rod with a note saying *You'll be next*."

Maura frowns. "Why didn't you come to me sooner? She's my sister, too, you know."

"I'm coming to you now. Who would do such a thing?" I fight the temptation to point out that if Maura hadn't blabbed to Inez, no one would know Tess is the oracle, and there would be no reason to target her.

"I haven't the foggiest." Maura's blue eyes narrow thoughtfully.

"Tess thinks someone's trying to discredit her. Make her seem too young and silly to lead."

"She *is* too young," Maura says. "If we were back in Chatham, she wouldn't even be attending teas or dinner parties yet. When the time comes that the Brotherhood falls—and that time is coming, mark my words—we can't put a twelve-year-old in charge of New England."

"I'm not against Tess requiring a regent until she comes of age, but—"

"But you think it should be you, not Inez." Maura kicks her gold slippers against the side of the desk. *Thud. Thud. Thud.*

"Actually, I think it should be Elena." The idea's been

spinning around in my mind for days, and the words come out before I think through the wisdom of sharing them.

Maura freezes. *"What?"*

"I'm not an ideal candidate. I know that. But Elena's brilliant. Strategic. Manipulative when she needs to be, but she can be kind, too. After Inez, she's the best witch we have. Her magic might not be as strong as ours, but she has more experience."

"You want *Elena* to lead until Tess is ready," Maura says slowly.

"Yes." I take a desk from the front row and turn it around so I can sit on the top, facing my sister. "I don't want it for myself. It's never been about that for me. I just want it to be someone who cares about people—all people, not just men, not just witches, and not just the rich. Someone who believes in equality."

Maura is staring at me like I'm a stranger. "Why, Cate, have you been reading political theory?"

I laugh. I'm not ready to make peace, far from it, but perhaps we can have a momentary truce? "Just the *Gazette*."

"I think Elena would be a good leader." Maura flushes. "But what about Inez? She's been so good to me. I can't betray her."

I clench my teeth as hurt lances through me. She can't betray Inez, whom she's known all of two months? She had no trouble betraying *me*. "What is it that she's done for you, besides flatter you and let you practice mind-magic?" I scowl, thinking of the men lying comatose in Richmond Hospital. "Made you responsible for murder?"

"We haven't murdered anyone," Maura snaps, jumping off the desk.

"As good as." I shake my head. "Do you even know what she's plotting now?"

Maura huffs. "If you're referring to Alice's ridiculous accusation—"

"I'm not," I interrupt. "Why has she been spending her afternoons at Richmond Hospital with Brother Covington?"

"I don't know what you're talking about." Maura plants her hands on her hips, but her shifty eyes give her away.

"I saw her there today with my own eyes, so there's no point in denying it. The nurses said she's been there all week." I raise my eyebrows as a thought occurs to me. "Was your mind-magic on Covington not entirely successful? Is there a possibility he could wake up and tell what happened?"

"Wouldn't that make you happy, to know I failed?" Maura's hands clench in her sapphire skirts. "I'm sorry to disappoint you, but that's not it."

"Well, whatever it is, Inez is hiding something. Maybe she's the one threatening Tess."

"No. She wouldn't do that." Maura lifts her chin. "She promised."

"That's the woman you'd have rule New England? One you'd have to beg not to hurt your little sister?" I snap. "You should never have told her Tess was the oracle."

Maura strides over to the window, her shoulders stiffening. She's quiet for a long moment, gazing out at the dreary winter garden. "It isn't Inez."

"Forgive me if I don't take your word for it."

Maura spins around. "She swore an oath to me, Cate. She swore on her husband's grave that she wouldn't hurt Tess."

"She . . . what?" I manage. "Inez was *married*?"

My sister nods. "In the Spanish territories. One of the Brothers' guards caught them sneaking across the border down in Maryland. The guard shot her husband in the head before her very eyes. So she compelled the guard to shoot himself." Maura shivers. "That brooch she always wears—it's got locks of her husband's hair in it."

Interesting. So it's not just power Inez has been craving all these years. It's revenge, too.

"Who else would want to discredit Tess?" I ask, refocusing on the matter at hand. "It would have to be someone who supports Inez. Someone like . . ." I trail off. I don't want to suspect Maura. She seemed genuinely surprised that the incident last night wasn't the first. But Alice has come around of late, Parvati isn't powerful enough, and frankly, I don't see any of the other girls having the initiative to plan a campaign like this.

"You're wondering if it was me, aren't you." Maura bites her lip. "Do you really think so little of me? You think I'd hurt *Tess*?"

"You hurt *me*." The words slip out before I can stop them.

"That's—" Maura pauses, but we both know what she was about to say. *That's different.*

Why? What about our relationship is so fundamentally broken that she would think that? What did I ever do to her?

I head for the door. "It's late, Maura. I'll let you get back to your friends."

• • •

The next morning, Tess is waiting for me in the hall between my illusions and advanced mathematics classes. "Cate!" she exclaims, grabbing me out of the crush of girls and pulling me into the library. "I have the most marvelous news! Guess what? Father's coming for Christmas!"

"Here? To New London?" I ask stupidly.

"No, to Indo-China. Yes, here!" She waves a letter in my face. "I wrote him last week and asked him to come and he—"

"Do you think that's a good idea?" I interrupt.

"Cate." She frowns at me, hitching her stack of books higher on her pink-clad hip. "We agreed to tell him the truth at Christmas. How can we do that if we don't see him? You promised."

"I know." Tess thinks it's past time to tell Father that we're witches, and I suppose I agree that he should learn the truth of it. But things seem so uncertain just now. Maura and I are barely speaking. How can we pretend to be a happy family for Father? Does Tess mean to tell him *everything*?

"He'll stay in his flat above the Cahill Mercantile Company." She bounces on her tiptoes, a grin spreading across her face, and I don't have the heart to argue. It's the happiest she's looked in weeks. "He said he expects to get in late on Friday, and we ought to come to the flat for dinner on Christmas Eve. He's bringing presents and a big surprise!"

"That sounds wonderful." But I can't help worrying. What if Father doesn't react the way she hopes? "Speaking of presents, I'm going shopping before I head to the hospital this afternoon. Would you like to come with me?"

"No, thank you." Tess puts her books down on a nearby shelf, straightening the fuchsia sash at her waist. "Vi and I are going tomorrow."

"Oh." I bite back my disappointment. "I don't have to go today. Perhaps we could play a game of checkers. Or I could help you bake scones for tea. Whatever you like."

"I've already promised to help Lucy with her Latin." Tess picks up the stack of books and edges her way toward the door.

"Oh. Well, perhaps I could—"

"Why don't you just shackle me to your ankle?" she snaps.

I stare at her, taken aback. "Tess, I didn't mean—"

"Forgive me." Tess flushes as pink as one of Mother's peonies. "I don't mean to be unkind. But if I want people to take me seriously, I can't be hanging on to your skirts all the time, Cate. You understand, don't you?"

"Of—of course." My fingers dig into the leather cover of my mathematics text. "I'll ask Rilla if she'd like to come with me instead."

"Perfect." Tess gives me a sunny smile, but my throat aches as I watch her walk away. It's natural that she wants to assert her independence, isn't it? She *will* be thirteen next year.

Somehow, though, it feels as if I'm losing both my sisters.

CHAPTER
11

VERY LATE ON THURSDAY NIGHT, PRUE, Rilla, and I head toward O'Neill's Stationery. Prue is eager to be reunited with her brother, and Rilla insisted on coming because she "refuses to let that conceited fop of a Merriweather" off the hook regarding her ideas for the *Gazette*. As we hurry along the frozen city streets, tucked into our cloaks and fur muffs, they chatter about their ideas for interviewing former Harwood prisoners. I smile, feeling confident in their ability to browbeat Merriweather into running some pro-witch pieces, but butterflies tumble through my stomach at the promise of seeing Finn.

The occasional phaeton rumbles past, carrying young men home from their carousing or whatever it is young men have the freedom to do late at night. Two guards stop us once we reach the market district, but we tell them we're on our way to Richmond Hospital to pray over the fever victims and they let us pass. No one seems to relish being out tonight. The wind whips furiously through my winter layers, numbing my thighs, sending my hair tumbling out of its careful braids. At least it isn't snowing. It hasn't since the night of the Harwood breakout. Has it been two weeks already?

The last two days have flown past. I've spent my mornings in class—illusions, advanced mathematics, and animations—and my afternoons nursing at Richmond Hospital. Inez has been strict in illusions, singling me out when my glamours don't hold, but otherwise she's been quiet. Too quiet, perhaps. This morning I caught her smiling in a way that sent terror tumbling through me. In the evenings, Sachi and Rory and I have been trying to determine what to do with the new girls. They can't stay at the convent indefinitely, but most of them have nowhere else to go.

Tess and Maura have both kept their distance. It hurts more than I'd like to admit.

The Brothers have begun to preach about the pestilence brought on by the witches. The *Sentinel* ran an article today claiming that the witches have cast a plague onto the populace. Yesterday, on the way home from the hospital, I ducked into a flower shop to buy some of the yellow tulips Rilla loves and overheard two well-dressed women gossiping about how the witches have done spells to make people sick. They wore bright, gauzy scarves tied over their faces because the fever has begun to spread into the market district, but it's a flimsy precaution. I suspect they think of the sickness as something that could only happen to other people—poorer, unluckier ones.

The alley behind Fifth Street is quiet. The wind has sent clouds scudding over the moon, plunging the night into shadow. I check to be sure there's no one nearby before using my key to unlock the back door. In the storeroom, I shuck off my cloak. I've forgone my Sisterly black for a dove-gray dress with a blue sash that I know looks well on me. I pause to pat my hair back into place, wishing for a looking glass.

"Do I look a mess?" I ask, flushing. If Merriweather could see me, he'd think I was a silly chit indeed.

Rilla reaches up to fix a strand of my hair. "No. You look lovely."

I lead the way down into the cellar, my eyes sweeping over the men assembled at the table: Merriweather, O'Neill, the ginger-whiskered Mr. Moore, a strapping man built like a dockworker but dressed like a dandy, and two others from last time. No Finn. My heart falls.

Merriweather crosses the room in three giant strides. "Prudencia!" he says, in a voice hoarse with emotion, and folds her into his long-limbed embrace. While he and Prue are having their tender reunion, I introduce Rilla to the others.

"Good to see you again, my girl," O'Neill says, after Prue extricates herself.

"Welcome back, Prue. How long did they have you in that place?" the tall man asks.

Merriweather whirls on him. "Good Lord, John, have a little tact."

"It was three years," Prue says, smiling. "I don't mind talking about it. In fact, I *want* to talk about it. I think people should know what we suffered."

"See?" Rilla's hazel eyes spark with the light of battle.

Merriweather sighs and turns to me. "Why did you bring this one? The other girl was lovely. Quiet."

"If you say women should be seen and not heard, I'll brain you myself," Prue threatens. "I think Rilla's idea is brilliant. Everyone who follows your paper knows where I was, Alistair, and they all know it wasn't because I was a witch; it was because I refused to tell the Brothers how to find you. Some of the other girls wouldn't want you using their real names, but you could use mine."

"Absolutely not!" Merriweather thunders. "I won't put you forward as a target."

Prue rolls her eyes heavenward. "You can risk your safety, but I can't? That's ridiculous."

The men around the table watch the siblings argue, heads swiveling back and forth as though they're at a lawn tennis match.

"The ladies have a point." Finn clatters down the stairs. He's wearing a chocolate-colored vest and a rumpled white shirt, and when his eyes meet mine, a grin spreads over his face, and I'm blind to anything else. "You weren't at the bazaar, Merriweather, but O'Shea had a nurse spinning stories about how well the Harwood girls were treated. The public ought to know the truth of it."

"And how am I supposed to get my hands on all these girls to interview them?" Merriweather demands.

"That's where we come in." Rilla's wearing one of her favorite dresses tonight, too. It's yellow brocade with enormous orange gigot sleeves and an orange taffeta bow at the breast. "I could interview them for you."

"What?" Merriweather's chiseled jaw drops. "*That's* ridiculous."

"It is not. It's past time you had a lady reporter on your staff. I would use a nom de plume, of course," Rilla plows on. "All the magazines from Paris and Dubai have lady reporters. Why not here?"

Merriweather runs a hand through his shaggy dark hair. "All the fashion magazines, you mean. I run a serious newspaper, Miss Stephenson, and I will not have it become a laughingstock."

Prue gives her brother a mutinous look. "I think it's a good idea."

"Of course you do." Merriweather folds his arms across his broad chest. "How do I even know she can write?"

"You'll see when I turn in my first interview, won't you?" Rilla brushes her palms together as if the matter is settled, and I can practically see Merriweather's brain explode. Poor man.

"I don't wish to tell you how to run your newspaper—" I begin carefully.

"Then don't. I beg of you, refrain from whatever it is you're about to say. I've had all I can take of managing females for the evening," Merriweather grumbles, glaring at Prue and Rilla. He pulls out a chair from the long wooden table and slumps into it.

"I'm afraid that wouldn't agree with my conscience." I take the empty seat between him and Finn. Rilla and Prue sit across the table. "I've spent the last four days nursing fever victims at Richmond Hospital. Are you aware that we're in real danger of an epidemic?"

"An epidemic?" Merriweather shakes his head. "I've heard it's gotten worse, but—"

I shake my head, terribly aware that Finn's knee is only inches from mine. "It's spread like wildfire all through the river district. It's bound to hit the market district next, and then what? It's three days till Christmas. Everyone's out doing their shopping."

John frowns, toying with his purple cravat. "I thought the accounts in the *Sentinel* were all just fearmongering."

Mr. Moore scratches at his whiskers. "My cousin lives out on the edge of town. Sent word yesterday that his kids are sick and might not be able to make it for Christmas dinner."

"See? People ought to be taking precautions, and they aren't, because the *Sentinel* is blaming it all on the witches. The hospital is a madhouse; they're turning people away for lack of beds. Talk to any nurse!" I glance around at the men lining the table: all gentlemen or tradesmen, by their dress. "When was the last time any of you went down by the river? For all your fine talk of equality and a vote for all men, do any of you ever interact with the poor?"

There's a moment of silence, and I grit my teeth.

"We don't get many customers from down by the river. Good writing paper and ink are luxuries," O'Neill admits, staring down at his wrinkled hands.

"If it's so bad, why wouldn't the Brothers be setting up quarantines? Or at least marking houses with the sick inside?" Merriweather asks.

"It might cause panic. That's the last thing O'Shea wants." Finn's brown eyes meet mine and then flick around the table. "He won't go anywhere without half a dozen guards. He's afraid of being assassinated or attacked—either by the witches or by someone inside the council. The Brotherhood is deeply divided right now."

The other men look suitably impressed by this information. "How so?" John asks.

"That last measure barely passed. They've caught ten of the sixty witches who escaped Sunday, but they haven't scheduled another execution. Some say it's because O'Shea's afraid of another show of power by the witches." Finn's freckled hand rests on his right thigh, just inches from mine, and I have to force myself not to reach out and twine our fingers together. It feels unnatural to be this close and not touching. "Others say it's because public opinion is against it. Some want to elect O'Shea permanently. Others want to call Brennan back and give him a chance to explain himself."

Merriweather straightens. "How many of them would side with Brennan now?"

"Hard to say." Finn leans forward to see around me, and his knee bumps mine. "Before the incident at Harwood, I think he could've gotten the vote. Now . . . I don't know. I feel damned guilty about the whole thing."

I suck in a startled breath. "Why would you feel guilty?"

Surely he isn't leading this conversation where I think he's leading it.

"Because I was there, not Brennan. Because it's my handkerchief they—ow!" Finn exclaims as I kick him in the shin. "I already told Merriweather, Cate, and I'm sure he told the others."

"Are you mad?" I swivel to face Merriweather. "You can't turn him in! Even if he confessed, they'd think he was making it up to clear Brennan's name. They'd hang them both."

"We know," Merriweather says. "We have no intention of turning him in. Come to think of it, though, Belastra, perhaps I ought to interview *you* about what happened at Harwood. Anonymously, of course."

I dart an uneasy glance at Finn. "He helped us bluff our way in. We were disguised as Brothers, but he was the real thing."

"I see." There's a curious gleam in Merriweather's eyes. "And then what?"

"We pulled the fire bell to get all the nurses in one place, and then we shut them in the uncooperative ward. It locks from the outside. But one of the nurses—the one who spoke at the bazaar—escaped and shot a patient. Finn helped me subdue her and then—"

"I appreciate your candor," Merriweather interrupts, "but perhaps you could let the man speak for himself?"

My heart sinks. He knows. Finn must have said something the other night, something that betrayed his lack of memory. Now Merriweather's bound to ask questions, he won't let it drop, and—

I throw a panicky glance across the table at Rilla.

"Why are you so interested in what Mr. Belastra did that night?" Rilla tosses her brown curls. "It was mostly us, you know. Witches. Women. Why not give us credit?"

"I give you plenty of credit. I've already thanked Cate profusely for saving my sister," Merriweather argues. "Don't you think Belastra deserves accolades, too, for risking his neck?"

Finn's brow is furrowed as he stands. "Cate, may I speak to you for a moment? In private?"

Moore chuckles behind his whiskers. "Lovers' quarrel?"

I can feel the prickly heat spreading up my throat and across my cheeks. I must look like a strawberry. Finn doesn't say anything and he's flushing, too, and the silence is horrible. I stand as he strides for the stairs. Leaving the meeting to chase after him will only make me look more foolish in Merriweather's eyes but—

"Go ahead. Prue and I can handle this," Rilla promises, waving a hand to encapsulate Merriweather and the rest of the men gathered around the table.

I go.

Finn is standing in the storeroom next to a lantern that throws a dim circle of light. The room smells of paper and ink and dust and now it feels right because Finn is here too, smelling of bergamot from his tea. He leans against a cabinet full of accounting ledgers, and I stand next to him.

He runs a hand through his hair. "This is a damned awkward thing to have to ask, but I don't see any way around it. What are we, Cate?"

"I— Pardon?" I ask stupidly.

"What are we to each other?" Even in the dim light, I see his ears go red. "Was that man right? Are—are we lovers?"

"We were in love. Engaged, briefly, before I joined the Sisterhood." I cast about. How can I explain what was between us in just a few sentences? It was trust and respect built on dozens of tiny moments—moments that he no longer has any memory of. "After that, it had to stay a secret."

Finn is so close that I can feel the heat radiating off him in the cold room, but I cannot read his expression. What must he be thinking? "Why?" he asks.

"They threatened you and my sisters if I didn't come willingly to New London. Because of the prophecy." I feel so bumbling. I bite my lip, terribly aware that Finn's eyes travel to my mouth. The air between us feels electric again, like the moments before a lightning storm.

"The prophecy?" he mutters. "Good Lord. Are you the oracle?"

"No. It's Tess." I say it without thinking.

His eyes are warm on my face. "You must trust me a great deal to tell me that."

"I do." More than anyone else in the world.

He nods, almost as if he hears the words I don't say. "Why didn't you come to me and tell me everything right away? The second you realized I wasn't myself?"

"I should have. I just—I couldn't bear it." My gaze falls to the wooden floor, and he reaches out and tilts up my chin so I have no choice but to look at him. "You don't remember being in love with me, Finn. How could I come to you and tell you that?"

A tear trickles down my cheek. Finn brushes it away with the pad of his thumb. "This must be very difficult for you."

"Not as difficult as it's been for you." I struggle against it, but another tear escapes. "I'm sorry. I am so sorry."

"Shhh." Finn draws me into his arms. I bury my face against the soft cotton of his shoulder. Perhaps he's only doing this because he feels obliged, because he feels guilty for not remembering me, but for a moment, I let myself pretend otherwise. I am pressed against him, our bodies touching from knees to shoulders, and there is nowhere else in the world I would rather be. He tucks a strand of blond hair behind my ear. "It's going to be all right. We'll figure this out together," he whispers, and his breath on my neck sends a not-unpleasant shiver through me.

I turn my head. "I've missed you." My lips almost touch his throat.

He lets out a little hum of pleasure, his hands moving on my back, burning warm through the gray silk. And I cannot help it. I press a kiss to the warm, smooth skin just above his collar. He tastes of salt and soap and Finn. His hands clutch at the fabric of my dress and I tilt my head and I'm not sure who moves first, but then we are kissing, we are kissing, and—

I am lost. I forget to go slow, forget this is—to him—our first kiss, forget about caution or reputation. My hand fumbles beneath his vest and I press a palm against the small of his back to anchor him against me. His lips move soft and hot and slow against mine. When I arch my neck, his mouth moves to my throat, making love to me until I curl my fingers though the crisp hair at his nape and pull his face back to mine. I nip at his bottom lip with my teeth and his tongue slips into my mouth and his hands are soft on my waist and—

It feels like it did before. It feels like the secret room, the gazebo, the conservatory. I can close my eyes and pretend that we are back in Chatham in the autumn rose garden, surrounded by hedges and the sweet scent of my mother's roses.

I can pretend that he still loves me.

Finn stills. He rests his forehead against mine, his breath coming fast. "Cate, we should talk about—" he begins, and then his eyes settle on something behind me.

"What is it?" I ask. His hands relax on my waist, but he doesn't entirely let me go.

The wooden floor is carpeted in rose petals. They're everywhere: drifting onto the shelves, blanketing the boxes of pens and the accounting ledgers. I run a hand through my hair, find one caught in my braid, and hold it in my palm. It's a deep scarlet, just like the ones in Mother's rose garden, and velvety soft. The scent is intoxicating.

I did this. Just like with the feathers.

But this time, Finn knows what I am.

"I lose my head around you. Always have," I confess.

"I suspect the feeling is mutual." Finn traces the line of my neck, and I shiver again. He winds his fingers through my blue sash and pulls me back against him. His mouth lowers to mine.

We are thoroughly lost in each other when the back door swings open and a man clad in Brotherly black bursts into the room. We spring apart, but the man's cold-marble eyes slide over us. Over my wrinkled dress and swollen lips. Over Finn's untucked vest and messy hair.

"So this is where you've been sneaking off to, Belastra?" Brother Ishida's lips twist into a sneer. "And you, Miss Cahill. What of your vow to the Sisterhood? Are you not meant to spend your life in chaste service to the Lord?"

Finn's jaw works. "Did you follow me?"

"I did, and what of it? You've been acting downright odd. I thought you were in league with those who've been working to bring Sean Brennan back into the fold." Ishida eyes me, stepping closer, and I press back against the cabinet. "I've been waiting out there in the carriage for an hour and I'm half frozen. And here you've just been dallying with this strumpet!"

"I'll thank you to keep a civil tongue in your head," Finn growls.

"It's plain as the nose on my face what you two have been up to. I was young once myself, you know." Ishida gives a lecherous smile. "But a member of the Sisterhood—this can't be shoved under the rug, Belastra. She's got to be made an example of."

"The hell she has." Finn steps in front of me.

I reach for my magic and find it hovering, ready. "It's all right," I say, pushing past him to open the back door. I focus on Ishida's lined face and narrow my focus, scalpel sharp. *Go back to your hotel. You weren't able to follow Brother Belastra tonight. You've no idea where he went. In fact, you've been quite silly to suspect him of anything. He's a loyal member of the Brotherhood.*

Brother Ishida nods and strides through the door. A carriage bearing the golden seal of the Brotherhood is waiting at the corner. I shut the door behind him with a sigh.

"What did you just do?" Finn's voice is low. I reach out to take his hand, but he backs away from me and repeats himself. "What did you do, Cate?"

I bite my lip. "I compelled him to forget."

Finn swears beneath his breath, and the look on his face—

"Finn." I step toward him, beseeching. "It's not like what happened to you. I only erased the last hour—him sitting out there in the carriage and then seeing us together. That's it. Nothing more."

But doubts swarm into my mind like bumblebees. This is the second time I've performed mind-magic on Ishida, and Tess compelled him once, too. How many times can a person's mind bear that kind of meddling before it breaks?

"He's a cruel man. He'd have been glad to see his daughters hanged," I insist, fighting my guilt. "He would have arrested me!"

"I wouldn't let that happen." Finn is looking at me like I'm a stranger again. "This isn't the first time you've used mind-magic, is it?"

"N-no," I stutter. My father. Finn himself. The night watch and nurses at Harwood. Ishida, twice now. "But only to protect myself. I will *never* use it against you. I swear."

"What if we have a fight? How can I trust you?" Finn's eyes collide with mine, full of anger and doubt. "You know who erased my memory, don't you? You've got to. You know everything else that happened to me that day, right up until the moment on the convent steps."

I nod.

"What else are you keeping from me?" Finn grabs his

cloak from the cabinet and throws it over his shoulders. Tears spring into my eyes, but he doesn't comfort me this time. "I don't know how the old Finn would have handled this, but the new one doesn't care much for secrets, Cate."

With that, he storms out into the cold.

I sink to the floor, burying my face in my knees, and that's how Rilla finds me a little while later: crying, surrounded by rose petals.

CHAPTER

12

I'M PUSHING PARSNIPS AROUND MY plate and thinking of Finn when someone rings the bell at the front door. Girls look up from their suppers with consternation. It's rare that we receive guests at the convent, and it's especially dangerous now, when we're harboring twenty-two fugitives. Inez stalks off to see who it is while Sister Gretchen ushers the Harwood girls upstairs via the back staircase. I turn, exchanging uneasy glances with Tess. Grace is trembling as she gets up from their table, and Lucy trails after her, leaving her roast chicken uneaten.

Inez is back in a minute, her pinched face unsmiling. "Miss Zhang, it's your father."

Mei rises, swiping her bangs out of her eyes. She looks across the table at Rilla and me. "Something's wrong. Baba's so busy, he wouldn't call here unless—" She bites her lip, and I wonder if it's her brother who's been arrested this time. Caught buying Merriweather's paper, perhaps.

"Don't borrow trouble. Go and see what it is," Rilla advises, reaching for her fork. "Perhaps it's good news. A letter from your sisters?"

Mei nods, straightening her shoulders as she hurries away. With her dark hair bound in one long plait down her back and her bright tangerine dress, she reminds me of the black-eyed Susans in my garden at home. Longing sweeps over me. I miss my garden. Miss having my hands in the dirt. There hasn't been any time to fiddle with the orchids in the conservatory lately, not between classwork and nursing and Resistance meetings.

I slump in my seat, remembering how Finn stormed out of the shop last night. Sachi and Rilla were right; I should have told him the truth sooner. He's got every right to be angry with me for keeping secrets. But at the same time, he's never made me feel ashamed to be a witch before. From the moment he found out what I was, he was awed and proud. Before, he knew I could do mind-magic and he never once worried I would use it against him. He trusted me.

How can I earn back his trust?

Is it even possible for him to trust a witch, after what Maura did?

I hear her low, bubbling laugh and glance across the dining room. Her red pompadour is next to Genie's mousy-brown head, and they're whispering. As I watch, she throws back her head and laughs as though she hasn't a care in the world, and fury cuts through me. How dare she be so merry when I am so miserable. Magic twitches through me and my fingertips go white against my water goblet. I'd like to throw its contents in her face.

"Cate!" Mei runs back into the dining room, stopping at the end of our table. "It's Yang. He's got the fever. It's bad. Baba thought—he doesn't want me exposed to it, but he thought I might want to come and—" She breaks off, her dark eyes shining with unshed tears. "He thinks Yang could die, Cate."

I rise and push in my chair. "I'll come with you."

"And do what, Miss Cahill?" Inez slithers toward us, black skirts rustling.

I plant my hands on my hips. "And heal him, if I can."

"You can't go around town using magic to heal people on their deathbeds," Inez snaps. "It would look a mite suspicious, don't you think?"

Mei's chin isn't as pointy as mine, but she can still look quite pugnacious when she wants. "I don't care how it looks! He's my brother."

Inez purses her thin lips. "Miss Zhang, how long have you known you were a witch?"

"Since I was twelve." Mei reaches into her pocket and begins counting the ivory mala beads she always carries.

"And in five years, you've never chosen to enlighten your family," Inez points out. "You didn't trust them with it. Why is that?"

Mei gives a sigh that blows her bangs askew. "I was worried Baba would disapprove. He's very traditional in some ways. But I don't care if he disowns me. Not if we can heal Yang." She starts toward the door. "I don't have time to argue. He's waiting."

Inez grabs her by the elbow, hauling her to a stop, and Mei trips over the blue rug. "How far do you suppose his disapproval would go? Do you trust your family with your safety? Not only yours—that of all your friends?"

Mei yanks away. "Yes. Baba would never do anything to hurt me."

"Be sensible," Inez pleads, her hands dropping to her sides. "If you heal one person, where does it stop? What if your mother takes ill next? Your aunt? Their friends? Word will spread of your brother's miraculous recovery, Mei, and it's dangerous for anyone to suspect what you're capable of. I know you think me a monster, but I'm trying to protect you, truly. Tensions are so high just now—"

"And whose fault is that?" I interrupt.

"I'm not going to let my brother die." Mei straightens the rug. "Cate, you can come with me or stay, it's up to you, but I'm going."

"Of course I'm coming with you." I dart past Inez, but she catches at my arm.

"Heal him if you must, but then erase their memories," she hisses, her breath hot against my ear.

I tug away without a response. Rilla pushes in her chair and chases after us.

"And where do you suppose you're going, Miss Stephenson?" Inez barks. "You've no affinity for healing at all!"

Rilla gives her an impudent grin, smoothing her chocolate

velvet gown. "All this talk of brothers reminded me that I forgot one of mine. I got Christmas gifts for everyone except Jamie, and he'll never forgive me. I'm such a cabbagehead!"

Inez eyes Rilla's half-full plate. "And you're going to remedy that now? In the middle of your supper?"

Rilla points at the clock on the mantel. "The shops will be closing soon, and my train to Vermont is first thing tomorrow. I've got to go right now, simply got to, or you can't imagine the row we'll have tomorrow night."

Inez steps aside. Mei runs ahead to get her things, while Rilla and I pause at the far end of the hall. "You got Jamie that book on botany," I remind her.

"I know." Rilla holds out her palm. "Give me your necklace. I'm going to see if Merriweather's at the shop. He ought to come see firsthand what witches and the fever are like."

A hired hack is waiting in front of the convent. Mei tells her father that I'm a nurse and she wants me to take a look at Yang. He examines me over half-moon spectacles, and I wonder what he sees. A tall, thin girl with blond hair straggling out of her simple chignon, wisps of it framing her pointy stubborn face, and sad blue eyes? I don't think I look terribly impressive. But he shrugs and says it couldn't hurt, and we ride the rest of the way in silence.

The carriage stops at the edge of the market district. Mr. Zhang climbs out and hands Mei and me down. The buildings here push up against narrow, cracked brick sidewalks. This block contains a general goods store on the corner, a milliner, a shoemaker, and—in the middle—a shuttered shop with a simple red sign reading ZHANG'S HABERDASHERY. Upstairs, candles burn in both front windows.

Mei opens the door to the flat and pounds up the stairs. She pauses to hang up her cloak and remove her boots, adding them to the row of shoes lined up beneath the hall table. I follow suit. "Mama?" she calls, weaving through a cozy parlor. It's cluttered with a mishmash of furniture: two tufted sofas and a battered settee all in bright clashing colors, several ottomans, a wooden chair with pineapples carved into the arms, and a host of small tea tables crowded with empty teacups. A pile of dresses lies next to a sewing basket beneath a lamp with no shade. A doll and several carved wooden animals are scattered across the hooked rugs.

"Mei?" A plump little woman bustles out of another room. She's wearing a bright orange paisley shawl over a brown dress. "Who's this?"

"Mama, this is my friend Cate." I smile as Mei takes her mother's hands. "How is he?"

Mrs. Zhang's eyes fill with tears. "Not good. You shouldn't have come. The fever is very contagious. I've sent the little ones to your auntie Yanmei's until—"

"Until he's better," Mr. Zhang interrupts, coming up behind us in his stocking feet. "Can I offer you a cup of tea, Miss Cahill? Jia, Miss Cahill is a nurse."

Mrs. Zhang pulls away from Mei, dabbing at her eyes with a lace-edged handkerchief. "Is that so? Do you think you could help Yang?"

"I—I hope so." I clasp my hands nervously behind my

back. What if I *can't* heal Yang, and he dies anyway, and they're furious with me for making promises I can't keep?

"Mama, Baba—there's something I need to tell you first." Mei draws her hand, wrapped in mala beads, out of her pocket. "Something I should have told you ages ago. I'm . . . a witch."

Her parents glance back and forth at each other, and I can't read them. I hope I won't need to compel them to forget this.

"Say something, please," Mei begs.

"We know," her mother says finally. She reaches up and tucks a wayward strand of black hair, streaked with gray, into her bun. "We've known for years, Mei."

Mei sags onto the violet sofa. "I— *How?*"

Mr. Zhang puts his hand on Mei's shoulder. "Quite a lot of strange things happened around here before you went off to that school."

"I'm sorry it took a situation like this for you to finally tell us." Mrs. Zhang's soft voice is full of reproach. "Surely you knew we wouldn't throw you out on the street?"

"We were so worried when you went away to that school. Proud of your scholarship, of course, but we didn't know what might happen if you did magic by accident in front of all those devout ladies." Mr. Zhang peers up at me. "You accept Mei as she is?"

Mei laughs. "Cate's a witch, too. They're all witches."

Her father's face scrunches into confusion. "Your auntie Yanmei went to the convent school when she was a girl. Before she was married."

"Who do you think told me they were all witches? She caught me turning Yang's hair pink while he was sleeping and suggested I learn how to control my magic before I got myself in trouble!" Mei explains.

"Yanmei is a witch?" Mr. Zhang takes off his spectacles and rubs them on the front of his gray vest.

A fit of coughing drifts out of the next room, and Mrs. Zhang darts a worried glance in that direction. "There isn't any truth to what the Brothers are saying, is there? That the witches set the plague on the people?" She twists her handkerchief in her hands.

"No! We would never do anything like that." Mei stands. "But healing is a type of magic, and Cate and I are both good at it. Cate's the best in the whole convent. If anyone can fix Yang, she can."

I bite my lip. "I might not be able to heal him entirely, though. The fever—it's rather resistant to magic."

"Anything you can do," Mr. Zhang says, wincing at the sound of more coughing. "We'd be very grateful."

Mrs. Zhang leads us into the small bedroom. She gestures at her son, who's lying in a small wooden bed with all the covers thrown off. The window is cracked open to let in fresh air, and my teeth are soon chattering, but Yang is flushed, his forehead beaded with sweat, his white nightshirt soaked with it.

His mother holds a glass of water to his lips and he drinks greedily, then coughs again. His breath is labored, rasping. Mrs. Zhang pushes damp black hair off his forehead. "I've been giving him ice baths, but he's still burning up."

"Let me try." I move to his bedside with a confidence I don't feel. "Hello, Yang. Remember me? I'm Mei's friend Cate." Yang looks up at me with dull, fevered eyes. His lips are dry and cracked. "It's all right. Don't try to talk. Let me just take your pulse." I pick up his damp hand and put my fingers on his wrist. His pulse is too fast. The second I touch him, I can feel the fever. It burns red in his lungs, coating his airways with infection. I push against it and it seems as though it pushes right back.

But I'm stubborn. I perch on the edge of Yang's bed and settle in for a fight. He hasn't had an easy time of it, having to go out to work instead of finishing school, putting his own ambitions aside in order to help his family make ends meet. And Mei's already lost two sisters to the prison ship. I won't let her lose her brother, too.

Magic pours out of me and into Yang. His airways clear first, and then his lungs, and the rasp of his breath eases. But his skin is still too hot. I push harder and my own muscles begin to go limp. "It's *almost*—Mei, can you help me?" I pant, as a bell rings downstairs.

Mei slides her hand into mine, and more magic rushes in, reinvigorating me. I heave and the fever shudders back, retreating. I yank on the last threads of magic running through me, twining through my body from head to toe, and it feels like pulling a frayed ribbon tight. Any moment now, I'll snap. My fingers scramble for purchase on Yang's wrist, and blackness begins to dance in the corners of my eyes as I *shove* the magic out of my body and into his. Yang's heart slows, strong and steady, as I fall sideways toward the wall.

"Oh! Cate!" Mei catches me just before my temple smashes into the headboard. She tugs me away from her brother and sits me in the high-backed wooden chair beside the bed. I tuck my head down over my knees until things stop spinning.

"What's wrong with her?" a voice demands.

I know that voice. Dimly, I hear Mei introduce her parents to Finn and Merriweather and Rilla, and then Finn impatiently asks his question again.

"There's a cost to healing magic," Mei explains.

"The fever's broken," Mrs. Zhang says from her son's bedside, and I can hear her smile.

"So she healed him, but it made her sick?" Finn sounds angry.

"That's how it works. She'll be right as rain in a few minutes. Here, Cate, Baba made you some green tea." Mei puts her hand on my shoulder, hauling me upright.

Nausea swims over me. I jump up, searching frantically for the washbasin, a hand clapped over my mouth. Rilla shoves it at me and I turn away and am ill right there in front of everyone. Good Lord. It's so mortifying, I'd cry if I had the strength.

"Give the poor girl a minute of privacy! This is a sickroom, not a circus!" Mrs. Zhang says, shooing them all away. Mei hands me a handkerchief, and I wipe my mouth.

"I'm not leaving until I see that she's all right," Finn insists.

I turn, forcing a smile that comes out like a grimace. "I'll be fine."

"Are you sure? You look rather—wobbly." Behind his spectacles, his brown eyes are full of worry. He might not love me—but he does care, at least a little.

Merriweather charges forward from the doorway, his dark hair windblown, his olive peacoat buttoned all askew. "You were able to heal the boy completely? Can you tell me what it felt like?" He runs a hand over his jaw. "If you can heal it, though—people might see that as proof."

"Proof of what?" Rilla demands, glaring up at him.

Merriweather shrugs. "O'Shea's claim that the witches created the fever, that it's some sort of dark magic."

"That's ridiculous." Mei stomps around me, jabbing her forefinger into Merriweather's broad chest. "We're helping people, not hurting them. It's more than the Brothers are doing. They only want to help those who can pay the hospital fees."

"It's true." Mrs. Zhang steps away from her son for a moment. "Baba went to the hospital earlier. The nurse told him all the beds were full, but then a Brother brought in a little girl and they took her right upstairs to see Brother Kenneally."

"See? That's what you ought to be reporting on!" Mei insists.

Merriweather arches one eyebrow. "That the Brothers and their families are given preferential treatment? That's hardly news, I'm afraid."

"Why?" I croak. "Why Kenneally?"

"He's the director of Richmond Hospital. It's all in who you know, isn't it?" Merriweather's rich baritone is full of disgust, but I shake my head, struggling to collect my thoughts.

"No. She means why would they come down to the hospital to see him, when it's full of infection and there's no cure?" Finn says, and I nod, relieved that someone else has caught at the heart of it. "What can Kenneally do that their private physician can't?"

"Ah." Merriweather steeples his long, elegant fingers. "That's a good question, Belastra. That might bear looking into."

Rilla swats at his arm. "*Cate* was the one pointing it out!"

I lean back against the wall, and Finn gives me his gap-toothed grin. There's admiration in his eyes—whether for my witchery or my wits, I don't know—but it makes my stomach flutter in an altogether different way.

CHAPTER
13

TESS HAS CALLED A FAMILY MEETING.

Frankly, I would have liked to refuse to come, but it *is* Christmas Eve.

"I think we ought to go over early for Christmas dinner," Tess says, standing awkwardly in the middle of her bedroom. It's the first time she and Maura and I have been alone together in weeks. "To talk to Father."

"Good luck to you with that." Still standing in the doorway, Maura rolls her blue eyes. "He doesn't know how to talk to us. Never has."

She's got a point. A month ago I would have said the same thing, in the same scornful tones.

"It's what *we* have to say to *him* that's important." Tess gulps, smoothing her green skirt. "We're going to tell him the truth. I—I'd like it if you'd come, too. I think all three of us should be there."

Maura stiffens. "What truth? You can't mean—"

"I do," Tess interrupts, ushering Maura in. Maura eyes me warily and then sits on Vi's bed, rumpling the fluffy white goose-down duvet. Tess shuts the door behind her. "There's something you ought to know. Something Mother kept from us. When they were first married, Father knew about Mother's witchery. She erased his memory. Zara told us."

Maura glares at us. It is not, I think, the reaction Tess was hoping for. "Tell me this—if he supported her, why would she need to erase his memory?"

Tess sits next to me on her bed. "After Zara was arrested, Mother was afraid she would be next. She thought Father might do something rash to get himself arrested right along-side her."

"Father?" Maura snorts. "He's hardly the impetuous sort. What did she think he would do, shoot Brother Ishida?"

I remember Marianne Belastra's kind brown eyes on the day she found out Finn and I were in love. *He may not have said the words, but I know my son. I saw the way he looked at you. Like he'd do murder for you.*

"He might," I snap. "It seems we don't really know *what* Father is."

"We do," Maura insists. "The way he's acted over the last three years says all we need to know about his character. He only cares for his books and his business."

"And Mother." I lean forward, eyes intent. "They were so in love. It never made sense to me that she kept such an enormous secret from him. When you love someone like that, with your whole heart"—*the way I love Finn, the way he*

194

used to love me—"how could you not want them to know you?"

Maura's eyes falter to the rich purple rug. "Still. If he'd stay home and open his eyes for two minutes together, he'd know what we are. Mrs. O'Hare knew. Even the maid suspected! If Father doesn't know us, it's because he doesn't care to."

Tess shakes her head. "I think you're wrong. Mother didn't give him the chance to be there for us, and I—I know she did it because she loved us, and she didn't want us raised by the Sisterhood and maybe separated. But I think he deserves the truth. I want to tell him."

"You're mad," Maura snaps. Tess recoils, though of course Maura doesn't mean it—not truly, not like that.

I fold my hands in my lap. "I agree with Tess."

"Well, you would." Maura tosses her red curls, sneering. "I don't have much of a vote, do I?"

I give her a cool smile. "It seems you're outnumbered."

Tess clenches a fistful of forest-green brocade in her hand. "This is important to me, Maura. I wish you could support me."

Maura's lips are a thin red slash in her angry face. "You've always been a cabbagehead where Father's concerned. You'd give up the entire Sisterhood's secrets to try and make him love you."

"He does love us. He might not know how to show it," Tess says, "but—"

I put a hand over Tess's smaller dimpled one. "Don't bother arguing with her. She only cares about the Sisterhood, as usual."

"And you don't care about it enough," Maura argues.

"The devil I don't," I retort. "Who led the Harwood mutiny? Who saved those girls from the gallows?"

Maura's mouth twists. "Who got Zara and Brenna killed with her fine plans?"

I leap up, fingers itching to slap her, and it's only Tess's sudden hold on my wrist that stops me storming across the room. "That's what she wants," Tess hisses, and I jerk to a stop, breathing deeply.

"That was uncalled for, Maura," Tess says. "It makes me think less of you, not Cate, for saying such a thing."

Maura shrugs. "That's nothing new, is it?"

Tess stamps her foot, clad in a pretty green slipper. "I wish things could just go back to the way they used to be! When we all got along."

"Well, it can't," Maura says, and for once I agree with her. We can never go back to the girls we were last summer. She's seen to that. "And telling Father won't give you the happy family you want. He'll break your heart, Tess, and one of us will have to fix it."

"You will not," Tess says very quietly, and there's something powerful and threatening in her voice. "I don't care what Father's reaction is, you will *not* undo this. You've already lost one sister. Do you care to lose two?"

Maura curls into herself. "No," she whispers. Then she stands. "Well, I hope you'll all have a merry Christmas Eve then. I'll see you tomorrow."

Tess's shoulders bow. "You don't mean that. Come for dinner, at least."

"No, thank you. You've made it clear how little you think of me, and it's sure to be a disaster anyway." Maura plants her hands on her hips.

"It's Christmas, Maura. We're family. We ought to be together." Tess throws me a desperate glance. "Cate, tell her."

I should. For Tess's sake. But I just shrug. "I don't want her there."

"And I don't want to be there. I'll have Christmas here, with Inez and the others who haven't anywhere else to go." Maura's voice catches, but only a little, and her blue eyes are hard as glass as she turns away.

"No." Tess's voice goes sharp. "I'm sick of you playing the martyr. You can spend Christmas with your family or not; it's up to you. If you don't, it's not because we tossed you over. It's because you're stubborn and selfish, and you chose this."

"Fine," Maura snaps. "It's my choice, then. The Sisterhood is my family. It's only right that I spend Christmas here."

The posh neighborhood around the convent is quiet as Tess and I head out to see Father. Occasionally a closed carriage rattles past, the horses' breath fogging the air. We watch as a family disembarks in front of a brick mansion with candles shining in all the windows. The father lifts the children down, and they race around each other on the sidewalk, the boy shouting about visiting Grandmother, the girl clutching a porcelain doll. The father's hands linger on his wife's waist as he smiles down at her. Her arms are full of Christmas presents tied with pretty red velvet bows.

If things were different, what would I have gotten Finn for

Christmas? Some rare book? A fine fountain pen? I picture him unwrapping a small package, that gap-toothed grin lighting up his face. I picture him pulling me into his arms for a long kiss.

I want *that* Christmas. Want it so much, it pains me.

Tess catches my hand in hers and squeezes. "Next Christmas will be better," she whispers.

It could hardly feel worse.

We pass into the market district, bustling with last-minute shoppers. I pause in front of O'Neill's. "Could we—that is, would you mind if—I'd like to go in here for a minute."

Tess doesn't ask any questions, bless her. "Of course," she says, though I can tell she's eager to get to Father's. Inside, she busies herself with a rack of calling cards while I turn in an uncertain circle.

"Can I help you, miss?" O'Neill asks, and then I pull my hood back and he recognizes me. "Oh, Miss Cahill! What a nice surprise."

"I was looking for a fountain pen," I explain. "For a gift. A bit last-minute, I know."

He leads me over to the glass case. "For a gentleman or a lady, if I might ask?" He gestures to the dozens of fine pens inside. Some are gold or silver plated and finely engraved; others are made of smooth wood; the most affordable are made of hard rubber. The nicest rest in cases like little satin caskets.

"A gentleman. My father," I lie, and I can feel my cheeks blaze.

I'm being stupid and sentimental. Finn doesn't trust me,

much less love me. He won't expect a gift—won't *want* it—and giving him one would be inappropriate as things stand.

"What about this one? It's our most popular." O'Neill slides open the back of the case and retrieves a gold pen. It rests in an ivory case and it seems altogether wrong for Finn; it's too fancy for him to use every day for his translations and letters to his mother.

I take it, weighing the heft of it in my hand, and shake my head. My attention is caught and held by a shining mahogany pen at the back. I tap the glass above it. "What about that one?"

"Ah, very nice." O'Neill hands it to me, and I remove one of my gloves, twirling the pen between my fingers experimentally, running a fingertip gingerly over the golden nib. "One of my favorites."

I can picture Finn using this. It's handsome, but still workmanlike enough to suit him.

How can I pretend he's not in my thoughts, in my heart, every moment? I simply can't let Christmas pass without giving him a gift.

"I'll take it," I decide, reaching in my pocket for my coins.

O'Neill nods and quotes the price. "A very good choice," he says, carrying it to the back of the room.

I follow him, a stupid smile still on my lips.

Father's flat is just a few blocks from O'Neill's shop, directly above the offices for the Cahill Mercantile Company. Tess takes a deep breath as she raises the brass knocker.

I hear boots stamping down the steps, and then Father

himself throws the door open, a grin stretching across his face. "Girls!" he exclaims, and then he frowns. "Where's Maura?"

"She can't come," Tess says quietly.

"She isn't sick?" I suppose he's been in town long enough to hear of the fever. Or has it already spread as far as Chatham?

"No. We'll explain later." Tess launches herself into his arms. "I'm so glad to see you, Father!"

"And I you," he says. He looks just the same as ever, really—blond hair gone silver, a red, green, and black plaid jacket that's quite out of fashion over a red vest and a pair of dark trousers—but his eyes are merrier than usual. Has he missed us?

"Cate," he says. The hug I mean to give is perfunctory, but his arms tighten around me, burying my nose in his neck, and he smells of dust and pipe smoke, and it reminds me so much of home that an ache rises in my throat.

"Merry Christmas, Father," I say, extricating myself.

He shuts the door and leads us up the stairs to his third-floor flat. It's warm and cozy and—

"It smells delicious! Are we having our dinner here? I thought we'd go to a hotel," Tess says, and I sniff appreciatively, taking in roasted goose and sage and onion stuffing. "Have you got a housekeeper?"

"I have, but I gave her the day off." Father smiles as he ushers us into the parlor. It's small compared to the rooms at home or at the convent, but it's handsome, with two tufted gold sofas and two leather armchairs and a red Oriental rug. A picture window looks out over the city, the curtains tied back with gold bows, and there are candles flickering in the windows. This is where he stays whenever he's in town for business. "I've got a surprise for you, girls. We'll be having a few guests joining us for—"

The pocket doors to the dining room crash open.

"Merry Christmas!" Clara Belastra shouts. She's in the midst of setting the table with a stack of Grandmother's blue china plates that Father must have brought from home. Clara's still tall and skinny, but she's settled into her arms and legs in the two months since I saw her last.

"Clara!" Tess cries, a glad grin stretching across her face. They're of the same age, and they became fast friends before I left Chatham.

Guests, Father said. My eyes count the seven table settings—the extra chair pushed in at one end—and fasten on the doorway beyond, my heart knocking like a wild thing. If *Clara* is here, then—

Marianne Belastra strides out of the kitchen, wiping her hands on her flowered apron and giving me a smile that doesn't quite reach her eyes. "Merry Christmas, Tess. Cate."

"Finn will be joining us later, for dinner," Father says, and my hand clenches around the shopping bag with the fountain pen inside.

"How lovely," Tess breathes. She looks back at Marianne. "Did you come into town yesterday, with Father? Have you— seen Finn yet?"

"We had dinner at his hotel last night. It was quite an interesting meal." Marianne's words are clipped, and her brown eyes, so like Finn's, narrow behind her wire-rimmed spectacles. *She knows.* My heart sinks. "Cate, could you help me in the kitchen? I'd so like to catch up with you."

"I—er—" I stumble. Marianne should have been my mother-in-law. She's a clever, kind woman who's raised a marvelous son, and I have a great deal of respect for her, but oh, I wish I could escape this conversation.

Tess comes to my rescue.

"There are some things we need to talk over with Father first, if you don't mind," she says, taking my hand and squeezing it.

"Come now, you can't have Mrs. Belastra doing all the work!" Father protests.

"Of course not. Do you imagine I'd let anyone else do all the cooking?" Tess jokes. "We'll both pitch in. But this—it's important, Father. It can't wait."

His brow furrows. "Does it have to do with why Maura isn't joining us?"

"Sort of," Tess allows.

Marianne nods, but it's clear she's granting me only a reprieve. She turns to Clara. "Let's give them a bit of privacy. Why don't you come help me in the kitchen until Cate's ready?"

Until Cate's ready. I don't suppose I'll ever be ready to explain to Marianne what my sister did, but there's no getting around it.

I turn to Tess, who looks as though she's about to face a firing squad herself. It is a day for reckonings, it seems. I sit beside her on one of the gold sofas. Across the room, the fire crackle-snaps. With the dining room doors pulled shut again, I can smell the pine boughs draped over the windowsills.

"Is Maura all right? You said it's not the fever." Father's lips twitch. "I know your sister can be a bit impetuous, but she hasn't run off with a sailor, has she?"

Tess forces a smile. "No, nothing like that." She toys with the green ruffles of her dress. "Now that we're here, I don't quite know how to start."

Father leans forward in his armchair. "Best just to have out with it, perhaps? You might not know it, but I can be a good listener. Your mother always said so." Pain flits across his face. "I know I've not been the best father to you girls. Having all three of you gone this last month—the house has felt so empty. It reminded me that I don't want to spend the rest of my life rattling around the place on my own. I know it's a natural thing, girls growing up and marrying and leaving home, but—I'd hoped to have more time with you and Maura yet, Tess."

Oh. It's the most heartfelt thing I've heard him say in years. *He missed us.* I look at Tess and find her lower lip trembling.

Father holds her heart in his hands now. If he rejects her, especially after this—this almost-promise of a different sort of relationship—she'll be devastated.

I wish there were something I could do to control the situation, to *make* him react the way she wants, but I know Tess's warning to Maura goes double for me. No magic.

She takes a deep breath. "There's something you ought to know—that is, we *want* you to know." Her heart-shaped face has gone pale. "We're witches. Cate and Maura and I. All three of us."

Father goes still as a statue. "That's impossible."

"It's true," I assure him.

"But—I know witches certainly still *exist*, but if all three of you were doing magic about the house, I would have noticed." He flinches. "I would have. Wouldn't I?"

"It's not your fault, Papa." Tess fidgets in her seat. "We kept it from you."

"I don't know if that's better or worse." He picks up the pipe lying on the tea table and turns it over in his hands. "How long has this been going on?"

Tess glances at me. "My magic manifested when I was eleven," I explain. My instinct is to keep my head down, but instead I raise my eyes to his—a pale blue like my own. I am not ashamed of being a witch, not anymore, and I won't act as if I am. "Mother helped me learn to control it and keep it a secret. When it was their turn, I helped Maura and Tess."

"Your mother knew?" Father walks to the sideboard next to the picture window. He pours a glass of amber liquor, then pauses with it halfway to his lips. "Magic is hereditary, isn't it? No one in *my* family—Anna never got on with her mother, she was raised by her grandmother, but she never said . . ."

"Mother was a witch. Like her grandmother." Tess swallows. "That's why she and her mother didn't get on. It skipped a generation."

"That's impossible." Father puts the glass down on the sideboard, staring at Tess as though she's grown horns.

"It's not. Watch." My magic is already stirring. I float his glass across the room and set it gently on the tea table without spilling a drop. "See?"

"Good Lord." Father's eyes go round as saucers. "Cate, you're a—a—"

"A witch," I supply, raising my chin. "Everything Tess is telling you is true."

He leans heavily on the sideboard, breathing fast, and for a minute I worry that he's going to have a fit of apoplexy. But he doesn't clutch his chest, just turns back to us, plainly puzzled. "I don't see why Anna would keep this from me."

"She didn't," Tess says. "Not always."

"We were married for fourteen years, Teresa. I think I would remember if my own wife had been a witch," Father snaps. He gets halfway across the room when it hits him and he stares at us, dumbfounded. *Or would I?*

Tess jumps up, reaching for his arm, but he flinches away. The look on his face makes my stomach hurt. It's too close to the way Finn looked at me two nights ago. It's as though Father doesn't know us anymore, as though his charming kittens have grown into fearsome tigers right before his eyes.

"Did one of you erase my memory? Like the Brothers are always preaching on about?" His face is flushed, his eyes dark and snapping.

"No!" Tess cries. Only—I *have* erased his memory. So has Maura. He has every right to look at me like that. "It wasn't us, Papa. I know this must be very hard for you to hear, but—"

"She wouldn't," Father interrupts Tess, his voice very sure, and I envy him that—that absolute certainty. He sinks back into his armchair. "Whatever my faults, I loved your mother. If Anna were a witch—if I'd known—I would never have turned my back on her. She wouldn't have needed to hide it from me. I—good Lord, whatever else you think of me, you've got to know that much. I would never have turned her in to the Brothers!"

Tess goes to him, kneeling on the soft red rug. "We know."

Father looks down at her. "I would have died before giving her up."

I cross the room and kneel on the other side of his chair. "We know. Mother knew, too. That was why she did it."

We do not tell Father everything; Tess thought it best not to overwhelm him with the prophecy or her visions. Still, Father handles the revelations far better than I had expected.

"What about Maura? Why isn't she here?" Father tilts the empty glass in his hands, watching the crystal catch the candlelight. Tess, curled up on the other chair, gazes at the floor. "Ah. Maura didn't want you to tell me," he guesses.

"We've had to be so cautious for so long," Tess explains.

"I'm sorry she didn't feel she could trust me. You can, girls." Father sets the glass down. His watery blue eyes meet mine and then travel to Tess's. "I've been remiss in not telling you this more often since your mother died, but I love you, and I'm terribly proud of you. You've been very brave to shoulder this alone."

I feel a warm glow that is not entirely from my proximity to the fireplace. "Thank you, Father," I say, and Tess's grin lights up the room. "But we haven't been entirely alone in it. Marianne's been a great friend to us."

Father's head swivels toward the kitchen. "Marianne is a witch, too?"

His disbelief is comical. "No. But she was one of Mother's best friends."

"She's always been quite progressive. And damned clever, too, for a woman," Father says. I chuckle at the outrage on Tess's face as I uncurl myself from the sofa and slide my feet back into my red slippers. Sachi insisted that I borrow a festive red plaid dress of Rory's instead of wearing my usual blues and grays. I gave in because I sensed she was feeling a bit homesick; I suppose even if your father's a tyrant and your mother's useless, you might miss them at Christmas. And now that I know Finn will be here, I'm glad I took a bit more care with my appearance. The dress brings color to my cheeks and darkens my eyes to thunderclouds.

"I'd better go help Marianne," I say. Tess starts to rise, but I wave her down. This is my reckoning, not hers. "Why don't you stay and chat with Father for a bit?"

Tess acquiesces easily enough. I follow my nose to the kitchen, where Marianne is peeling potatoes and Clara's just started to roll out a piecrust. "It smells delicious in here."

"Thank you, Cate." Marianne swipes a stray curl from her flushed face. With the goose in the oven, the small kitchen is very warm. "Clara, would you finish setting the table, please? I'll take care of the pie."

Clara scurries off. "I'm no good with pies, but I think I can manage the potatoes," I offer.

Marianne nods. "Is everything all right with your father?"

I pick up the paring knife and set to work. "We told him the truth. That we're witches."

"It went well? No . . . extraordinary measures were employed?" Marianne's use of the rolling pin is more vehement than necessary.

"It went very well. Even if it hadn't, we wouldn't—" I set the knife down and turn to her. "I won't lie to you. Tess wouldn't have let me alter his memory. I would have done it in a heartbeat if I thought it were necessary to protect her."

"Is that what happened to Finn?"

"No! I would never— It wasn't me. I swear it."

"But you were involved somehow, weren't you?" Marianne turns to me, brown eyes blazing. "I told you once that we can't choose who we love. And I like you, Cate, I do. But this is my son, and now—well, I daresay I wish he'd chosen differently. This would never have happened if he hadn't come chasing after you to New London."

I flinch away from her recrimination, setting to work again. There's a long silence broken only by the snick of my knife. Words and tears build a knot in my throat until it feels like I can't breathe unless I let something escape.

"It was Maura," I whisper.

Marianne has sprinkled flour over the crust and fit it into the pie tin, then poured a mixture of apples, cinnamon, and sugar into the shell. Now she sprinkles a crumb topping over it. It's only after she slides the pie into the oven that she turns to me, and I realize her careful movements belie a mother's fury. "Why?"

"I don't know if I'll ever really understand that. She claims it was to protect us, because we can't trust any Brothers. Any men. She refused to come today because she didn't want us to tell Father the truth. But, honestly, I think she attacked Finn to punish me. Our relationship has always been . . . complicated. Some days it feels like there are a hundred petty rivalries between us. But this—I don't think I can ever forgive this." I look into her eyes, begging for understanding. "I want to make things right with him, Marianne."

Marianne runs a hand over her face, leaving a smudge of flour on her cheek. "Then you have to tell him everything." She purses her lips. "You know he won't turn her in. He would have every right to want her punished, but angry as he is, he wouldn't want her killed for it."

"I want to tell him, but it still feels like a betrayal. It's the stupidest thing." I let out a mirthless little laugh. "She betrayed me without a second thought. Making him forget me was the worst thing she could have done to me. And yet I still have the most ridiculous urge to protect her." Unthinking, I run the tip of my thumb over the sharp edge of the paring knife. It stings.

"That promise to your mother still weighs on you, doesn't it?" Marianne's eyes have softened. "Anna would want you to be happy, too, you know."

Her kindness brings tears to my eyes. I'm like a leaky faucet lately. "I hope so. I—I worry that I'm disappointing her, all the time. I've tried so hard, but Maura—she's become—I don't even recognize her anymore. And I can't help wondering if it's something I did, or didn't do. I know I couldn't replace Mother, but—"

"No." Marianne wraps her arms around me and lets me sob onto her shoulder. "You've done your very best, Cate. As a mother, I can tell you, that's all you can do. Anna would be proud."

The clink of china and crystal and silver stops in the dining room, and footsteps make their way toward us. Marianne and I draw apart, and I wipe the tears from my cheeks. "Thank you," I say, a little embarrassed.

"Mama!" Clara calls. "Finn's here!"

CHAPTER
14

FINN AMBLES INTO THE KITCHEN carrying an armful of gifts. My heart lifts at the sight of him. "Merry Christmas, Mother!" he says, giving her a one-armed hug. I hang back, waiting for him to notice me. It's strange to feel so tentative with him; it makes me realize how accustomed I was to taking the lead, before.

"Hello, Cate." When Finn notices my tearstained face, he whirls back to Marianne. "Mother, what did you say to her?"

"It was nothing," I insist. "I'm fine."

"It's not nothing, not if she's making you cry. I'm a grown man. I don't need my mother fighting my battles," Finn grumbles. His waistcoat and trousers are charcoal gray, his shirt a crisp snowy white. It looks well on him. He's even combed his hair down neatly.

"It wasn't like that." I turn to Marianne with a smile. "She was kinder than I deserve."

Marianne tsks. "Cate, you're twelve times harder on yourself than anyone else is. Now, why don't you help Finn take those presents into the parlor? Send Tess and Clara in to help me. You're no use in the kitchen at all, are you?"

I send the girls into the kitchen, then pile the presents beneath the front window while Father pours Finn a glass of scotch. They settle in the leather armchairs, and I sit across from them on the golden sofa, toying with the tassels on a pillow and trying not to be terribly obvious about watching Finn. My ears perk up when their conversation turns to the outbreak of fever.

"Had no idea until I read about it in the *Gazette* this morning," Father says. "Hasn't hit Chatham yet, thank the Lord. Have you seen much evidence of it here?"

"It hasn't made inroads to the council yet, but Cate's seen her share of it at the hospital." Finn takes a sip from his tumbler.

"I've been volunteering. As a nurse," I explain. "The hospital's been packed to the gills with patients from the river district—and yesterday there were some from the market district, too. You've got to be careful, Father. If you start to feel ill, you must send for me at once."

"You, a nurse?" Father laughs.

His words strike a chord, reminding me of the time Finn fell off a ladder working on our gazebo. I wrapped his ankle so Mrs. O'Hare wouldn't catch sight of the illegal pistol strapped to his shin.

He won't remember that.

"I have an affinity for healing magic." Father darts an anxious look at Finn, and I smile. "It's all right. He knows. Anyhow, I'm glad Merriweather finally urged people to take precautions."

Father looks dumbstruck. "You read the *Gazette*?"

This time I feel a pinprick of irritation. "I'm not illiterate," I snap, mortified that he's making me out to be such a dunce in front of Finn.

"Of course not. I didn't mean . . ." Father chooses his words carefully. "You're a very capable girl. More capable than I dreamed, it seems. But you've never been one for politics. It's good that you're taking an interest—more women ought to be informed."

Finn gives me his mischievous grin. "Cate's well informed, all right. She's the one who introduced me to Merriweather and the Resistance movement. Did you read that feature today about the boy who was sick, couldn't get a bed in the hospital, and was healed by a witch?"

"Yes." Father rubs a hand over his jaw. "Do you mean to tell me *you* were the witch?"

I nod, gratitude rushing over me. Even though he's angry with me, Finn is still flying to my rescue. And he's such a progressive where women are concerned—far more than Father or Merriweather. That's down to having Marianne as a mother, I suppose. Another reason to thank her.

Father is frowning. "Merriweather's a wanted man. I don't want you putting yourself in danger to—"

"Father," I interrupt him, voice gentle this time. "I'm a witch. That makes me a wanted woman."

"You're still my daughter. I'm no supporter of the Brother-hood, but I want you safe first and foremost." He stares past me at the candles on the windowsill. "I do miss the old days, though." He sighs, and I wonder if his second glass of scotch is making him sentimental. "Back before Christmas trees were outlawed—I've told you about that, haven't I? My father and I would go out into the woods and cut one down ourselves. My sister spent a week making paper cornucopias to put stuffed dates and sugared almonds in, and Mother made snowflakes out of lace."

"My father said it was a beautiful tradition." Finn looks somber. He must miss his father, just as I miss Mother, on days like this.

"Close your eyes, both of you," I say, struck with sudden inspiration.

"What? Whatever for?" Father blinks at me owlishly.

"Just do it. I've got a surprise for you." They do, and I let magic pour through me. The illusion is easy enough. I don't know that it will last through Christmas dinner, but after the year we've had, we all deserve some extra cheer. "All right. Open."

Father actually gasps. "It even smells like a fir tree!" he marvels, standing and examining it from every angle. It's as tall as him, a fat pine with strands of popcorn and lace snow-flakes and little paper cornucopias adorning its branches.

"Oh, drat. I forgot something." I pick up Father's glass from the tea table and transform it into a feathery angel with a bright tinsel smile. I hand it to him. "Would you do the honors?"

Father takes it and perches it gingerly atop the tree. Then he stands back and stares, awestruck. "It's perfect."

"It is," Finn says, grinning.

I smile, too, because it's not the tree Finn's looking at.

Our Christmas dinner is a feast: roasted goose with sage and onion stuffing, mashed potatoes and gravy, cranberry sauce, Brussels sprouts, baked onions, and roasted chestnuts. By the time we get to dessert, I'm nearly groaning—but not enough to forgo a bit of gingerbread. The conversation around the table is a lively mix of literary talk and gossip about our neighbors; Father is scandalized when Tess mentions offhand that Sachi and Rory are sisters. It is strange to have Finn surprised by the news all over again.

After dinner, Tess strengthens my spell so we can open presents beneath the Christmas tree. She and I went in together to buy Father a handsome magnifying glass with a mahogany handle. He seems pleased by it; the footnotes in some of his books are quite small. I give Tess her stationery, and she's bought me a book on human anatomy that scandalizes Father again. He gives us money to buy new dresses, and he grows rather sentimental when he hands Tess a book of Romantic poetry that belonged to Mother. Marianne receives perfume from Finn and a strawberry pincushion from Clara, while Clara gets drawing pencils and a set of watercolors. Finn, of course, gets books.

I tuck the bag containing the fountain pen beneath the sofa. It doesn't feel right to give it to him here, in front of everyone. After the gift exchange, Tess and Father play a game of chess while Clara shows Finn some of her sketches. I page through my anatomy book, and Marianne does the dishes. It's dark outside when I regretfully suggest we ought to be going.

"I'll walk you home," Finn offers.

We bundle up in our cloaks and exchange good-byes with Clara and Marianne. Father walks us downstairs and gives us hugs before releasing us onto the cold, quiet streets.

I pause on the brick stoop of the Cahill Mercantile Company. "You're very kind to offer, but you can't walk us back to the convent," I explain to Finn.

He smiles at me behind his upturned collar. "I suspected as much. I just wanted to have a moment alone."

Ever perceptive, Tess has already dawdled down the street to examine the windows of a candy shop. "Oh," I say stupidly, heart hammering.

"I had a drink with Merriweather last night after we left the Zhangs'," he continues, and my disappointment that he's talking about the Resistance instead of us mashes up against worry. He shouldn't be seen in public with Merriweather; it's too dangerous. I bite my tongue before I chide him. I haven't the right to do that anymore. "He's planning a surprise for the Brothers at church tomorrow."

"At the cathedral?" I wince when Finn nods. Richmond Cathedral can fit over a thousand worshippers, and its congregation is chock-full of Brothers and the upper-class denizens of New London. They're the least-receptive audience Merriweather could possibly choose. "Is he mad? What kind of surprise? If they catch him—"

"They won't." Finn chuckles. "He's too clever for that. It's low risk, but I daresay it should make an impact. I'm sorry I won't be there to see it—Mother isn't one for churchgoing, you know. You'll have to tell me about it."

Alistair *is* clever—but he's a good deal too convinced of his own cleverness. What if he's overestimated it this time around? He'll get himself killed and we'll lose a valuable ally.

"He's a good man, Alistair. Thank you for introducing us." Finn rubs his gloved hands together for warmth. "You should read that feature he did on Yang. His indictment of the Brotherhood for not making more care available to the poor—for their nepotism—was absolutely scathing, and then he took them to task for making ridiculous accusations about witches instead of focusing on the science of prevention. He made you and Mei both out as heroes." His eyes rest on my face. "You were quite extraordinary, you know."

I beam at him. "Thank you." He moves to walk past me down the steps, and I summon up my courage, reach into my bag, and pull out the pen in its satiny case. "Wait. This is for you. It isn't wrapped—I didn't know you'd be here—but—"

"Oh, I—" Finn flips open the case. Runs a finger along the gleaming wooden barrel. "This is splendid. Really. But I didn't get anything for you."

"That's all right." I clear my throat. "I didn't expect that you would."

He puts a hand gloved in black leather on my arm, and I cannot help but remember the softness of the leather stroking my face while he kissed me in the convent garden. "This is a queer Christmas, isn't it? It must be for you, too. Here instead of home, and with me all wrong, and your sister not here—"

"You're not all wrong," I insist, smiling up at him. "You're still you."

"I don't feel like it." Finn hesitates as he slides the pen into his bag. "Why *isn't* Maura here? She's not ill?"

"No." I bite my lip, remembering Marianne's words. "Frankly, she wasn't wanted."

"But it's Christmas! You must have had an awful row to—" Finn runs his hand through his hair, his eyes growing wide. "What was it about?"

I watch him carefully. "You."

He grips the wrought-iron railing as the full realization of it hits him. "*Maura* took my memories?"

"Maura." I nod. "I'm sorry I didn't tell you sooner. She's my sister, and I suppose I—I felt responsible, somehow. You don't love me, I know you don't, but I suppose I hoped that you *might* again, someday. But the fact is, you're in danger whenever you're with me. You deserve to know that and to make any—any decisions you might make, from there. I have enemies within the Sisterhood, and they wouldn't hesitate to attack you again in order to hurt me."

Across town, the bells begin to toll the hour, and Finn pauses. *One.* He's deciding it isn't worth it. *Two.* That *I'm* not worth it. *Three.* How could he trust me, when I can do mind-magic? *Four.* When I've lied to him, by omission if not by my words? *Five.* When my own sister is the one who attacked him? *Six.* Kissing me was a mistake. *Seven.* He's going to tell me so any second now.

I take a deep breath and speak before he can. "I'm sorry I didn't tell you everything weeks ago. You really—Finn, you ought to find some nice, ordinary girl and marry her. Your mother said as much tonight."

Finn hesitates, his brown eyes inscrutable behind his glasses. "Is that what you want?"

I let out a miserable little laugh. "Of course not. But it's what I *should* want. For your sake."

"But I don't think that's what I want, either." He takes my hand—right there on the steps, right where anyone could see us. "I think I might want a girl who's rather more extraordinary. A girl who would risk her own life to help people and to right wrongs—a girl with a scandalous aptitude for magic and nursing—and kissing."

I blush at the way his voice dips, a little rough, on *kissing*. "You mustn't romanticize—"

"Shhh." Finn puts his leather-clad finger over my mouth before I can recite my failings. "There's so much I don't remember, Cate. I don't feel the way you do—not yet—but give me time to catch up?"

"All the time you need," I promise. My heart feels like a balloon, soaring into the sky, ready to burst from happiness. "I'll tell you anything you want to know. No more secrets."

"I'll take you up on that. Not now, though. It's freezing out here." He trails a finger over my cheek and gives a wicked grin when I shiver, as though he knows it's from his touch and not the cold. "I do remember some things, you know. Like last Christmas?"

"Last Christmas?" I echo, confused. We barely knew each other then.

"You came to the shop to buy a book for Tess. I picked out the *Ramayana* for you. It was the first time I noticed you. The first time I thought about kissing you." Finn's eyes dart down to my mouth. "I know the other night wasn't our real first kiss, but I've got to say—it more than lived up to my expectations." He looks across the silent street before leaning down and brushing his lips over mine, butterfly-quick. "Merry Christmas, Cate."

It is the best Christmas present I could have wished for.

"Merry Christmas, Finn."

Back at the convent, I'm surprised to find light and noise spilling out of the front parlor. The private sitting room is where girls usually gather; it's far more comfortable in there. "Cate! Come join us!" Rory hollers.

"Rum punch?" Prue offers, leaning unsteadily out the door.

"What are you doing here?" I ask as I hang up my cloak. "I thought you'd be with your brother."

Prue frowns and takes a swig from her glass. "Alistair refused to let me spend Christmas with him. Said it was too dangerous. He still blames himself that I was stuck in Harwood. Stupid patronizing creature."

A tiny white kitten comes barreling out of the room, slides across the wooden floor, and plows into the wall. It shakes its tiny, furry head and sits there, looking perplexed. Vi comes chasing after it. "Cate, Tess, look what Papa gave me!" She scoops up the kitten and cuddles it to her bosom, beaming.

"There are two. I've named this one Noelle, and her brother Nicholas, on account of being Christmas kittens. Come see!"

We follow her into the parlor, where Grace is knitting in the silk chair by the fire, her needles flashing. Lucy and Bekah are playing with the other kitten and a pink hair ribbon. There's a pewter punch bowl on the tea table, half full of some sweet-smelling concoction. Rory hands me a glass.

"What are you doing in here?" I wonder, joining Sachi on the settee.

"I couldn't stomach watching your sister lord it over everyone for another minute." Sachi rolls her dark eyes. "Something's put her in a good mood."

"I can't imagine what." And although I tell myself it's Christmas and I don't want Maura miserable, the truth is I hoped she'd be lonely without us. I take a sip of the punch, which tastes of oranges and sugar with a kick of something stronger.

"Elena and some of the other governesses are drinking mulled wine and singing carols in the library, so we decided to make this our headquarters." Prue flings out her arm, sloshing punch onto the brown carpet. "Livvy plays beautifully, but if I hear one more badly tuned Christmas carol, I'll scream. I'm not feeling very merry."

"She's a bit foxed," Rory whispers loudly. "Put out at her brother for babying her."

"Well, that's Alistair for you," I admit. Now is obviously not the time to tell Prue that her brother is planning some sort of scheme for tomorrow.

"Oh, and Alice sent a message. Her father's taken sick, so

she's going to stay with him tonight." Sachi traces the flowers etched into her glass. "The fever must be spreading like the dickens if it's reached a wealthy neighborhood like Cardiff."

"The convent felt so empty this morning." Most of the girls who could afford it went home. Mei is spending the day across town with her aunt and little sisters. Pearl and Addie took the train to Addie's family's dairy farm in Pennsylvania, and Rilla left this morning for Vermont. She interviewed Livvy and Caroline about their time at Harwood before she went—and gave me strict instructions to watch while Merriweather read her article.

I watch as Tess strokes the second kitten's wriggling back. Nearby, Prue stretches out on the carpet. I wonder where her brother is tonight. He must be missing her. For all that he is a conceited, condescending fop, Merriweather's heart is in the right place. He loves his sister; he wants to protect her. I can understand that.

"Jennie Sauter and one of the other new girls ran off," Rory says. One of the kittens makes a mad dash out into the hall, and Lucy and Tess scramble after it.

"Why?" I ask, taking another sip of the punch. "Jennie didn't seem unhappy here."

"Maybe they were homesick." Rory shrugs. "It *is* Christmas. If you've got anywhere else to be—well, you'd want to be there, wouldn't you?" Her brown eyes are sad. Is she thinking of her drunk of a mother—or remembering her dead stepfather, who was by all accounts a kind man? She glances down at the empty serving tray. "I'm going to fetch more gingerbread."

I look to Sachi, wondering if she's missing her parents, too.

"How are you managing?" she asks me, smoothing her frock—a bright fuchsia with turquoise polka dots. "You must be missing Finn."

"Actually . . ." I launch into the story of our reconciliation. I'm at the bit about him needing more time when Lucy comes running pell-mell into the room.

"Cate! Come quick. It's Tess!"

I dart down the hall, the others scrambling after me, to find Tess crumpled on the first-floor landing in a heap of green brocade and blond curls. "What is it? What happened?"

She isn't crying this time, but her face has gone pale as milk and she's shaking like a leaf. "The—the kitten," she says, pointing at the limp little body lying at the foot of the stairs.

Vi falls to her knees, scooping it up in her hands. But it doesn't wriggle or meow or lick her with its sandpapery tongue. It doesn't do anything. My heart sinks.

"It was dead. Right in my hands. I picked it up and it was all—all broken and bloody." Tess shudders.

Vi's plummy eyes are filled with tears, but she blinks them back valiantly. "It's dead, but—" Her hands search its spotless white fur. There is no blood, no wound save the obvious. Its little head droops at a strange angle.

"She dropped it." Lucy wipes away tears with the backs of both hands, and draws in a deep breath. "Tess picked it up, and then she just—dropped it."

"It was already dead!" Tess stands, hanging on to the

wooden railing. "I thought—it *looked* dead. There was blood all over my hands."

She holds up both palms, as if to prove her point—but they're spotless, too.

I turn to Lucy. "Did you see the illusion?"

Lucy shakes her head, caramel braids swinging. "No."

"Nothing at all?" I press. "Was anyone else in the hallway?"

"I don't think so." Lucy twists her pudgy hands together. "I looked up when Tess cried out, but then she dropped it and—it was too late. It tumbled right down the steps."

"I saw it!" Tess's voice is anguished as she makes her shaky way down to us. "I swear I did. I'm not making it up, and I'm not going mad!"

"Course you aren't!" Bekah sounds indignant. "You'd never."

"Vi, I'm—I'm so sorry," Tess says.

"I know." Vi is staring at the kitten cradled in her hands; she doesn't meet Tess's eyes.

Bekah links her arm through Tess's. "Come on, let's go back to the parlor," she suggests, leading her away.

"Why don't you give him to me?" Sachi holds out her hands, and Vi brushes her fingers over the kitten's furry head one more time before she relinquishes it. Tears spill over her cheeks. "It's all right. Get Noelle and take her upstairs. I'll take care of this."

She and Vi go their separate ways, but Lucy lingers on the bottom step. "Is there something else?" I ask.

Lucy toys with one of her braids. "I don't want to be a tattletale."

224

"If it's about Tess, I need to know so I can look after her," I say.

"I'm worried about her." Lucy's gaze is still trained on the floor. "On Tuesday, we were going up to my room so she could help me with my Latin, and she swore she heard music."

I lean against the wooden banister as dread blooms through me. "What kind of music?"

"A funeral dirge. Only I didn't hear a thing. I even ran down to check if Livvy was playing the piano, but no one was there. And then yesterday morning, Tess asked me to come in and help her do up the back of her dress. She was looking in the mirror and she started screaming. She said—" Lucy gulps. "She said the front of her dress was all covered in blood. She tore it off and threw it in the fireplace. I tried to stop her, but—"

My hand flies to my mouth. "No one was there but you? No one else saw?"

"No. But all of these—episodes—they've got one thing in common, haven't they?" Lucy whispers, her brown eyes enormous. "It's like she's preoccupied with—"

"Death," I finish. Fear shivers up my back. Is this how madness begins? Is this how it started for the oracles before Tess?

"You mustn't tell anyone else. Let me handle this," I insist. "Promise me."

Lucy nods. "I promise."

CHAPTER
15

I KNOCK LIGHTLY ON MAURA'S DOOR just after dawn.

She opens it a few inches. "What is it? Parvati's still sleeping."

I crook a finger, beckoning her out. "I need to talk to you."

She tiptoes out in stocking feet, closing the door softly behind her. Her hair falls in bright curls to her waist. She's already dressed in a black wool frock with rabbit fur at the wide belled sleeves. "I thought you and Tess washed your hands of me."

I don't know what to say. We're sisters, and no matter how angry I am, that still means something. I've been awake half the night, worried sick about Tess. What if her worst fears are being realized, and she *is* beginning the slow descent into madness? Brenna's brokenness was due in part to Alice's mind-magic gone wrong, but Brenna wasn't the first oracle to go mad. And Tess—brilliant, capable, curious Tess—how could she bear it?

Tess saw something that Brenna feared would break her. Something Tess confessed she couldn't keep from me forever. Did she foresee her own madness?

"It's Tess," I say finally. "Are you *absolutely certain* Inez isn't terrorizing her?"

Maura sighs, propping one hand on her hip. "I told you, it's not her. What's happened now? It must be something awful for you to come to me."

"You asked me to come to you." I purse my lips. "But you've got to promise—before I tell you, Maura, I want you to swear you won't tell Inez. That you won't tell *anyone*. Swear it on Mother's grave."

"Good Lord," Maura breathes. She knows that for me to invoke Mother, it must be serious. "What—very well, I swear on Mother's grave that whatever it is, I won't breathe a word of it to anyone. Will that do?"

"Thank you." I twist Mother's pearl ring round and round on my finger, avoiding Maura's eyes. "There have been other episodes. Several of them now. And I'm—well, I'm afraid it may all be in her head."

"That she's going mad." Maura steps closer as she utters the words I can't bring myself to say aloud.

"I don't know what to do," I whisper, sinking back against the green flowered wallpaper. "She must be so scared."

Maura's shoulders slump. "I would be terrified."

"Me too." Not being able to trust my own senses—I can't

even imagine it. "We've got to look out for her, without letting her know. She needs us."

"We?" Maura squints up at me. "You want us to work together? Does that mean you're willing to put the past behind us?"

I set my jaw. "I'm willing to try and work with you. For Tess's sake."

Maura laughs her new, brittle laugh. "How gracious of you. Cate, do you even hear yourself? How condescending you are?"

"What do you expect? *You erased me!*" My hands vibrate as magic hums through me, and I clasp them tightly behind my back. "Perhaps if you apologized . . ."

Her blue eyes meet mine as she shakes her head. "No."

I gape at her. *No?* I offer her an olive branch, and she throws it to the ground and stomps on it.

I try. I try and try and even when I swear I've turned my back on her, I wind up trying again.

She won't tell me she's sorry because she's not. Maura's never been one for a polite lie. She's never had my compunctions about mind-magic, never thought it wicked or wrong. She didn't hesitate to use it on Father or the O'Hares. Her friends, Finn, the Head Council: They've all been recipients of her ruthlessness. Maura wouldn't hesitate to—

Another puzzle piece fits into place. "What did you do to Jennie Sauter?"

Maura folds her arms across her chest, smirking. "She ran off. Didn't you hear?"

"Did she really? Don't lie to me." I smooth my black skirts, hands trembling.

Maura tosses her head, curls dancing. "They're not witches, Cate. Having them here put us all in danger. I was rectifying *your* mistake."

My anger simmers like a teakettle, but I ignore the jab. "If anyone recognizes them—if they're arrested—they'll be executed without a trial. Did that occur to you?"

"We only erased their memories from the last few weeks— since the night of the Harwood breakout. They won't know how they escaped, but they'll know enough to be careful," Maura explains, in a tone that implies she's done them a great kindness.

"Who is 'we'?" I ask.

"Parvati and me. She needed to practice." Maura lifts her chin, forestalling my outburst. "I stand behind what I did. To them, to the Head Council—and to Finn. I'm not ashamed of any of it, so don't you stand there and judge me."

"I do judge you!" It tears from my throat. "If Mother could see you, she would be ashamed of you. *I'm* ashamed of you."

Maura recoils as though I've slapped her. "How dare you speak for her! Do you think she would be proud of *you,* turning your back on me over a man? A man who doesn't even *remember* you, at that? What kind of great love affair do you suppose you had, if he could forget you so easily?"

I lunge for her. In the fury of the moment, I forget magic and simply throw myself at her, knocking her back into the wall, the way I would have when we were children. I don't care if we wake the entire convent.

"What is *wrong* with you two?" Elena whisper-shouts, storming down the hall. She grabs Maura's arm and whips her around. Her chocolate eyes are snapping; every line of her elegant body is tense. I've never seen her like this. Not when I lied to her about my mind-magic. Not when I dismissed her and threw her out of the house.

She glares at Maura. "I heard what you said. Bad enough that you did this to her, but to *taunt* her about it?"

Her defense only makes me angrier. It brings back memories I'd sooner forget.

"You're one to talk." My throat feels rusty. "You threatened to compel Finn once yourself. Perhaps that's where Maura got the idea."

Elena hardly spares me a glance. "I didn't mean it, Cate. I wouldn't have."

I want to grab her, shake her until her teeth rattle in her pretty head. As threats go, it was damned convincing. Convincing enough for me to get up on the dais and announce that I'd join the Sisterhood instead of marrying Finn.

Lord, where would I be if she hadn't threatened Finn? Married. Happy. It's her fault as much as Maura's. Hers and Cora's and— I take a deep breath as my magic rises again. I can't lose control or I don't know where it will stop. It won't be innocuous, snow and feathers. If I lose control now, there will be blood.

I can picture them flying down the hall, splintering the

stained glass window above the window seat, falling to the cobblestones three stories below. Their bodies thump like heavy bags of flour to the ground. Maura's red hair and Elena's coral dress are bright against the pillow of snow that fell overnight; Elena's black hair and Maura's dress are shadows against it. Their bodies are bent at horrible, unnatural angles.

For a moment, I am lost to the violence of it. Then I blink, shoving the magic down into the hidden spaces between muscle and bone.

That's not what I want.

Was it just a few weeks ago at Harwood that Brenna said I would kill, and I believed in my heart of hearts I could never hurt either of my sisters?

I could now.

"This has to stop, Maura," Elena hisses. "Cora would have exiled you for it."

"Cora's dead." Maura's voice is careless, but her eyes don't quite match. "Lucky for me, I suppose."

"Don't you disrespect her like that." Elena is two inches shorter than Maura and petite where Maura is voluptuous, but she seems to tower over Maura nonetheless. "She took me in when my parents died. She was a good woman."

Maura's mouth twists. "Better than me, you mean."

"Better than both of us put together." Elena shakes her head. "Maura, you can't let Inez make you—"

"Inez believes in me." Maura lounges against the green-papered wall as if she hasn't a care in the world, but I can see the way she draws in great gulps of air. This has unsettled her more than she'd admit. "I know why you hate her. You thought you'd be next in line after Cora. You've always been ambitious."

"And because of it, I've made mistakes. I've hurt people I cared about." Elena reaches out, her fingers curling around Maura's black sleeve. "I'm sorry, Maura. I never should have lied, never should have pretended that that kiss didn't mean something when it did."

Maura wavers. She sways toward Elena, erasing the inches between them. "Why are you doing this?" Her eyes are wary. Elena is so lovely, her brown skin glowing against the coral silk of her dress, her black hair in perfect ringlets. "Why now? You haven't spoken to me like this in ages."

"Because you made it abundantly clear you wanted nothing to do with me." Elena throws up her hands. "I thought you needed time. But I can't stand by any longer. Erasing the council's memories, attacking Finn, tossing Jennie out onto the street—that's not the girl I fell in love with. I care for you too much to let you go on like this."

I cringe back against the nearest doorway. It's the wrong thing for her to say. Maura will go right past "in love with" and only hear—

"*Let* me? I hardly need your permission." Maura scowls. "You chose Cate over me, remember? You gave up any right you had to weigh in on my decisions."

Elena tosses a glance over her shoulder. My presence here isn't making this easier for either of them.

"Cate doesn't mean half what you mean to me, and if you weren't so utterly consumed by this rivalry between the two of you, you'd see it. For Persephone's sake, Maura," she swears. "Why do you think I'm standing here embarrassing myself like this? You're the one that I want, the only one I've ever wanted, and you're the only one too stupid to see it."

Elena curls her hand behind Maura's neck, pulls Maura's face down to hers, and kisses her.

Maura looks stunned, her blue eyes wide. Stunned and— ravenous, somehow. Her eyes flutter shut; her mouth begins to move hungrily against Elena's.

Anger rushes through me. Part of me wants to scream and shout and stamp my feet. She doesn't get to have this! Not after what she's taken from me. It isn't fair.

But this might be the only thing that can save her.

And Elena's been my friend.

So I slip back down the hall and into my room, and I shut the door.

Half an hour later, I'm back in the hall, hammering my fist on a different door.

Sachi opens it. She's already dressed in a black-and-white houndstooth gown festooned with black lace. "Rory and Prue are still asl— What's wrong?" she asks as I march to the window.

I shove the pink-pinstriped curtains open, letting the weak December sunlight spill into the room. Prue sits up, blinking and groggy, reaching for her spectacles.

"My sister's a monster," I explain.

Rory sticks her rumpled head out from beneath her quilt and groans. "You woke us up to tell us that? We already know that, Cate. Go back to bed."

"I can't. I've got to go to church." I pace around their room, sidestepping slippers and petticoats and books dropped helter-skelter. It's a pleasant change from pacing around my own room for the last thirty minutes, waiting for it to be late enough to wake them. "Finn said that Merriweather is plotting something and I'm afraid Alistair will get himself arrested. But Prue, we can't leave you alone. Someone has to stay with you, every moment, until we get word to your brother. He'll want you with him once he finds out you aren't safe here."

Prue swings her bare feet onto the floor. "I'm not safe here?"

Sachi catches my elbow, hauling me to a stop. "Cate, you're not making any sense and you're making me dizzy. What's Maura done now?"

I went to Maura for help with Tess and somehow she turned everything around, the way she always does, and made it about her. And now—now I've got to worry about whom she and Parvati might take it into their heads to attack next. I'm afraid the leading candidate is sitting right in front of me on her trundle bed.

"Jennie and Elsie didn't run off of their own accord." My voice is tight. I am ashamed to say it out loud. How could my sister do such a thing? "Maura and Parvati erased their memories and threw them out. They don't trust anyone who's not a witch. I wouldn't put it past Maura to go after you next, Prue. We had a huge row, and if she wants to get back at me—"

"She wouldn't hesitate to attack one of your friends." Rory

sits up, straightening her red flannel nightgown. "Your sister's a right bitch, Cate."

I slump onto the bench in front of their dressing table. "I know."

"All right then. Church it is." Prue shucks off her nightgown and rummages through the armoire. She's still too thin from her time at Harwood; I can see the knobs of her spine through the white muslin of her shift.

"What if someone recognizes you?" I protest. "I'd have to glamour you. My illusions are better than they used to be, but maintaining it the whole way through church would be tricky." Particularly considering how little I've slept and how splintered my focus already is—furious with Maura, frightened for Tess, annoyed with Merriweather. "You're better off staying here with Sachi and Rory."

"Is she?" Sachi's taken up my pacing. Her feet, clad in black silk stockings, whisper against the wooden floorboards. "Parvati can't go to church. What if she tries to attack Prue? She could compel us to step aside and we'd have no choice in it."

Prue's pulled the black dress over her head. Now she turns her back and gestures for Sachi to fasten the hooks. "My brother's smart, but he isn't infallible, and that church will be overflowing with Brothers. If it were your sister taking such a mad risk, you'd go, wouldn't you?"

She's got me there. I sigh. "All right. I'll ask Tess to help with the glamour."

Sachi grabs my elbow again. Her smile is chilling. "I know

Maura's your sister, Cate, but if she does anything to hurt Prue, she'll have to answer to me."

"I won't let that happen," I promise.

I only hope I'm not telling a lie.

Despite the *Gazette*'s warnings about the fever, Richmond Cathedral is packed. Christmas Day is for prayerful commemoration of the Lord's birth—and for showing off one's finery to one's neighbors. The air is cloyingly fragrant with the scents of perfume—lavender, lemon verbena, and rosewater. Girls wave at friends with their satin gloves and matrons toss their heads to display new earbobs, while men ostentatiously check their new pocket watches.

"I don't see him," Prue complains, glancing around anxiously. We've waited until the last moment to take our seats so she could search the crowd for her brother.

"Maybe he changed his mind," I suggest.

She raises her eyebrows. "I find that unlikely."

We start down the central aisle, but an old woman in a white fur cloak jostles me and I stumble, grabbing Prue's arm to right myself. My focus wavers. Her newly pudgy, dimpled hands stretch into long, thin fingers with nails cracked from lack of proper nutrition.

"Are you all right?" she asks.

"Of course." It's fixed in a trice. A small thing, barely noticeable. I push down a jolt of worry. I'd counted on Tess's help, but she stayed home from services; Vi said she was up half the night crying over the kitten.

I head toward the Sisterhood's customary pews, searching

for Elena. Maura sits in the first row with Inez, but Elena's nowhere to be seen. It's not like her to miss church. Keeping up appearances is important, she would say; Sisters are meant to be devout. I tap Sister Celeste, one of the governesses, on the shoulder. "Have you seen Elena?"

"She went across town. Her aunt's taken sick," Celeste explains.

Blast. I nod and thank her while cursing Elena's aunt. The services are about to start; we can't rush out now. I motion Prue into the last row, next to Lucy.

Lucy looks askance at the seeming stranger. "This is Lydia," I explain, gesturing to the plump, pretty blonde with brown eyes and round apple cheeks who looks nothing like Prue Merriweather. I should have made the illusion less complicated. I didn't realize I'd be solely responsible for keeping it up.

I look up at the ceiling, praying that I can manage this.

Brother O'Shea climbs the dais, his long horse's face unsmiling, and wishes us all a merry Christmas. At his command, we reach for the Bibles tucked on the back of each pew. I open ours to follow along with the customary prayers—and a leaflet falls out, fluttering to the floor. Prue picks it up, and I peer over her shoulder as she reads:

This reporter has obtained records from Richmond Hospital confirming that over three hundred people have died of fever in the last week alone. Yesterday's Gazette *urged the Brotherhood to cancel services and other public gatherings until the threat has passed. This reporter has learned that the* Sentinel *intends to print a rebuttal charging us with shoddy journalism intended to stir the populace against the Brotherhood. However, it is the* Sentinel *which has ignored the science of prevention in favor of blaming the witches. This reporter has borne witness to witches healing the fever—that of a poor boy, a tailor's son, who was denied a place in the hospital. The Brotherhood dismissed the outbreak because it originated in the river district, whose inhabitants don't contribute to the Brothers' coffers. The Brothers' refusal to set up temporary hospitals, to make available more medicine and nurses to treat the city's poor, has allowed the fever to spread across the city into your fine neighborhoods. If I print lies—why are so many of your fellow congregants coughing?*

Wishing you all a very merry and healthful Christmas,
Alistair Merriweather
Publisher & Editor in Chief, New London Gazette

I meet Prue's eyes and her lips twitch.

No one is paying attention to Brother O'Shea now. Whispers slither through the pews along with the restless movements of the congregation. The sermon is punctuated by dozens of deep, hacking coughs—and each time, heads swivel to locate the culprit and everyone near the afflicted person inches away.

It was rather brilliant, slipping those leaflets into the Bibles. Rilla will be sorry she missed it.

Still, the service stretches on and on, interminable. O'Shea seems oblivious to his flock's preoccupation. He recounts the story of the Lord's birth and then launches into a sermon on suffering hardship joyfully. Somehow, this becomes a judgment on the starving poor and those who would not sacrifice their daughters gladly.

I stand and sit at the appropriate cues, mumbling the responses. An hour passes, then two, and then the bells in the neighboring council building mark three. For all Brother Ishida's shortcomings, the Christmas sermon in Chatham was never so long as this. Two rows ahead of us, old Sister Evelyn's head droops like a fuzzy dandelion. Snores and the shrieking of tired children begin to mingle with the coughs of fever victims. Keeping up Prue's illusion becomes a matter of endurance, and an exhausting one at that.

Finally, Brother O'Shea begins the familiar ritual of leave-taking.

"Let us clear our minds and open our hearts to the Lord," he intones.

"We clear our minds and open our hearts to the Lord," the congregation echoes, rising and stretching. People wake the elderly and small children.

"You may go in peace to serve the Lord," O'Shea declares, raising his hand in farewell.

"Thanks be." Even the faces of the black-cloaked Brothers up in the chancel—all forced to spend Christmas in New London away from their families because of the never-ending National Council meeting—show relief.

People rush for the three processional doors at the back,

practically knocking one another over in their haste to escape. The marble floor is littered with hundreds of crumpled leaflets, but judging by the quick exodus, I daresay they've done their work.

I beam at Prue—still blond-haired and brown-eyed and plump. "Let's wait a minute till it's not so crowded."

The other Sisters join the crowd without a backward glance, eager to go home and break their fast. Only the most faithful congregants remain in their seats, heads bowed in prayer. A few dozen Brothers mingle on the dais. I wait while the elderly totter down the aisle with their canes, moving at a snail's pace.

I've no sooner stepped out of the pew than I'm accosted.

"*There* you are," Alice hisses. "I was waiting outside forever."

Beneath her cloak, she's still wearing her Christmas Eve finery—an amethyst gown with a low, square neckline that doesn't befit a Sister at all. Her golden hair tumbles out of its pompadour, wisps framing her cheeks, and there are dark shadows beneath her eyes.

"What's wrong?" It must be grave for her to go out looking such a mess.

"My father." She rubs a tired hand over her cheek. "He's ill. All the servants have fled in fear of the fever and I don't know what to do. He's a bit of a tyrant; I don't blame them for going. But he's all the family I've got left. I can't just leave him."

I feel a pang of sympathy. "Of course not. How bad is he?"

Alice makes a face. "Well, he's been sweating like a pig all night. I can't get him to eat anything but a little broth. It's the fever, I'm sure of it. Four houses on our street have yellow ribbons nailed to their doors." She lowers her voice. "I hear some of the Brothers' guards are going round and ripping them down. Why wouldn't they want people to know where the sickness is? Don't they want to stop it?"

"They don't want people knowing it's reached Cardiff," I explain, remembering the wealthy man we met in the hospital. "No one cared so long as it was just river rats dying. The rich will be furious that O'Shea didn't set up a quarantine. Now it's too late."

My mind fills with grim images of a city decimated by fever. Of shops closing, people out of work. Of fathers confined to their sickbeds for weeks and families going hungry.

"In the *Sentinel* this morning, O'Shea outright denied that it's anything but a plague cast by witches. He says the *Gazette* was just trying to stir up trouble," Alice whispers.

"I heard." I hand her Merriweather's leaflet.

What if Merriweather's efforts aren't enough? Coffins will be piling up in the churchyards again. I can't save them all. I could barely save Yang. I'll have to stand by and watch people die and—

I've had to see too many people die.

Mother—her face and body swollen with child, blue eyes staring, asking me for promises I could not keep. Zara—the smell of pennies on her breath, coppery skin hot against mine as she begged me to help her die. The woman from Harwood who lost her baby—her blond hair matted with blood as her life seeped out onto the cobblestone street.

O'Shea sweeps down the aisle from the chancel. He and his retinue pause to greet their wealthy parishioners, laying blessings on their heads, chuckling at something a well-dressed man says. He looks utterly unconcerned by the weighty responsibilities of state, by the hundreds of people dying in his capital city while he doesn't lift a finger to stop it. While he lays the blame at *my* doorstep.

He pauses before us with his reptilian smile. "Merry Christmas, Sisters!"

Prue and Alice go to their knees, but I hesitate. The idea of kneeling before him makes my stomach roil. I do not want this man to touch me. He would have murdered Sachi and Rory and Prue. He would order me and my sisters and all my friends killed if he knew what we were. He would watch us hang and cheer our deaths.

O'Shea stares at me with his pale eyes. "Sister Catherine, isn't it?" he says.

I grit my teeth and kneel. He blesses Prue, then Alice, and then lays his plump, sweaty hand on my forehead, and oh— the moment he touches me, I sense his headache. Perhaps he is not as unaffected by Merriweather's stunt as he pretends. My fingers twitch along the marble floor.

If anyone deserves pain, deserves suffering, it is this man, who doles it out so gleefully.

"Lord bless you and keep you this and all the days of your life," he says, and I cannot help wishing the exact opposite for him.

"Thanks be," I murmur, yanking on the threads of magic

running through me. His headache flares, burns a fiery scarlet. He stumbles back.

It's not enough. I wish I could make his head explode, crack his skull wide open.

I did not know I contained such violence.

"Brother O'Shea, are you unwell?" I hear someone ask, and I feel a grim satisfaction—along with a wave of dizziness. My vision blurs.

"Cate?" Alice whispers, her hand on my shoulder. There's a note of alarm in her voice.

"Isn't that the newspaperman's sister?" a woman's voice shrills. "The one who was supposed to be hanged?"

Oh no. I struggle to my feet, but it's too late. I am such a fool.

Prue stands before me, utterly herself again. My illusion has disappeared.

"That's her. Prudencia Merriweather," a man declares, starting toward us.

But the guards get there first.

Four of them surround Prue. Two grab her roughly by the arms. I can tell by the look on her face that they hurt her, but she doesn't cry out.

The well-to-do man strides up to her, his gilded cane tapping along the marble floor, Alistair's leaflet crumpled in his fist. He shakes it in her face. "Is this your doing, too? Making a mockery of the Lord's birth?"

Prue lowers her eyes to the floor.

Good Lord, what have I done?

Alice's eyes are on me, but there are a hundred people left in the cathedral. Far too many to mind-magic.

Prue's already been convicted; now they'll use her to roust out Merriweather and hang them both. What a prize I've handed O'Shea.

"What have we here?" he asks, voice echoing. He turns to me, his smug smile restored. "Is this girl a friend of yours?"

"I—" I croak. Prue's gray eyes are wide with fright, but she gives the tiniest shake of her head. She's telling me to abandon her.

But this is all my doing. My promise to her—to Sachi, to look after her—

Despite my best intentions, I never seem able to keep my promises.

"Speak up, girl!" O'Shea barks.

A burly guard puts a hand on my shoulder, hauling me around. His fingers will leave bruises. My temper—so carefully leashed all morning—cracks. Splinters. And breaks wide open.

"Don't touch me!"

My magic surges up and out in a burst so powerful, I've never felt the like. Brother O'Shea and his guards are flung backward. Their bodies fly through the air like rag dolls, or trees uprooted by a tornado. They fly and flail and don't stop until they hit pews, landing with a series of sickening crunches.

At the same time, there's a deafening crash—and then another—and another—and another. The people still left in the cathedral scream—men and women alike—on and on, shrill and hoarse and *terrified.* I look toward the sanctuary in time to see the image of the Lord ascending to heaven shatter, shards of stained glass flying everywhere.

People cower behind the mahogany pews, hands thrown up to protect their faces from the rain of glass.

I look to Alice. A bit of glass has nicked her cheek, but she is utterly still.

There is fear in her blue eyes, too.

Alice is scared. Of me.

CHAPTER
16

"GO!" I URGE, YANKING THE KEY FROM around my neck and tossing it at Prue. "Prue knows where. I'll meet you. *Go!*"

The second *go* seems to galvanize them. They run down the aisle, boots clattering. No one tries to stop them. One of the guards is slumped against a marble column; another lies sprawled atop several pews; a few appear to be unconscious—or worse.

"Guards!" O'Shea hollers. His bald head peeks above a pew several rows away.

I glance toward the doors. Prue and Alice are almost out.

Two guards run out of a door near the sanctuary. I fling up a hand, and everyone in sight cringes. "Stay back. I don't want to hurt anyone else."

Wisely, the guards halt.

"You can't hide. We'll find you," O'Shea promises, rising to his feet. His blue eyes glitter from inside the shadow of his hood. "We'll put you to death for this sacrilege."

I run. The glass cuts through my black slippers. Three more guards dart out from behind pillars and try to stop me. It isn't hard to stop them instead. My magic hovers just beneath my skin, pulsing through my body in time with my heartbeat.

In this moment, full of fear and anger and *power,* I feel more alive than I ever have.

More guards rush in from outside. "Sister, what's happened? Are you all right?" they ask, rifles at the ready, eyes frantically searching the central aisle for danger. What must they think it was—an assassination attempt on O'Shea?

"There was an explosion," I pant, dashing between them.

"Witchery!" O'Shea roars behind me. "Stop her!"

But I'm slipping out into the bedlam. Guards are trying to prevent a group of Brothers from reentering the church. I pause at the back of their flock, head down, and when I raise my face to the sun, I've transformed into a man with coffee-colored skin and fuzzy black hair. Brother Sutton, of Chatham.

Fortunately, most people seem to have headed directly home after the long service instead of mingling about on the steps. Guards are trying to herd the remaining members of the congregation across the street into Richmond Square. I pass a woman sitting on the steps, heedless of the commotion around her, applying a gray glove to a jagged gash on her son's forehead to stop the bleeding.

I take in the amount of colored glass littering the steps, casting rainbows onto the cobblestones below, and realize that it could have been much worse.

I head down the street. The moment I turn a corner, my glamour changes. *Rose,* I think, and I become my old neighbor Rose Collier, dressed in a fine pink wool cloak. At the next corner, I'm Lily: the meek, cow-eyed maid who informed on us to Brother Ishida. I go on like this for blocks, zigzagging my way toward Fifth Street, running through half a dozen disguises, but I don't slow my strides.

I can feel the magic sapping my strength, dragging at my feet. My head swims, vision tunneling, but I can't rest. Not until I'm somewhere safe. I stumble forward into the alley behind O'Neill's shop, begging my magic to see me through one last transition.

"Merry Christmas, Hugh!" a man says cheerfully, hauling boxes inside a shop two doors down.

I turn to him, face transformed into O'Neill's weathered visage, white hair stark against my tanned face. "And a very merry Christmas to you!"

I wait until the neighbor's gone inside before I knock twice at the storeroom door. When it opens, I practically fall into Prue's arms.

"Cate! Oh, thank heavens!" Prue lowers me to the floor.

I press my face to my knees to keep from swooning. "How did you get out?" Alice asks.

"Not important. You have to go to the convent, Alice. Hurry. Get Maura and Tess out of there!" I gulp air, lifting my face. "O'Shea knows my name. He'll come looking for me and when he finds out I've got two sisters—all he'll have to do is look at the registry of students—"

"The prophecy," Alice breathes. "Three sisters, all witches. They'll know it's one of you. You were *powerful,* Cate."

She means it as a compliment, but all I can think is that I was powerfully stupid. I can't take this back. I can't go home—not to the convent or to Chatham—not unless I want to put everyone I care about in danger.

I broke Mother's cardinal rule: *Never* do magic in public.

And now the Brothers will descend on the convent, interrogating girls, searching the rooms, looking for any hints of witchery. If Alice doesn't get there first—

The consequences are too awful to imagine.

"You have to go warn them. Now. *Please,*" I beg, voice shrill.

Alice takes me by the shoulders and shakes me. "Don't you dare go into hysterics. When your magic's back, go to my father's. I gave Prue directions. All the servants are gone, and he's half out of his mind with fever; you'll be safe there." She presses the key into my hands. "I'll bring Maura and Tess to you."

So canny. She's like Elena, always planning. I'm grateful for it now. "Hurry! The entire convent—"

"The Sisters have contingencies for this sort of thing. Don't follow me, Cate. You'll only wind up getting yourself or someone else killed. Do you understand?" She stares at me until I nod, and then she transforms herself into a pretty brunette and swirls out the door.

I struggle to my feet, turning to Prue. "I'm sorry. What happened at the cathedral—"

"You got me out of there. That's all that matters." Prue smiles. "There's a note on the front door that the shop's closed for Christmas. O'Neill's gone to his daughter's. I'd like to let Alistair know where I'll be, but I don't suppose I should leave that information lying around."

"I can write a note in—" *Code,* I mean to say, but my mind catches up to the phrase *his daughter.* "My father! Prue, my father's here in New London. The Brothers will go after him next. I've got to warn him!"

Grisly images of Father being tortured fill my mind. Prue hops down off the cabinet. "How long will it take for your magic to come back?"

I bite my lip. "I don't know."

I pound on the door of Father's flat, praying that I'm not too late. It took an hour—sixty torturous minutes—for my magic to return. What if the Brothers have already sent soldiers for him? What if they're waiting for us? What if they've already beaten him and dragged him off to their prison in the basement of the council building? *What if—what if—what if?* Doubts pulse through me in time with the hammering of my fist.

Prue catches my arm. "Stop," she hisses. "You're going to roust all the neighbors."

Father throws open the door, beaming. "Maura! It's good to see you, girls. What's—?"

Guilt stabs through me at his smile. "Not Maura," I say, dropping both illusions as we push past him. "And not Tess.

This is Prudencia Merriweather, Alistair's sister. We're—we're in trouble."

"Well, you can stay here for as long as you need," Father says. The three of us stand crowded in the tiny entryway. Two cloaks hang on the pegs just inside the door. A pair of leather gloves lie on the hall table where he dropped them—likely when he came in from church. I'm so grateful we caught him at home.

"I can't. Neither can you. You have to leave. But you can't—" I catch both of his hands in mine and squeeze them. Father's hands are soft, a gentleman's hands, unused to hard labor or even the reins of a horse. "You can't go back to Chatham. They'll look for you there. They might arrest you—hurt you—to draw me out."

"The Brothers?" Father asks, and I nod. His grip tightens. "Where are your sisters?"

"They're still at the convent. I sent someone to fetch them—someone I trust." I run a hand over my windblown hair. It's strange to refer to Alice as such, but she's proved herself worthy of it. "You've got to go, Father. They could come for you any minute now."

Father takes the steps two at a time. "Tell me what happened while I pack a few things."

I follow him, and Prue scurries after both of us, right into his bedroom. He pulls his valise from beneath the bed and begins stuffing things into it—books from his bedside table, a daguerreotype of Mother when she was my age. Prue goes to his armoire and begins to take out shirts and vests, tossing them on the bed. She's dead helpful in a crisis, I'm learning. I just pace.

"I was supposed to be glamouring Prue at church, but I lost focus. Someone recognized her and the guards tried to arrest her. They would have hanged her, Father. They started questioning me, and I—I lost my temper and—" I take a deep breath. "I smashed all the windows in the cathedral."

"*Richmond* Cathedral?" Father pauses with his hands full of crisply ironed shirts.

"And tossed Brother O'Shea and a dozen guards halfway across the church," Prue adds.

"O'Shea recognized me. We've met before—at the convent, when he came to speak to the headmistress. He'll come looking for me. Not just for what I did today, embarrassing him like that, but because of the prophecy. When he finds out I have two sisters—" I break off as the tide of worry threatens to pull me under. "We've got to go into hiding, all of us."

"You're the oracle, then?" Father asks.

"Tess," I explain. "Wait. How did you know about the prophecy?"

"I haven't been living in a cave." But Father gives me a sheepish look as he snatches pants and unmentionables from his dresser. "I talked to Marianne after you left last night."

Marianne! Oh, Lord, is there no end to the lives I can ruin? "She should go back to Chatham straightaway. I don't want her and Clara coming to any harm."

"I'll stop and warn her." Father puts a hand on my shoulder. It's strange to realize that he is only a few inches taller than I am. I suppose I still think of him as the towering giant he seemed when I was a child. "What about you? If the Brothers could be here any minute, you ought to be on your way. Surely you're in more danger than anyone else."

I exchange a quick look with Prue. "I'll see you safely out." I'll be damned if I let the Brothers imprison him without a fight.

Father zips the valise and strides into the parlor. "Let me fetch money from the safe and we'll be on our way."

I bite my lip. "Where will you go?"

Father removes the portrait of his parents hanging above one of the golden sofas. Behind it, a small metal safe is set into the wall. He spins a combination, opens the safe, and takes out a small bag. Judging from the way he lifts it, there must be quite a bit of coin in there. "Can never be too careful," he chuckles, noting my surprise. "Don't fret about me, Cate. A man of means can stay hidden in a city the size of New London without too much trouble. Look at Prudencia's brother, there. I'll start at the Golden Hart. It's down near the river; no one would look for me in a place like that. Not for a while, at any rate."

I gulp, imagining Father in a tawdry inn populated by— who? Pickpockets and prostitutes? I've never seen either, though I've heard tales. I'm more concerned about sickness. "Be careful. The fever—"

"I'll send word for you if I take sick." He shoves a sheaf of documents into his bag along with the money pouch. Then he turns to me. "I don't want you checking up on me. It's not a fit place for a young lady."

A young lady! I don't know whether to laugh or cry.

Prue recites Alice's address for him as we clamor back down the stairs. "That's where we'll be for the time being."

"Cardiff, eh? And if I see Finn whilst I'm telling Marianne the news, should I pass that along?" Father pulls on his gray cloak. "He'll be worried."

I blush. What, precisely, did Marianne tell Father? "I don't want him involved in any of this."

"Are you sure of that, Catie?" The childhood nickname almost sends me into tears. It reminds me of Father kneeling and checking beneath my bed for monsters. *Nothing there, Catie,* he'd say, before giving me a smacking kiss on the forehead. No one else has ever called me that—and I haven't heard it from him since I was very small.

I picture my bedroom back in Chatham: the quilt and curtains with the blue daylilies, the rose-patterned rug next to my bed, and Mother's violet settee. Will I ever see any of it again? I can't go back, at least not with the Brothers in charge of New England, and despite all of Inez's schemes, we do not seem very close to ousting them at the moment.

"I'm sure," I say. But my voice trembles on the lie.

Father pauses, looking me straight in the eye. "I haven't been a good father to you, Cate. My advice may not be welcome, but I'm going to give it nonetheless and hope you'll indulge me. A man like Finn—he won't take well to being coddled. A marriage requires a meeting of equals. Your mother—well, I wish she'd told me the truth and trusted me to make my own decisions."

"I—I'll keep that in mind." I give him a quick embrace,

inhaling the scents of leather and pipe smoke. "Keep safe, *please*. I feel as though we've only just found you, in a way."

"I do, too." Father's voice is gruff. "Take care of yourself, now."

"I will. And I'll look after Maura and Tess, too."

Father smiles. "Never had any doubt of that."

I almost break my promise to Alice three times over.

"I can't wait and do nothing!" I complain, pacing the Auclairs' grand foyer. Above me, the crystal chandelier catches the last rays of sunlight.

Prue throws herself in front of the door. Again. "You've got to."

"I could move you if I wanted," I point out, frustrated.

Prue leans back against the door, arms crossed over her chest. Her gray eyes, fringed with unfathomably long lashes, practically dare me to try. "I know you're worried, but you've got to think this through. The convent will be crawling with Brothers. If you go back, it will only complicate things. Alice is probably on her way home with Maura and Tess right now."

"What if she's *not?*" I sink onto the bottom step of the great, gleaming staircase, my mind filling with nightmares. "It's been hours! They should have been back by now. I don't know what could be keeping them, unless the Brothers got there before Alice did and there was a battle. O'Shea will have a registry of students. When he sees three Cahill sisters on that list—"

"Don't think of it," Prue interrupts. I glance up at the

ceiling, covered in the same deep blue floral paper as the walls, bridged by a cornice of sculpted cherubs. I can't stop thinking of it: guards restraining my sisters, knocking them unconscious so they cannot use their magic. Beating them. Breaking their fingers the way they did Brenna's when she refused to cooperate. Leaving scars and bruises and worse. I think of what was done to Parvati and others at Harwood and my stomach lurches.

Maura would fight back, and Lord knows she's formidable. But Tess—Tess, whose magic is the strongest of all—

"Tess hasn't been herself lately," I fret. "I'm afraid she might do something foolish."

Even if she has no sense of self-preservation, she knows what the prophecy says: If the oracle falls to the Brotherhood, we're all lost. Surely that would rouse her to fight. Wouldn't it?

Prue rummages through the hall table for a match, then lights the exquisite little blue crystal lamp. It's growing dark outside; it must be nearly half past four. What's taking them so long?

"They'll be all right, Cate. Besides, you're exhausted. How much more magic do you suppose you can do today?"

I glance into the silver mirror over the table, noting my pallor and the tired droop of my shoulders. She's right. I barely managed to get us across town in our disguises before I collapsed onto Alice's kitchen floor. Prue scrounged up some bread and cheese from the pantry, but I couldn't bring myself to eat. It took an hour before I was able to go upstairs and attend Alice's father.

"I don't care. I don't care about anyone but Maura and Tess," I mutter.

"Liar," Prue says. "If that were true, you would have let them arrest me. You would have let us all hang. No—you would have let us all rot in Harwood, or suffer whatever other fate the Brothers had in store for us."

I sigh as Prue presses my cold cup of tea into my hands. A few months ago, Tess and Maura were the only people who truly mattered to me in the world. I would have been incapable of staying here and entrusting their safety to anyone else. Now—well, it's driving me mad, but I do recognize the sense in Prue's argument.

The front door crashes open. My heart lodges in my throat when I see the tall, gray-haired man standing in the doorway.

"Oh, good, you're here." Alice drops her disguise, closing the door behind her.

She's come alone.

My heart plummets. "Where are my sisters?"

"Hidden away." Alice shivers into her cloak. "It's freezing in here! How's Father?"

"Sleeping peacefully. I eased his fever. He's past danger now." I frown, gripping my teacup with white-knuckled hands. "Are they still at the convent? Are they safe?"

"Yes, and yes—at least for the time being." Alice strides into the parlor—a large room with a thick rose-colored rug and curtains the pale pink of the inside of a seashell. She sits on a plush pink settee identical to the one at the convent, and I wonder if she prevailed upon her father to buy her *two*. I cannot imagine growing up in this cold mausoleum of a house. It's lovely but impersonal—no books or papers or slippers scattered about, no family portraits on the walls. It seems a lonely place for a child.

"Isn't the place swarming with Brothers by now?"

"Dozens of them." Alice reaches up to pull the bell for a servant. Her hand falls as she remembers there's no one to call. She makes a face and gets up to light the fire herself. "But it turns out there's a suite of rooms hidden behind Cora's. The door is in the back of her privy closet, and it's glamoured so no one would ever suspect it was there. I've been living at the convent for years and I never knew. Dead clever, isn't it? Stocked with everything you'd need for a few days—blankets, privy pots, candles, even some of Sister Sophia's canned goods. I don't know that they'll be very comfortable, but they won't starve. Gretchen got everyone in just as O'Shea himself marched in, demanding your arrest."

I sink onto a pretty gold chair. "Thank the Lord you got there in time."

"There wasn't a minute to spare. Girls were rushing around, casting illusions over anything forbidden, while Inez stalled the Brothers at the door. She put on a good show of being shocked by your betrayal. Meanwhile, Gretchen was upstairs shoving all your strays into the secret rooms." Alice sighs and throws up her hands. "Can one of you start this blasted fire?"

Prue kneels beside her and takes up the tinderbox. "Was anyone arrested?"

"No. Not yet, anyway. When I left, the Brothers were still there, questioning everyone and making dire threats. Of course everyone was claiming they hadn't the foggiest notion where you might have gone, or when your sisters disappeared, or that you were in league with the Merriweathers." Alice settles back onto the love seat, kicking off her fine velvet slippers and tucking her feet beneath her. "Cate, you don't keep a diary, do you?"

I frown at her. "Of course not. Do you think I'm stupid?"

"No?" Her voice leaves room for doubt. "The Brothers found one when they searched your room. In it, you claim responsibility for the attacks at Harwood Asylum and Richmond Square—as well as the assassination of the Head Council. You boast about how easy it was to pull the wool over the good Sisters' eyes, how the convent provided the perfect ruse."

"What an excellent villain I am." I grit my teeth, clenching the carved wooden arm of the chair. "Inez must have planted it."

"She's quick, I'll give her that." Alice smiles. "Fortunately, she's not immune to a bit of flattery. I made out like you and Prue escaped together, and begged her forgiveness for going against her at the hanging. I think she believed me."

"Clever," I say, because Alice is clearly expecting it. "You're certain Maura and Tess are all right?"

"As long as they stay put and don't do anything reckless," Alice says. "O'Shea's keeping a squadron of guards at the convent. He's furious! You should have heard him thundering about the Sisterhood making him look a fool, nursing a viper in its bosom!"

"How did you manage to sneak out?" Prue rocks back on

her heels as the fire blazes. "I assume they aren't letting girls walk out willy-nilly."

"I told them the truth: that my father's sick and I was going to nurse him. When they heard who he was, they were happy enough to let me go. He donates quite generously to their coffers, so they wouldn't want him turning up his toes." Alice frowns. "One of them suggested I take him to see Brother Kenneally, but I don't know what good that could do, exposing him to the riffraff down at the hospital!"

"That's not the first time Kenneally's name has come up. Merriweather's trying to see what he can find out." I sigh, tracing a finger over the wallpaper, which is all pink stripes and roses. This is the most garishly feminine room I've ever seen—even worse than Mrs. Kosmoski's dress shop back in Chatham. "Your father should be right as rain in a few days. I didn't heal him entirely; I didn't have enough magic left. I'll need a few days to figure out where to go next anyway."

"You can't spend the rest of your life in hiding." Alice's blue eyes are piercing. "You're a very powerful witch, Cate. If I ever doubted that—and we both know I *did*—I saw proof of it today. The Sisterhood can't afford to lose you."

"I'm not leaving New London. I'd never leave Maura and Tess." Or Finn.

"This affects more than you and your sisters," Alice snaps. "You've cast doubt on the entire Sisterhood. It gives O'Shea the perfect excuse to toss us all out into the streets. Then what will we do? I for one have no intention of marrying some empty-headed dandy selected by my father. And if we disperse, it'll be impossible to organize properly and over-throw the Brothers."

"At least you have somewhere to go. Options. Most of the others don't," Prue points out.

She and Alice are both staring at me as though pearls of wisdom will fall from my lips at any moment.

"We've got to do something," I agree slowly. "Soon."

I've just got to figure out what. Before we lose our chance.

We're in the midst of a makeshift dinner of fried eggs and salted ham when there's an odd series of knocks on the kitchen door: one short, one long, one short, one long. Alice startles, but Prue jumps out of her chair and races for the door with a laugh. She flings it open to reveal her brother, stamping his feet to keep warm, breath clouding the air.

"Pru-dennn-ci-aaaaa!" he sings, echoing his knock.

She throws her arms around his waist, hugging him tight. "Hurry up, come in, before anyone sees you."

"Just in time for dinner, I see," he notes. "Good evening, Cate. Glad to see you here and not dancing at the end of a rope. The whole town's buzzing about what happened."

I wince at his jest and glance back at Alice. "This is Alice Auclair. This is her father's home."

"Oh, I know. *Everyone* knows George Auclair." Merri-weather gazes around the immense kitchen, which boasts a shining new range and extravagantly tiled walls. "One of the Brothers' most generous supporters. Made a bundle off his contracts with them."

"There's no need to be vulgar," Alice says crisply, but she flushes, obviously nettled. "Besides, you're hardly one to talk!"

I squint at them in confusion. Merriweather bows low, theatrically. "The Merriweathers were rich as Midas before yours truly sank it all into the newspaper. All thanks to Walter Merriweather, head of the Brotherhood, 1816 to 1818. Our august ancestor was the last man to order witches hanged— up until O'Shea, of course."

"Marvelous legacy," I say dryly.

"Isn't it?" he returns.

"Have you eaten? Shall I make you a fried egg?" Prue picks up the skillet.

"My, how domestic. Mama would be proud." Alistair steals Prue's seat at the rectangular wooden table, his back to the crackling fire. "No, thank you. I can't tarry; I've got to redo the front page of the paper. I'd take a cup of tea, though."

Prue reaches for the china teapot and pours. "Are you writing about Cate?"

Her brother steals a bite of her ham. "Yes. The *Gazette* will draw a distinction between those responsible for the attack on the Head Council and those responsible for saving the Harwood girls. I daresay I'll be accused of favoritism, seeing as how you've saved Prue's neck three times now, Cate. But I *am* grateful." He reaches up and tugs on her braid, eliciting a yelp. "What were you doing in church anyway, you heathen?"

"I heard a rumor that you were up to something," Prue explains. "Nice work with the leaflets."

"I'm grateful for your support," I say, ignoring Merriweather's preening. "I hope it will mean something to those who'd normally be fearful of magic."

"The working class, you mean." Alice rolls her eyes.

"That attitude is precisely what's got the Brothers in trouble. The working and merchant classes are your best bet for change," Merriweather argues. "They're suffering. They'd turn on the Brothers quick enough if they thought their day-to-day life would be better under a new government. I'm suggesting that new government ought to be composed of a triumvirate—like the old days of Rome—consisting of a Brother, a witch, and a commoner. That way, everyone's concerns will be represented."

"Magic's still illegal, you know. Don't you think repealing those laws would make a better first step?" Alice tosses her golden hair. She's bathed and dressed in a fresh gown of royal-blue wool. "They'll laugh you out of town."

"Why not go whole hog if we're advocating for reform?" Merriweather waves Prue's fork as he talks. "The witches are too powerful to ignore. You were only trying to protect a friend—one who would have been put to death, after suffering through three years of false imprisonment."

"Are you suggesting that women have the vote, too?" Prue asks. "If you really want to effect change—"

Her brother eyes her warily. "I wouldn't go that far. Where's your friend Miss Stephenson? I expected she'd be here, sharing in your misfortune, ready to berate me for my patriarchal ways."

I smother a smile. "Rilla's gone to her family in Vermont for Christmas."

Merriweather clears his throat. "You ought to fetch her a copy of tomorrow's *Gazette* so she can see her name in print. Pen name, at least. The chit has a way with words, believe it or not."

"Alistair! Was that a compliment? For a lady journalist?" Prue's gray eyes go wide behind her spectacles.

"If you repeat it, I'll disown you," he mutters. He steals another bite from Prue's plate, and she swats at him. "Cate, I don't suppose you could get me an exclusive interview with the oracle, could you?"

I take a sip of my tea. "I could not, as she's currently in hiding."

"One of your sisters, then?" Merriweather raises his eyebrows at me. "That is—if you're still maintaining that it's not you?"

"I would swear to it." My voice is tart. "And I'll thank you to leave my sisters out of your paper. They're in enough trouble as it is."

Merriweather shakes his head, a lock of black hair falling over his pale forehead, just as there's another knock at the kitchen door. "That'll be Belastra."

Alice glares at me, and I shrug, though my pulse races.

"I'm going to show him our printing press," Merriweather explains. "Told him to meet me here."

I open the door, glad to find Finn on my doorstep. "I badgered the address out of Merriweather this afternoon," he explains, his brown eyes searching me as if to make certain

I'm still here and still whole. "I had to see for myself that you were all right."

"Now that you've seen, you can go away again," Alice says waspishly.

"This is Alice Auclair," I explain. "And you've already met Prue."

"Evening, Prue. It's a pleasure to meet you, Miss Auclair," Finn says, bowing. He doesn't reach for me, but stands closer than is proper. Only an inch separates his shoulder from mine.

"The pleasure is all yours." Alice swivels in her seat. "I don't want a member of the Brotherhood in my house, Cate."

"Really?" Merriweather drawls. "I hear your father plays a regular card game with some of them—despite the measure against gambling."

"Five minutes, Alice, please?" I give her a beseeching look. "In exchange for healing your father?"

She rolls her eyes. "I thought providing you sanctuary was payment enough."

Finn ignores her. "Are your sisters all right?"

I nod. "They're safe. Did your mother and Clara leave for Chatham?"

"Put them on the train this afternoon. I suspect the Brothers will be paying her a visit soon, though." He runs a gloved hand through his coppery hair. "Brother Ishida and I were both questioned this evening. Berated, really. O'Shea claims we let the oracle slip right under our noses. Of course Ishida made out like he's been suspicious of you all along. Said you're too educated for your own good—and then threw it in my face that you'd probably bought your books on magic from our shop."

I twist my mother's pearl ring on my finger. "I'm sorry. I never meant to involve Marianne in any of this."

"It's Ishida who brought her into it. I should have clocked him," he seethes. His freckled cheeks are flushed from anger and the icy December wind. "Fortunately, our interview was cut short. Some urgent business at the hospital."

"Speaking of the hospital . . ." Alice takes a sip of tea. "Have you heard anything about the Brothers developing medicine to treat the epidemic? I was advised to take Father to see Brother Kenneally."

"That can't be a coincidence." Merriweather drops his fork with a clink against the china plate. "I've asked my sources in the hospital to look into it."

I turn to Finn. "Can you ask around, too? If they're with-holding medicine from the sick, that's awful."

"But if we could prove it, there'd be a nice public outcry," Merriweather muses.

"I'll look into it." Finn turns to face me, ears flushing, and lowers his voice. "I'm sorry I wasn't able to get here sooner. I went to Alistair's lodgings as soon as I heard, hoping he'd know where you were, but then I had to see Mother off. And when I came out of the train depot, there was a guard waiting to escort me back to the hotel for questioning. I've been wor-ried about you."

My eyes collide with his. "I'm all right. Better now that I've seen you."

"Well." Merriweather clears his throat, rising with an

elegant swirl of his greatcoat. "We ought to be going. Loads of work to do tonight. Thank you for the tea and hospitality, ladies. Prue, you know how to reach me." He pats his sister on the head like a puppy and is out the door.

Finn brushes his hand over mine before following. It's a sweet gesture, but it reminds me how far apart we still are. A few weeks ago, he would have kissed me.

CHAPTER
17

PATIENCE HAS NEVER BEEN ONE OF my virtues.

By midmorning, I'm driving Prue and Alice mad with my pacing. Alice is lounging on the love seat with a fashion magazine, wearing a rose-colored brocade embroidered with gold leaves. The fire burns merrily in the hearth; a plate of freshly baked cranberry scones and a steaming pot of tea sit on the table where Prue left them.

I can't seem to settle. Unlike Alice, I'm not well suited to idleness, and unlike Prue, I've no useful domestic talents. I'm practically twitching with pent-up energy.

I should be at the hospital, nursing, but I can't leave the house without an illusion, and it would be impossible to do any significant healing magic while maintaining a glamour. I've got to find something to occupy myself with.

"Would you go pace somewhere else?" Alice snaps.

I go in search of Prue, following my ears to the music room across the hall. It's papered with pretty blue and yellow scrollwork, but it's obvious that this room isn't often used; the grand piano is covered in a fine layer of dust, and brown petals have fallen from a vase of pink roses. Prue sits on a stool next to the harpsichord, playing and singing softly. She stops when I come in.

"Go on," I urge, leaning against the piano. "Don't mind me."

She's just begun to sing in a high, beautiful soprano when there's a knock at the front door. I pull the music room door mostly closed, peering out through a small crack. Could someone be paying a call on Mr. Auclair? Alice tacked a yellow ribbon onto the front door last night to indicate sickness within, but perhaps a good friend or a business associate would come to check up on him?

Alice opens the front door. Immediately, I can tell from her haughty expression that it's not the Brothers. My heart leaps, hoping for my sisters, before I recognize Rory's voice.

I lean out into the hall. "Is everything all right at the convent?"

"Strange is what it is." Rory strides over and air-kisses both my cheeks.

"The guards have all left," Sachi says. "They had half a dozen soldiers stationed on each floor last night and more patrolling the street out front. Then, right after breakfast, the sergeant told Gretchen they'd been given orders to leave."

"Why?" This seems far too good to be true. "Do you think it's a trap?"

Alice darts a glance toward the front door. "You weren't followed, were you?"

"Please." Sachi plants her hands on her slim hips. "We aren't novices at sneaking, you know."

Something strikes me. "You said the guard reported to Gretchen? Where's Inez?"

"That," Rory says, tracing her name in the dust on top of the piano, "is an excellent question. She went off last night and we haven't seen hide nor hair of her since."

"Peculiar, isn't it?" Sachi adjusts the ivory cummerbund of her apple-green dress. "You wouldn't think she'd leave the convent crawling with guards. She said she had business to attend to at the hospital."

"Perhaps she'll take sick and die," Rory suggests cheerfully.

I narrow my eyes. Perhaps Inez is visiting Covington and the other members of the Head Council again.

"How are my sisters?" I ask, collecting the fallen rose petals in my palm.

Sachi and Rory exchange glances, and my breath quickens. "Tess had another episode last night. A vision or a nightmare, we're not sure which. She didn't seem certain herself," Sachi says carefully.

I crumple the rose petals in my fist. "What was it about?"

"It's hard to say. She seemed a little batty, to be honest." Rory dots the *i* in *Elliott* with a star.

Sachi elbows her. "Tess kept saying that the city was going

to burn. That there would be fire and death and she couldn't stop any of it. It was—a trifle disturbing."

Rory gives an exaggerated shiver. "It was eerie, being shut up in that room all night without a clue what was going on, with Tess prophesying all sorts of death and destruction."

"Everyone's in a panic," Sachi sighs. "Sister Gretchen has teachers stationed at every exit to catch anyone coming or going. She nearly refused to let us leave, but we thought you'd want to hear the news."

"There's going to be some sort of proclamation at noon in Richmond Square," Rory explains.

I frown. "Finn stopped by last night. He said O'Shea was called away to the hospital in the midst of interrogating him and your father. You don't suppose they've seen through Inez's pretense with Brother Covington and arrested her, do you?"

"Perhaps they'll hang her!" Rory's rabbity smile turns bloodthirsty.

"Better hope that's not it. She'd give us all up to save her own neck," Alice says.

"We need to go find out what's happening," I declare, dropping the rose petals into the wastebasket and heading for the front hall. Behind me, Sachi is rubbing out Rory's name in the dust.

"I was hoping you'd say that. I'm dead tired of being cooped up," Rory declares.

"Do you suppose you can keep your temper under control this time?" Alice needles.

"Yes." I glare. "I don't make the same mistakes twice, Alice."

• • •

Alice creates a glamour that turns her hair brown and thins her hourglass figure and heart-shaped face. It's just enough that no one would recognize her as the same girl who was in the cathedral yesterday. She uses more of her magic to turn me into a willowy Indo girl with glossy brown hair and caramel skin. I could pass for Parvati's sister.

The cobbled streets of Cardiff are quiet. Several of the neighboring houses sport fluttering yellow ribbons

Once we reach the market district, there's an abrupt change in mood. Soldiers lurk on every street corner, stopping us every few blocks to demand that we lower our hoods. It's obvious that they're searching for someone.

Searching for me.

I know that Alice has a powerful affinity for illusions, but I can't help trembling every time the soldiers peer into my face. I'm placing an enormous amount of trust in someone I considered an enemy a week ago. If she wanted to destroy me, she could do it so easily.

Newspaper boys loiter next to shops that have shuttered early for the lunch hour. "Assassination attempt on Brother O'Shea! Dangerous witch on the loose! Richmond Cathedral damaged in the attack!" they shout, waving copies of the *Sentinel.*

I stop to purchase a paper, fearing all the while that someone will see through the illusion and shout my name and the soldiers will drag me away. I must be mad, brazenly walking down Church Street when all of New London is searching for me. And yet Alice was right. I can't hide in her father's house forever.

"Good Lord," Rory swears. A sketch of me, Maura, and Tess is plastered on the front page of the paper. It's based on a photograph we sat for two summers ago, and the likeness is quite good. Maura sits in a tall armchair, while Tess kneels at her feet and I stand behind them, my hand on Maura's shoulder. Tess still wore pinafores and her hair in braids then. She kept the picture tucked into the corner of her mirror; the Brothers must have found it when they searched the convent.

Right above the photo, a headline screeches out: WITCH RESPONSIBLE FOR ASSASSINATION ATTEMPT ON O'SHEA IDENTIFIED. The first sentence declares that a substantial reward *and* immunity will be given to anyone who comes forward with reputable information regarding the whereabouts of Catherine Cahill. Then it notes that my sisters—also witches—are missing and presumed complicit in the attacks on the Head Council, Harwood Asylum, Richmond Square, and Richmond Cathedral. Alistair and Prudencia Merriweather are mentioned as fellow fugitives, presumed dangerous.

Rory lets out a low whistle. "That's a hefty reward. It's a good thing I like you."

On my other side, Alice scowls. "Perhaps Maura has the right idea, getting rid of those girls. I don't know many people who'd resist a sum like that."

I let her take the newspaper, and shove my hands in the pockets of my blue cloak. I don't want to believe that the Harwood girls would betray me after I saved them twice over. But after being locked up again last night—even for their own safety—well, the promise of freedom and immunity must be tempting.

Maura would be delighted to have all her accusations about the untrustworthiness of the Harwood girls and my gullibility proven correct—if she survived it.

As we walk down Church Street, more shopkeepers are locking up so they can watch the proclamation. I glance at the cathedral. They've swept the broken glass from the front steps, but the damage is clear: All the beautiful windows are gone, the gaping holes boarded up. It was sacrilege, what I did, destroying a place of worship like that.

I pray that my sisters won't be punished for my transgressions.

A crowd has already gathered in Richmond Square, though it's only half past eleven. Liveried guards with bayonets at the ready are patrolling the entrances and grouped in clusters throughout the square. Hundreds of Brothers stand at the front of the crowd, right before the gallows—so many that it looks as though the entire National Council has turned out. Finn will be there somewhere.

A single noose dangles in the center of the gallows stage.

Fear grips me. It's to be a hanging, then.

A witch? Obviously they're prepared for trouble.

"Well, this explains why there are no guards left at the convent. Every soldier in New London is downtown," Rory whispers.

We take up a position near the front. The crowd is growing every minute, but the mood is different today. Somber.

There are no vendors selling roasted chestnuts or hot cider to take away the chill. No children playing tag. The crisp air is filled with hacking coughs, and people look anxiously at their neighbors before nestling deeper into their upturned collars. I don't see any other Sisters present, but perhaps they, too, are glamoured. The few women in the crowd have their hoods up and scarves wrapped around their mouths.

Alice elbows me. "Look, they're coming!" she hisses, pulling her hood lower.

A squadron of guards moves slowly down the steps of the National Council building. At its center are three figures cloaked in black, indistinguishable in the distance. Two of them walk side by side while the third trudges behind them, head down and hands bound, with guards close on either side. Could that be Inez? It's impossible to tell whether the figure is male or female.

As they enter the square, whispers slink and skip through the crowd. People fall to their knees, shouting—what? I cannot make it out.

I stand on my tiptoes, trying to see over the shoulders in front of me.

When I finally catch a glimpse of the man climbing the gallows, I gasp.

"That's impossible!" My voice is lost in the shocked murmurs of everyone around me.

The broad shoulders, the sharp cheekbones, the black hair gone gray at the temples—the charismatic carriage—his way of wearing the Brothers' robes as though it's the finest suit money could buy—

It's Brother William Covington, back from death's door.

"It's a miracle!" someone shouts.

The air fills with amens and hallelujahs.

As Covington takes center stage, another figure ascends the gallows. She turns to face the crowd, her sharp beak of a nose and dark eyes instantly familiar. The wind catches at her hood, revealing chestnut hair pulled back into a tight chignon. Inez.

But her hands are free, clasped piously before her. Then, who—

The third figure climbs the steps, a guard's rifle at his back. My breath strangles in my throat when he lifts his face and I recognize the icy blue gaze of Brother O'Shea.

How has Inez managed this?

"The Lord works in mysterious ways," Brother Covington begins. His honeyed drawl is a trifle hoarse, and the crowd goes silent, pressing forward to hear him better. "I should not be standing here before you today. I have spent the last three weeks lying in a bed in Richmond Hospital, stripped of my dignity. The witches' horrific attack left me unable to recall my own name, unable to perform the most basic functions. All previous victims have lived out the rest of their days in this state. It is nothing short of a miracle that I stand here, fully recovered, with all my faculties intact. Thanks be!"

The crowd echoes him, and I bite my tongue. Miracle, my foot. If his faculties were truly intact, his memory returned, he'd never be standing next to the woman who attacked him in the first place.

How is this possible? He ought to be drooling in his hospital bed, being spoon-fed his meals and changed like an infant.

Covington gives a broad smile. "I am humbled. And I feel certain this miracle would not have occurred without the incredible devotion—the tireless prayers—of this woman. I would like to publicly thank Sister Inez Ortega, headmistress of the Sisterhood, for praying by my side every day." He gives a low, chivalrous bow. I clap with the rest of the crowd. Next to me, Alice gives a little hiss through her teeth.

This is the result of all her hours at his bedside. Somehow, she's compelling him.

Inez wants Brother Covington awake and leading New England. But why? How does this fit into her plans? A mixture of fascination and fear washes over me. I've never heard of such powerful compulsion, but nothing else makes sense.

"After successfully completing a battery of tests, I have reassumed my duties as head of the Brotherhood," Covington says, and pauses while the crowd cheers. The people of New London have always liked him. "The last few weeks, New London has been under attack. We have now learned the identity of the witch responsible: one Catherine Cahill. I urge you all to buy a copy of today's *Sentinel* and examine her picture closely. This girl is extremely dangerous. Just look at the damage she did to our beautiful cathedral!" He makes a sweeping gesture behind him. "We have reason to believe she's still in New London, and I will not rest until she and her accomplices are found. Justice will be served!"

He shakes his fist in the air as the crowd cheers again.

What on earth is Inez playing at?

And if she's capable of this—what's to stop her from doing it again, to anyone who stands in her way? She's never been able to compel me, but I've always been on my guard with her. What about my sisters? My friends? Finn?

Covington's full mouth tilts into a frown. "My pursuit of justice has led me to a disturbing revelation. A revelation that someone I trusted has betrayed me—has betrayed us all!—in the worst possible manner. I hereby charge Edward O'Shea with treason against New England." The guards push O'Shea forward. All his bantam courage has deserted him; his shoulders slump as he fixes his eyes on the floor. "Yesterday, guards found Miss Cahill's diary concealed in her bedroom at the convent of the Sisterhood. In it, she confessed to the attacks on the Head Council as well as Harwood Asylum and Richmond Square. She admitted—unsurprisingly—that noted seditionist Alistair Merriweather aided her in these attacks. But she also wrote that, in the interest of furthering his own ambition, O'Shea helped her plan the attack on the Head Council. Cornered, she turned on him yesterday inside the cathedral—and he let her escape! His betrayal and lies— indeed, his abuse of power—must be punished to the fullest extent of the law."

The crowd murmurs. O'Shea is not well liked. But to put a man—a member of the Brotherhood—to death without a trial? On such flimsy evidence as the word of a witch? Down front, the Brothers' calm has devolved into angry whispers, like the buzzing of a hundred furious bees. I hear murmurs of Sean Brennan's name. Is this Inez's plan? Divide and conquer?

"Let this be a warning to you all. Anyone aiding or abetting the witch known as Catherine Cahill will be put to

278

death." Covington points an accusing finger at O'Shea, while I marvel at Inez's talent for mimicry. She has his theatrical gestures, the smallest inflections of his voice, down pat. How long has she been planning this?

Covington and Inez leave the stage as two guards advance on O'Shea. One pushes his head into the noose, while the other tightens the knot. O'Shea's hood falls down; his bald head glints in the sun.

"By executive order of Brother William Covington, you have been convicted of treason against New England. Your sentence is death by hanging," one of the guards proclaims. Then they both step backward.

The crowd is silent.

One of the guards pulls a lever. The trapdoor beneath O'Shea's boots gives way. His body falls, jerking to a sudden stop.

The crack of his neck makes a sound like a wishbone breaking in two.

Sister Inez—a witch—is now in charge of New England.

One might think that cause for celebration.

But now that two of the people standing in Inez's way have been disposed of, is there any doubt that I will be her next target?

Around us, the crowd has gone silent. Their faces are averted from the spectacle of O'Shea's body, swinging in the icy December wind.

Alice grabs my elbow with pinching fingers. "We've got to get you out of here."

CHAPTER
18

WE'VE BARELY TAKEN OFF OUR CLOAKS when there's a pounding on Alice's front door. Mei and Rilla tumble in, windblown, dressed in their Sisterly black. Rilla is carrying her battered suitcase; she must have come straight from the train station.

"What are you doing here? You were supposed to be gone a week!" I cry as she drops her bag and wraps me in a fierce hug.

"I didn't feel right being away, between the fever and all the unrest," she explains. "I sent Mei a telegram. She met my train and filled me in on what's been happening." Rilla's freckled face is full of worry. "I'm so relieved you're safe."

Alice leads us into the parlor, while Prue bustles off to make a pot of tea.

"Is she safe, though? I told Maura and Tess where she is, in case they needed her." Alice has settled into her corner of the pink love seat, her legs crossed elegantly at the ankle, gold slippers peering out beneath her rose-colored skirts, but she's frowning.

I sit on a wooden chair near the fire, shivering. "Maura wouldn't tell Inez. She's still my sister."

On the other end of the love seat, Sachi raises her eyebrows in silent skepticism. "That may mean something to you." She straightens the apple-green feather in her hair. "But Maura's proven it doesn't mean much to her."

"'One sister will murder another,'" Alice quotes, and my stomach twists. "It's in your stars, isn't it? She doesn't have to put the noose around your neck herself."

If Maura told Inez where I am, she wouldn't have to. Now that Inez has blamed me for the attack on the Head Council, I'm the witch all of New England will fear. Even now, word will be spreading throughout the country that I am the monster the Brothers have been preaching against all my life: a witch with mind-magic, capable of compelling others to do my bidding. It wouldn't be enough to lock me up and throw away the key. They will have me killed, and people will spit on my body, and Inez will cheer at my death.

Surely that isn't what Maura wants.

She can be impulsive, but she must know what the consequences will be if she tells Inez my whereabouts.

"She doesn't hate me that much," I say, praying that it's the truth.

"She knew what Inez was planning to do with Covington, didn't she?" Rory is perched on the arm of the love seat, her bright orange dress clashing wildly with the wallpaper of pink stripes and roses behind her.

I remember the way Maura refused to meet my eyes during our conversation about Inez's visits to the hospital. "I think so."

"Then she's already been a party to murder," Rory says.

"The murder of a terrible man who would have seen us all hanged gladly," I point out.

Mei's sitting in a high-backed blue chair opposite me. "I'm not saying what Maura and Inez did was right. Far from it. But . . . this is our chance, isn't it? The Brotherhood is rudderless. They'll be even more divided now—those who support Covington versus those who put O'Shea in charge versus those who want to call Brennan back from exile. And the people *want* change. I saw how bad things are when I was with my parents for Christmas. Our neighbors are sick, dying in droves. My brother would have died if it weren't for Cate. People can't afford proper food, much less medicine to help fight the fever—and only the rich are being admitted to the hospital now. People are starving because sick men can't work and the Brotherhood never delivered the Christmas rations they promised. We have to do something!"

"I don't argue that." I look around at my own version of a war council. My heart twists a little, missing Tess. She ought to be present for any decision we make. In her current state, though, is she capable of helping? "But I don't have any answers."

Alice fiddles with her topaz earrings. "I don't understand what Inez is trying to accomplish," she admits, her blue eyes puzzled. "She claims she wants to put the witches back in power, to have us rule New England the way we once did. I used to believe all her grand talk. But this ruse with Covington—what is it she intends to do? Provoke a civil war? His leadership would have to fail *spectacularly* for people to consider the witches an option. They're far more likely to elect another Brother, no matter how bumbling and corrupt she paints them."

"True. It's not as though she wants them to call Brennan back so we can all work together." I snort at the very idea.

"But *we* do. I've been thinking about Merriweather's suggestion." Alice tucks a flyaway strand of golden hair back into her pompadour. "A triumvirate that consists of a Brother, a witch, and a commoner. I think he might be on to something."

Sachi raises her eyebrows again. "*You'd* be willing to share power with a Brother?"

"And a commoner?" Mei sounds equally incredulous.

Alice shrugs. "It's more power than we've got now."

Footsteps sound in the hall. Multiple pairs of them. We all swivel toward the doorway as Prue, carrying the silver tea service, leads her brother and Finn into the room. "Look who I found in the kitchen!" she declares, making introductions.

Merriweather gets right to the point. "What in the devil is going on? Has Covington been miraculously resurrected, or is this some sort of witchery?"

"Compulsion. But we can't expose Inez without exposing the entire Sisterhood." I slump in my chair. "She's dangerous. Unpredictable. She loathes me for opposing her. And Finn, she—" I falter, though everyone but Merriweather already knows the truth of it, and perhaps Finn has told him, too.

"She's the one who suggested Maura erase your memory. I daresay she's only biding her time before she has you arrested for treason. You're not safe in the Brotherhood anymore."

Finn takes a moment to digest this news, then turns to Merriweather. "Looks like I need another line of work. Do you have need of a new reporter?"

"I can always use a good writer." Merriweather claps him on the back while offering Rilla a cheeky grin. Across the room, she flushes with pleasure.

"I'm not certain you realize the danger you're in," I point out. Finn's smiling like a madman.

He pulls off his black cloak. Beneath it, he's wearing gray herringbone trousers with a matching vest and a crisp white shirt that clings to his muscled shoulders. "I've hated every moment of being a Brother. I'm glad to be rid of this," he confesses, pulling off his silver ring of office and tossing it into the fire.

"Don't be hasty, now! That could be of use." Merriweather strides over to the fireplace, picks up the poker, and slides the ring out of the flames. "Tell them what you found out."

"Ah." Finn rubs a hand over his jaw. Already, his bearing seems lighter. "The Brothers have a store of medicine that's been proven to cure the fever in a matter of days. They're keeping it in Richmond Hospital under Kenneally's watch, in case the National Council falls sick."

Mei jumps to her feet. "They must have hundreds of doses, then!"

"Yes." Finn's mouth is pressed into a grim line, but behind his spectacles, his eyes are still smiling.

"Those bastards," Rory swears, reaching for a leftover cranberry scone.

"Rory!" Sachi elbows her sister.

"I *am* a bastard. I might as well get to use the word," Rory insists. "They're watching hundreds of people die and they're sitting on the cure!"

"Brothers and their families can afford rest and other costly medicines like quinine and salicin to help reduce fevers and ease their pain," Mei complains. "This isn't fair. The people who really need that cure—"

"Ought to have it," I finish, standing, smoothing my black skirt. "You've been at the hospital more than anyone. Do you know where they'd keep such a thing?"

She nods, a grin spreading over her face. "All we've got to do is find Brother Kenneally."

"Cate." Rilla is perched on a round blue ottoman next to Mei. "You can't waltz into the hospital. Everyone in New London is looking for you!"

"No one would suspect I'd be daft enough to show up there, then, would they? And Mei can't do it by herself. She'll need a witch with compulsion." I glance nervously at Finn. "Just in case things go wrong."

"Perhaps we can bluff our way in." Finn picks up the ring and slides it back onto his finger. "I can play at being Brother Belastra one last time."

"There are swarms of guards downtown today. You don't think they'd come running if there was a disturbance in the hospital?" Alice narrows her eyes.

"If word got out that this medicine existed . . ."

Merriweather offers up a mischievous smile. "There would be a riot. All I'd have to do is suggest it in the *Gazette* and—"

Mei clenches fistfuls of her black skirt. "People are dying. We can't wait for tomorrow's paper!"

Rilla bounces up, a grin spreading across her freckled face. "What if there was another way?" She grabs Merriweather's elbow, her words rushing over themselves. "What if you printed up some leaflets right now?"

"There's still the matter of distributing them," Merriweather says, but his gray eyes are curious. "My newspaper boys can't be seen passing them out on street corners. They'd be arrested."

"What if we used magic?" Rilla kneels, digging through her suitcase until she comes up with a book. She grimaces as she rips out a few pages. "Watch."

We all stare as she casts a silent animation spell, and the torn pages swirl through the air, landing all over the room. "Like that. Only on a much grander scale. Sachi and Rory and I could send them all over the city."

Merriweather picks up the page at his feet, balancing it thoughtfully in his palm. "It could work. Then, on the way out of the hospital, Cate could hand out the medicine to the poor."

"Are you mad?" Finn steps closer to me, protective. "She'll be arrested!"

"Just listen." Merriweather is several inches taller than Finn, but Finn looks half ready for a brawl. "The *Gazette*'s reported that she wasn't responsible for the attack on the Head Council. I painted her as a friend of the powerless, the disenfranchised. What better way to prove it than to have her steal from the rich and give to the poor? She does this, and she wins the loyalty of every family she helps. They'd take a bullet for her."

"They might have to!" Every line of Finn's body is tight with anger. "The minute the guards recognize her, what's to keep them from—"

"I'll do it," I interrupt. "I've already got a price on my head. I might as well make it worth something."

Three hours later, Mei and Finn and I walk to Richmond Hospital. Neither of them are glamoured, but beneath my black hood, my hair is darkened to chestnut, my pointy jaw has gone square, and my eyes are the brilliant green of spring grass. Once I cast the illusion, Alice gave me an appraising look and pronounced me quite pretty.

"Not as pretty as she is without it," Finn insisted, looking affronted on my behalf, and I fell a little more in love with him.

A harsh wind has picked up, and our small white leaflets are scattering like autumn leaves across the cobblestone streets. Children chase after them. Horses mark them with dirty hoofprints. Most important, people are reading them.

"All this folderol about caring for their flock! They don't care one whit about us." A lean blond man shakes the pamphlet in his fist as he leaves a tobacco shop.

"Content to watch us drop like flies, and not doing a thing to stop it," his dark-haired friend agrees.

"Hospitals are meant to care for the sick, ain't they? Not just the rich! Let's go give 'em hell, Jim!" They race ahead, glaring at us as they pass.

The scene outside the hospital is heartbreaking. People beg for the medicine, cradling sick children and citing elderly mothers. The guards remain impervious, insisting that everyone move along, that no secret cure exists. They stand shoulder to shoulder on the sidewalk in front of the hospital, forming a protective barrier that allows no one in or out. Inside, patients and white-capped nurses alike peer out the windows facing the street.

"It's nothing but a hoax," a silver-haired sergeant insists. "That newspaperman trying to stir up trouble again!"

"Let's search the hospital, then!" a thickset woman insists, and the crowd roars its approval.

Another guard snorts. "This is a place for the sick, not a treasure hunt!"

Finn shoulders his way through the crowd. "What's going on here?" he asks pleasantly, shoving his spectacles up with his index finger.

The sergeant sighs as he hands the leaflet to Finn. "Some nonsense about the hospital having a secret stash of medicine. Lord knows how many of these were printed up. I'm afraid we're going to have a mob on our hands soon."

Finn gestures to Mei and me. "I've got two Sisters here to nurse, and I'm supposed to take a shift for Brother Diaz in the chapel. Can we get through?"

The sergeant's blue eyes dart down to Finn's hand, taking note of the silver ring of office on his finger, and then he nods. "Of course, sir. Go on." At his signal, the guards part to let us pass.

Behind us, the crowd hurls epithets.

An orderly unlocks the hospital doors and admits us.

Mei leads the way up the wide staircase. "Kenneally's office is on the fourth floor," she advises, "near the matron's office. We could try there first."

But we only make it to the second-floor landing before a voice rings out. "Mei! Thank the Lord you're here. We're awfully short staffed. Half of my girls are sick and the male nurses are useless. We need you in the men's contagious ward." Mrs. Jarrell eyes Finn. "I'm sorry, sir, but a crisis is no time for excessive modesty."

"I couldn't agree more, ma'am." With his hood down, Finn looks young and boyish. "The three of us are here to help."

"Wonderful." Mrs. Jarrell plunks her hands on her hips. "I hope you'll forgive me for saying it, but we've got plenty of prayer; we need more hands. I don't suppose you'd let me put you to work emptying bedpans?"

Finn gives her his most charming smile. "Perhaps some other time. We've got an errand to run upstairs."

Mrs. Jarrell is unmoved. "I need these girls. People are dying left and right!" She swivels on Mei, the cap she wears over her short brown hair tilting precariously. "Don't tell me you're too shy to care for male patients."

"Course not. I've got a brother at home," Mei insists. "It's only—"

I follow my instincts, stepping closer to the petite nurse. "Do you really want to help people? As many people as possible?" We are alone outside the doors to the female contagious ward.

Mrs. Jarrell nods. "That's my job, isn't it?"

I pull a crumpled leaflet out of my pocket and press it into her hands. "Then how do you reconcile yourself to this? Keeping medicine from the people who need it most?"

She scans the leaflets, then glances up at us. Her eyes linger on Finn. "This is nothing but nonsense. If a cure like that existed—right here in the hospital—I would know about it."

Finn shakes his tousled head. "The Brothers have kept it secret because they don't know when the next shipment will come in from Britain. You know how the fever's been spreading. If four men come down with it, the entire National Council will fall like a stack of dominoes. They're hoarding it all somewhere in the hospital, and Brother Kenneally is doling it out to those with the right connections."

"If that were true"—Mrs. Jarrell shoves her hands in the pockets of her white apron, scowling—"it would be a crime. But I don't understand. Why are *you* telling me this?"

Finn looks only too pleased to shatter his reputation as a devout Brother. "Because I think it's criminal, too, and I want to do something about it. So do Mei and Cate. That's why—" He freezes, realizing what he's said.

Mrs. Jarrell's brown eyes go wide. "Sister Cate?" She takes a step backward, and I wince, hoping my instincts were correct, that I won't have to compel her not to run, not to raise a warning. I *like* this feisty little woman. "That's you? You're the—the witch they've all been talking about?"

"She's the same girl who's been here all week, working right alongside me," Mei says.

"But she attacked the Head Council!"

"No." I raise my chin. "I've never hurt anyone when I

could help it, I swear. I don't mean you any harm. We just want to get the medicine and give it to the people who need it."

Mrs. Jarrell glances between Mei and me. "You knew what she was all along, didn't you? Because you—you're *both* witches. It makes sense now. The ones who recovered faster than the others—you haven't been nursing my patients; you've been healing them!"

"Don't tell anyone. Please," Mei begs, her dark eyes pleading.

Mrs. Jarrell straightens her slim shoulders. "I'll do better than that. Come along. If this cure exists, I'll bet you anything it's in the fourth-floor storeroom."

She leads us upstairs, passing harried nurses and orderlies and the occasional doctor. They all nod at her respectfully, and she sings out cheery greetings, and no one gives us a second glance. We follow her down a warren of twisting white hallways. She stops outside a door with an enormous red-haired chap standing guard outside.

Mrs. Jarrell is nonplussed. "Hello, Willy. Increased security, I see? I suppose it's because of this garbage?" She waves Merriweather's leaflet at him.

"That's it, all right." Willy snorts. "I ain't never heard anything so foolish in all my life. Da's sick, you know. I'd hardly be standing out *here* if there was a cure sitting right in there."

Mrs. Jarrell clucks sympathetically. "I'm awfully sorry to hear about your father. I hope he'll be back on his feet soon." She reaches for the doorknob, but Willy steps in front of her.

"Sorry, ma'am. Got my orders from Brother Kenneally himself not to let anyone in without his say-so."

"Of course." I turn to Finn. "Give him the note."

Finn stares at me blankly. "The note?"

"The note from Brother Kenneally. You put it in your pocket," I remind him.

"That's right." He pulls the leaflet the sergeant gave him from his pocket, and I hide a smile as he reads it. I've glamoured it to look like instructions from Kenneally, counting on the fact that Willy isn't familiar with his handwriting.

Willy squints at the signature at the bottom, flushing, and it occurs to me that the poor man probably can't read. "All right then," he agrees, stepping aside.

The storeroom is a jumble of boxes and bottles and medical equipment.

"What's this?" Mei crows. In the back of the room stands a tall, padlocked metal cabinet. She puts her hand over the lock and it clicks open.

We crowd around her as she removes the lock and opens the door. Inside sit hundreds of small vials of medicine. Each bottle is perhaps three inches tall, stoppered shut with a cork, and looks to contain a few ounces of the same clear liquid.

"Marvelous," I declare.

"Why, those rats!" Mrs. Jarrell mutters. Then she crosses herself, looking worriedly at Finn. "Forgive me, Brother."

"They *are* rats." Finn opens his satchel and begins to stack bottles in it, wrapping them carefully in the linens we borrowed from Alice's house. When he's finished, Mei and I take turns filling our empty bags. Mrs. Jarrell counts each bottle as it's packed.

"Three hundred," she declares as we finish.

I hover with my hand over the zipper. "Do you want to keep a few for your girls?"

"No, dearie." She shakes her head. "They're all good, sturdy girls. Likely they'll be fine. And they know the risks of what we do."

"You're angels, all of you," I proclaim. I remember how powerless I was to help Zara and Brenna and my mother, and imagine facing that with good cheer day after day. "If you ever fall ill yourself, you send for us straightaway."

"That I will." She gives me a quick hug, then flushes, straightening her white cap and apron. "It's a shame you can't work your magic openly. You could save so many lives."

Mrs. Jarrell takes her leave of us on the second floor, grasping my hand and then Mei's in turn. "Bless you, girls," she says, before bustling back to her work.

Downstairs, we peer out the front window at the mob. Its numbers have grown exponentially while we've been inside. People are shouting and pressing against the makeshift wooden barricade the guards have erected. The soldiers look a trifle panicked to be so outnumbered. Though they have guns, they do not seem to be firing them into the crowd. Yet.

Truth be told, it is the guns that worry me most.

Mei will be next to me the whole time. She can heal me if I'm injured.

Not, of course, if I'm shot somewhere crucial. I know all too well that some injuries are stronger than our magic.

"I'd go out the back, sir," the guard says to Finn.

Finn squares his jaw. "I'm not afraid of these people."

The guard shrugs and unbars the door. "It's your funeral."

The crowd turns hateful at the sight of Finn in his black cloak, handsome and strong and healthy. They curse him and surge toward the blockade, and the guards beat them back with truncheons.

"Why should he get medicine when my husband can't? What makes you any better than us?" an old woman shrieks.

"I'm not." Finn pulls off his cloak. He's abandoned his jacket, and his shirtsleeves are rolled up, exposing the freckles on his forearms. He pushes past the astonished guards and vaults over the barricade, then turns to me, looking like the boy who worked in our garden again. "Coming?"

I clamber after him, and he sets me down gently on the other side. Mei hands us our satchels before Finn helps her down.

"What the devil are you doing?" one of the guards yelps. "They'll kill you!"

Finn shoulders his way through the crowd. People throw elbows and tramp on my feet. Someone steps on the back of my cloak and I trip forward, falling into a woman who shoves me back and curses me. I clutch Mei's hand and pull her along after me. Finn turns when we've made it to the middle of the street. His spectacles are crooked and his lip is bleeding where someone hit him, but he's grinning. "Ready?"

"Ready." My heart is racing. When I was up on the barricade, I spotted Sachi, Rory, and Alice at the back of the crowd, ready to help at a moment's notice. Sachi will do an animation spell to keep the front doors of the hospital shut, to prevent the guards inside from coming to the aid of the soldiers outside. But it wouldn't take more than a moment for this crowd to shove me down and trample me. What if my desire to help results in nothing but a passel of broken limbs—or worse?

"The Brothers are lying to you!" Finn shouts, but only the people directly around us can hear over the noise of the mob. He gives me a worried look, wiping the blood from his chin.

"Try again," I urge, and this time I use my magic to amplify his voice so his words boom through the crowd:

"The Brothers are lying to you! The medicine *does* exist. We've seen it, and we think you have a right to it."

That gets the mob's attention. I glance over my shoulder. I can't see most of the guards through the press of people, but one is climbing up on the barricade—presumably to try and hear Finn, or to find out why the crowd is suddenly hushing.

"The Brotherhood is your enemy. Not the witches. Everything the *Sentinel* is saying about Cate Cahill is a lie. She didn't attack the Head Council. She was only saving innocent girls from being locked up in Harwood. Most of those girls weren't even witches, just unlucky. Girls like Prudencia Merriweather, whose only crime was that she didn't give up her brother," Finn says.

"What's this got to do with us?" a bony old woman shouts.

"What about the medicine?" a short Chinese man yells.

"We've got the medicine here. Hundreds of doses of it." Finn raises his satchel, and the crowd presses toward him, pushing, shoving one another, hands grasping at the handle and trying to tear it away from him. Finn spins around, trying to defend himself from every side.

My magic twitches through my fingers at the threat to his safety. I didn't want him putting himself at risk, but he refused to let me do this alone. And—tiresome as it is—I had to admit people would be more willing to listen to a man.

A fat man with a thick walrus mustache grabs Mei's elbow and yanks her toward him, just as I feel a painful grip on my own wrist.

"Let go of me!" Mei cries, and I narrow my eyes at the mustached man and *heave.* My magic pushes everyone around us backward as though they're skating on a frozen pond. They windmill their arms, trying to catch their balance, and fall into each other. It leaves Finn, Mei, and me standing with a foot of empty space around us.

"Don't put your hands on us." I've dropped my illusion, and I am myself: tall, blond, skinny, sharp-jawed. Undeniably the girl whose picture is splashed all over the morning's headlines.

The crowd is gasping, murmuring my name, and then one of the guards fires into the air. One of our friends freezes him like a black-and-gold statue atop the barricade.

"I don't want to hurt anyone," I warn. "If you'll queue up, we'll hand out the medicine. If you push and shove, no one will get any."

"How do we know this ain't a trick? That it ain't poison?" a man asks as I fumble to open my satchel.

Mei already has a vial in her hand. She pops open the cork. "If it were poison, I wouldn't drink it myself, would I?"

she retorts, tilting the bottle to her lips. She makes a ghastly face. "Tastes awful, though. It's better if you put a few drops in your tea."

Mei and I stand back to back, handing out the medicine. Finn hovers a few inches from my elbow. The people reach out gingerly, staring at me as though I'm a two-headed troll, mumbling their thanks and fleeing with vials clutched tightly in their fists. No one violates the barrier of space I've created around us.

I glance up at the barricade. Three guards now stand frozen. Some of the others, including the sergeant, have vaulted over the barricade and are tussling with the crowd.

A woman carrying a roly-poly baby girl in a pink knitted hat is the next person in my line. The baby's chubby cheeks are flushed pink and she squirms restlessly in her mother's arms, trying to escape her blankets, but she doesn't cry. Her blue eyes stare listlessly at the crowd, her breath coming in unhealthy rasps.

"Bless you, miss." The woman cringes as the baby lets out a wet, wheezing cough. "I been at my wits' end with Susannah so sick."

I hesitate. Who knows whether the medicine—made for grown men—is safe for a child that size?

"I could heal her completely. With my magic," I murmur. "If you'll let me touch her?"

The woman hesitates for a moment before moving closer and nodding. I reach out one finger, and the baby curls her fist around it, the way Tess used to do when she was small. Blocking out the sounds of the crowd, I focus on the baby's

297

tortured breath. I can feel the congestion in her tiny lungs, and I push against it. Gradually, her breath eases. Her hot skin cools. I sway on my feet.

"That's enough, Cate," Mei says, voice sharp.

I pull my hand from the baby's grip. She kicks her feet as her mother stares down at her—at the bright curiosity in her eyes, at her plump creamy cheeks—and presses a kiss to her forehead.

The woman presses the vial back into my hands. "Thank you."

I can hear the rasp of her lungs, too. "Keep it for yourself, in case you have need of it next."

"Cate!" Finn shoves me, hard, and I fall backward into Mei, almost toppling us into the crowd. He crouches low and I'm confused, my stomach spinning from the healing, my head pounding, until he draws the pistol from his boot and fires. A guard shouts and drops his rifle, clutching his left shoulder. The guard next to him, swinging a truncheon to clear their way, freezes as a blond man snatches up the rifle and points it at him. Another man pulls the truncheon from the soldier's hands.

"We've got to go. It's not safe anymore." Mei tosses a few more bottles at the crowd and then hands her entire satchel to a skinny woman nearby.

Alice has obviously come to the same conclusion, because as I rise, I notice a strand of black hair falling over my shoulder. My cloak goes blue. I leave my satchel behind.

This time, there's no need to push. The crowd parts to make way for us.

• • •

"That was too close," Finn says, pacing Alice's foyer. "He wasn't going to fire into the air. He was going to shoot you!"

I'm sitting on the bottom step of the staircase. "I'm glad you shot him first, then."

Finn looks a bit frazzled—his shirt untucked at the back, coppery hair standing up even more than usual, lip swollen, and the knuckles of one hand bruised. "I've never shot an actual person before. An actual living human being."

"He'll be all right unless you hit an artery." Mei doesn't sound terribly concerned. "Then he might lose the arm."

"I was aiming for his chest," Finn admits.

"Do you think we've made any difference?" My voice is small as I tuck my arms around my knees. "The way they looked at us—they were *scared* of me."

Finn sits next to me, lacing his fingers through mine. "You were magnificent."

"I was scared silly," I admit, uncurling myself.

"But you did it anyway. That's what bravery is." His thumb strokes the back of mine, and my breath catches. I bring his knuckles to my mouth and press a kiss to the middle one. At my touch, the bruises disappear, and the look he gives me—

It's the way he used to look at me. Before.

"I don't mean to interrupt the celebration, lovebirds, but I've got news," Merriweather says, striding into the front hall.

Finn doesn't let go of my hand. "What now?"

"I thought it strange there weren't more guards at the hospital, fending off the mob, so I called on a source of mine. A footman for the Brothers. After the hanging, he heard

Covington order most of the guards pulled from their patrols and sent to the river district." The line of Merriweather's broad shoulders is stiff; his usual elegant slouch is gone.

"Perhaps they're worried about a riot, once more people find out about the cure," Finn suggests.

I stare at the flickering light of the blue glass lamp. Something about this doesn't make sense. "But it sounds like Covington gave the order *before* they saw our leaflets."

"Turns out they're setting up barricades all along Prince, Munroe, and Fifty-Seventh. Cordoning off the whole district." Merriweather sketches three sides of a rectangle in the air. The river itself would make up the fourth.

Rilla pops out of the parlor. "Do you think they're setting up a quarantine?" She hands me a cup of steaming tea.

"It's a little late for that now. The fever's all over the city," Mei mumbles between the hairpins in her teeth. She's twisting her hair up in a chignon in front of the silver mirror.

"Another of my sources, enterprising soul that he is, saw a caravan of army wagons pass the barricades and followed one. Knew I'd pay him for good information with good coin," Merriweather says. "They stopped at a warehouse down by the port."

"What were they carrying?" Finn asks.

Merriweather paces the hall, his boots echoing against the wooden floors. "Turpentine and kerosene, supposedly. Do you think they're hiding the rest of the cure in the barrels?"

"No, if they were going to take it out of the hospital, they'd want it somewhere close at hand, near the city center." Mei skewers pins through her black hair.

Rilla frowns, smoothing her yellow dress. "Dozens of people are dying every day. Shouldn't the Brothers concern themselves with how to stop the fever? They haven't even told people to take basic precautions."

"I have. Stay inside if you can; cover your face and wash your hands if you can't."

"Boil your clothes," I add, remembering how Mei boiled our dresses each night when we got home from the hospital. "Or burn them. During the influenza outbreak when I was little, my mother went out to nurse and came home and burnt her dress in the kitchen fireplace."

Finn's hand flexes, squeezing mine painfully. "Do you remember the Bowers? No, you would have been too young, probably—but their whole family came down with the flu. All the servants, too. They all died. Later, the Brothers sent guards in with barrels of kerosene and burnt the farmhouse to the ground. Said it was cursed with the contagion."

"Do you suppose the Brothers intend to burn the dead? That could account for all the wagons," Mei suggests.

Finn's forehead rumples. "They wouldn't need to set up a quarantine for that, or keep it a secret."

"Good Lord." I drop my teacup, and it shatters, shards flying across the wooden floor. The tea soaks my skirt and scalds my knees. I stare into Finn's brown eyes, horrified. "What if it's not the dead they're after? What if the Brothers are going to burn the river district with the sick people in it?"

CHAPTER
19

"THE BROTHERS?" MEI ASKS. "OR INEZ?"

No one suggests that I'm wrong, or that she would be incapable of such cruelty.

Finn shoots to his feet, ignoring the crunch of broken china. "No one will suspect she's behind it. If Covington's ordered the guards to burn the river district, everyone will blame the Brothers. Between this and hoarding the cure, it could start a civil war."

Merriweather stuffs his hands in the pockets of his olive peacoat. "But the Brothers will only claim Covington's gone mad—that he came back wrong—and toss him out of office. She'll lose control of the city."

Rilla kneels to clean up the shards of china. "What kind of person tries to set a fire and barricade people inside?"

"The same kind who'd let dozens of innocent

girls hang because it interfered with her plans." I'm pacing around the hall, heedless of my wet skirts.

Mei slides on her black cloak. "We have to stop this."

Merriweather runs a hand over his square jaw, thoughtful. "Can we enlist the guard?"

"We're witches, and progressives, *and* fugitives!" Rilla gives him an exasperated look. "We can't go strolling up to the master of the guard and expect him to believe Covington's being compelled. Besides, even if they knew what was happening, are you sure the guards would try to stop it? You should hear the way they talk about river rats."

I put up a hand to stop Merriweather's rebuttal. He and Rilla would argue all day if we let them. "We can't rely on the guards. For all we know, Inez has compelled them, too. We have to stop this ourselves."

"How do you plan to do that?" Merriweather snaps. "The people wouldn't believe us if we told them to evacuate on such flimsy evidence. And we don't even know where to start in terms of stopping the fires. We could search all the warehouses, but that would take forever; there are dozens of them."

Mei frowns. "I don't know that we can stop the guards from setting fires if that's what Inez has compelled them to do. But we can use magic to put them out."

Finn pulls back the curtains and gazes out at the inky sky. It's only half past five, but it's December; the sun has already set, and wind sends the trees in the front yard whipping against the windows. "They'll wait until people are in for the night. The fire will spread quicker if there are only a few night watchmen to see it."

"The wind's kicked up something fierce." Mei pulls up her hood. "Fire in three or four warehouses could take down half the city on a night like this."

Merriweather's jaw goes tight. "Prue's down there." Alice, Prue, Sachi, and Rory took the rest of the medicine in Finn's satchel and went to call on some families that Alice and I often visit on Sisterly missions of charity.

"My family's not far from the river district, either." Mei opens the front door and shivers against the sharp wind.

"Let's hire a hack to take us there first. *They'll* believe us," Merriweather says.

Rilla blows out the lamp. "I'll go to the convent and see if I can rouse more girls to help. Once those fires start, we'll need all the magic we can muster."

I've stopped stock-still in the process of putting on my own cloak. "Where is the Golden Hart?"

Merriweather sputters. "What do you know of the Golden Hart?"

"That's where my father's hiding." I swallow. "It's by the river, isn't it?"

Merriweather nods. "Attracts all the sailors that way. Situated in a plum spot between a tavern and a—" His voice drops. "A cotton warehouse."

Finn takes my hand again, sensing my distress. "I'll see you safely to the convent and then I'll go find your father."

The notion of them both being at risk sets my stomach tumbling. I make a silent vow to myself: When this is over, Inez will never put anyone I love in danger ever again. I don't care what I've got to do to ensure it.

• • •

The hack stops outside the convent and Rilla clambers down before the wheels have even stopped turning. Finn tugs on my wrist, pulling me down for a quick, hard kiss. Behind his spectacles, his brown eyes are worried. "Be careful, Cate."

"You too." I want to ask him to wait, not to go down to the river without me, but I can't tie him to my apron strings. He may not have my strength, but he has his own. He is still my clever, resourceful Finn. "I'm sorry I've gotten you mixed up in all of this."

"Don't be." He shakes his head. "If it weren't for you, I wouldn't be able to help change things. I'm making a difference, Cate. That's worth a lot."

I hesitate, but I have to say it. Just in case. I brush a hand over his stubbled cheek. "I love you."

I step down to the carriage block without waiting for an answer. He can't say it back. He doesn't mean it. Not yet. Three weeks ago I didn't think anything could be worse, and now—

Well, things can always get worse, can't they?

As I step onto the sidewalk, I give a laugh as bitter as any of Rory's.

There are two lonely guards patrolling the marble steps of the Sisterhood. They raise their rifles as I sweep toward them with eyes narrowed. "Go away, and don't come back here tonight," I snap as Finn's carriage rolls away.

They turn, ambling down the street obediently. Rilla is already pushing the front door open. She rushes down the hall toward the sitting room, which should be chock-full of girls studying and chatting before supper.

305

"Where's Inez?" Rilla demands.

"Lord knows. Not here," Vi says. "Have you been to see Cate? How is she?"

"I'm here." My entrance is received with both glares and cheers.

"What are you doing here? Haven't you made enough trouble already?" Parvati seems to have taken possession of Alice's queen-bee spot on the pink love seat.

"Oh, I'm only starting to make trouble," I declare, pulling off my hood.

Tess rushes at me, throwing her arms around my waist, burying her face in my hair. I pull back and look at her: really look. We've only been apart for two days, but it seems forever, and I see her with new eyes. She's grown thinner. Her new curves and the rosy flush of her cheeks are both gone; there are purple shadows beneath her eyes. Even her blond curls seem lifeless. My baby sister looks *haunted*.

"I heard about the vision you had," I tell her. Tess shrinks away. "The one about fire and death. It wasn't a nightmare; it was a prophecy. Inez is going to try to burn the river district."

Maura stands, resplendent in an ivory gown embroidered with green leaves. "That's nonsense."

"They set up a quarantine this afternoon, and guards were seen carrying turpentine and kerosene into warehouses down by the river. She's the one giving orders, isn't she?" I search Maura's face, but she looks genuinely shocked by this turn of events. "She's going to make it look like the Brothers murdered the people in their beds to prevent the fever from spreading."

Whispers hum and buzz through the room.

"She'll kill thousands of people." Tess is trembling, pressing a hand to her temples. "I thought it was just a nightmare. I should know the difference by now."

Lucy is sitting on an ottoman at her sister's feet. "It's not your fault." Grace's knitting needles never pause.

"I should know the difference," Tess repeats, her voice anguished. "I should have been able to warn everyone. I—I just haven't been feeling *myself* lately."

"This is going too far, even for Inez." Maura's blue eyes dart around the room, searching out allies, but no one else speaks. It is telling, I think, that not a single other person— not any of the teachers leaning in the doorway, not even old Sister Evelyn—leaps to Inez's defense. "It's got to be something else."

"She's ruthless, Maura. It's past time you admitted it." Elena wraps an arm around Maura's waist to soften her words.

"We need to get down there. We might be too late to stop the fires from being set, but we can help keep them from spreading." Rilla's voice is crisp, without her usual bounciness. "Alice and Mei and Sachi and Rory have already gone."

"I'll tell Father to get the horses ready," Vi says, scrambling from the room.

"We'll have to work in teams of two or three." Elena smooths her pink silk dress. "That area isn't safe for girls alone at night."

"Safe?" Genie echoes. "You're asking us to do magic in public. We'll all be arrested. Or murdered!"

"I don't think so. I think the people—especially the working-class people who live down by the river—are sick of the Brothers. It's a risk, certainly." I lift my chin. "I'm willing to take it. We're powerful. It's time we stopped hiding it."

"Hear, hear!" A grin spreads over Elena's face as she turns to Maura. "Be on my team?"

Maura pulls away, scowling. "No. I'm going to the council building, and I'm going to get the truth of it from Inez. She wouldn't do this. I know she wouldn't."

My stomach sinks as Maura stalks out of the room, but I don't go after her. Neither does Elena. "What about you, Parvati? Are you coming?" I ask.

Parvati rises from the love seat, her brown eyes enormous in her thin face. "My grandmother lives down there. It's one thing to target the Brothers, but if Inez is the sort of person who would burn an old woman alive . . ." She swallows hard. "Well, then I was wrong about her."

All around me, girls are stepping into their boots or rushing to fetch them. I look for Tess, to tell her Finn has gone to warn Father, and I realize she's gone. Out in the hall, Sister Gretchen is organizing the teachers and governesses into teams to lead the younger students. Unlike the Harwood mission, there's no talk of leaving anyone behind. Tonight, we will need the full might of the Sisterhood.

I peer into the front hall, where girls are pulling on their cloaks. No Tess. Perhaps she went upstairs for her mittens? I hope she hasn't gone chasing after Maura.

Pausing near the parlor, I hear a tiny, strangled sob from within.

It's not Tess, but I go in, closing the door behind me. "Lucy? Are you all right?"

Lucy raises her blotchy, tearstained face. "No. I'm a terrible wicked girl, Cate."

I haven't time for this, but I can't walk away from a crying child.

I perch next to her on the olive settee. "Are you scared? You and Bekah can go with Sister Gretchen or one of the other teachers. They won't let anything bad happen to you."

Lucy lets out another wail. "S-stop being so nice to me. I don't deserve it!"

I stifle my impatience. "Lucy, it's perfectly all right to be frightened." I remember Finn's words from earlier. "Being brave is when you're frightened but you do something anyway, because it's the right thing to do."

She wipes her nose on her sleeve. She is all brown today—a chocolate wool dress and big brown bows tying her caramel braids—like a plump little sparrow. "I've got to tell you the truth, then. Even though it will make you hate me," she says, meeting my eyes. "I'm the one who's been haunting Tess."

I go very still. My hand—just inches from Lucy's knee—freezes. "Explain."

Her eyes fall to the brown carpet. "I cast illusions to make her see and hear things that weren't there. Cyclops hanging from the curtain rod in her room. Her bed on fire. Blood on her dress. The funeral dirge. The—the kitten."

She sniffles, wiping away fresh tears, but all my sympathy has vanished. "Why?" My hand has clenched into a fist.

Lucy is only twelve, I remind myself.

But so is Tess.

Tess, who's been terrified that her worst fears were coming true.

"Why would you do that?" I demand.

"Inez said if I didn't, she'd turn Grace over to the Brothers and they'd hang her," Lucy whispers. "I—I couldn't let that happen. I'm sorry, Cate! I never wanted to hurt you, or Tess."

My anger hardens into something bright and icy. So much for Inez's oath to Maura that she would never hurt Tess.

"Why those *particular* illusions?" My voice is a little softer. Only a little.

Lucy fidgets. I reach out and snatch her chin, wet with tears, and turn her face toward me. My fingers are not gentle. She chokes on another sob. "Tess had a vision!" she blurts out. "About you. She had a vision that she was going to—to hurt you."

The realization slams into me, knocking the breath from my body. Like being run down by a carriage.

"Tess had a vision that she was going to kill me."

My voice is dull, but I feel almost relieved.

I don't want to die. There are loads of things I want to do first. Small things, like planting roses, or seeing the finished gazebo on the hill near Mother's grave, or beating Mei at a game of chess. Big things, like hearing Finn say he loves me again, and marrying him, and having a house of our own.

Becoming a mother. Practicing magic openly. Seeing Tess and Maura grow up into beautiful, clever, strong women.

Only—we can't all three grow up, can we?

Not according to the prophecy.

Perhaps it's good to finally know the truth of it.

"Yes," Lucy says softly. "It broke her heart. She couldn't understand how she would ever do it, unless—"

"Unless she was mad." I take a deep breath. "And you told Inez, and she decided to use that against Tess. To make her think her worst fears were coming true. You're her best friend, Lucy! She trusted you with her greatest secret."

"I know." Lucy begins to cry again. "I'm sorry."

"It's not me you need to apologize to." I stand. "Do you know where she is?"

"Sh-she went to the bell tower, to ring the fire alarm." Lucy buries her face in her dimpled hands.

The bell tower is atop the National Council building— where every guard has no doubt been ordered to memorize our pictures and arrest us on sight. I pray Tess has the sense to use a glamour.

"Why would she do that?" I demand. "Why would she go by herself?"

"B-because I told her to," Lucy admits, her words muffled by her hands. "Sh-she felt like it was all her fault. I said she could help make it right."

I grab her by the shoulders and shake her. "Inez asked you to do that, too, didn't she? Why?" I let her go and back away before I'm tempted to shake the answers right out of her.

"I don't know!" Lucy yelps. She's stopped crying, but she

looks terrified of me. "Inez said—she said this was the last thing she'd ask me to do. She promised!"

"Good. Because if you ever do anything to hurt Tess again, you will answer to me, and I will see you and Grace both put on a prison ship for the rest of your miserable lives. Do you understand?" I glare at Lucy until she nods, and then I pull open the door. "Go tell Rilla everything you've told me. *Now.* And tell her I'm going after Tess."

It's surprisingly easy to gain access to the council building. There are precious few guards on duty tonight. As I wait for the elevator, I hear the fire bell begin to peal, piercing even from this distance. A man racing down the curving marble staircase gives me an odd look. I press a hand to my face, reassuring myself that my glamour hasn't given way. But this is an easy illusion. Brother Ishida's face is one I know well; it's haunted my nightmares since I was a child. I step onto the newfangled brass elevator, and in a few moments, it cranks and clanks its way to the ninth floor. The heavy door that leads up to the bell tower is locked, but my magic makes short work of it. I open it and climb the spiral staircase beyond.

The tower is open on all four sides to the elements. In the center, high above me, the enormous cast-iron bell hangs from a beam right below the steeply pitched roof. Despite the fierce gusts of wind that send clouds scurrying over the moon, the great bell has gone still. Has Tess already left?

A lantern sits on the brick floor, casting a small circle of light among the shadows. It's the only clue that she's been here.

To the west, fire is already blazing on the horizon.

I hurry to the low wrought-iron fence, trying to get a better look, but it's impossible to tell anything from so far away. It could be one fire; it could be half a dozen.

Damn Inez.

I've got to find Tess and get to the river district.

"Tess?" My voice is swallowed up by the night.

"I'm here." Her voice is so close behind me that I jump.

I whirl around. "What are you doing?"

"Waiting for you," she says.

There's something in her voice—something *off*.

I take a few steps forward. The hair on the nape of my neck prickles, as if my body can sense danger before I can.

I should not be here.

The wind sends my cloak flapping like the wings of a great black bird. I've hardly braced myself against it before I'm pitched backward.

I fling out my arms, grasping, trying to catch hold of something, anything. There's nothing within reach. My boots slide across the brick floor without gaining purchase. I throw myself forward, but it doesn't work. An invisible hand is pushing on my chest, shoving me toward the edge and the ten-story drop to the street below.

I scream as my thighs bump into the wrought-iron railing behind me.

"No! Tess, help me!"

But she doesn't. She can't.

Tess is the one trying to kill me.

CHAPTER
20

IT ALL HAPPENS SO QUICKLY. I HIT THE railing and begin to fall.

My eyes never leave Tess's, but her gaze is no longer hers. I have the eerie sense of Inez peering out at me, cold and uncaring and *triumphant*.

The prophecy is coming true, and I am going to die.

I want more time.

Another scream claws its way out of my throat. There are no words this time, just inchoate rage.

Someone grabs my wrist and yanks me forward. I fall to my knees, scraping my palms against the brick. Opening my eyes, I see my sister's face: bright and beautiful and *furious*.

Maura.

Across the tower, Tess lies in a heap of black skirts. As I watch, she pushes herself to her feet, smoothing her cloak calmly, meticulously, as though I haven't just narrowly avoided death at her hands.

I am shuddering, shaking, sick.

"Tess. Look at me." Maura strides forward, trying to snag her attention, to distract her from the task Inez has set her.

But Tess has always been extraordinarily focused. I am pushed slowly, inexorably backward. I scramble to my knees and grab the cold iron railing with both hands, curling my fingers around it as tight as I can.

Maura tosses Tess through the air again. Tess's small body crumples as it hits the door that leads downstairs. "Don't hurt her!" I cry.

"She's trying to kill you!" Maura snaps, pulling me to my feet.

Tess struggles up and stalks forward like a small blond wolf hunting her prey. Maura turns to me, her face full of panic, and it's obvious that her magic isn't working this time.

I try an immobilizing spell, with no effect.

Our sister is strong. The strongest witch in all of New England.

Maura thrusts her hand into mine. I press my skin against hers, merging our power. Magic crackles through me like lightning as Maura casts and Tess flies through the air a third time.

"Stay down," Maura commands. "Inez has gotten inside your head. You've got to fight. You're stronger than her, Tess. You're stronger than anybody."

It's a desperate admission, coming from Maura.

Tess sits up, and something overhead cracks. Maura and

I look up into the bell tower in time to see two massive bolts pop free and clatter to the ground. Tess is trying to unlatch the beam that holds the bell in place. If it falls, it will crush us.

Maura clutches my hand again. Tess rises to her feet, her lips pursed in concentration.

"Intransito," I cast, and she freezes.

Maura sags in relief, looking up at the bell.

I step closer to Tess, careful to keep some distance between us, half afraid she might reach out and snap my neck. Only her gray eyes move, darting here and there. "Tess," I say, voice gentle.

Then there's a noise—a huge, terrifying crack—and I whirl around to see the slim white spire of Richmond Cathedral falling right toward us.

All I can think is that Tess, unable to move, will be crushed. I cast silently, freeing her, just as Maura tumbles into me, shoving me toward the door.

Then something smacks into my shoulders, and I trip forward.

Everything goes black.

I don't know if it's been two minutes or two hours.

Something heavy lies across my back, pinning me to the floor. My left cheek is pressed into the brick. The floor is covered with rubble. Nearby, something shifts and dust scatters through the air. I cough.

"Cate?" It's Maura's voice, hoarse but alive.

"I'm here." I try to move my arms, but I can't. Pain stabs

through my left shoulder and splinters down my arm and I bite back a cry. I concentrate on the weight across my back. Try to move it. My magic feels far off, overwhelmed by pain and the nausea spinning my stomach. I cast again, focusing with all my might, and the weight lifts and shifts and I roll to the right, out from beneath it. This time I can't help the whimper that escapes my lips. My left arm is definitely broken.

"I can't move." Maura again.

"I'm coming." I scramble to my knees, ignoring the wave of dizziness that threatens to drag me under again, and search the rubble for my sister.

My heart sinks when I see her.

Just a glimpse of bright curls beneath a pile of brick and stone and splintered wood. I crawl over the debris to reach her, heedless of the shredded skin on my palms. Warmth trickles over my cheek and I swipe it away and it stains my fingers red. I use a combination of magic and sheer will-power to lift the bit of roof that's hiding Maura, hoping against hope that beneath it she'll be uninjured and—

No. I press my fingers to my lips.

Maura lies on her back, her right side still trapped beneath an enormous wooden beam. Her heart-shaped face is dusty, save a clean trail at the corner of each eye. There's a gruesome cut across her right cheekbone, and her right collarbone— clavicle, I correct myself, from my anatomy lessons—has punctured through her skin and the ivory fabric of her dress.

"I'm here." I collapse at her good side. "It will be all right.

I'll heal you." I reach out and touch her chin with my fingertips.

I almost jerk away as I feel her injuries. Her collarbone I could fix, but that's not the worst of it: shattered humerus and radius, broken right femur. I can't tell about her spine; her stomach is a haze of red that indicates broken ribs. Has one of them punctured her lung?

I can't kill again. I cannot kill my sister, not even to ease her suffering.

Please, Lord, don't ask that of me.

Her hand wiggles out from beneath her cloak and clasps mine. "Does it hurt very much?" I ask.

Her voice is a dreamy wheeze. "It did, but not anymore. Now I can't feel anything." Her grip is weak. Her hand slips away. "I think I'll be all right. Just need a little nap."

"No! Stay awake, Maura. Where's Tess?" I glance around wildly. "She'll—*together*, we can—"

"Gone when I woke up." Maura's fingers clutch at my black skirt. "I—was wrong. About Inez."

I smile through my tears. "You saved my life, silly. Don't worry about that."

"You were wrong, too." She's as stubborn as ever. "About Elena. She's *good*. Makes me want to be—better."

"You're already the best." I capture her hand again. "If Merriweather gets his triumvirate government, Elena won't just lead the Sisterhood. She'll help govern all of New England."

Her breath rattles. "She'll like that."

Maura's blue eyes flutter closed, and I grab her hand

318

tighter. Her pain is fading as her body shuts down. "I love you!"

I lean over her. Her voice is threadbare; I feel the words against my cheek more than I hear them. "Love you too, Cate."

My tears fall onto her chest. "Don't die. Please don't die." But she can't hear me.

My little sister—who used to toddle after me, stuffing my toys into her mouth; who used to hide romance novels under her floorboards; who had the most beautiful laugh in the world—is dead, and I won't ever laugh with her again.

For a while I just sit there with her. I'm not certain how long. The clouds move over the moon. My arm throbs, and the back of my head aches, but it's nothing compared to the hurt in my chest. I don't know why I'm trying to keep the tears back. There's no one here to see me. Eventually I stop fighting them. Racking sobs trail into quiet tears that wend a stinging path over my raw cheeks.

Eventually, something shifts above me, sending dust and bits of rubble raining down. I look up at the part of the cathedral spire that's still wedged precariously against the bell tower. I suppose the roof could fall in at any moment, but I cannot bear the idea of leaving Maura alone on this cold rooftop.

I was supposed to die, not her. That's what Tess's vision foretold.

Except—it's impossible to change the future, isn't it?

What did Tess really see in her vision?

I've spared little thought for her, but now I wonder where she went, and why. Did she think she'd accomplished Inez's task when she saw me lying amid the rubble? If she's herself again, free of Inez's compulsion, she must be racked with guilt. Did she think Maura and I were both dead? How else could she have left us? If Tess hadn't gone, perhaps—

I stop that thought before it starts. Maura's injuries were too grave. And if Tess were here, likely she would still be trying to murder me.

Inez.

Inez is the one responsible for this, not Tess.

I let go of Maura's hand, which has grown cold. Her red curls have fallen out of their perfect pompadour. I tuck one behind her small seashell ear. She's wearing the pearl earrings she stole from me weeks ago. I like the thought that something of mine will stay with her. When I bring my hand to my mouth, I find a trace of her sweet citrusy scent, from the lemon verbena she always dabs at her throat and wrists.

I struggle to my feet, head spinning, and that's when I see the red blazing on the horizon. The fire—fires?—are burning higher and hotter than they were before, and I suddenly remember the other people that I care about. Finn is down there. My father. My friends.

I can't lose anyone else tonight.

I begin to pick my way across the rubble toward the door. My arm hurts with every small movement; it's hard to keep it from being jostled. I bend down and rip at my petticoat. The thin cotton tears easily enough. I knot it into a sort of makeshift sling around my neck and slide my wounded arm into it, gasping at the pain. This would be easier if I could heal myself, but healing magic doesn't work that way.

At the door, I pause and look over my shoulder. It's not really Maura anymore, I remind myself. Her sense of humor, her ferocious temper, her desperate desire to be loved— everything that made her Maura—those things are already gone. I'm not leaving her. It was the other way around. She's gone ahead of me, into a place I can only wonder about, and she won't be alone there. She'll have Brenna and Zara and Mother.

Tears slip over my cheeks again. I want my mother. Want someone to hold me and stroke my hair and whisper that it will be all right.

But I'm not a child anymore, and even if someone told me that, I wouldn't believe it.

Tonight feels like a crucible.

Before, with Maura.

And *after,* without.

The council building seems to have been evacuated. Everything is still and silent as I make my way downstairs. Outside, I glance up at the cathedral's broken spire, wedged mid-fall against the bell tower. Eventually, I suppose gravity will do its work, and it will all come tumbling down. It's for the best that there isn't a crowd here gawking.

The heart of the city has an eerie, abandoned quality. Only a single lanky guard patrols the sidewalk in front of Richmond Square. He hastens over when he sees me.

"Sister, what are you doing? Didn't you hear the evacuation order?" He takes in my bedraggled state as he draws on his cigarette. "Were you hurt in the accident?"

"I'll be all right." I smile through gritted teeth. "I'm looking for Sister Inez."

His breath fogs the cold air. "She took a carriage down to the river district. Heard her talking about a fire that might disrupt the quarantine. Most of the guard was sent down to barricade the river district this afternoon." He gives me a patronizing smile, though he can't be much older than me. "I say, keep the river rats where they belong. Keep 'em from spreading disease to the quality."

And I suppose he thinks *he's* an instance of quality. I make a low, noncommittal noise at the back of my throat. "Have you seen a little blonde? Another convent girl? We were separated in all the confusion."

He nods. "She asked after Sister Inez, too. Seemed awful upset. I offered to fetch her a hack, but she didn't want help. Can I get one for you?"

So Tess went after Inez on foot. If I go by carriage, perhaps I can overtake her.

"No, thank you. I can manage." I walk two blocks uptown, where carriages and wagons are rattling past. A hired hack trots past and I flag it down. A lady would never ride in one alone, but I'm well past worrying about being a proper young lady. "Could you take me to the river district, please? To the Golden Hart?"

The mustachioed driver looks askance at me, and I'm not certain whether it's because I've asked him to take me to a house of ill repute or because I've got a broken arm, a cloak covered in dust, a scraped-up cheek, and swollen eyes. Possibly both.

"River district's closed off, miss. Quarantined. And there's a fire at one of them big warehouses near the Golden Hart. Can I take you somewhere else?" The big bay snorts and paws at the ground restlessly, and I wonder if he can smell smoke on the wind.

"Just take me as far as you can in that direction. I'll walk the rest of the way."

"Are—are you sure you don't want to go to the hospital, miss?" The driver's brown eyes are worried.

"Quite sure. Just as near as you can get me to the river district." I half climb, half fall into the carriage.

I will see to it that Father and Finn are all right, and then I will find Inez. It's well past time for us to have a reckoning.

The carriage pulls up in front of a row of houses on Fifty-Sixth Street. Ahead of us, an army wagon blocks the way to Fifty-Seventh. I climb down and hand the driver coins, but he waves them away.

"Can you tell me how to get to the Golden Hart?" I ask, pulling my tattered hood up over my hair.

His olive skin flushes. "It's down by the river, miss. River and Seventy-Second. But that's right where the fire is."

I thank him and hurry toward the barricade. The air smells of smoke—not the pleasant smell of wood smoke from the chimneys, or the waxy smoke of a candle, but something heavier, more acrid, and more dangerous.

Behind the wagon, the barricades have been knocked down. So much for the supposed quarantine. I spot two guards who've been immobilized. They stand at the checkpoint, hands clenched around missing rifles and truncheons. Witches have been here.

As I make my way into the river district, people flood past me in the opposite direction. Mothers carry frightened children; fathers lug suitcases full of valuables. People on foot hurry alongside those on horseback, choking the narrow streets and making it near impossible for wagons to pass. Several carriages sit abandoned in the middle of the street. The sidewalks are littered with dropped toys and clothing and pots and pans. Above it all, smoke clouds the air, and to the west, orange flames leap into the night sky.

I've walked half a dozen blocks when I encounter the first fire. Two city blocks lie smoking, reduced to rubble. A line of firemen directs water from three steaming fire engines onto the ashes, trying to prevent the sparks from reigniting. One block has been utterly flattened, so much that I can't tell what the buildings once were. In the second block, a row of brick chimneys still remains—and at the nearest corner, one brick edifice, toothless and eerie without its windows and doors.

How many fires were set? How many lives have already been lost? I hasten my pace, heedless of the pain in my arm and the now constant throbbing of my skull. I pray that down by the river, the firemen and the witches are working together peacefully. What if I was wrong and the people don't want our help?

I'm three blocks nearer the river, walking up Bramble Hill, when I hear an explosion. People around me scream and point wildly, and I follow their fingers just in time to see the great wooden water tower at the top of the hill crack wide open and water flood out.

The way it breaks—that isn't the work of firemen. That's magic.

As I get nearer, the gutters run with water and my boots sink in the mud of the streets. Bramble Hill is the highest elevation in the river district, just before the streets slope down toward the river. Several ramshackle tenement buildings sat right below the water tower on overgrown lots choked with weeds. On our Sisterly missions to the poor, Mei and Alice and I visited families in some of those buildings. Two and three generations lived crammed together in little two-room flats with no heat and rags stuffed into the cracked windowpanes to keep out the wind. Now the buildings are nothing but charred, blackened wood. Smoke pours off the remains and water rushes downhill, flooding several more blocks.

At the bottom of the hill, several buildings are in states of partial collapse. People hang out second-story windows and climb onto porch roofs, crying for rescue. I spot Vi's father, Robert, shouldering his way into a small clapboard house. Vi and two other witches stand in the street next to a wagon, and as I watch, two toddlers float off a porch roof, away from their astonished mother, and safely into the back of the wagon.

No one objects to the witchery. No one attacks the girls

openly doing magic in the street. I pause for a moment, warring with my conscience, but it seems as though Vi and the others are doing well enough. The fire here has been quenched. I hurry on.

As I near River Street, the scene takes on an increasingly nightmarish cast. Two hulking warehouses, several blocks apart, are on fire. Sparks arc out over the river like fireflies. Flaming bits of docks bob on the water alongside pieces of ruined ships. Down the street in each direction, fire brigades pass buckets and fire engines hiss, but these blocks in the middle seem to have been abandoned.

Even from across River Street, the smoke is choking, and the heat makes it feel like June instead of December. As I near the intersection with Seventy-Second, my heart pounds. The fire has already eaten away at the entire block of shipping offices and taverns and the inn. I watch, coughing, as a roof collapses with a shower of sparks.

This is where the Golden Hart was.

A girl dashes past, dressed in the black cloak of the Sisterhood. Her hood is down, and I recognize the fuzzy black braids wound around her head. "Daisy?"

Daisy Reed—Bekah's older sister—whirls at the sound of my voice. "Cate?"

I join her, lengthening my stride to match hers. Daisy was part of the Harwood mission. She would know Finn by sight. "My father was staying down here at the Golden Hart, and my—Finn came to warn him. Do you know if everyone got out of these buildings in time?"

"I think so. Rilla and some of the others tried to stop the

fire here, but it was impossible. That was a lumberyard, and it went right up." Daisy gestures to the smoldering lot between this block and the warehouse ahead, then jerks a thumb over her shoulder. "I saw Finn with a group of Brothers working for the fire brigade. The fire's been contained down by the train depot; we're all moving this way."

"There are Brothers down here helping?" I ask, astonished, and Daisy nods. At least Finn is all right. I proceed to the next worry. "Have you seen Tess?"

Daisy shakes her head. "Maybe she's with Bekah and Lucy. I'm going to look for Bekah now. They were paired up with Sister Gretchen, but I heard Gretchen got shot by a guard."

We're passing the second warehouse. The roof has collapsed; flames leap from the debris and have spread to the shipyard in the next block. Out on the river, ships in various stages of construction have been set loose. There is a terrible beauty in the flaming skeletons of those still on the dry docks.

Across the street, a row of witches—Sister Mélisande, old Sister Edith, and two of the governesses—stand with their hands linked as they direct the wind out to sea instead of inland. Firemen train their hoses on the tenement houses across River Street from the shipyard. The bucket brigade is hard at work, scooping water near the docks. And at the end of the longest pier, two figures gesture angrily. One is Elena, and the other—

Even this far away, I can make out Inez's hawkish profile.

The image of Maura, lying pale and broken beneath the rubble, flashes through my mind.

I barrel toward Inez.

CHAPTER
21

IF I STILL HARBORED ANY DOUBTS about whether I am capable of murder, they are dismissed.

I would use the strength of my own arms or any magic at my disposal to do it. I don't care if all of New London witnesses Inez's death at my hands.

I push past the men filling buckets at the edge of the river. The clatter of my boots on the long wooden pier is lost in the shouts of the fire brigade and the roar of the flames and the hiss of the hoses.

I'm still three yards away when magic explodes from my body. Inez staggers back toward the edge of the pier and the six-foot drop to the water below. At the last moment, she catches herself on a wooden piling and turns. When she sees me, her brown eyes go wide with shock, but she recovers quickly.

"This is all your fault," she seethes, and her

ability to playact, to manipulate the situation, hardens my resolve. "Exposing us like this? How *dare* you take such a step without consulting me."

"How dare *you* act as though you didn't try to have my own sister murder me!" I shout.

Elena freezes, then swipes black curls away from her face. "Maura?"

Pain seizes through me at the sound of her name, at the knowledge that I won't ever call it and hear her respond. Such a small thing. "Tess."

Inez turns to Elena. "This is nonsense. Tess has been unstable. Everyone's seen that. She's going mad, like Brenna Elliott. I've got nothing to do with it."

"Liar." I push her backward again, but this time she anticipates my attack and doesn't move. "Lucy told me the truth. You threatened her into tormenting Tess. Then, when you'd convinced Tess she was going mad, you compelled her to kill me. Aren't you the one who's been saying she's a *child*? She's twelve years old!"

Elena folds her arms over her chest. Despite her tiny stature, she radiates power. "Is this true?"

Inez throws up her hands. "Cate has been a liability from the moment she set foot in the convent. Tess had a vision she would kill her sister. It was inevitable. The prophecies are never false."

"But oracles can be mistaken." Tess has crept up behind us. I spin around, establishing a wary distance, but her stormcloud eyes are hers again. Right now they're wide with wonderment. "You were so still, Cate. You didn't move when I called you. I thought you were dead. It was just like my vision; I thought I'd killed you." She reaches out, as if to reassure herself I'm not a ghost, and I let her touch me.

"No." My voice chokes a little, thinking of Maura, how she saved me. "I'm alive."

Tess whirls on Inez, her blond curls flying out behind her. "Stay out of my head, Inez," she hisses. "I can feel you poking around, looking for a way in. I will never attack my sister again. If you know what's good for you, neither will you."

Inez's mouth twists. "Listen to the child! Do you think I'm frightened of you? You were so easy to manipulate. So easily frightened. So *weak*."

"Weak?" Tess frowns, and quick as that, Inez tumbles backward with a splash.

She paddles frantically to keep herself above the waves, but each time she reaches toward the dock, the waves push her back and Tess dunks her and she comes up choking.

"I could keep this up for *days*," Tess says, and there's something new and vengeful in her voice. "I daresay your arms would give out before my magic does."

"Tess," Elena reproaches.

Inez's chin has sunk below the water now, the weight of her boots and heavy skirts and cloak pulling her down. Elena steps toward the edge of the pier and kneels.

"She doesn't deserve your help," I warn.

Elena ignores me, stretching a hand down to Inez. "It's terrible, what she tried to do to you. To both of you. But you can't *drown* her."

"Can't we?" I cast, and Elena sprawls backward on the dock. "I think I could, actually."

Inez uses the momentary distraction to clamber back onto the pier. She is dripping and panting, her brown hair plastered over her chiseled cheekbones, but her brown eyes are narrowed and unafraid. Around us, the wind kicks up. The flames in the shipyard leap higher. Sparks scatter into the sky.

"I haven't lost yet." Inez sneers. "I might not lead the Sisterhood directly, but Maura will be my voice. She's a very tractable girl, your—"

"Don't say her name." I break two pilings and send them flying toward Inez from either side. They seem to hesitate in the air before her, then rocket back toward me. She's quick; I'll give her that. But so am I. I cast, batting them aside, and they clatter to the dock and roll into the river.

"Where is Maura?" Tess grabs my sleeve. "Cate, *where is Maura?*"

"She's dead," I say, my voice brittle. Nearby, the skeleton of a great schooner collapses into the water. The pier beneath us rocks.

Elena flinches as though someone has dealt her a bodily blow. "*How?*"

Tess's shoulders hunch; her hands press over her mouth. "No. I never meant—but you're here. You're all right. Maura can't—"

"I watched her die." I stalk toward Inez. Behind her, one of the remaining pilings begins to smolder. "You swore to

Maura on your husband's grave that you wouldn't hurt Tess. How do you reconcile that?"

Inez reaches for the ivory brooch at her throat. "I am sorry about your sister. She was a clever witch. But I made an older oath to avenge him."

I focus on the high neck of Inez's black dress, peeking out from beneath her cloak, and the cold glint of ivory there. I cast, and the brooch rips from Inez's bodice and arcs into the river. Inez cries out—a high, eerie shriek like a trapped animal.

I am unmoved.

"Jump in after it," I suggest.

She turns to me, eyes narrowed over her hawkish nose. The wind shifts. The bucket brigade and the firemen begin to move back, but before they get clear, the buildings of the shipyard collapse. Several men are trapped beneath the flaming wreckage. Debris whips across River Street, sailing over the heads of the witches and firemen. The roofs of the tenement buildings begin to billow black smoke.

"This entire district will go up in flames, and the Brotherhood with it," Inez vows. I can understand her better now than I ever have before. There is a part of me that could stand back and watch everything burn and revel in the destruction. My sister is dead. Why should the world go on turning?

"We won't be hunted anymore," Inez continues. "Soon we'll be the ones everyone fears."

"No," Tess says, and the last section of the pier snaps, separating Inez from the rest of us. Tess's face is unforgiving, implacable.

"Elena!" Inez reaches out as the dock tilts crazily beneath her. "You've always been an ambitious girl, you—"

"I loved her," Elena interrupts. She turns her back on Inez, tears falling over her cheeks. "I let ambition ruin that."

Inez turns to Tess. "You don't want to be a murderer."

"No," Tess agrees. She hesitates—just for a moment—and hope lights up Inez's face. But then Tess casts, and Inez stumbles back into the flaming piling. Her wet skirts begin to smoke, and she shrieks and slaps at them with her gloved hands. The pilings snap, leaving the dock unmoored, and she's thrown off balance. She topples into the river, surrounded by jagged, charred bits of wood.

"I don't want to be a murderer, but you made me one," Tess says. Inez thrashes for a moment, her black cloak and skirts ballooning out around her. Tess reaches for my hand. "I think the Lord would forgive me this."

Inez stops thrashing and seems to go still. Immobilized, she bobs there for a moment. Then she sinks like a stone beneath the dark water.

"Did—did Maura suffer, do you think?" Elena asks.

"No," I lie, remembering her tears. I wrap my good arm around Elena's waist. "She was very peaceful, at the end. Like she was going to sleep. And some of her last words were about you. She told me she was wrong about Inez, but that I was wrong about you—that you were good. That you made her want to be better."

Elena cries harder. "She was good, too. I know she made some terrible mistakes, but—"

"None of that matters now." I find that I mean it. Maura was no saint, but she was my sister, and in the end she saved me. None of the dozens of ways we hurt each other—big or small—will be what I remember her by.

Tess is crying, too. "I'll never forgive myself."

I look down at her. "I love you, and so did she. We both knew that wasn't you."

Tess hangs her head, blond curls obscuring her face. "I should have told you about my vision. I was so confused— I thought I was going mad, and I didn't want you to know. I never once suspected that *Lucy*—and I couldn't imagine ever hurting you, but the prophecy—oh!" The realization hits her then. "I thought we could change it. I wanted us to be able to change it."

"I know." I let go of Elena and pull Tess toward me, patting her back, wincing at the stinging of my mangled palm.

"We should get you to the infirmary," Elena says, noticing my makeshift sling. "Mei's set up a nursing station in a park a few blocks east."

"Help!" Our heads snap up at Rilla's shout. I scan the burning shipyard and those still fighting the flames at the tenements, but I don't see her anywhere. She must be using the amplification trick I used on Finn at the hospital. Was that only this afternoon? It feels a year ago. "Help needed immediately at Seventy-Seventh and River, at the city orphanage."

I frown. "Surely they've evacuated all the children?" That's only three blocks from the fire. "We should go see what we can do."

"I don't suppose I can persuade you to go to the infirmary

first?" Elena asks. I shake my head and she sighs. "Stubborn. Just like your sister that way."

We all smile through our tears, and the three of us dash up the pier and through the street littered with bits of ash and wood and other debris from the shipyard. The three blocks between the tenements and the orphanage are filled with working-class housing that won't provide much resistance to the flames. The fire engines have moved down the street. Some of the firemen are injured—they've got cuts and scrapes across their sooty faces, and wet cloths wrapped around burns on their arms and hands—but they keep working. Some wear handkerchiefs wrapped around the lower halves of their faces to make breathing through the smoke easier.

Rilla stands in the street before a five-story brick building with a silver plaque out front declaring it the NEW LONDON CITY ORPHANAGE #3. She's directing firemen and bucket brigaders and witches alike to go into the building.

She gives a quick smile when she sees us. "Thank heavens you're here! Brother Coulter—the headmaster—he's locked the children in their rooms."

"Why?" Tess demands.

"Because witches are out here and he thinks we mean to eat them," Rilla says crisply. She throws up her hands. "Really, he'd rather see them burn than come down into the street with us. We thought they'd been evacuated ages ago, but a fireman went to make sure and—never mind. We've got to get them out is the thing. We've got witches unlocking the doors and firemen and bucket brigaders knocking them down."

I eye the orange flames and billowing black smoke headed this way. "Is there time for all that?" I remember the children that Vi floated to safety above the floodwaters. "Could they jump out the windows if we help them down?"

"I'll buy you as much time as I can." Tess is squinting up at the night sky. "Can you get me higher? Up on the roof, maybe?"

"Absolutely not!" I've lost one sister tonight. I can't lose two.

"I'm not letting hundreds of children die because I'm too cowardly to put myself in harm's way," Tess snaps.

"Cate." Finn appears at my good arm. A group of Brothers follows him, and for a moment my heart pounds with fear. Are they here to try to arrest us all, *now*? "What can we do to help?"

"See if there's a way to get Tess up on the roof so she can get a better view of the fire and try to hold it off until the children are out," Rilla commands. "Can you and the Brothers do that?"

"Sure." A lanky blond man with a green silk cravat wrapped around his sooty face nods and charges into the building. "Let's go, gentlemen!"

Tess follows them, but I hang back. "Those are all Brothers?"

Finn gives me a sheepish grin. "Your father and I went to two of the inns where most of us are housed during the council meeting. Lots of men wanted to help when they heard how bad things were getting and how badly we needed more manpower. The rest are fighting the fire a few blocks over."

I'm stunned—and a little ashamed of myself for it. Of course not all Brothers would sit back and cackle in glee while the river district burnt. They can't all be monsters.

"They aren't—?" I swallow. "They don't object to our magic?"

"Not right now." Finn shrugs. "Or if they do, they're not saying so."

"Cate, I need you," Rilla says.

"Go. I'll look after Tess," Finn promises.

Rilla amplifies her voice again. "Children! Children inside the orphanage, look out the west windows. Can you see me?" Small faces press against the windowpanes, and she waves at them with a freckled grin. "Don't be frightened. There are firemen coming to help you. And the witches are helping, too. Don't pay any mind to what silly Brother Coulter told you. Those of you on the fifth floor—we want you to open your windows. Can you do that?" A few windows inch up tentatively. "Open them farther. All the way! Now, I want to see, who's the bravest person on the fifth floor? I want you to lean out the window and wave at me."

Immediately, a girl with blond pigtails leans out one window in the south wing, waving, and in the north wing, a dark-haired boy flaps both hands. Elena and I dash beneath their windows and wave back. "Hmm. I don't know which of you is braver," Rilla muses. "Let's find out. These are my friends Cate and Elena. If you jump, they'll use their magic to help you land safely. Haven't you always wondered what it would be like to fly? Whoever jumps first wins."

The boy hesitates. It must sound positively mad, asking

them to jump five stories and trust witches—whom they've no doubt been taught to hate and fear—to catch them. But the pigtailed girl pushes her window up and climbs onto the wide windowsill. She wears a navy dress and white pinafore and she can't be more than ten. "Here I come!" she shouts.

The girl jumps—and plummets toward the ground. She screams. I reach up with my magic, cradling her, slowing her descent until she seems to float rather than fall. She hovers above the ground for a second, then touches down gently.

"You're a real witch!" Her blue eyes are round; her face is full of wonder.

"I am," I admit.

"That was fun!" She looks up at the dark-haired boy, still framed in the window above Elena. "Come on, Jamie! Don't be a scaredy-cat!"

"What's your name, honey?" Rilla asks.

"Mary Fowler." The girl grins.

Rilla raises her voice. "Mary Fowler is the bravest girl in the whole orphanage! Who wants to come down next?"

Rory and Sachi come charging up next to me. "The fire is out over by the train depot. The tracks served as a natural fire break," she announces. "What's happening here? Why haven't the children been evacuated?"

I explain what Brother Coulter did.

"That bastard. I'd like to get my hands on him," Rory seethes, and this time Sachi doesn't chide her for her language. To our left, children are trickling out the front door. Some of them clutch blankets or rag dolls in their hands, and when they see the nightmarish sky and the flames licking at the building next door, they begin to cry. Bekah stands at the door and directs them farther down the street.

Meanwhile, Jamie jumps and is guided down by Elena. He looks a bit pale, but he raises his arms and cheers when he lands. "Come on, lads!" he shouts as other faces fill the windows.

"Girls are braver than boys!" Mary hollers, and another little girl positions herself above me.

"My friends Sachi and Rory are here to help, too. Four children at a time, please," Rilla instructs as Sachi and Rory wave. "Let's see who gets out first: boys or girls!"

Children line up at the windows to jump, one after the other. Sachi and I catch all thirty-seven girls before Rory and Elena catch the thirty-seventh of forty boys. Some of the girls cheer, while the defeated boys bluster, but most seem to recognize the gravity of the situation once they're on the ground. These were wards full of the oldest children in the orphanage, anywhere from eight to fourteen, and some beg to be allowed to go back inside to fetch younger siblings and friends.

Bekah grabs a wriggling boy determined to save Susie, his four-year-old sister. He hits and kicks at Bekah until a fireman picks him up and sets him down in the street. Rilla tries to direct the children to a tavern that has promised to feed and shelter them for the time being, but some flat-out refuse to go until they see their friends come out. There's a great reunion when Susie finally emerges, one of a handful of children led by Sister Edith.

Daisy and her friend Alexa run out, each carrying a squirming baby. "The roof is catching on the other side. We don't have much time," Daisy informs us breathlessly. She thrusts one baby at Rilla while Alexa hands hers to one of the older orphans waiting in the street. "We've got the third and fourth floors clear—they were the four- to seven-year-olds— but there are still babies and toddlers on the second floor. We need to form a brigade and pass them out."

That's it. I can't carry babies with a broken arm and I'm not going to just stand here. "I'm going up to the roof to help Tess," I announce, hurrying into the building, squeezing past a snaking line of firemen, Brothers, and witches passing cherubic babes from arm to arm. Most of the Brothers have shed their black cloaks in the hot, close quarters, and without them, they look like—well, like regular men instead of the villains of my nightmares. They are helping, their shirtsleeves rolled up, sooty faces streaked with sweat, indistinguishable from the firemen except for their rings of office and their upper-class speech.

I run to the far stairwell, which is beginning to fill with smoke. I pound up the steps and pause on the third-floor landing, trying to draw a proper lungful. I cough and keep going. On the fifth floor, a ladder leads up to the roof. I crawl up it with a sense of déjà vu. Truth be told, I am none too eager to stand on another rooftop tonight.

"Tess?" She stands near the edge of the roof, staring out over the city. The wind has died down to nothing. The air feels perilously still, the way it sometimes does before a storm. The muscles of Tess's neck and arms are taut as she fights the wind. The far side of the roof is smoldering, fire licking at the drain spouts. Finn and a few other men—Brothers? fire brigaders?—are trying to beat it out. Water from a relocated fire engine arcs onto the roof, forming a great puddle in the center, but it's not enough.

Tess is trembling, every ounce of her energy focused on battling the fire, but she's losing ground. She opens her eyes when she hears my boots next to her. "Let me help," I say, slipping my hand into hers.

She takes my remaining magic—and with it, most of my strength. It suddenly requires an inordinate amount of effort to remain standing. My eyes sting and tear, and the sound of my own wheezing breath reminds me horribly of Maura's last moments. I look down as a wagon clatters up and several firemen leap out, running to gather children into the back. They need more time.

Cinders fall all around us. One falls on Tess's shoulder and I let go her hand for a moment to slap at the smoking spot before her cloak can ignite. She barely reacts. The wagon clatters away down the street below us, full of older children and firemen holding babies, and then comes barreling back a few minutes later. Bekah and Daisy lift toddlers into the wagon. Rory stumbles out the front door, leading Sachi by the hand. My vision is tunneling again; my legs are shaking with the effort to stay upright.

Tess thwacks me on the back of the head. "Your hair!" she shrieks, beating out a spark.

"Don't worry about me! *Focus*," I insist as the wind surges around us.

Finn rushes across the roof. The other firemen have already gone. "Everyone's out. Let's go, ladies." The bump on the back of my head hurts something fierce, and spots dance before my eyes. I try to draw in a deep breath, but everything tastes of ash and my throat burns. It's so hot up here. Finn unties a wet handkerchief from around the lower half of his face—it makes him look rather like a highwayman from one of Maura's novels—and ties it gently around mine. It makes breathing easier, but I flinch when he touches the back of my head. "You've got a hell of a goose egg back there. Can you make it down the ladder?"

"I've got a better idea." Tess steps onto the ledge. "Elena! Can you catch us?"

"You've got to be mad," I mumble. But a gust of wind sends the flames closer toward the ladder, and Elena is waiting below us.

I jump.

It is terrifying. Not like flying at all—like dropping, like that horrid half-asleep sensation of falling. I shriek as the street rises up below me at an alarming rate. My boots touch down gently enough, but my knees buckle. I am not half as brave as ten-year-old Mary Fowler.

Rilla wraps a steadying arm around my waist as Elena helps Tess and then Finn to the ground. "We've got to get you to the infirmary. You look ready to collapse."

"I'll take her." Finn scoops me up in his arms, and I yelp as pain surges through my broken arm. "I'm sorry, sweetheart. I'll try to be careful."

He called me sweetheart. I try to smile up at him, but it comes out more a grimace.

"I'm taking Sachi to Mei, too," Rory says, marching up

to us and practically dragging her sister behind her. "She can't see."

"It's all the smoke," Sachi insists, but the whites of her eyes are flushed red, and she can't seem to focus on Rory's face.

"Prue?" I ask.

"Already at the infirmary. She got a dreadful burn on her back earlier," Sachi explains.

I twist my head back to Finn. "Father?"

"Took some of the orphans to the Green Dragon. Tess is going to meet him there. I'll take you when you're healed," Finn promises, striding down the street. I look over his shoulder and gasp. The orphanage is engulfed in flame already.

I relax into him, trying not to wince against the jostling of his steps, comforted by the rumble of his voice through his chest as he and Rory talk. When we reach the park, he stops and sets me down on a patch of grass. The park is crowded with people—the injured, with their burns and cuts and broken limbs; witches from the Sisterhood with some healing magic; and working-class women with some nursing skill. Finn slides his cloak beneath my head as a makeshift pillow.

He sprawls down on the grass next to me, stretching out his long legs. "Three of the four fires are out," he announces. "And the firemen are making another stand on the far side of the orphanage. I think they'll get that one soon. It could have been much worse."

He's right, I know. Things could *always* be worse. Still, my eyes fill with tears.

"What is it?" He leans over me. "Where does it hurt?"

"Maura." I close my eyes, but tears trickle out from beneath my lashes. "She's dead."

"Good Lord. How?" Finn takes my hand.

I tell him everything. "There was nothing I could do besides sit with her," I say. Finn wipes away tears that are rolling toward my ear. "I know she—she was awful to you, and you must hate her, but—"

I break off as the truth of it hits me. If Finn can't grieve with me—if he's *glad* of her death—I don't see how we can survive this.

"No." Finn runs a hand through his wild hair, sending bits of ash flying. "What she did to me—to *us*—was awful. But she was still your sister, Cate."

"I love you," I whisper. "But I loved her, too."

"Of course you did." He brushes another tear from my face with the pad of his thumb.

I thought I was all cried out, but it turns out I'm not. Finn picks me up again and—heedless of the impropriety of it—holds me against him, stroking my hair while I sob.

"Things are going to change," he says. "The Brothers can't continue to outlaw witchery, not after what's happened tonight. The people won't stand for it. Witches and common people and Brothers have been working together all over the city. Look. It's happening right here, in this park. Things are going to be different after tonight."

CHAPTER

22

TEN DAYS LATER, WE GATHER IN Chatham for Maura's funeral.

It is strange to be home when, two weeks ago, I thought returning was impossible. It's even stranger without Maura. I expect to hear her voice calling me in for dinner, to see her running down the stairs to share some madcap scene from her book or popping into my bedroom to ask me to tie a troublesome sash. Last night, I sat at her dressing table, surrounded by old hair ribbons and the ghost of her laughter. In her jewelry box, I found a rhinestone bracelet she wore everywhere when she was little—she loved the way it sparkled when it caught the sun—and I burst into tears.

Now I stand in the family cemetery, surrounded by Cahill graves and sobbing mourners, and my eyes are dry. To our right is Mother's tomb—*Anna*

Elizabeth Cahill, beloved wife and devoted mother—and the five small stones marking the babies she lost. Next to them is a gaping grave and a mound of dirt and a mahogany casket from which I avert my eyes.

Elena stands beside me in her finest black brocade. Father was surprised when I asked that she be treated as family, but when I told him it was what Maura would have wanted, he agreed readily enough. Tess stands on my other side, her small face pale, next to Father; our housekeeper, Mrs. O'Hare; and our coachman, John. Mrs. O'Hare is dabbing at her eyes with a frilly white handkerchief, her gray curls bobbing as she cries. We only arrived yesterday; she has not had much time to get over the shock of Maura's death.

Not that we are very used to it yet ourselves.

Brother Winfield refused to allow the funeral of a known witch to be held in the church proper, but Father prevailed upon Brother Ralston to perform the service. Father was furious that we've been banned from church, but I wasn't bothered by it. Maura would have liked this better; she hated every moment she spent in that stuffy clapboard room, listening to sermons about our wickedness. It's a pity we can't have her funeral in a bookstore. She'd like that best of all.

Brother Ralston strokes his brown whiskers, then clears his throat. "Blessed are those who mourn," he begins, "for they will be comforted. We have come here today to remember before the Lord our sister Maura, to give thanks for her life . . ."

I bite my lip. Truth be told, I do not feel very much like giving thanks at the moment. I shift and my footsteps crunch on the grass beneath me. It snowed yesterday as we were driving into Chatham. The ground is covered in four inches of sugary white that glistens whenever the sun hits it right—just like the rhinestone bracelet tucked into my cloak pocket.

I prick the tip of my thumb on the white rose I'm holding. Soon, we'll drop our roses on the casket and the gravediggers Father hired will lower Maura into the ground. It seems impossible. It feels as though any minute she'll come banging out of the house and dash up the hill, yelling, "Wait for me!"

A mound of white hothouse roses already rests on the coffin, along with an enormous bouquet of imported white tulips. Merriweather sent them; they must have cost a fortune. He didn't come, but he sent Prue with Sachi and Rory.

I glance across the gravesite, where my friends stand. Neither Mei nor I have been able to heal the stubborn infection in Sachi's eyes. She's meant to rest them completely—no reading, no needlework, nothing taxing at all. She oughtn't even be out in this bright sunlight. She can see blurry shapes now, but nothing more, and the specialist isn't sure if she'll ever fully regain her sight. Mei was able to heal Prue's burns, though, and Rory escaped the fire unscathed. She sees me looking at her and tilts her head. She's wearing a white feather in her hair, and beneath her black cloak, a white hem peeks out. Mei told her about the Indo-Chinese custom of wearing white for mourning, and Rory's decided to adopt it for her own. She says she's spent too much of her life wearing black already.

Rilla and Vi are here, too. Rilla stands with a motherly arm around Vi, whose eyes are as bloodshot and swollen as

Sachi's—though hers are from crying. Two days ago, we attended Vi's father's funeral. Robert was trying to save a little boy trapped in a house when the roof collapsed on them both. He was the only family Vi had; now she's an orphan.

I glance at my father. He has been very present these last few days—not like after Mother's death, when he disappeared into himself. He wants to spend most of his time in New London now; he plans to rent a proper house in Cardiff, and he has asked Tess and me to come live with him. We are considering it. Truth be told, I am not terribly used to having him fussing around us so solicitously; it feels equal parts comforting and annoying. Tess likes it, though.

"The Lord is my Shepherd; I shall not want. He maketh me to lie down in green pastures; He leadeth me beside the still waters; He restoreth my soul," Brother Ralston recites.

My mind catches on "still waters." I look at the pond, covered in a thick layer of ice. We used to go skating every winter when we were young—or rather, I did, with our neighbor Paul McLeod, and sometimes Maura tagged along. I was always racing Paul across the pond, while Maura twirled graceful figure eights and pretended to be a ballerina.

Paul sent a sweet note of condolence about Maura's death. He wanted to come to the funeral, but he's laid up in New London, recovering from the fever. I thought perhaps his mother would come, but Agnes McLeod is terribly devout. If she's heard what Maura was—well, likely she'd turn up her nose and cross herself and think the world better off for being free of one more witch. The papers—even the Brotherhood's mouthpiece, the *Sentinel*—have been full of news of the great fire in New London and the madness of Brother Covington, who's slipped back into a coma.

Brother Brennan has returned from exile and ordered two squadrons of guards stationed at the convent—not to restrict our movements, but to protect us. The papers have reported on the shocking truth of the Sisterhood, and while some people are full of gratitude for our help with the fire and the fever, others hold deeply to their hatred. Rilla and Tess and I—commended in the firemen's reports for our bravery in saving the orphanage—might well have targets painted on our backs. Finn and Father would prefer that I have guards trailing after me at all times. For this trip, they've let the matter rest, but I suspect we've not had our last argument on the subject.

Finn stands with his mother and sister and a bearded Brother I've never seen before. Finn is wearing an old black greatcoat instead of his Brotherly cloak, and his coppery hair shines in the sun. He and I haven't seen each other alone since the fire.

"We thank You for Maura, the years we shared with her, the good we saw in her, the love we received from her," Brother Ralston prays.

Love you too, Cate. Maura's last words—more breath than sound—flutter against my cheek. I look up into the cloudless blue sky—a brilliant blue like Maura's eyes—as other mourners bow their heads.

"Now give us strength and courage to leave her in Your care . . ."

I do not want to leave her in the Lord's care. I cannot help feeling as though He has already failed her. Or perhaps it was I who failed her. I remember the girl who used to sing bawdy songs and play her mandolin when Father was away; who would spend rainy afternoons with her tea going cold while she curled up on her window seat, enchanted by the exploits of dukes and governesses; who sent ghosts popping out of my closet to terrify me; who was enraptured with Elena's velvet slippers and satin underthings when they first met. The girl who, to her dying day, believed that her magic was a gift, never a curse.

Maura was far from perfect, but then so am I.

No matter what I do, it never feels enough. I want so badly to protect the people I love from harm, but my love is not strong enough.

How can I learn to make my peace with that? How does anyone?

Fifty-seven people were killed the night of the fire; hundreds of homes were destroyed. The worst fire—the one that consumed the orphanage—was put out by Wednesday evening, twenty-four hours after it started. It could have been much worse, I know. If the witches hadn't immobilized or compelled the guards to open up the quarantine checkpoints—if Alice hadn't put out the fire on Bramble Hill—if the fire engines hadn't reached the fire closest to the market district so quickly—if the train tracks hadn't provided a natural fire break—if Tess hadn't held the winds back until the orphanage was evacuated—hundreds could have been killed.

Still, the cost to the Sisterhood seems high. Alice was

killed after she collapsed the water tower. Genie and Maud—both only fifteen—were killed when a building caved in. One of the Harwood refugees, little Sarah Mae, was badly burnt when she tried to rescue a kitten. Livvy broke her leg so badly we couldn't heal it; the physician isn't sure if she'll ever walk without a limp. Old Sister Evelyn had an attack of apoplexy and is bedridden in the convent. And Sister Gretchen was fatally shot by a soldier when she tried to open up one of the checkpoints.

"We now commit her body to the ground: earth to earth, ashes to ashes, dust to dust . . ." Brother Ralston says, and I startle to attention. I have avoided looking at the coffin, but now it's time to place our roses on top of it. Father goes first. Then Tess. Then it's my turn.

Everyone's eyes are on me. It is not so very difficult, Cate. Put one foot in front of the other. It's only five steps.

I get as far as the coffin, and then I can't seem to make myself move. I stand there, frozen, breath strangling in my chest. Panic sinks its sharp teeth into me. I feel such a fool, clutching the white rose in my ungloved hands, staring blindly at my sister's casket. I am not the sort of girl who falls to pieces, even in moments like this. But my corset feels cinched too tight and I cannot breathe and—

Footsteps crunch across the grass, and someone takes my arm. A freckled hand stained with blue ink pulls the rose from my clenched fingers and sits it lightly on top of the casket. Finn escorts me back to my family and wraps an arm around my waist. "Breathe," he whispers, his lips very near my ear.

Brother Ralston's voice eventually stops, and the mourners begin to make their way back to the house. I can hear them offering Father and Tess their condolences. I ought to hurry in and help Mrs. O'Hare lay out the food. But the notion of making small talk with our neighbors is dreadful, and I know Marianne and Clara and Rilla will be eager to help.

Finn doesn't rush me.

"Take as long as you need." Behind his spectacles, his brown eyes are solemn. "I'm here. Or I can go, if you want a moment alone."

"I don't know what's the matter with me." I flush, pulling away from him and huddling into myself. "I didn't fall to pieces when Mother died. Maura and Tess needed me. I couldn't."

Finn's brow rumples into the upside-down V. "You've lost your sister, Cate. Grieving her doesn't make you weak. I cried when my father died. Perhaps it's not manly to admit it, but I did. Do you think less of me for that?"

I scowl up at him. "Of course not."

"Then stop being so hard on yourself." He tucks a strand of blond hair behind my ear. "It's only been ten days. You need time." I shove my hands in my cloak pockets, miserable, and he chuckles. "That was the wrong thing to say, wasn't it? Your face is transparent as glass sometimes."

I've never been good with words—not like Tess—but now they rush out of me, raw and urgent. "I can't help feeling lost, somehow. I *promised*, Finn. I promised Mother I would look after both of them, keep them safe, and that promise has been everything to me for the last four years. And then there was the prophecy. I haven't gone a day without thinking of it for months, but I couldn't stop it, and now Maura is gone and—I just don't know!" I falter.

"Now what do you do, you mean?" Finn suggests.

"Yes," I whisper. "Am I terrible for thinking it?"

"You are never half as terrible as you think you are," he promises, grinning at me. "I actually wanted to talk to you about that, but I wasn't sure it was the right time."

"About me being terrible?" My lips tilt into—not quite a smile. But close.

I turn, noticing the bearded Brother standing in our gazebo. "Who is that?"

"Ah. I wanted to introduce the two of you. He's got to get back to New London, but he wanted to pay his respects." Finn adjusts his spectacles. "It's Sean Brennan."

"Brother Brennan?" I wince. "He's just been standing out here in the cold, waiting for me?"

Brennan sees us approaching and steps forward. "Miss Cahill." He bows. "I'm very sorry for your loss."

"Thank you." I pause, uncertain whether I ought to kneel in order to receive the customary blessings. In the end, I do not. "And thank you for coming. I daresay you have more important things to do."

He shakes his head. He's perhaps thirty-five, with a closely trimmed brown beard and kind brown eyes. Laugh lines radiate from his mouth and crinkle the corners of his eyes. "Actually, speaking with you was one of the first things on my agenda. I don't wish to intrude on your grief, though. If you don't feel ready to discuss—"

I wave away his polite assurances. "You came all this distance. I'd like to hear what you have to say."

"Very well." He folds his hands in front of him. "I came back into the city the day after the fire, and since then I've been meeting with members of the Resistance as well as members of the National Council, trying to figure out how we can move forward. Covington's orders regarding the quarantine and the fires were a travesty. Even before that, the public was unhappy with the Brothers' most recent measures." He glances at Finn. "Measures that I voted against. Brother Belastra can vouch for me."

"Mr.," Finn corrects. "I've left the Brotherhood."

"I'm still hoping to change your mind on that. We could use a man of your character," Brennan says, before turning his attention back to me. Every other Brother I've met has treated me with casual condescension, assuming that I am some mindless, submissive creature—or ought to be. But he speaks to me with the same quiet respect he shows Finn. "I think repealing the measure against women working will make a vast difference in the lives of ordinary families. I'm planning to make aid available to those who were hit hardest by the fire and the fever. And as soon as possible, I'd like to pass a new measure that makes witchery legal."

I smile my first true smile in days. "That would be wonderful."

"I understand that, in the past, compulsion may have been a necessary evil to guarantee your own safety. But going forward, it will be illegal—a crime tried by a jury and subject to a prison sentence. Any crimes of that nature committed before the measure is passed will be pardoned." Brennan is solemn. "Does that seem fair to you?"

"It does. If I can be of any help—if you need a recommendation for a liaison between the witches and the government—" I begin.

"I was hoping you might serve as that liaison, actually," Brennan interrupts. "You've been highly recommended by Alistair Merriweather. Frankly, I was hoping you'd be more than a liaison—that you would join the two of us on a new governing council. You've proven that you have the best interests of New London at heart, Miss Cahill."

I glance at Finn, eyes wide, and then back at Brennan. "I—thank you, sir. I'm flattered. But that's never been something I aspired to. If you'd like a witch on the council, though, I know someone who'd be perfect for the position. My governess—Elena Robichaud—she's just heading back to the house." I point to where Elena and Mrs. Corbett are striding down through the gardens.

Brennan nods. "Belastra guessed that you might turn me down, but I had to ask. I'd be happy to speak with Miss Robichaud." He hesitates. "There is one other matter. According to the prophecy, one of the Cahill sisters is the oracle. If anything should come up—anything that I, or the government of New England, ought to know—I hope you will come to me. In return, I will do my best to honor your privacy."

I nod, rather amazed at his restraint. "I think that can be arranged. Thank you, sir."

"Thank you, Miss Cahill, for allowing politics to intrude

on such a sad day. I'll take my leave now." He nods at Finn and makes his way down the snowy hill toward Elena.

"He's a good man," Finn says. "New England will be far better with him in charge."

I run a finger over the snow on the wooden railing. Maura would be happy about this. Cautious about the notion of working with Brothers, of course, and a little suspicious about any council that involved two men against one woman. But making magic legal—that would go a long way toward earning her trust. "Are you sure you don't want to work with him?"

"I've had my fill of politics." Finn smiles. "Merriweather's going to be able to sell the *Gazette* properly now, you know. He's asked me to come on as a reporter."

"That's wonderful." I smile back, though my heart sinks a little. Finn's already made his decision, without discussing it with me? "He offered Rilla a job, too. She's terribly excited."

"And you?" Finn asks. "What are your plans?"

My smile splinters. "I—I'm not sure yet." I turn away, trying to hide my disappointment. I thought he understood how rudderless I feel with Maura gone and Father—well, actually being a proper father to Tess. "I'd like to do more healing work. As a nurse, perhaps."

"But you intend to go back to New London?" Finn presses.

"Does it matter?" I immediately loathe myself for the frost in my voice.

"It does." He grasps my elbow and turns me to face him. "Cate, I can't say what you want to hear. Not yet. I want you to know that—*when* I do, I'll mean it. Completely. Irrevocably."

"When?" I ask, voice small but hopeful. "Not *if*?"

"When." He takes my cold hand in his. "I'm falling in love with you more every day. I don't know if they were the same things I loved about you before, but now—the bit of red in your hair. The way you tilt your chin when you get angry, like you're charging into battle. How fiercely protective you are of the people you care about. How big your capacity for forgiveness is. You're an amazing woman, Cate Cahill. And to that end—"

He takes something from his pocket and holds it out. The red jewel catches the sunlight. It's his mother's ruby ring—the ring he gave me when he proposed—only now it's linked through a silver chain. "I found this in my desk. It's my promise to you that we'll work our way back to where we were—or somewhere even better. Will you wear it and keep it safe until I ask you to put it on your finger?"

I didn't know that happiness and sadness could mingle this closely. "I will." I turn, and he drops the chain around my neck and then fastens the hook. I clutch the ring in my fist for one second, then let it drop down between my breasts.

When I turn back around, his brown eyes take in every bit of me.

"May I kiss you?"

I launch myself at him, my mouth reaching for his. He trails a finger down my bare neck and I shiver and press closer. "Not," I whisper against his lips, "if I kiss you first."

• • •

A bit later, we walk hand in hand down the snowy hill and through the garden. I'm surprised Father hasn't sent someone out to fetch me yet, given how fatherly he's been of late. But as we turn the corner past the rose garden, a voice calls out.

"Cate? Is that you?" It's Tess.

Finn squeezes my hand. "I'll go in, and give you two a moment."

"Thank you." I walk into the rose garden—our old sanctuary, our one safe place. Tess has brushed the snow from the marble bench at the foot of the statue of Athena. She looks cold and miserable; her shoulders are hunched and her lips faintly purple. "What are you doing out here?"

"I wanted to be alone." She gestures to the tall hedges that surround the garden; no one can see us from the house. I hesitate, but she pats the bench. "You don't count, silly."

I perch next to her. "How are you?"

She purses her lips. "Sad. Guilty. Happy. And then guilty again."

"Tell me about the happy bit," I suggest.

"Father said Vi could come and live with us in the new house. He thinks he's found just the place—he said there's a room that would make a magnificent library, and one of the bedrooms has a turret with a window seat, and he said that could be mine. And there's a great big kitchen and he said Mrs. Muir—that's his housekeeper in New London— wouldn't mind me poking about. He even said Vi could bring her kitten." A shadow passes over Tess's face. "I'd like to have Vi with me. We've become so close over the last few months, rooming together. Like sisters, almost. Only— do you suppose that Maura would think I was trying to replace her?"

"No." I give a firm shake of my head. "She wouldn't suppose she was so easy to replace."

"She isn't." Tess smooths her black cloak. "I'll miss her forever."

"I know." I put my hand over Tess's and we sit there for a moment, quiet together.

"Part of me feels like I don't ever want to do magic again," Tess confesses. "I haven't since the fire."

"What?" I stare at her. "That's not what Maura would want. She *loved* being a witch. Sometimes I was jealous of how happy it made her, especially when I felt like my magic was such a dreadful burden."

Tess leans forward, propping her elbows on her knees. "Do you still feel that way? Like magic is wicked?"

"No." I'm a little startled to find that that's true.

Tess's heavy sigh blows blond curls away from her face. "All I can think of is the terrible things I did. I don't see how magic will ever be fun again."

A memory flashes through me as I look around the dreary winter garden. "What good is all this, anyway, if we can't use it to make things more beautiful?" I ask.

I cast, and the rosebushes burst into color: bright pink and scarlet flowers framed by deep green leaves.

Tess frowns. "Did I say that? That sounds like something I'd say."

"You did, and you were absolutely correct. You usually are." I gesture at her. "Your turn."

She hesitates.

I elbow her. "I dare you. Maura would, too, if she were here."

Tess stands, and for a minute I think she's going to flee. Then she turns, and the statue of Athena is wearing a white clematis skirt. Tess giggles.

I cast, and Athena receives a giant sunflower hat.

Tess casts, and there are yellow daffodils *everywhere*. The harbinger of spring. Maura's favorite flower. They pop up between the rosebushes and coat the marble bench and dot the walkway outside the rose garden. We peek out and see a carpet of them stretching away up the hillside.

Tess grins. "Are you going to tell me to put it back? I'm breaking the rules, you know."

"No." I breathe in the summertime perfume of wild roses and feel my heart lighten. "Those rules don't apply to us anymore."

ACKNOWLEDGMENTS

SENDING A SERIES OUT INTO THE WORLD IS an enormous team effort. Thank you to everyone who's supported the Cahill Witch Chronicles over the last four years. Special thanks to:

Jim McCarthy, my agent, for your wise advice every step of the way.

Ari Lewin, my editor. Working with you has taught me so much; I'm a better writer because of how you push me. Thank you for loving my witchy girls almost as much as I do.

Katherine Perkins, for your editorial help and for the dozens of behind-the-scenes things that I'm not even aware of. Anna Jarzab, Elyse Marshall, Jessica Shoffel, and the rest of the marketing and publicity teams, for helping to connect the books with readers. Everyone else at Penguin, for all your hard work and enthusiasm about the Cahill witches.

Andrea Cremer, Marie Lu, and Beth Revis—my wonderful Breathless sisters—for giving me role models for the kind of author—and the kind of person—I want to be.

Liz Richards, Fiona Paul, and Kim Liggett—for being on the receiving end of my flailmails.

My amazing critique partners—Kathleen Foucart, Andrea

Colt, Miranda Kenneally, Caroline Richmond, Tiffany Schmidt, and Robin Talley—for reading so fast and telling me when I make you cry. (Yay!) Also for retreats filled with wine and cheese and gossip. You are the best.

My family and friends, who have been such fantastic champions of me and my work, and hand out bookmarks at every opportunity.

My brilliant playwright husband, who brainstorms with me at four in the morning when he would really rather be sleeping. Thank you for helping me untangle all my plot knots. I love you.

This book is dedicated to my sisters, Amber and Shannon. Four years ago I had a dream that we were fighting over a magical locket from our mom, and although there's no magical locket in these books, the idea of writing about that complicated mix of love and sibling rivalry stuck. Thanks for helping to inspire Maura and Tess.

And to my friends Jenn Reeder, Jill Coste, Liz Auclair, and Laura Furr, who are the sisters of my heart—thank you for always being there for me, celebrating the ups and commiserating with the downs. I'd be lost without you, and it's because of you I couldn't imagine a world where Cate doesn't get to have brilliant, talented friends.

To the librarians, booksellers, sales reps, and bloggers who recommend my books and put them into the hands of readers—thank you a million times over. You are my heroes.

And last but never least, to my readers. It's been a dream come true to write this series for you. Thank you for sharing Cate and her sisters' journey with me.

THE CAHILL SISTERS' STORY BEGAN IN

TURN THE PAGE TO READ A SAMPLE CHAPTER!

CHAPTER

OUR MOTHER WAS A WITCH, TOO,
but she hid it better.

I miss her.

Not a single day goes by that I don't wish for her
guidance. Especially about my sisters.

Tess runs ahead of me, heading for the rose
garden—our sanctuary, our one safe place. Her slippers slide on the cobblestones, the hood of her gray
cloak falling to reveal blond curls. I glance back at
the house. It's against the Brothers' strictures for
girls to go out of doors uncloaked, and running isn't
considered ladylike. But we're concealed from the
house by tall hedges. Tess is safe.

For now.

She waits ahead, kicking at the dead leaves

beneath a maple. "I hate autumn," she complains, biting at her lip with pearly teeth. "It feels so sad."

"I like it." There's something invigorating in the crisp September air, the searing blue skies, the interplay of orange and scarlet and gold. The Brotherhood would probably ban autumn if they could. It's too beautiful. Too sensuous.

Tess points to the clematis climbing up the trellis. Their petals are brown and crumbling, their tired heads bowing toward the ground.

"See, everything's dying," she says mournfully.

I realize what she intends a scant second before she acts.

"Tess!" I shriek.

I'm too late. She squints her gray eyes, and a moment later, it's summer.

Tess is an advanced caster for twelve—much more advanced than I was at her age. The deadheads spring up, whole and white and luscious. The oaks sprout new green leaves. Magnificent peonies and lilies sway toward the sun, glorying in their resurrection.

"Teresa Elizabeth Cahill," I hiss. "You put that back."

She smiles winsomely, skipping ahead to smell the fragrant orange daylilies. "Just for a few minutes. It's prettier this way."

"Tess." My tone doesn't brook any argument.

"What good is all this, anyway, if we can't use it to make things more beautiful?"

As far as I can tell, "all this" is good for precious little. I ignore Tess's question. "Now. Before Mrs. O'Hare or John comes outside."

Tess mumbles a *reverto* spell under her breath. I assume that's for my benefit. Unlike me, she doesn't need to speak aloud to cast.

The clematises' flowers droop on their vine; the leaves crunch beneath our feet; the impatiens fall to pieces. Tess doesn't look happy about it, but at least she listens to me. That's more than I can say for Maura.

Footsteps strike the cobblestones behind us. It's a man's quick, heavy stride. I whip around to face the intruder. Tess moves closer, and I resist the urge to put my arm around her. She's small for her age, but I'd keep her this way forever if I could. An odd, pretty child is safer than an odd, pretty woman.

John O'Hare, our coachman and jack-of-all-trades, lumbers around the hedge. "Your father's wanting you, Miss Cate," he huffs, his bearded cheeks red. "In the study."

I smile politely, tucking an errant strand of hair beneath my hood. "Thank you."

I wait until he's gone. Then I turn, tugging Tess's cape up over her curls, bending to brush the dust from her ragged lace hems. My heart is pounding. If he had come two minutes earlier—if it had been Father, or the Brothers paying an unexpected call—how would we have explained this corner of the garden springing back to life?

We couldn't have. It was magic, plain and simple.

"Best to see what Father wants." I try to sound cheerful, but the unexpected summons makes me uneasy. He's only been back from New London for a few days. Does he mean to leave us again so soon? His time at home gets shorter every year.

Tess looks longingly down the cobblestone path toward the rose garden. "No practicing today, then?"

"After that display? No." I shake my head. "You know better."

"No one could see us from the house, Cate. We were behind the hedges. We'd have heard them, like we heard John coming."

I frown at her. "No magic outdoors except in the rose garden. That's what Mother taught me. She made the rules to keep us safe."

"I suppose," Tess sighs. Her thin shoulders slump, and I hate that I've taken this small happiness away from her. When I was her age, I liked to run through the gardens, and I suppose I was careless with my magic, too. But I had Mother to look out for me. Now I have to play mother for Tess and Maura, and ignore the wild girl that still bangs in my heart, begging to be let out.

I lead the way back to the house, and we troop through the kitchen door, hanging our cloaks on the wooden pegs inside. Mrs. O'Hare is bent over a bubbling pot of her dreadful fish chowder, humming a snippet of an old church song, her curly gray head bobbing in time to the music. She smiles and gestures toward a pile of carrots on the table. Tess washes up and sets right to work chopping. She loves bustling around the kitchen, dicing and mixing and measuring. It's not proper for girls of our station, but Mrs. O'Hare gave up on proper a long time ago with us.

The heavy oak door to Father's study is slightly ajar. I can glimpse Father at his desk, shoulders rounded in exhaustion, as though what he'd like the very most is a nap. But there's a stack of thick leather-bound volumes on his desk, and I have no doubt that when our business here is concluded, he'll go right back to them. And when he finishes those, there are dozens more on the shelves ready to take their place. He is a businessman, yes—but a scholar first and foremost.

I rap on the door and wait for permission to enter. "John said you wanted to speak with me?"

"Come in, Cate. Mrs. Corbett and I thought you should have a say in our new venture, since it affects you girls." Father gestures toward the corner of the room, where Mrs. Corbett sits like a fat spider on the plush red sofa, spinning her helpful little schemes.

"New venture?" I echo, striding up to his desk. Mrs. Corbett had precious little interest in us before Mother died, but she's been full of neighborly advice ever since. Her last suggestion was to send me off to a convent school run by the Sisters. I had to compel Father and modify his memory so he wouldn't make me go. He only remembers deciding it wasn't wise to send me away, not so soon after losing Mother.

Invading his mind is the wickedest thing I've ever done. But it was necessary. How could I keep my promise to look after my sisters if I was in New London? It's a two-day journey.

"I think—that is, Mrs. Corbett suggested—" Father hems and haws but eventually gets to the point. "A governess! It would be just the thing."

Oh no.

I jut my chin at him. "For what?"

Father's thin face flushes. "For your education. I'm going back to New London next week, and I'll be gone most of the autumn. That's too long for you girls to be away from your lessons."

My heart sinks. Hours snatched here and there to correct our

French pronunciation and Latin translations are the only time we get with him anymore. Now we won't even have that. I learned not to count on Father years ago, but Tess hasn't. She'll be heartbroken.

I brush dust from the lamp at the corner of his desk. "Maura and I can teach Tess while you're gone. I don't mind."

Father tactfully refrains from pointing out that Tess's Latin is worlds better than my own. "If that were the only—that is to say—you're sixteen now, Cate, and—" He looks helplessly at Mrs. Corbett, who is only too pleased to jump in.

"There is more to a young lady's education than foreign languages. A governess could give you girls a bit of polish," she asserts, eyeing me up and down.

I clench my hands into fists. I know how I look: a high-necked navy frock unadorned with any frills or frippery, the scuffed boots I wear to work in the garden, hair plaited neatly down my back. It doesn't do me any favors. But it's better to be thought dowdy than to attract too much attention.

"We have our piano lessons in town every week," I remind Father.

Mrs. Corbett smirks, her eyes disappearing into the fat folds of her face. "I believe your father was thinking about more than piano lessons, dear."

I should lower my eyes like a good girl, but I don't. That sugary, overly familiar "dear" sets my teeth on edge. I square my shoulders and lift my chin and stare right into her beady little hazel eyes. "Such as?"

"May I be frank with you, Miss Cate?"

"Please." My voice is syrupy steel.

"You're of an age to be thinking about your future now, yours and Miss Maura's. Your intention ceremony is coming up soon. It won't be long before you'll have to make your choice: marry and raise a family, Lord willing, or join the Sisterhood."

I fiddle with the gold tassels on the lamp shade, a flush rising on my cheeks. "I'm well aware of my choices." As if I could forget. It feels like I spend half my days batting the fear away, refusing to let the rising panic consume me.

"Well, you may not be aware that you girls are getting a reputation. As—eccentrics. Bluestockings. Miss Maura more so than you—she's always got her nose in a book, doesn't she? Always popping in and out of that bookshop. You two don't go visiting or receive callers. It's understandable, without any mother to guide you—" Mrs. Corbett looks sadly at Father. "But regrettable. I thought it my neighborly duty to tell your father what I've been hearing."

Of course she did, the snooping, meddlesome—

Eccentrics, she said. Have the old cows in town been gossiping about us? What if the Brotherhood has heard? Father's a Latin scholar of some renown, and he's respected by the Brothers. Before Mother died, before he inherited his uncle's shipping business in New London, he taught at the boys' school in town. But that's not enough to place his daughters above suspicion. These days, no one is above suspicion.

I thought keeping us secluded would be safer. Perhaps I've been going about it all wrong.

My face falls, but Father takes my silence for assent. "Mrs. Corbett knows of a young lady who would do. She's fluent in French—painting, music—" His voice drones on, but I stop listening. Our governess will excel in all the pretty, useless things young ladies of our station are expected to embrace.

And she'll be living here. Right here in the house.

I grit my teeth. "Have you already retained her, then?"

"Sister Elena will be here Monday morning." Mrs. Corbett smiles.

Sister? It's worse than I thought. The Sisters are the feminine arm of the Brotherhood, only without any power: they do not preside over legal disputes, or create addendums to the morality codes, or judge the cases of girls accused of witchery. They live isolated in convents in the cities and dedicate their lives in service to the Lord, educating girls in their elite boarding schools, occasionally serving as governesses. I've never met a member of the order before, but I've seen them passing through town in their closed carriages, dressed all in black. They always look pinched and joyless. Mrs. Corbett's daughter Regina had a Sister for her governess before she married.

Is that Father's intention? Does this governess specialize in marrying off hopeless girls, like Maura and me?

I turn to Father, accusations on my lips. He wanted my input, did he? He's already made his decision! Or had it made for him by someone else.

He sees the anger on my face and droops like the poor clematis flowers in the garden.

Blast. I can't argue with him; since Mother died, there isn't enough of him left to argue with.

"If the decision's already been made, we shall make the best of it. I'm sure she'll be lovely. Thank you for thinking of us, Father." I give him my most charming smile, full of daughterly devotion. See? I can be sweet as Tess's strawberry pie when I want.

Father smiles back uncertainly. "You're welcome. I only want what's best for you girls. Would you like to tell your sisters the news, or shall I tell them at dinner?"

Oh. *That's* why he summoned me. He never intended to ask my opinion. It was only a pretense because he doesn't have the courage to tell them himself! This way, when Maura throws a tantrum and Tess sulks, he'll be able to comfort himself with *Cate agreed it was for the best.* As if I had any real say in the matter.

"No, no. I'll tell them." Better they're rude to me than to Father. "I'll be off to do that now. Good day, Mrs. Corbett."

Mrs. Corbett brushes invisible lint from her heavy wool skirt. "Good day, Miss Cate."

I curtsy and close the door behind me, cursing her black soul. She has no notion of the peril she's just put us in.

THE CAHILL WITCH CHRONICLES
READ THE SPELLBINDING TRILOGY.

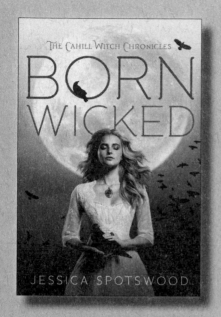